END GAME

STEELE RIDGE: THE BLACKWELLS

SPECIAL EDITION

TRACEY DEVLYN

WWW.TRACEYDEVLYN.COM

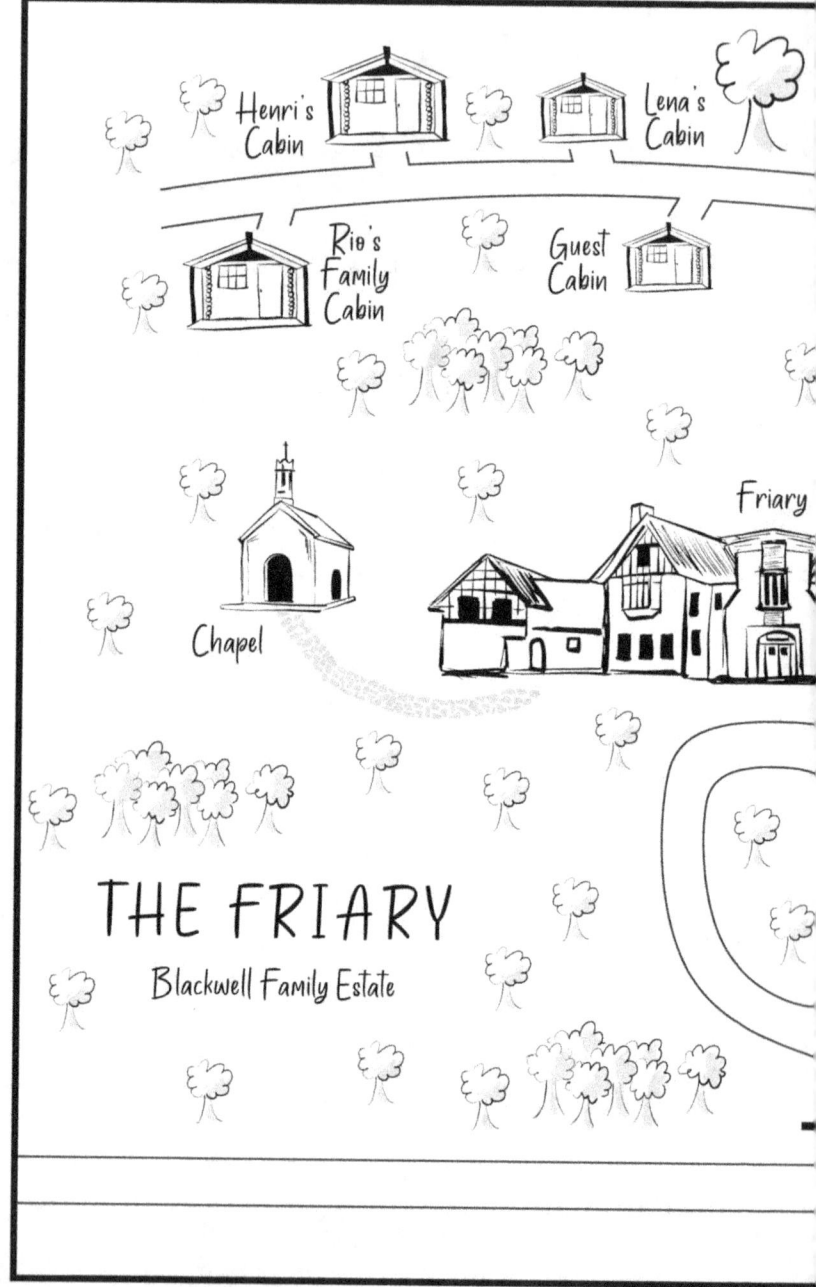

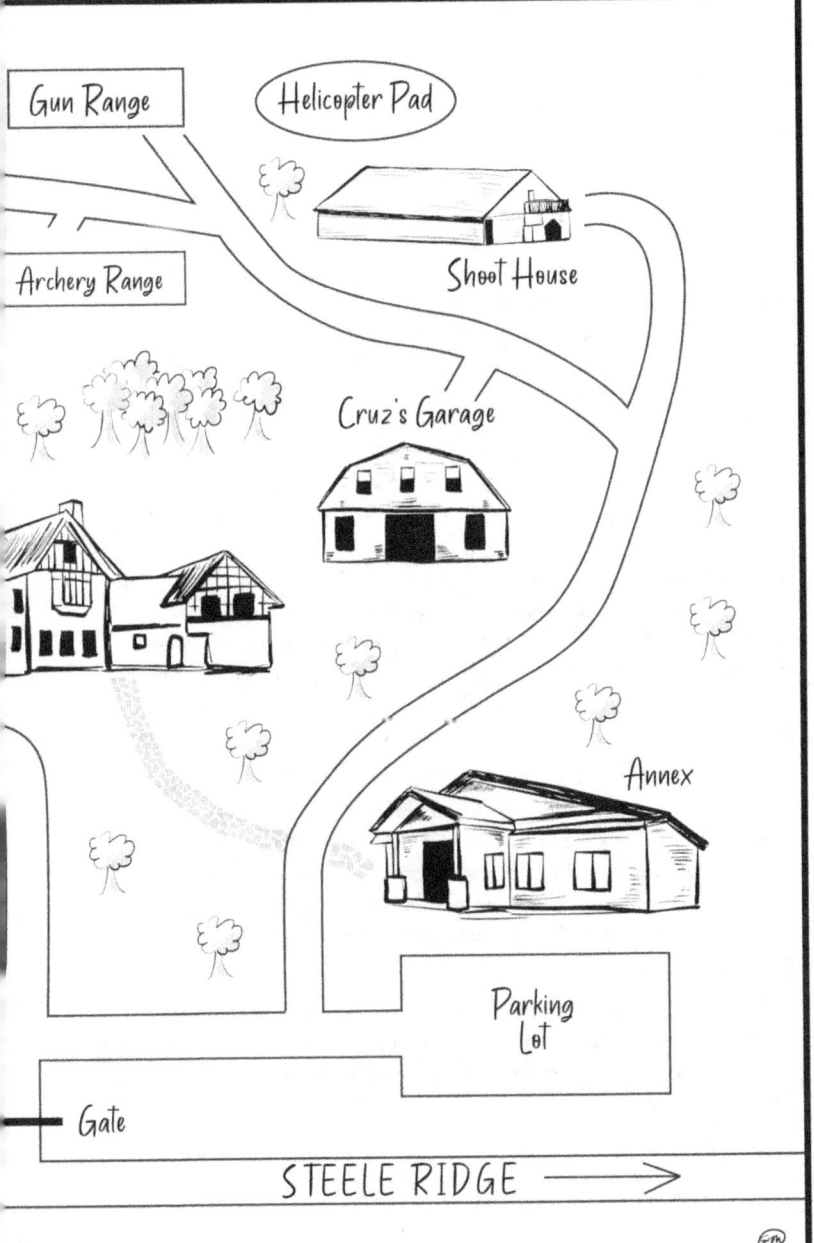

Print Edition, January 2026, ISBN: 978-1-940677-26-2
Digital Edition, January 2026, ISBN: 978-1-940677-22-4

For more information contact: tdccreationsinc@gmail.com

DISCOVER MORE STEELE RIDGE

STEELE RIDGE: THE STEELES

The Beginning, A Novella

Going Hard, Book 1

Living Fast, Book 2

Loving Deep, Book 3

Breaking Free, Book 4

Roaming Wild, Book 5

Stripping Bare, Book 6

Enduring Love, A Novella, Book 7

Vowing Love, A Novella, Book 8

STEELE RIDGE: THE KINGSTONS

Craving Heat, Book 1

Tasting Fire, Book 2

Searing Need, Book 3

Striking Edge, Book 4

Burning Ache, Book 5

STEELE RIDGE: THE BLACKWELLS

Flash Point, Book 1

Smoke Screen, Book 2

Cross Roads, Book 3

Crash Course, Book 4

End Game, Book 5

STEELE RIDGE CHRISTMAS CAPERS

The Most Wonderful Gift of All, Caper 1

A Sign of the Season, Caper 2

His Holiday Miracle, Caper 3

A Holly Jolly Homecoming, Caper 4

Hope for the Holidays, Caper 5

All She Wants for Christmas, Caper 6

Jingle Bell Rock Tonight, Caper 7

Not So Silent Night, Caper 8

A Rogue Santa, Caper 9

The Puppy Present, Caper 10

For the Love of Santa, Caper 11

Beneath the Mistletoe, Caper 12

ALSO BY TRACEY DEVLYN

NEXUS SPYMASTER SERIES

Historical romantic suspense

A Lady's Revenge

A Lady's Temptation

A Lady's Secret

A Lord's Redemption

A Lord's Bargain

BONES & GEMSTONES SERIES

Historical romantic mystery

Night Storm

TEA TIME SHORTS & NOVELLAS

Sweet historical romance

His Secret Desire

END GAME

STEELE RIDGE: THE BLACKWELLS

SPECIAL EDITION

TRACEY DEVLYN

WWW.TRACEYDEVLYN.COM

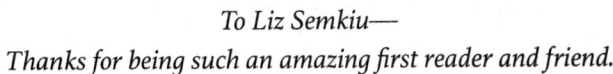

To Liz Semkiu—
Thanks for being such an amazing first reader and friend.

AUTHORS' NOTE

Dear Reader,

Thank you for purchasing our special edition of *END GAME*! We hope you enjoy Ash and Kayla's love story.

END GAME is the fifth and final book in our Steele Ridge: The Blackwells series. A truly bittersweet moment for us.

The seed for this series took root six years ago when we converged on Tracey's house to brainstorm plots for the final two books in The Kingstons series (*Striking Edge & Burning Ache*) and sketch out our next series, which, at the time, was *not* The Blackwells. As often happens during our brainstorming sessions, someone threw out a random comment and the Blackwells were born.

It took us several more years to slot these black sheep of Steele Ridge into our production schedule. In May 2022, book 1, *FLASH POINT*, hit the shelves, and we've been torturing the Blackwell boys ever since. We loved getting to know the Blackwell clan and introducing the guys to the fantastic women who transformed their lives.

Thank you for taking this journey with us. Everything you do—buying our books, recommending them to your friends and libraries, sharing fun pics on social media, and posting your reviews—has all contributed to helping us get the word out about this series.

We appreciate you so much and hope you enjoy this wild, romantic ride through Steele Ridge, North Carolina.

— Tracey & Adrienne

1

_____

THE SLICE ACROSS HIS FLESH TOOK HIM BY SURPRISE. PAIN seared through subcutaneous layers with such speed that Special Agent Asher Cameron Blackwell—Ash to his family and Cameron to his colleagues—flicked his hand hard in a futile attempt to stop the flow of torture.

"Dammit." He slammed the cabinet door shut on the deadly manilla file folder and stuffed the pad of his injured thumb into his mouth. The metallic taste of blood spread across his tongue.

Better there than on the paperwork he'd just completed.

He hated paperwork.

With. A. Passion.

Eileen Tao, the new FBI director, seemed to equate the quantity of forms, reports, and daily logs to an agent's level of productivity. What she did with all the data, he didn't know. But he would have liked to tell her where she could shove her new procedures.

He'd much rather be out in the field, tracking down leads, talking to his confidential informants, or being undercover. Hell, he'd even swap a night surveillance in twenty-degree weather for logging phone calls.

A quick tap against the metal frame of his cubicle brought his head around.

Senior Resident Agent Mitch Lawson stood at the opening, a blond eyebrow lifted at the sight of one of his agents with his thumb stuck in his mouth.

If Cameron had still been stationed at the Charlotte field office, his supervisor there would have made a joke about him regressing, and he would have responded in kind. Tit for- tat. Since relocating to the much smaller resident agency in Asheville six months ago, he hadn't yet crossed that line from no-nonsense professionalism to friendly banter with Lawson.

Maybe he never would.

He lowered his thumb. "Can I help you, sir?"

"I need you to follow up on an unofficial complaint the Bureau received."

Lawson's use of *unofficial* caught his attention, but he let it ride for now.

"Anonymous?"

"No, the complainant is a member of the Engel County School Board." Lawson shifted on his feet. "She believes another board member is going to sell her vote on an upcoming agenda item in exchange for a piece of artwork."

Cameron's interest sparked. After Special Agent Olivia Westcott left the Bureau to work for his brother at Blackwell Asset Recovery Services, aka BARS, he'd jumped at the opportunity to slide into the vacancy she'd left behind in Asheville. Partly because it was the opportunity he'd been waiting for since joining the Bureau five years ago and partly because it would put him closer to Steele Ridge.

Home.

Or what used to be home. Didn't much feel like it anymore. Not with the unending tension between him and his brother Zeke.

A situation he intended to remedy. Soon.

If he could get his hardheaded brother on board.

Due to Cameron and Liv's success with recovering stolen art over the past couple of years, Special Agent in Charge Shanice Williams had decided North Carolina could use its own art crime squad. Now, he and two other agents could prioritize art and cultural cases over others that might cross their desks.

But someone using artwork to swing a school board vote didn't seem like a job for the FBI, let alone his team.

"Isn't that an issue for the Board's superintendent to sort out?" he asked.

"Under normal circumstances, yes."

He lifted a brow. "And these aren't?"

"The complainant believes the offending member and the superintendent are having an affair."

"What about the sheriff?"

A look of exasperation crossed the SRA's features, as if he'd already run through the gamut of FBI-alternatives. Which he probably had.

The verdict on whether or not he liked Lawson as an individual was still out. But there was no denying the man's keen intelligence and agenting skills.

"According to the complainant, the sheriff and super have been best friends since high school."

Too bad this incident wasn't in Haywood County. Sheriff Maggie Kingston was friends, friendly, or related to most of the folks under her jurisdiction. She'd figured out how to navigate sticky relational issues and still get the job done.

"Who's being accused of buying the board member's vote?"

The SRA consulted a document inside the folder he held. "Krowne. Kayla Krowne. Owns a lobbying firm by the name of Krowne and Associates."

Cameron's heart whipped the blood in his body into a frenzy, giving him an insta-headache. He fought to keep his gaze steady, his muscles loose, when all he wanted to do was explode into violence.

He forced himself to draw in a slow breath, once, twice. When the urge to break things passed and his heart rate returned to normal, he was left feeling cold and unsteady.

"Know her?" Lawson asked, eyeing him closely.

He shrugged. "Not really. We've exchanged a few words." *Verbal barbs, heated glances.* "She's friends with my brother's fiancée."

A long heartbeat stretched out before Lawson asked, "Liv?"

Only years of conditioning kept the cringe off his face. One of the reasons Olivia Westcott had traded her FBI badge for a position with BARS, as their provenance expert, was because of Lawson's growing romantic interest in her.

To his credit, the SRA had never acted upon his feelings, but Liv, a single mom, had worried that her boss's iron will would eventually corrode and break. And where would that leave them when she said no?

Rather than gamble, she'd left on her own terms and couldn't be happier, especially since the new gig allowed her to spend more time with her son Brodie.

"Yes," he said, confirming the SRA's suspicion.

The skin over Lawson's cheekbones whitened a moment before he asked, "Is Zeke still pissed at you about your role in the Lederman-St. Martin case?"

The Lederman-St. Martin case had forced a tenuous alliance between the Bureau and BARS in order to stop a huge shipment of nasty drugs from being dumped into small towns across Western North Carolina, including Steele Ridge.

He hesitated in answering Lawson's question, not wanting to air out his family's dirty laundry. Zeke had been ticked off at him long before his involvement in the case. "Hard to say."

"I'll take that as a no, which means you shouldn't run into any familial obstacles while investigating this complaint."

He wasn't so sure. If Zeke found out about him nosing around in Kayla's business—and he would—his brother would have one more reason to believe he'd written off his family.

Kayla had been instrumental in a couple of recent asset recoveries. In Zeke's eyes, she was practically family. Plus, Liv and Kayla were best friends and Phin did work for the lobbyist. Neither of them would ever forgive him if his involvement led to her arrest.

"Might be best if you take this one," he said.

"Why's that?"

"I have another connection to Ms. Krowne. My youngest brother, Phin, works part-time for her lobbying firm."

"Fucking small towns." Lawson tapped the file folder against his thigh as he considered options. "I can't. The complainant is my cousin."

Guess that explained the *unofficial* part of the complaint.

"I'll have Gomez or Finch look into it." The other two members of his art crime squad.

"Aren't they headed to Quantico for some training?"

Shit.

He nodded. "Slipped my mind."

Short straw.

Lawson eyed him. "You can be objective?"

If his family hadn't been involved, he would've jumped on the opportunity to go toe-to-toe with Kayla Krowne. But she'd rooted herself in with the Blackwells now, which would make investigating her challenging for him on a personal level. But not impossible.

"Of course." His headache intensified, as he held out his hand. Lawson slapped the file folder into his palm. "I'd like to say keep me updated, but given the circumstances, it might be best to stick to highlights only. I'd prefer not to have to lie to my cousin."

Cameron nodded, and Lawson left.

He pinched the bridge of his nose and squeezed his eyes shut. "Shit, shit, shit."

"Having a bad day, hon?" a female voice asked.

He dropped his hand and looked up to find the happiest, most energetic person he knew standing in the opening of his cubicle. Liv had dubbed her Peppy Patsy. It fit.

Some might find the office assistant's constant positivity and casual manner grating. Liv confessed as much to him, even though she liked the older woman. But Cameron appreciated Patsy's happy countenance and distinctive laugh for the blessings they were.

He produced a smile. "Not anymore."

"Now, aren't you sweet." Her hazel eyes lit with excitement. "I have someone here who'll perk up your day."

Wariness made him sit straighter. He rarely got visitors, and those who did come here were generally invited by him.

"Who?"

Patsy glanced to her left as she stepped aside. A tall, broad-shouldered man came into view. "Morning, Ash."

With those two words, Zeke Blackwell sucked every square inch of air out of the office. Cameron didn't even have the breath to correct his brother's use of his first name.

He could think of only one reason why Zeke had entered enemy territory.

To deliver bad news.

2

CAMERON SLOWLY ROSE FROM HIS CHAIR. "THANK YOU, Patsy."

The assistant must have sensed his brother's visit wasn't the welcome relief she'd thought it would be, for her excitement dissipated and she glared at Zeke with unusual ferocity as she brushed past him.

"Protective," Zeke observed.

"Steadfast." He threw the word down between them, knowing the subtext wouldn't be lost on his brother.

Zeke's jaw tightened, and they stared at each other for a long, taut moment.

"Did something happen to Grams?" he asked, breaking the tense, visual battle.

"No."

"Mom?"

"No?"

"Who then?"

Instead of answering, Zeke surveyed the elements that warmed up Cameron's workspace. Framed certificates, newspaper clipping of his first solved case, the ubiquitous

Smokey Mountain landscape, the stark cleanliness of his desk. His Academy graduation picture with his family, minus one.

Ever since Cameron left the Blackwells' repo business to become a special agent, Zeke had made his hatred of the FBI clear. The Bureau had disrupted his brother's vision of the future. A future that had included Cameron at the helm of a business for which he had no passion, with Zeke sitting in a comfortable position to his right.

Cameron's so-called betrayal had set off three years of near radio silence between him and his brother. It wasn't until the Bureau had yanked them both into the Lederman-St. Martin case, where Zeke had been forced to work with Liv Westcott, that rooms no longer iced over when they both entered.

By the end of the drug-smuggling case, Zeke had found the love of his life in Liv and Cameron had wedged his foot in the door before his brother could shut it again. Cameron wanted to be able to see his family without feeling like an outsider. Soon, he and Zeke would have to have a long, difficult discussion.

But that day wasn't today.

"Ezekiel?" he prompted, tempering the frustration and fear roiling in his chest.

Zeke cleared his throat before crossing his corded arms over his chest. Then he scowled at Cameron, as if his dilly-dallying around were Cam's fault.

"I need a favor," Zeke growled out the words.

Cameron stared at him for a stunned moment, barely aware of the relief drowning out his thundering heart. Then he mentally shook himself, instinct telling him that whatever had dragged Zeke to his doorstep would alter his world.

"You have my attention." He nodded toward an empty, adjacent cubicle. "Grab a chair and sit down."

Zeke shifted on his feet, then glanced around again before hooking his thumb toward the exit. "Can you get out of here for half an hour?"

Checking the clock on one of his new 24-inch dual monitors, Cameron realized he'd missed lunch. Maybe some fresh air and food would stop the hammering that had set up shop in his head since his discussion with Lawson.

He snatched his suit coat from the back of his chair and shouldered past his brother. "You've got thirty minutes."

They left the federal building and, as if by mutual consent, zigzagged their way to Carmel's on Page Avenue and snagged an outside table. It was a beautiful spring day, not a cloud in the sky. A fact Cameron would regret within minutes.

His navy-blue coat absorbed the intense Carolina sun, making it feel like eighty-five instead of seventy. Removing his garment meant exposing his service weapon. Something he tried to avoid in public.

When the server arrived with their drinks, Cameron's request to move inside dried up on his tongue when he keyed in on his brother's already caged expression.

After loosening his tie and unfastening his shirt's top button, Cameron prayed for a bank of clouds to roll in. When the sky remained a pure, unobstructed blue, he asked the server to bring out a pitcher of ice water.

Once they placed their orders, silence cratered around them. Cameron let it stretch out for a good two minutes before he prompted his brother. "What's this about a favor?"

Zeke took a long pull of beer. "I need you to talk some sense into Kayla."

What the hell? Was this Kayla Krowne Day?

"Me? I barely know her." And what he did know of the lobbyist, he didn't much care for.

"Which makes you the best person for the job."

"I don't follow." Sweat gathered between his shoulder blades.

Zeke took another hefty drink, his irritation—or was it nervousness—palpable. "Aunt Joan visited Mom the other day."

An image of the petite matriarch of the Steele clan came to mind. Like many his age, Cameron carried fond memories of the former elementary school teacher. He regretted that their families hadn't been closer while growing up. It would've been nice having cousins to beat up.

"Something to do with Uncle Eddie?"

His mom, Lynette Blackwell, and her brother Eddie Steele had grown closer since his surprising return from isolation a few years ago.

Zeke shook his head. "What I'm about to tell you, I'm sharing with my brother, Ash, not that G-man prick Cameron."

"That G-man prick has been pretty damn helpful to the Blackwells on some recent recoveries."

"Promise me that you'll listen as a family member, not the FBI."

Family member. Right. It seemed Zeke only remembered that fact when he needed the Bureau's resources, these days.

"I'm the same person, Zeke. You can't get one without the other."

"Promise me." His brother's knee jackhammered beneath the metal table.

Unable to do anything else, he nodded.

"A friend on the school board of a nearby county confided in Aunt Joan their belief that Kayla was attempting to influence a colleague's vote on an upcoming agenda item."

Déjà-Kayla-vu.

Coming from his Aunt Joan brought a helluva lot more validity to the accusation. His empty stomach knotted, and he forgot all about his melting body. "How?"

"According to this other board member, Kayla gifted her peer with an expensive Celtic artifact."

Lawson had said "artwork." His own bungling of words? Or his cousin's?

"The board member knows this, how?"

"Evidently, she overheard the two discussing the arti-fact, which she recognized from attending a recent event at Kayla's home. A few days later, the other board member was gushing about the fact her curator son had managed to secure a ten-thousand-year-old artifact for the grand opening of the new natural history museum in Asheville."

Cameron's mind flashed back to the file folder sitting on his desk. "What do you want me to do, exactly?"

"Find out if there's any truth to the situation and, if there is, convince Kayla to fix it."

"Why not ask Liv? They're best friends. If anyone can put the lobbyist straight, it would be her." Investigating a potential pay-to-play scheme in an official capacity would be hard enough. Interrogating a family friend was another thing all together.

"No," Zeke said, uncompromising. "I don't want Liv involved with this. If Kayla has stepped over the line, it would stress out Liv. Something I want to avoid at all costs, right now."

Cameron frowned. As a former special agent, Liv had dealt with far more stressful situations than this without falling apart. What was going on *right now* that had triggered his brother's full-on protective mode?

He let it go for now. "Why do you think I'll be able to get through to her?"

"I don't know. Flash your badge. Impress upon her the seriousness of the situation."

"Kayla's been a lobbyist for a long time. I'm sure she understands the consequences of tampering with votes."

They fell silent while the server delivered their lunch.

Once she was gone, Cameron said, "If this board member is right and Kayla's putting her career on the line, she's either taken a personal interest in the issue or there's something much bigger at stake."

"Agreed."

"Did Aunt Joan indicate what the vote was for?"

"Something related to the book ban issue. A parents' bill of rights policy." His left knee pumped with the right now.

Did Kayla have a friend whose kid attended a school in Engel County? Was she on a crusade to protect young readers' access to books? Or did she have an author friend whose book had been banned?

He didn't know her well enough to answer his own questions. A result of spending the last few years avoiding the lobbyist.

"I don't know, Zeke. I haven't been exactly cordial to her during our few encounters. Phin might be better suited for feeling her out."

"God knows why, but Phin's enjoying the work he's

doing for her. I don't want something like this jeopardizing their relationship." Zeke tapped the blunt tips of his fingers against the table. "Will you talk to her? Kayla's done a lot for our family. We owe her."

Cameron's jaw clenched at his brother's invocation of family again.

His instincts warned him to keep his investigation professional, keep family out of it. But he couldn't easily say no to his brother. Especially since Zeke had checked his ego and tamped down his tsunami of emotions in order to ask for his help.

Cameron tapped his forefinger against his condensation-slick glass. His mind buzzed with all the ways he could screw this up, personally and professionally.

But he couldn't get around the fact that Kayla had tapped into her extensive list of contacts and extraordinary resources to assist BARS, several times, without recompense or apparent benefit to herself.

He glanced up, saw the storm of disappointment rising in his brother's gaze. Before Zeke could bolt, he nodded. "I'll speak to her, but don't expect a miracle. Our feelings toward one another aren't what you'd call conducive to discussion, let alone persuasion."

Amusement lit Zeke's eyes. "I have faith in you, brother."

And with that bombshell, Zeke dropped money on the table and walked away, leaving Cameron drenched in sweat and a serious case of déjà vu.

AT HIS APARTMENT, CAMERON SET A TAKE-HOME BAG FROM Carmel's on the smooth gray concrete countertop. Hands on hips, he stared down at the recycling bin at the end of the island for a long, procrastinating minute before step-ping on the lid lever and reaching inside.

He pulled out a four-by-six linen card and did what he hadn't bothered doing yesterday. He read the card's elegant script.

You're cordially invited
to a fundraiser for the preservation of the
Gorekin Cove natural area.
Special Guest Governor Victoria Stokes
Hosted by Gordon and Jillian Krowne.

CEO and CFO, respectively, of Krowne Hotels & Resorts, aka Kayla's parents.

After Kayla's assist with the Lederman-St. Martin case, he'd started receiving invitations from her family for various events. He had no idea why. He'd never met Mr. and Mrs. Krowne and he couldn't imagine Kayla orches-trating his attendance.

Why would she? They weren't on friendly terms. Correction, he wasn't. He couldn't be. She'd caused him too much grief with her political meddling.

For whatever reason, he'd never been able to put on a professional game face around her. He'd smiled and shook the hands of crooked politicians, drug lords, arms dealers, and art thieves. He had no problem playing a part.

But not with her. A condition that seemed to amuse her.

He tapped the invitation against the countertop and worked to halt the conflicting emotions roiling through his body. He had no doubt the lobbyist would be in atten-dance. The über-wealthy Krownes were known to be a close-knit family and supportive of each other's pet projects.

Stretching his neck left, then right, he worked to extinguish the building tension.

"You're a professional, Special Agent Blackwell. You've dealt with far more difficult, more life-threatening cases than Kayla-fucking-Krowne's."

The pep talk didn't help. Dread fermented in his stomach like a batch of kimchi.

Drawing in a resigned breath, he texted his RSVP to the number indicated before dropping the card in the trash again and heading for the liquor cabinet.

Tonight, he would have dessert before dinner.

3

Sharks don't sweat.

With infinite patience, they circle their prey in ever-tightening circles, evaluating, calculating, lulling their soon-to-be dinner into a false sense that they have nothing to worry about.

The Great White below is simply taking in the waters, enjoying the view.

Nothing to worry about down here.

Until something triggers the beast's instincts, and it surges upward, lightning quick, and takes a massive bite out of its target before drifting away.

Kayla Krowne had been swimming in one shark tank or another for the entirety of her life.

First preschool, then boarding school, university, the White House, and now North Carolina's General Assembly, dinner parties, and fundraisers. The sharks were circling.

But not around her.

In the past ten years, she'd made it clear that if anyone tried to take a chunk out of her, she'd remove an arm and two legs in retaliation.

Tonight, the sharks encircled North Carolina's Governor Victoria Stokes. The woman gearing up to lead the Tar Heel State for another four years. If she won reelection.

It was Kayla's job to make sure she did.

By feeding the sharks. Or fending them off. Whichever served the governor's path to reelection best.

Kayla followed the attending donors with a strategic eye. Some she would allow to approach the governor. Others, she would blast out of the surrounding waters with her own version of an electrical shock.

She zeroed in on one of the local mayors, wife in tow, swimming between guests. To the untrained eye, his course seemed meandering, without purpose.

But Kayla recognized a predator honed in on a scent when she saw one. She flashed on what she knew about the mayor. How she could pair his wants to the governor's. She almost always found something that would benefit both parties.

The politicians and businesspeople present saw in Governor Victoria Stokes a potential vote for their various causes or, if they were on the other side of the fence, a danger to promises they had made to constituents or shareholders. Anyone interested in influencing current policy would seek to curry Vicky's favor, because, well, it never hurt to have a governor on speed dial.

But Vicky's friends—her true friends—wanted nothing from her but love.

A distant memory surfaced about the mayor. An unpleasant rumor about domestic abuse that had just enough meat to it to cause Kayla concern. Politicians were always easy targets for the rumor mill. Some of it absurd, some of it disgustingly true.

The mayor whispered something to his wife. A pained look tore across her plain features before she drew her phone from her black clutch, broke away from her husband, and took up a position opposite the governor.

With a nonchalance she'd mastered years ago, Kayla sipped her champagne as she strode toward a quartet of sixty-something women dressed in their finest. All of them friends since their university years. All accomplished, wealthy, influential women. Women Kayla loved and respected like favored aunties.

Kayla wrapped a hand around the governor's waist and squeezed her close. "Good evening, Aunt Vicky."

Victoria's face lit up and she pressed her cheek to Kayla's. "Hello, sweet pea."

One would never know by interacting with the governor that she came from Old Money. She presented as someone you'd walk by on the street and smile at without stopping. Brown hair, indistinguishable eye color, average height, accessible and warm to everyone who met her.

Only on further acquaintance would one detect the boarding school education, the family tree that went back ten generations, the houses in Montford and six other cities around the world, and the weight of the most powerful position in the state.

Kayla lowered her voice. "I'm here to save you from Mayor Ward and his impromptu photo op."

Ever the professional, Vicky didn't turn and search for the approaching mayor. "How bad?"

When Kayla worked on Vicky's first gubernatorial election, they'd come up with a series of hand signals, code words, and rating systems to alert her to possible shitstorms.

"If rumors of how he treats his wife are correct, a ten plus."

"I continue to be in awe of your network of spies." Vicky's hold around her waist tightened. "Thank you for having my back."

"Always." Out of her peripheral vision, Kayla watched a scowl appear on the mayor's face before he veered off toward the open bar.

Kayla held back a smile.

The mayor's wife dropped her phone back in her purse and stalked off in the opposite direction of her husband. Kayla made a mental note to talk to Liv about Mrs. Ward's situation. Her friend had experience with assisting domestic abuse victims.

"Coast is clear." She gave her honorary aunt a final squeeze before shifting closer to another member of the quartet. "Amazing turnout, Mama. As always."

Jillian Krowne's slender fingers folded over Kayla's. "I'm so glad you could make it."

One look at her mother, and Kayla grew concerned. The dark lavender gown complemented her coiffed blond hair, though the garment seemed to hang rather than mold. Her public smile dragged a bit and no amount of concealer could hide the dark shadows at the corners of her eyes.

"Have you been getting enough sleep?" she whispered, knowing Jillian always had trouble sleeping the week leading up to a big event like this.

"Oh, dear." She lifted a hand to her cheek. "Do I look tired?"

"A little." She smiled, then lied. "Only a daughter would notice."

"Of course she made it," a tall, black-haired woman

interrupted, stepping forward to wrap Kayla in a warm hug. "Saving wild things is one of our girl's many passions."

Aunt Sybil had one of those personalities that eclipsed everyone in the room. She had used her sharp mind, droll humor, and fearless attitude to open many boardroom doors, and now she helmed the state's top pharmaceutical company.

"Glad you could pull away for the evening," Kayla said, returning the embrace.

"Anything for Jillie and Vicky."

Tonight's benefit would increase the governor's exposure while raising enough funds to purchase a thousand-acre plot of land on the north side of Asheville. The developer who owned the property had established a sales office and cleared about twenty acres for an internal road system for the first phase of the development before going belly-up.

Local conservation groups had long believed the area housed several endangered and threatened species, but the developer's survey hadn't indicated a single species. Once the property went up for sale again, three independent surveys revealed an astonishing plethora of important plants and animals on the site.

Unfortunately, no one organization had the financial resources to buy such a sizable parcel. So they had approached the Krowne Foundation, which was known for its generosity toward local issues.

As much as Kayla believed in and supported conservation initiatives, she'd originally declined her mother's invite. She had three more votes to secure for an upcoming bill. Time was ticking. To get the votes, she needed to be in Raleigh, the capitol, where all the dark magic happened.

"Harper threatened to put blue dye in my pool if I didn't make an appearance," Kayla said.

Vicky laughed. "Your sister can be quite persuasive."

"Sounds like Harper got to y'all, too." Kayla stepped forward to embrace the petite woman beside Sybil. "Maybe I should take a lesson out of her playbook."

"Don't you dare," Aunt Elsie said, with a smile and warm hug.

As she always did for social events, the fashion designer had tamed her riot of red curls and concealed her freckles. Kayla thought of this version as her Nicole Kidman red carpet look. Sleek, polished, classic Hollywood.

Kayla much preferred her aunt's natural and wild, let-your-freckles-fly look.

"For you, persuasion is an art form," Elsie said. "You customize your approach to each person's basic needs."

"Harper, on the other hand," Sybil said, "goes right for the fear factor."

"I'm for whatever tactic brought us all together," Kayla said. "It's been too long."

Everyone nodded and held their drinks up in a silent salute.

Kayla addressed the governor. "I hope Mama's guests aren't pestering you too much."

Vicky smiled. "No more, no less than usual."

"I've counted one snide remark," Sybil said in an affronted voice, "two veiled threats, and four impassioned pitches for why she should support one cause or another."

The governor's smile widened. "As I said."

"What has gotten into people, these days?" Jillian asked. "It's as if civility is a foreign concept. A romantic notion only practiced in bygone days."

"People feel more empowered," Kayla said. "They have platforms where they can voice their concerns."

"Sharing is one thing," Sybil said. "Being an ass about it is quite another."

"How are your efforts going with the Engel County School Board?" Elsie asked. "Are the votes there yet?"

Kayla sensed Jillian stiffen beside her. Focusing on her aunt, she conjured a secretive smile.

"How did you do it?" Sybil asked. "My source told me Rhodes was a solid yes."

Kayla's heart began a slow slide into the depths of her stomach.

A seasoned lobbyist, she maintained her pleasant expression, while attempting to discern the meaning behind her aunt's question. Curiosity? Suspicion? Envy?

"Ms. Rhodes understood why it would be in her community's best interest to table the Board's response to SB49 until they had time to work through the new law's complicated mandates." Slapping a Parents' Bill of Rights policy together for the sole purpose of complying with state law was not only irresponsible, in this case, it could create a dangerous environment for some students.

Jillian clasped Kayla's hand in a tight grip and smiled at the aunties. "Y'all look so skeptical." Her free arm snaked around Kayla's shoulders and gave her a little shake. "This is the same woman who sweet-talked us into going roller-skating for her thirtieth birthday. She changed four hard noes to yeses."

The aunties' expressions cleared, as each no doubt recalled how much fun they'd had, despite their many reservations.

"Speaking of votes." Kayla returned her attention to the governor. "How'd your meeting with Representative Gladwell and Senator Orston go? Are they going to back HB821?"

The Women Entrepreneur Empowerment Act would provide each approved candidate twenty-five thousand dollars for startup or improvement expenses and access to training and mentor centers across the state.

Vicky grimaced. "We've run into an issue."

"Issue?" Kayla searched the other women's faces. None of them looked surprised by the governor's revelation.

"Some new data has come to my attention that my office is looking into."

"What sort of data?"

An emotion Kayla couldn't pinpoint skittered across the governor's features, as her gaze swept the crowded room. "Nothing I wish to discuss here."

"But you still plan to support the bill, right?" Kayla pressed.

"I will do what's best for my constituents, as I have always done." Vicky nodded to the group. "Now, if you'll excuse me, I should mingle."

A heavy silence clung to the small group, after the governor strode away. Still holding Kayla's hand, Jillian gave it a squeeze. "Don't let your fear win. She'll stay the course."

Kayla hoped so. Much was riding on the passage of HB821. She motioned to one of the four interns stationed around the room to shadow the governor. A frequent attendee at functions such as this, Gemma Niles, a seasoned fourth-year, would keep Vicky out of any political sand traps.

"Or Assembly leadership will run roughshod over her and kill the bill," Sybil mused.

Kayla didn't agree. Vicky had a good working relationship with Gladwell and Orston. Against all odds, the trio had managed to find common ground on several important issues. A prime example of the good that could be done for the people, when politicians put their oath to the Constitution before loyalty to their party.

"Good evening," a familiar masculine voice said on Kayla's other side.

She turned to find Phin Blackwell, displaying his most charming smile. An answering grin tugged at the corners of her mouth. It was difficult to do anything else when around this impeccably dressed rogue.

She placed a free hand on his solid shoulder. "Phin, are you acquainted with my mother's friends?"

"I haven't had the pleasure."

After making the introductions, she asked, "Is Maddy with you?"

He shook his head. "She couldn't make it, but I did arrive with someone."

"Oh? Who?"

"Cameron."

Ash.

An image of his handsome black-haired brother filled her mind, and she experienced a familiar quickening in her chest. He'd finally accepted a Krowne invitation. Excitement set her heart to racing—until she ran into a red flag. *Why now?*

Phin filled the ladies in on his FBI brother. Kayla half-listened, as she scanned the expansive room for the unmistakable eldest Blackwell. The man, for reasons she didn't understand, had taken an instant dislike of her. Which made him all the more intriguing.

She spotted him at the bar, wearing a sleek black suit. Drink in hand, he turned to face the crowd and his penetrating blue eyes snapped to hers like metal to a magnet.

As it had done the first moment she'd spotted him jogging through Pack Square Park with Phin, her pulse drummed in her ears, silencing the world around her.

When he continued staring, she lifted a brow, amused despite the visual tension.

Taking her silent inquiry as an invitation—or challenge, he pushed away from the bar and prowled her way.

4

CAMERON'S BLOOD PRESSURE SURGED AS HE CLOSED IN ON HIS quarry.

One taunting eyebrow from the lobbyist. That's all it had taken to knock tonight's plan off its rails.

He'd intended to mingle, to slowly make his way to her side. Split her off from the pack. Tease out a believable denial or a night-altering confession with a promise to mend her stupidity.

Simple. Clean. Unemotional.

Right.

He cursed himself for allowing her to get under his skin as he wove through a kaleidoscope of primped and tittering high-profile guests.

The lobbyist's taunting expression never wavered.

The agent in him boiled at the sight of her. If not for her behind-the-scenes witchery, Eileen Tao would never have been appointed as FBI director, and he wouldn't be pivoting every couple weeks because the director tweaked a policy or modified a procedure or made an unannounced visit to his office. And let's not forget the damn forms.

But the man in him *burned* for her any time they were in a room together. He felt her presence first. She all but vibrated with intelligence, confidence, and unmatched beauty. Her habitual amusement regarding everything around her, no matter how serious, intrigued him as much as it infuriated him.

Tonight, she wore her long blond hair down, the sides clipped high at the back of her head by a sparkling barrette that probably cost more than his vehicle. She looked stunning in a strapless, shimmering powder-blue dress and silver stilettos that did amazing things to her toned calves.

Realizing the direction of his thoughts—and his sight line—he jerked his attention up and caught the slight twitch in her smile. His normal response would have been to avert his eyes, throw back a searing gulp of his drink, or deliver a scorching death stare.

He did none of these.

He was here to gather intelligence. In order to do that, he had to play nice. He had to engage her in cordial conversation. So he softened his features and locked eyes with hers.

A stocky man stepped in front of him, eclipsing the lobbyist's faltering smile. "Special Agent Blackwell?"

Cameron hesitated, reflexively scanning the room. "Who's asking?"

"Evan Barclay." He thrust out his hand. "Close friend to the Krownes."

In his mid-thirties, the man had a ruggedness about him that some women might find appealing. Coal black hair shaved tight at the sides, square jaw, thick torso, lean hips. But the absence of a neck eliminated him from any Top Ten lists.

Cameron cared less about his looks and more about

how he knew him and just how close Mr. No-Neck was to one particular Krowne.

He shook his hand. "Name isn't familiar. Have we met?"

Instead of answering, Barclay produced a card. "If you're ever interested in doing some side gigs. Give me a call."

He read the card. "Gradient Enterprises. Private security?"

Something sparked in the man's eyes. "That's right."

"I'm not in the market, but thanks." He pocketed the card. Babysitting high-profile, wealthy people was not how he'd ever spend his free time.

"The pay is top-notch. Would be a nice supplement to your government salary."

"I'll keep that in mind." Arrogant prick. "Now, if you'll excuse me."

He took the fifteen feet separating him from his quarry to shrug off his encounter with Mr. Ultra-Networker. Rather than take a position on Phin's free side, he paused just behind his brother and the lobbyist.

"There you are." Phin shifted to the left to make room for him, as he knew his little brother would. "Let me introduce you to our hostess."

Cameron rearranged his features once again. This time conveying polite anticipation, while Phin made the introductions.

When his brother nodded toward the tall beauty next to the lobbyist, he recognized Kayla in her features a second before he heard her name. He noted the keen way the older woman assessed him as she shook his hand.

"Thank you for coming, Mr. Blackwell," Jillian said. With an elegant, slim hand, she introduced her two friends, then indicated Kayla. "You know my daughter, I assume?"

Drawing on acting skills he'd honed onstage with the Montford Park Players for two summers in high school along with his Bureau undercover work, he infused warmth into his features and looked at the lobbyist for the first time since joining their circle. "We're acquainted, yes."

The laugh lines around Kayla's eyes curled tighter, and Cameron realized he'd moved the congeniality needle too far in the opposite direction. She was used to his scowls and barely contained civility. Anything approximating friendliness would, of course, draw her suspicion. And increase her damn amusement.

He cursed his rookie move. Why did he always feel off-balance around this woman? Why did every cell in his body nudge him closer to her, while his brain slammed on the brakes and threw him in reverse?

For the thousandth time, he cursed Zeke for forcing a promise on him and Lawson for backing him into a corner. Nothing he'd learned at the FBI Academy could have prepared him for Kayla Krowne.

The likelihood that she would divulge anything of substance to him was next to nothing. He flattened his features.

A master at reading body language, Phin turned the conversation toward the event. "With such a full house, I suspect you'll hit your fundraising goal."

While his brother did damage control, his mind worked through different scenarios on how to get Kayla alone, so he could question her about the board member's accusations. He had the sensation of responding to inquiries, while his mind kept working the problem.

Right when he decided the direct approach was his best option, the back of a large hand smacked his bicep.

"Where the hell did you go, bro?" Phin said in a low, irritated voice.

Blinking, he glanced around and realized with some shock that the three older women had moved on. Feeling a shift in the air beside him, he turned to find the lobbyist walking away, her head bent toward her phone.

In two giant steps, he was at her side. "I need to talk to you."

When she lifted her head, her eyes had that faraway look a person gets when their mind was still engaged elsewhere. Phin muttered something beneath his breath before leaving them alone.

Kayla lifted a blond brow. "That's not the impression I got while you were standing next to me, aloof for ten full minutes."

"I was ... thinking."

Her lips twitched, and he braced himself for one of her sharp barbs. But she surprised him by putting on her professional hat instead.

"Call my office tomorrow and my assistant will get you on my calendar."

"Why not find a quiet spot now?"

She rocked her phone back and forth between her thumb and middle finger. "I have to meet with someone."

Irritation bubbled, and his pleasant façade slipped. He held out his business card. "Text me when your meeting is over."

Her amusement disappeared, as she accepted it. "What's this about, Ash?"

"Cameron."

An expression he couldn't quite name flashed across her features. If it had been anyone else, he might have thought his correction had hurt her.

He shook off the thought. This was Kayla Krowne. He knew from experience that the lobbyist's skin was as thick as a rhino's.

She raised an inquiring brow, waiting for an answer.

"I'd like to get your opinion on a piece of art," he improvised.

"I'm sure your expertise far exceeds my own. What could my input add to the equation?"

He tamped down another surge of irritation. "Meet with me and find out."

"Such mind game tactics don't work on me, Mr. Blackwell. Now, if you'll excuse me, I really must go." She glided away, exiting through a set of French doors that led to what he assumed was an outdoor veranda.

Mr. Blackwell.

"Way to build trust, G-man," he growled before socking back the rest of his drink.

He stared at the multipaned glass doors. It was dark outside. All he could see was his own pensive reflection staring back at him. Was she meeting a client? A politician? Evan No-Neck Barclay?

He clinked his empty glass down on a passing server's tray.

"Only one way to find out."

He slipped through the French doors.

5

SMALL SOLAR LIGHTS LIT THE PATH LEADING TO HER MOTHER'S treasured gazebo. Kayla's mind wasn't on the tidy pebbles beneath her feet, but on the gorgeous, perplexing man she'd left inside.

Everything about her brief encounter with Ash—Cameron—had been off. From his ridiculous effort at flirtation to his odd stillness to his attempt at getting her alone. She didn't buy his lame reason for needing a private audience with her. She would be the very last person he would go to for an opinion on art.

But damn, he looked good in his evening finery. Dark hair smoothed into place, clean-shaven, black tie, tailored suit molded to his broad shoulders and powerful hips.

How many nights had she lain awake pretending her hand was his as she pleasured herself until her aching cry pierced the shadows of her lonely bedroom?

She would never forget that infinitesimal moment of raw connection they'd shared when they first met. The moment before her friend Liv Westcott had introduced them. The moment his admiring gaze had taken in every inch of her.

His desire had penetrated her armor and hadn't stopped until it reached her very core. Not before Asher Cameron Blackwell had entered her life, and definitely not after, had she experienced anything so powerful, so exhilarating, so pulse-pounding with another man.

Etched even more permanently in her memory was when his desire had blinked out as soon as he heard her name. She would have given away her entire fortune to have been anyone else but Kayla Krowne, in that moment.

His insistence that she use his FBI alias hurt. She'd sat in on intense BARS meetings and hilarious Blackwell family dinners. She wasn't a stranger, dammit. Yet she couldn't say the two of them were friends, either.

What they did have, no matter how hard he tried to scowl it away, was sizzling attraction.

She pushed away thoughts of Cameron—hell with it, Ash—and his odd behavior to mentally prepare for whatever awaited her at the end of the path. Getting a text from one of her aunties wasn't unusual. In fact, the trio had made a habit of checking in on her. Almost as if they each had entered "Text Kayla" on a specific time and day in their individual calendars.

But tonight's text from Vicky had a clandestine quality to it.

Meet me at the gazebo in ten minutes. Alone.

Did the governor want to update her on HB821, away from prying ears? Why? She'd been surrounded by trusted souls. What had been so earth-shattering that she couldn't speak of it in front of her friends?

Or did Vicky want to speak to her about something

more personal? Maybe she wanted Kayla to act as an intermediary again with her estranged daughter.

Four years separated her and Linda. Kayla had been like an older sister to the girl, even pulling duty as a sitter when her teenage schedule allowed.

When Vicky decided the time was right to run for governor, Linda had been right there, doing what she could to support her mother's ambitions. However, not long after Vicky's husband died in a tragic accident, Linda's adulation of her mother slowly devolved into something venomous.

Where once mother and daughter had finished each other's sentences, now Linda seemed to despise everything her mother stood for. Maybe even her mother.

Kayla didn't understand her friend's shocking transformation. In many ways, Linda was the same. Her favorite color was still orange, she still had a soft spot for abandoned dogs, and she still measured every sci-fi horror flick against the classic *Aliens* film.

Yet her politics colored her worldview in such a way as there was no room for gray. Only pitch-black and stark white.

If not for Vicky's pleas of assistance, especially now that Linda was expecting her first child, Kayla would have distanced herself from Linda long ago. But for Vicky, she kept trying to reconnect with that teenaged girl who had adored her mother and loved spending Saturday afternoons browsing art museums with her friend.

As far as Kayla knew, Vicky had kept Jillian and the aunties in the dark about the severity of her fractured relationship with her daughter. For all her many positives, the governor was a proud woman and her failed relationship with Linda wasn't an area of her life she'd want dissected.

Nearing the gazebo, Kayla frowned when she realized

the interior lights were off. Her mother always lit up the structure, inside and out, for guests who needed to escape the crush.

She could have sworn the lights illuminating the gazebo's dome had been on when she'd stepped off the veranda. Wariness slowed her steps and her pulse kicked up a notch. Her attention left the path and skittered from shrub to tree to endless shadows.

With each step, she questioned her memory. Maybe she hadn't seen the dome lit up at all. Maybe she'd mistaken the gazebo for their neighbor's back patio. They used similar party lights on their ginormous pergola.

The more she thought about it, the more she convinced herself of the mistake. Feeling ridiculous, she crossed the structure's threshold and reached for the switch.

"Leave it off, please," a familiar female voice said from the depths of the wooden structure.

"Aunt Vicky, why are you lurking in the dark?"

The governor peeled away from the shadowed back wall. "Kayla, thank you for coming."

"Of course. Is everything okay? Where are Glenn and Ford?" The governor's security detail was never far away.

"They're taking a long bathroom break."

It wasn't unusual for Vicky to dismiss her bodyguards in order to have a private conversation, but they generally just hovered farther away.

"This must be serious."

"There's something I need to tell you. Something you must keep to yourself. For now."

Kayla moved deeper into the gazebo. "I would never break a confidence. You know this."

"Promise me." She hesitated a moment. "Not even your mother."

Kayla's heart gave a hard beat. What could be so sensitive that Vicky would cut out her friend? Something inside her warmed at the thought that Vicky, the governor, trusted her with the information above all others. "You have my word."

A small smile appeared on Vicky's face, and she reached for Kayla. "Thank you."

Kayla rushed forward to take the older woman's trembling hands. "Of course—"

The pointy toe of her silver stiletto caught beneath the floral outdoor rug that covered much of the gazebo's floor. She stumbled, but managed to break her nosedive by grabbing the arm of a nearby chaise longue.

Righting herself, she lifted her gaze, amused embarrassment stretching across her mouth.

Until she spotted the perfect hole drilled into the center of Vicky's forehead. A trickle of dark blood oozed from its center.

The governor—her godmother—crumbled to the floor, as if every bone in her body had turned to dust.

Kayla screamed.

6

THE DISTINCTIVE *TICK-THUMP* OF A SUPPRESSOR REACHED Cameron's ears seconds before a sharp, piercing wail erupted from somewhere deep within the garden. The loud, pulsing calls of whip-poor-wills, spring peepers, and katydids cut off.

Kayla?

He pushed away from the exterior brick wall, rushed across the veranda, and plunged down the garden path.

Another scream. This one choked off suddenly.

"Kayla!"

After she had exited the French doors for her meeting, he'd waited a full minute before following. Seeing the tiny white lights framing the dome of what he assumed was a gazebo and Kayla's meeting place, he'd positioned himself in a shadowed alcove, where he'd had a perfect line of sight on the garden path. He wouldn't let her slip away again before she'd answered his questions.

Within seconds, the now darkened gazebo appeared. He removed his Glock from his shoulder holster, keeping his forefinger on the outside of the trigger guard. "Kayla?"

No response.

The unnatural silence seemed to amplify his footsteps against the gravel path.

As he approached the gazebo, he heard a shuffling sound from within. Then, about a foot above the floor, a pale, slender arm speared through the opening, frantically waving him forward.

The hairs on the back of his neck woke up, and his gut tightened. After a quick scan of the garden, he bent low, entered the structure, and turned in the direction of where the disembodied arm had disappeared.

Kayla sat huddled against the low wall, tears coating her face.

"What's wrong?"

"Aunt V-vicky—the governor." She pointed a shaky finger toward the back of the gazebo. "Dead."

"You're sure?"

She nodded. "Gunshot."

His head snapped back to her. "Are you injured?"

"I'm fine."

Tension he didn't realize he'd been harboring eased its grip around his chest.

"Did you see the shooter?"

She shook her head. "I didn't even hear the gunshot."

Unlike in the movies, suppressors didn't completely silence a gun's report. However, if she'd never heard one before, the sound might not register.

"Do you have your phone?" he asked.

"I dropped it and haven't been able to locate it in the dark."

"Here." He handed her his. "Call nine-one-one."

When he pivoted on the balls of his feet, she grasped his arm. "Where are you going?"

"To check on the governor."

"I told you. She's g-gone."

"I understand." He motioned toward the phone. "Make the call. I'll be back in a second."

For a moment, her eyes pleaded with him to stay. Then she blinked, and some of her normal mettle returned.

Staying low, he rushed to where the governor's body lay on its side. She looked almost peaceful, except for the vacant stare and the hole in her head. He checked her pulse to be sure.

Nothing.

Judging by the size of the entrance and exit wounds, the shooter had used a 9mm handgun or a pistol-caliber carbine rifle.

Making his way back to the lobbyist, he asked, "Are the police on their way?"

She nodded.

"Sure you're okay?"

Another nod.

An electrical current buzzed in the back of his skull, urging him to sweep the garden, to make sure the threat was gone. But another part of him couldn't leave her alone, unprotected.

Sirens blared in the distance.

"Did you see anything?" he asked, keeping his attention on their surroundings. "Hear anything out of the ordinary?"

"No, nothing."

"Tell me what happened."

"The governor texted me, requesting that I meet her here."

"How did she seem when you arrived?"

"Anxious."

"Why did she want to meet you?"

She hesitated for a brief moment, then said, "She wanted to tell me something." Her eyes filled with tears, though they never fell. "But she didn't get the chance."

"Any idea of what she wanted to share?"

Another hesitation, followed by a negative head shake.

He would drill into that topic later. Right now, he wanted to get Kayla to safety.

"The sirens have likely scared off the shooter. We need to get you inside."

"I don't want to leave her."

He had no way of knowing if the governor or Kayla was the shooter's intended target. No doubt both women had made enemies on their climb to the top.

Cameron heard the rapid footsteps a second before a tall, distinguished gray-haired gentleman, hemmed in by two men in near-identical black suits, rushed toward them. The older man appeared to be vying for the lead position and having little success.

He rose to a standing crouch, using a thick support beam as cover. "FBI. Stay right there."

The trio skidded to a halt.

"Glenn Ziller." The suit in front lifted his hands in the air, one held a gun. "My partner Ford and I," he jerked his head toward the other suit bringing up their flank, "are part of the governor's security detail. My creds are inside my jacket."

Cameron motioned the man to proceed with his gun. "Slowly."

"Kayla!" The distinguished gentleman's voice was breathless with fear as he tried to push past Suit Number One, but the younger guy simply held out a muscular arm, barring his way.

"Daddy?" Kayla scrambled to her feet and, before Cameron could stop her, she ran into the older man's arms.

Gordon Krowne hugged his daughter close. "Are you all right, Pepper?"

With an odd combination of relief and envy, Cameron observed how her father's endearment seemed to calm her.

"Fine," Kayla said. "Where's Mama?"

"Entertaining our guests. I didn't want to say anything until I knew more." He cocked his head, listening to the sirens. "A decision I will pay for shortly when the police arrive on our doorstep."

Cameron checked the creds of each bodyguard, though he kept his handgun aimed at Glenn's center mass. "Where were you while the governor took a bullet?"

"Bullet?" Gordon echoed.

"Aunt Vicky's d-dead," Kayla said, her voice breaking.

"My God."

Ford cursed, and the two guards shot forward.

"Stop, or I'll blow you into the rosebushes." Cameron widened his stance. "Answer my question."

Ford's already chiseled jaw turned to granite. "The governor ordered us to take a restroom break."

"At the same time?"

"Yes."

"Don't blame them, Agent Blackwell," Kayla said. "Governor Stokes would've given them hell if they'd done otherwise. She liked her privacy."

Cameron lowered his arm, and the guards attempted to push past him. He stepped in front of them. "I confirmed she's dead. No need for more people trampling the crime scene."

The sirens were loud and close.

"Wait here," he said to Kayla. "I'll be back in a minute."

"Where are you going?"

"Perimeter check. I want to make sure the shooter is gone."

"No, please don't." She latched on to his arm. "Let the police search the property."

For a moment, he thought her concern might be for his welfare and warmth spread into his chest. Then he brushed the thought away, realizing the more likely scenario was that she had less faith in him than the police.

Or did she have something to hide?

He detached his arm from her grip, signaled for Glenn to follow and pushed into the darkness.

7

KNEELING ON THE GAZEBO'S FLOOR, KAYLA DIVIDED HER attention between her beloved godmother and the dark garden. Her heart sat heavy in her chest as she waited for Ash to reemerge. The thought of him meeting the same fate as Vicky made her stomach tangle into a mass of writhing snakes.

Ash wouldn't like it when he found her at Vicky's side again, but she couldn't leave her alone. Couldn't reconcile the woman's still warm hand and the absence of her beating heart. The entire time, she waited for the vacancy to leave her godmother's eyes and for her to focus on Kayla's face.

The bullet wound in Vicky's head mocked her for a fool.

Ford stood outside, guarding her and Gordon, or the crime scene, or maybe both. Neither Ford, nor her father, had been successful in keeping her from Vicky's side.

Kayla's heart sank at the thought of her mother's reaction to learning about her friend's violent death. She closed her burning eyes. Sweet Mary, she would have to notify the other aunties, too.

The powerhouse quartet had been friends for nearly four decades. They'd supported one another through the trials and triumphs of each of their lives. But death among them? How would they survive it?

The heavy weight on her chest became crushing. Her breathing more difficult. It was then that Ash returned, extending his hand in her direction.

"All clear," he said in the gentlest voice he'd ever used with her. "Come, you shouldn't be here."

She grasped his hand, and the heat of his skin penetrated her chilled fingers. Noticing the temperature difference, he shrugged off his coat and wrapped it around her shoulders. She hadn't realized she was shaking until that moment.

He pressed the backs of his fingers against her clammy neck, and Kayla leaned into his touch, seeking more of his warmth, his comfort.

But he lifted her chin and flashed the bright beam of a Maglite across her eyes. She reared back, blinking away the echo of his light. "Why'd you do that?"

His brows slashed together, and he gently pried her hand from the governor's and ushered her over to the chaise longue. "Lie down," he ordered, pointing to the raised end. "Put your feet up on the arm—back—whatever you call it."

Police and paramedics filtered into the gazebo.

"I'm fine," she said through chattering teeth.

"No. You're not." He forced her to sit down. "Your body is going into shock, which means your organs aren't getting enough blood and oxygen. We need to get your feet up."

"I'm just chilled from sitting on the floor for so long. I'll warm up in a few minutes."

Her head suddenly felt bloated, and two frustrated Ashes wavered before her eyes. She reached out to stop her world from spinning. Heard his oath and shout to the paramedics. Then . . . nothing.

TWO HOURS LATER, KAYLA SAT IN THE CORNER OF A LARGE plush sofa located in her father's study. Still wrapped in Ash's jacket, she watched Gordon pace and Jillian wipe away tears that wouldn't stop falling. Sybil and Elsie sat nearby, equally distraught.

A governor's apparent murder was no small thing. State and local law enforcement officials of various expertise and standing cluttered the house and front lawn of her parents' home. Thanks to Ash, the garden and gazebo had been secured before the curious could trample precious evidence.

Kayla experienced a twinge of guilt, but consoled herself that she'd been careful to retrace her steps back to Vicky.

After collecting the guests' contact information, the police had shooed them away. As for Kayla, she was now giving her eyewitness account for the umpteenth time. Exhaustion was shutting off the lights in every cell of her barely functioning brain.

"Ms. Krowne," the forty-something detective said. "I'm sorry to put you through this again, but I need to record your statement."

"I understand." Her gaze flicked up to the silent, dark-haired man looming above the seated APD detective. Ash's features were set in grim lines and his hands were fisted beneath his crossed arms.

Ash had tried to postpone this latest interview, but the detective had been adamant about talking to her while the incident was fresh in her memory.

As if it would ever go stale. The image was seared into her mind.

At least the detective had agreed to taking her statement here, instead of the police station. She refocused on her interviewer. An attractive man, with sandy-blond hair, brown eyes, and wide shoulders. He wore a gray pressed shirt, a black tie, and slacks.

"Before you begin," Kayla said, "can you tell me if the governor's daughter, Linda Collier, has been notified?" Vicky's husband had died three years ago, and she never remarried, nor did she have any romantic attachments, as far as she knew.

"Several attempts to reach Ms. Collier have been made," Detective Damon Morgan said, "with no success. We'll keep trying."

Kayla frowned. Linda was notorious for never being far from her phone, especially at this time of the night. A thought occurred to her. "She's seven and a half months pregnant. If you continue having trouble reaching her, you might try the hospital."

Detective Morgan nodded at his rookie partner, whose sole role seemed to be taking notes.

"Let's start from the beginning," Morgan said, turning his attention back to Kayla. "How did you and Governor Stokes come to be in the gazebo tonight?"

"I received a text from her, asking to meet with me."

"What time?"

"Eight thirty-three." She'd confirmed the time during her first interview.

"What did she want to meet with you about?"

"The message didn't say." Sharing her thoughts on what Victoria might have wanted to speak with her about wouldn't do anyone any good. Speculation on her part could send the police on a wild goose chase. "She never got an opportunity to tell me."

"How did she seem to you?" Morgan asked, interrupting her rabbit hole of unknowns. "Upset? Happy? Scared?"

"I would say more anxious."

"About what she wanted to discuss with you? Or being seen meeting with you?"

A jolt went through her body. "I-I'm not sure."

"Do you remember seeing anyone else in the garden, on your way to the gazebo?"

She paused to think. "No, not that I recall."

"Hear any unusual noises?"

"No."

"Walk me through what happened the moment you entered the gazebo?"

Kayla's stomach clenched into a tight ball, shielding itself against another emotional punch. "When I first entered, I didn't immediately spot Vicky. She was standing against the far wall, almost as if she were—"

She cut the thought off. The events of the night were stirring up her imagination.

"Were what, Miss Krowne?" Morgan prompted.

"Nothing, I . . . "

"Listen to your instincts, Kayla," Ash said in a quiet voice.

"As if she were hiding. She wouldn't allow me to turn on the gazebo's lights."

"Any ideas why?" Morgan asked.

She shook her head.

"You entered the gazebo, then what?"

"I went to greet her, but my shoe caught on the area rug, and I stumbled."

The detective glanced down at her stilettos, where they lay haphazardly on the floor beside her. The pointed, rhinestone toe glittered in the study's bright light.

"Go on."

"When I straightened, I saw the—" She touched her own forehead, unable to say the words.

Instinct had her lifting her gaze to Ash, almost as if looking at him would give her the reassurance, the courage she needed to continue. Which was ridiculous. She barely knew the man.

Why hadn't she looked to her parents instead, two people who had never let her down?

Then she'd recalled Ash's gentle care with her after finding her huddled on the floor. His fierce protection.

"Are you of a similar height to the governor?"

"Nearly the same. Without heels, she's an inch taller."

Ash and Morgan shared a meaningful glance. The agent's jaw turned stone hard.

Despite the warmth of her borrowed coat, anxiety tacked down her spine.

"What?" she asked.

"Did the governor say anything to you, prior to your stumble?" Morgan asked.

There's something I need to tell you. Something you must keep to yourself.

Her fingers toyed with the coat's button.

Promise me. Not even your mother.

A promise Vicky wouldn't have exacted lightly. Her

godmother knew how close she was to Jillian. Requesting she keep something from her mother was a big ask.

Kayla needed to figure out what Vicky wanted to tell her. It might not have had anything to do with her murder. Maybe it concerned one of the other aunties or even Jillian.

The last thing they needed right now was the police nosing around into their private affairs.

"Nothing outside of a greeting," she said.

"Can you think of anyone who would want to kill you, Miss Krowne?"

"*Me?* I'm not the one you should be worrying about."

"You might be right, but based on what you've told me, I suspect you were the intended target. If you hadn't tripped on the carpet when you did, the bullet would have assuredly hit the back of your head."

8

"THANK YOU FOR THE RIDE," KAYLA SAID, THE MOMENT ASH put his vehicle in park.

Normally, at this point, she would say something to ignite his irritation. Some time ago, and quite by accident, she'd discovered the slight narrowing of his eyes and the clenching of his jaw heated up every one of her woman parts. The man was sexy as hell when peeved.

If only he knew his attempts at intimidation and suppression had such a stimulating effect on her, he'd probably laugh more in her vicinity.

But tonight, on the heels of seeing one of her aunties killed, literally before her eyes, she didn't have a single provocative thought in her head.

As a matter of fact, not much of anything was moving around upstairs. She couldn't recall the last time she didn't have the next dozen steps already mapped out.

This void would have unnerved her under normal circumstances, but Kayla wasn't unsettled. She was tired. A bone-deep, out-before-your-head-hits-the-pillow exhaustion had consumed her body.

For this reason, she didn't compute Ash's continued presence at her side until he closed and locked the front door behind them.

"What are you doing?" she asked, noticing the pistol in his hand.

"Making sure you're safe." He nodded toward the alarm panel. "Arm it."

The intensity carved into his features as he scanned the foyer and the long hallway leading into the interior of her house compelled her to do as instructed. When he grasped her hand and made for the upstairs, the switch from shock to WTF clicked over.

She dug the heels of her Jimmy Choos into the stair runner and disengaged her hand from his. Albeit reluctantly.

"My wits have returned." She motioned toward his weapon. "Explain yourself."

His chest rose on a deep inhalation, but he continued to surveil their surroundings. "I'm escorting you to your bedroom, then I'm going to clear this enormous home."

"Why?" she asked. "If someone was here, they would have tripped the alarm."

"No security measure is one hundred percent fool-proof." He indicated the stairs.

Lifting the hem of her gown, she followed a half-step behind him. A calico cat sat at the top of the staircase, her yellow-green eyes intent on Ash.

When they reached the top stair, Ash asked, "Which way?"

She took a moment to brush Crispy's forehead and felt the feline's answering pressure against her palm. Straightening, she turned to the right, but Ash, with a gentle hand, maneuvered her behind him, again. His protective instincts made the flutter in her stomach intensify, and even more so the closer they got to her bedroom.

Once they entered her suite, he flipped on the overhead light and took a moment to glance around, then motioned for her to stand behind a chair while he cleared the bathroom and walk-in closet.

Kayla felt a little ridiculous, almost as if she were on the set of a Bourne movie. Crispy seemed to agree with how ludicrous her mistress looked hiding behind a chair. The feline limped straight across the middle of the room, tail held high, until she reached her bed, where she curled up and closed her eyes.

Kayla stayed put and allowed Ash to do his job. To be honest, she appreciated the extra caution, even though she hadn't bought into Detective Morgan's speculation about her being the killer's actual target.

Who would want to kill her? No one she could think of.

If she had been the target, why wait for her to reach the gazebo? Why not pick her off on the garden path?

She stilled as another thought struck. Had they both been the shooter's target? One bullet, two kills. Was that even possible?

A shiver rippled down her spine. Thank God for rhinestones and rugs.

Emotion gripped her throat at the selfish thought. She would give anything—even her own life—for Vicky to still be alive. For her godmother to be able to hold her first grandchild in her arms.

Despite her rocky relationship with Linda, Vicky had set up a baby room in the governor's mansion, full of toys and books and the most adorable bassinet.

Why would anyone want to kill Vicky? Although some would consider her biased, Kayla truly believed Victoria

Stokes was—had been—the best governor for the citizens of North Carolina.

Kayla would wait to see what forensics had to say before she started drawing up a list of Vicky's potential enemies. And hers.

Ash reemerged and pointed at the balcony doors. "Are they on sensors?"

"Yes. All the exterior doors and windows."

He whisked the curtains closed. "Got your phone?"

Patting her clutch tucked in the crook of her arm, she nodded. One of the officers had found her phone at the base of a large planter. Other than needing a new screen protector, it had survived its smash-and-slide with the flag-stone floor.

He strode to her door. "Lock this behind me and don't open it to anyone but me. Stay away from the windows and keep the lights off. No sense providing a beacon of your whereabouts."

"Lights? Wait, where are you going?"

"To clear the rest of the house."

"But—"

"Lock it." The door closed quietly, but not before he flipped the light switch off.

Thrown into darkness, Kayla robotic-armed her way to the door, fumbled to engage the lock, then pressed her ear to the wooden barrier between them. Absolute quiet descended on the other side. She backed away from the door and tried to rub warmth back into her cold fingers.

After shrugging off Ash's coat and folding it over a nearby chair, she slid her phone from her silver clutch and tapped the icon to engage the flashlight. Bright light flooded the darkness, guiding her to the walk-in closet. Once inside, she turned on the light and kicked off her high heels. When the entirety of her foot touched the carpeted floor, a moan escaped her lips, as it always did upon removing her armor.

She shucked off her evening gown, then drew black yoga pants and a long-sleeved tee from one of the many drawers along the wall. In all of her homes, her closets were designed the same way.

She kept her casual clothes, pajamas, and undergarments in the exact same drawers. Her power suits, sundresses, and evening gowns hung in the same alcoves. Her shoes stood in the same slots. Her jewelry nestled in the same protective cases.

Everything was designed in a way that required little thought, little decision-making, other than, *which one*? Even that took minimal effort. Her schedule dictated style, comfort, and color.

She arranged her homes in this way to reserve all her mental energy for strategizing and executing action plans for her clients.

A lot rode on her ability to convince policymakers that her client's campaign was in their constituents' best interests. Or, in many cases these days, their future reelection's best interest. Political aspirations could fold on a dime after one wrongly backed initiative, one can-I-get-a-selfie-with-you picture, one ill-judged post.

Policymakers had to be convinced over and over and over before agreeing to back an initiative. Lobbying was one part strategy, one part networking, one part patience, one part investigative, and one part rooting out a legislator's passions and weaknesses.

Kayla's structured existence helped her be a damned good lobbyist.

What she wasn't good at was inaction.

She hooked two fingers around a pair of black runners and slid her bare feet into the no-tie shoes with foam insoles. Heaven on rubber.

She stood in the center of her closet, motionless. Every cell in her body shouted at her to *move*.

But Vicky's face *after* kept creeping into her mind like a phantom haunting her. Taunting her, pointing a finger at her.

What if she was wrong and someone really wanted her dead? Had something she'd done, said, not done, not said, caused one of her favorite people to die?

The possibility weakened her knees. Knees that had held her upright when friends deserted her, when clients lost faith in her, when competitors outmaneuvered her.

Marching into the bathroom, she grabbed a hair tie out of the top middle drawer and scooped her blond mass up until she had it secured in a sloppy bun at the back of her head. She would save washing the makeup off of her face until after Ash left.

Speaking of Ash, where the hell was he? With every minute he was gone, her security system lost another percentage point of her trust.

Returning to her closet, she stared at the back corner. The mental ticking clock urging her to do something besides busywork until he returned.

If he returned.

She couldn't stop thinking about how everything in her life was normal until a single bullet shot her world into an entirely new direction.

What if the shooter had been waiting for her to return home, and Ash had found them.

Another spiral, another direction, another new hell.

"No one will take care of you, but you, Kayla Krowne."

She marched into the depths of her closet, depressed the upper lefthand corner of the tall cabinet, and entered a six-digit passcode. The lock disengaged, and she pulled open the narrow steel door.

Inside the ten-by-ten safe room hung a specially made Kevlar vest with an attached cross-draw pistol holster. She threaded her head and arms into the vest, secured it, then reached for her Glock 43X. Checked the chamber and clip before securing the weapon in her holster.

Every fourth Sunday afternoon for the past five years, she'd gone to the range to train, something Liv had introduced her to after a mugging Kayla survived in Raleigh. A mugging that had left her with a fractured rib.

At the time she'd bought it, she'd thought the body armor was a bit much. But now, she took comfort in its solid weight against her chest and the pistol helped bolster her natural confidence. Something she needed desperately at the moment.

Drawing in a fortifying breath, she fast-walked to her bedroom door, unlocked it, and stepped into the hallway, listening for any signs of Ash.

Something belowstairs clattered, then went silent.

"Ash," she whispered, her heart galloping in her chest.

An image of him bleeding out on her tile floor burrowed into her mind and, before she knew it, she'd flattened herself against the wall and drawn her handgun. She slid along the wall until she reached the wide staircase. With sloth-like slowness, she eased forward until the first level came into view.

Everything seemed normal. No slinking shadows, no grip of shoe soles against marble tile, no sound of hand-to-hand combat. No crackle of gunfire.

One slow step at a time, she descended the stairs and

focused all of her senses outward, scanning her surroundings for the unfamiliar.

She made it all the way to the spacious entryway without dying. Now she had a decision to make—left or right? Left took her to the rooms where she entertained guests and cemented multimillion-dollar promises. Where she was Kayla Krowne, results-driven lobbyist.

The right led to the kitchen. A room that had witnessed catastrophic culinary attempts and masterpieces in equal measure, depending on whether she'd followed a recipe or leaned into her non-award-winning tastebuds and eye-measuring ability.

Mentally tossing a coin in the air, she took the hallway to the right of the stairs.

With the same precision of movement, she inched her way toward the kitchen, keeping her ears alert for any bit of sound that might give away the intruder's or Ash's location.

As she passed the downstairs bathroom, she caught a movement out of her peripheral vision. She swung her pistol around, then choked back a gasp when she nearly put a bullet through her reflection in the mirror above the sink.

Lowering her weapon, she released a shaky breath. She didn't have a chance to feel the full relief of her near mishap.

Something hard and unforgiving slammed into the side of her head. Pain splintered her thoughts and her knees weakened. A blurry image of her attacker's imposing silhouette filled the mirror, then . . . lights out.

Again.

9

KAYLA'S RISE TO AWARENESS CAME SLOWLY, PAINFULLY.

Her head throbbed as if someone had squeezed her brain like a therapy gel ball, while prying her eyes from their sockets. With an ice pick.

A sixth sense cautioned her to remain still. To force her bruised mind to go back in time. To remember . . .

The images came fast and violent.

The gazebo, the dark hole in Vicky's forehead, Detective Morgan's questions, Ash's concern for her, feelings of helplessness, her search for Ash.

Excruciating pain.

Kayla's heart smashed into her ribcage before retreating into a quivering ball. Was her intruder the same person who'd killed Vicky and presumably meant to kill her? If so, why was she still alive?

Or was she that unlucky—to be shot at and assaulted by two different people in the same evening?

Ash. Oh my God, where was Ash?

Heart in her throat, she forced herself to calm down,

which was damn hard. Every cell in her body, screamed at her to move, find Ash, make sure he was safe.

Alive.

She needed to assess her surroundings, identify the danger zones. It was the smart thing to do. But the physical inaction was killing her.

She drew in a long breath, analyzed the scent, but didn't identify anything alarming. No mustiness, no foul body odor, no metallic scent of death. Only an intense coldness beneath the left side of her head.

The contraction of her left hand confirmed that she rested on a bed. Could she turn over? Or would bindings restrict her movement?

She didn't detect any cold metal or hard plastic around her wrists or ankles. But she hadn't moved enough to be sure.

Feeling buoyed by what she'd ascertained so far, she rolled to her right side. Not only was she not bound to the bed, the sheets were made from the highest thread count and the duvet was so soft that she could've nested in it for days.

Unnerved by her findings, she blinked her dry eyes open and came face-to-face with Ash Blackwell.

"'Bout damn time," he said, his gruff voice belying the concern bracketing the corners of his eyes. His tone softened. "You're safe."

"Where am I?" she asked, wincing as she made to sit up. She glimpsed a familiar nightstand, crystal chandelier, and calico cat before scrunching her eyes shut against the sharp jab of pain behind her left ear.

"Easy," he said, pressing his fingertips against her shoulder until she laid back down. "You might have a minor concussion."

She touched the small aching bump behind her ear and was surprised to find the area cold, until her hand brushed against a gel pack positioned between her head and pillow.

"Leave it," he ordered, when she made to remove the pack. "It's keeping the swelling down."

"My head is numb."

He pried her fingers away, gently. "Just a while longer."

Crispy batted at his hand, ripping the skin.

"Okay, okay," he muttered, rubbing his knuckles. "Blood-letting feline."

Kayla noticed several more scratches. "Crispy gave you those?"

"Crispy? What kind of name is that for a savage guard cat?"

Five years ago, she'd agreed to foster the calico after a devastating fire had killed her human family and left the five-month-old kitten's right rear haunch badly burned. At seeing her singed fur and damaged leg, one of the young volunteers at the animal shelter had joked about the kitten's close call of becoming a crispy critter.

The name had stuck.

Crispy's leg still bore a significant burn scar, which caused a slight limp. But she was otherwise whole, hearty, and freakishly attuned to Kayla's moods.

After three months and not a single inquiry to take on an injured cat, Kayla had decided to make the fur baby's stay permanent. The calico hadn't been the first animal she'd fostered from the shelter, but Crispy was the only one she'd ever adopted.

"Did you catch who attacked me?" Kayla asked.

As if sensing her unease, Crispy nuzzled her cold, wet nose against Kayla's cheek. She tunneled her fingers into the calico's soft fur, and the low thrum of anxiety in her chest calmed.

Mission accomplished, the cat curled up by her feet.

Ash sat back and seemed to brace himself. "In a manner of speaking, yes."

She studied his features. "What manner would that be?" The answer came to her in an instant of clarity. "You knocked me out."

This time, it was his turn to wince. "Sorry."

"Why?"

"Why were you downstairs? Wearing all black? And in tactical gear, for chrissakes?"

When he put it like that, she could understand why he'd acted first, thought later. She'd been operating on instinct. A compulsion to find and protect. Given the circumstances, she was lucky he'd only rendered her unconscious.

"I heard a noise."

"Doesn't answer my question."

"I was worried something had happened to you."

The hard lines around his mouth softened . . . a little.

"I could have killed you, Kayla."

Her name on his lips momentarily stunned her speechless. She couldn't recall having ever heard him say it before. It was nice. Blood warming, even.

Until she registered the barely suppressed terror edging his voice. "I'm sorry, Ash. Really. I couldn't stand hiding away while you faced a danger meant for me."

He slouched back in the chair he'd dragged up to the side of her bed and stared at the ceiling.

While she'd been unconscious, he'd removed his jacket and rolled up the sleeves of his white button-down shirt. His broad chest rose on a deep inhalation.

The moment his chest returned to its natural position, he said, "I've trained for situations like tonight. A lot. It's second nature to me." He lowered his chin and his beautiful blue orbs locked onto her face. "And I expect my orders to be obeyed."

Obeyed.

There were no words in *Merriam-Webster* to describe how much she loathed the word.

"Don't get your feminist knickers in a bunch, Ms. Krowne. I expect the same from any person under my protection."

She counted backward from five, a technique she'd picked up in college when trying not to deck every male student in her political science class.

Five, four, three, two, one.

"I understand," she said, the words drying out her mouth like a handful of sawdust. "But know that inaction goes against every drop of H_2O in my body."

His lips twitched as if he were about to smile, then he seemed to recall they weren't on friendly terms and shot out of his chair. He scraped two white oblong pills off the bedside table and picked up a glass brimming with water.

"Take these. They'll dull your headache."

"How'd you know?"

"I've been there. Plus," his index finger waggled before her eyes, "the squinting is a dead giveaway."

Kayla flared her eyes wide. The action released the tension she hadn't realized she'd been storing. She sat up slowly and took the proffered tablets, washing them down with the water.

He eased the half-empty glass from her shaky grip. "Try to get some sleep."

If only.

The second she closed her eyes unwanted images would plague her, making sleep impossible. Just as well. Every creak of the house's joints would likely send her imagination into overdrive. Sounds she'd heard a hundred times would be new and mysterious and absolutely maddening.

"Thanks for everything you did tonight," she said, handing him the gel pack. "Well, except the head bashing."

No reaction.

The guy never laughed at her jokes. It was good she loved a challenge.

An unexpected worry crowded aside her amusing pet project. Would he stay if she asked? She glanced down at his right hand, where he rhythmically tapped his forefinger against the side of his thigh.

A nervous habit. A tell. One that had *escape* written all over it.

Setting aside her own wishes, she took pity on him. "I'm fine now. There's no need for you to babysit me any longer."

"I'm not worried about your head. I know how hard it is."

She lifted one brow at the insult. "What are you worried about then?"

"Unwanted visitors."

"You really think the bullet that took"— she cleared her throat, still unable to say the words —"was meant for me?"

"It would be unwise to rule it out."

"The house alarm system is armed and there are surveillance cameras all around the property. There's no sense in you staying any longer."

"That's a lot of security."

"Your point?"

"Seems like you were anticipating trouble."

"There's always a losing side in what I do. And the loser is never my client." She knew the statement sounded arrogant, but she spoke the truth. Not everyone accepted losing. "I also have a sizable art collection in the house, if you recall."

"Which is why I'm crashing on your couch tonight."

"What?" She bolted upright and got a meat cleaver through the brain for her efforts.

"Don't worry, Ms. Krowne. Your virtue is safe with me."

Pity.

He sat in the middle of her sofa, balancing his pistol on his leg.

"Are you going to stare at me all night?"

Although she couldn't see his eyes in the gloom, she felt their thorough glide down her body, as if he could see through layers of bedding and clothes.

"There are worse ways a man could spend his evening."

10

THE MORNING WAS ALREADY IN FULL SWING BY THE TIME Kayla eased her legs over the side of the bed. A situation she occasionally indulged in on the weekends, but never during the workweek. Evidently, experiencing not one but two traumatic events in a single evening had a sedative effect on her.

She still wore her black leggings and tee. Her hair had escaped its tie and now fell around her face and she was tempted to stay hidden behind the blond veil, but that wasn't her way.

Unable to put the moment off a second longer, she brushed her hair aside and turned toward the sofa, only to find it empty. She scanned the rest of the room for Ash's tall, imposing figure, but found no evidence of him anywhere. Crispy had abandoned her, too.

If not for her Kevlar vest draped over one of the high-backed chairs near the cold fireplace, and the tender spot on her head, she might have convinced herself that last night had been nothing but a vivid nightmare.

She didn't know whether to feel relief or disappointment at finding Ash gone. It had taken awhile for her to fall asleep last night, not being used to having others in her private space. But once she succumbed, she'd slept through the night, though her dream state mind produced a vivid reenactment of the governor's assassination, replacing Vicky's face with Ash's .

Rising, she padded across the expansive room and pushed open the curtains. Rather than her normal adrenaline-pumping anticipation to get the day started, she felt a strange nervousness.

A reluctance.

The small display of pictures lining the mantel drew her attention. One photo near the middle snagged her attention. A younger version of herself smiled at the camera, her arms wrapped around Sybil and Elsie on her left and Jillian and Vicky on her right. The Hungarian Parliament building's imposing red dome and stunning Gothic towers soared above their heads as they drifted along the Danube River, day one of their weeklong getaway to celebrate Kayla's twenty-fifth birthday.

The trip that changed her life, her worldview, forever.

A trip she would later learn had been initiated by Vicky, not Jillian. She was still processing that fact. Still didn't know how she felt about it. Maybe she never would.

That day seemed like a lifetime ago, now.

Kayla wasn't the same bright-eyed, bend the world toward goodness person. A decade as a lobbyist had opened her eyes to the fragility of democracy, the flexibility of morality, the power of hope.

She traced the tip of her index finger across Vicky's laughing face. Her throat contracted, making it hard to swallow, to breathe, to think of a life without one of her greatest cheerleaders.

Her dearest auntie.

Her godmother.

Her friend.

She loved them all, but there had always been something special about Victoria. Though no one had ever acknowledged it. Not Kayla, not Vicky. Not Jillian or the other aunties. They all knew of her and Vicky's special bond.

Maybe it was the godmother-goddaughter connection. Maybe they just clicked better.

The constriction around her throat crept downward to engulf her chest. It squeezed and squeezed, daring her to release the grief bottled up in her heart, making her eyes burn.

Kayla wouldn't let the tears fall. She hadn't earned that right. Her auntie's killer was out there. Free. No doubt congratulating themself for removing whatever threat Vicky had posed to them.

No matter what Ash or Detective Morgan said, Kayla didn't buy their hypothesis that a scuffle between a rhinestone and a rug had saved her from assassination. If the killer had wanted her dead, they had only to pull the trigger for the second time. She'd given an experienced killer ample time to take her out before she'd thought to drop to the floor.

Kayla didn't know who would want Vicky dead, but she would use every bit of her abundant resources to find them and avenge her auntie's murder. Fire gathered in her center, filling her with new purpose and replacing her earlier reluctance to meet the day.

Somehow, she would figure out who'd stolen North Carolina's beloved governor from the people of this great state.

From her.

And make them pay.

11

Standing at the bay window in Kayla's kitchen, Cameron sipped from a steaming cup of black coffee. The graphic on the side depicted a sassy, blinged-out chicken with the inscription, *This chick's still got it.*

An entire cabinet full of mugs and cups and not one a solid, boring color. The lobbyist had a definite mischievous side. One he'd done his damnedest to ignore. And mostly failed.

If she'd been anyone else, he would have enjoyed giving as good as he got from her. Nothing sexier than a woman with a sense of humor. But with him, she always seemed to be harboring something else beneath the surface of a well-delivered barb.

Meeeoow.

Cup near his mouth, Cameron turned to find the cat with the creepy yellow-green eyes staring at him. She lifted her pert pink nose, with its drop of black in the center, and sniffed the air.

"You like bacon?" He picked up a thin slice cooling on a plate beside the stove. "Is this what you want?"

She rose on her hind legs, stretched her body upward, and placed a soft paw against his knuckle to brace herself.

"Ah ah ah, not so fast." When he made to pull away, her sharp claws sank into his flesh. Air hissed between his teeth.

Her nails curled deeper.

"Here's the deal," he gritted out. "You get the bacon if you tell me one of your mistress's secrets. Let's start with—"

The feline snatched the bacon and ran to the nook housing her food and water bowls.

"You play dirty." He rubbed the torn flesh on his hand, hoping bacon wasn't to cats what grapes were to dogs. "Just like she does." He turned back to the window and let the coffee roll down his throat.

Images from the previous evening flashed through his mind. The devastation on Kayla's face when he'd found her next to the governor. The pain clouding her beautiful eyes when she awoke after he'd bludgeoned her with his pistol.

His stomach roiled at the thought of having hurt her. No matter how much she annoyed him, he would never have intentionally caused her harm.

Eggs crackling in a pan on the induction stove redirected his attention. Using a spatula, he raised each one to check their level of brown before covering the lot with a lid. By the time he dropped four pieces of multigrain bread in the toaster, Kayla swept into the room.

She wore her long blond hair in a low ponytail and a black business suit with a lavender silk shirt. The air in the room charged to life, and he suddenly felt at a disadvantage with his finger-combed hair, scruffy jaw, and day-old clothes.

Spotting him at the island counter, she stopped short. "What are you doing here?"

"Good morning to you, too." Her eyes cut from his, as if embarrassed. Or was that nerves he detected? Interesting. "The better question is why are you dressed for work?"

"It's Friday."

"Don't you think it's too soon to return?"

"No, why?"

"You watched someone you care about die before your eyes, violently. Not to mention the lump on your head."

"Which you put there."

He kept his focus, despite her provocation. "Give yourself time to grieve." *To heal.*

"Better I go into the office than sit here with my thoughts, twiddling my thumbs."

"Somehow, I knew you wouldn't stay home. Have a seat," he said. "These are almost done."

On her way to the massive fridge, she paused at the sight of the serving tray sitting on the counter. A fork and knife, napkin, butter, and blueberry preserves already nestled inside.

The area around her eyes softened as her gaze shifted from the tray to him. Her lips parted as if to say something, then the moment passed. She opened the fridge door and pulled out a tumbler filled with something creamy and slightly purple. "I appreciate the gesture, but I drink one of these for breakfast."

A drink no doubt made of some kind of alternative milk, like oat or almond, fruit, nuts, and a heaping tablespoon of protein powder. He wouldn't mind having one of those, too.

"Save it for the road. Eat while we wait."

"Wait for what?"

Ignoring her question, he nestled two eggs and a slice of bacon on a warmed white plate and plucked a lightly toasted bread slice from its slot. He set it on the counter and moved everything from the serving tray to near her place setting.

"Bon appétit."

She heaved a heavy sigh before sliding onto one of the island chairs. Her stomach growled.

A satisfied smile rippled at the edge of his mouth. "How's your head?"

"Tender to the touch, but otherwise fine."

"No headache?"

Instead of answering, which was an answer in and of itself, she said, "I'm fine, Ash. No need to worry."

Ash.

He didn't know if it was brain fog from lack of sleep or the novelty of serving her breakfast in her own kitchen, but it seemed to him that she spoke his name with a sweet melody. One he could have replayed, over and over.

Suddenly, inexplicably, he missed hearing his name. Missed being Ash Blackwell.

Why now? Why this woman, this *lobbyist*?

He was saved from delving any deeper by a sharp rap against the sliding glass door.

Ash stepped over and unlocked the door. Phin slid the heavy glass back, stepped inside, and lifted his nose in the air. "Smells delish."

"Lock it, then come have a bite before you go."

"No complaints from me." Phin smiled at Kayla. "Morning, boss."

"Would someone tell me what's going on?"

Setting four eggs and three strips of bacon on a plate in front of Phin, he said, "I got the same reception."

Phin lifted a brow. "Might have something to do with keeping her in the dark."

"Her highness just appeared."

"One more comment as if I'm not sitting here, and I'm throwing you both out and keeping the food for myself."

Opening the fridge, Ash pulled out a bowl of cut fruit and set it between them. Kayla looked at his offering as if she expected a bug to crawl out of the center. "You've been busy."

"I had a lot of hours to fill."

"You didn't sleep?"

He plucked his black evening coat from the back of a chair. "Don't leave her side today. Text me if you detect anything suspicious."

"Ten-four."

"No," Kayla said, glancing between the two of them. "Absolutely not."

Grabbing a bacon-to-go for himself, he tossed the last slice to Crispy after confirming she was still breathing. The cat stared at his offering for a full second before deigning to accept.

"Did you just feed my cat bacon?"

"She likes it."

"I'll leave tonight's litter box for you to clean up."

He pointed his bacon at her. "You either let Phin shadow you today or I talk to Detective Morgan about assigning someone to you. It'll put an extra burden on a department that's already criminally underfunded and understaffed, but—"

"I don't need anyone following me around like a duckling."

"Hey!" Phin grumbled around a mouthful of eggs.

"Protection," Ash corrected.

"I have a full schedule today, as does Phin, I'm sure. We can't be in each other's pockets."

"I moved some appointments," Phin said, stabbing a chunk of juicy pineapple. "I'm all yours."

"Then it's settled." Ash grasped the sliding door's handle.

"Wait," Kayla said. "Where are you going?"

"Hunting."

12

_____

AFTER A POWER NAP, SHOWER, AND FRESH CLOTHES, ASH returned to the Krowne residence to walk through the crime scene without the filter of fear for Kayla's safety clouding his analysis.

By the time he drove from the gate to the mansion's front entrance, Jillian Krowne awaited him on the massive ten-foot-wide stoop, framed by large ceramic vases containing evergreen topiary and clusters of purple, yellow, and maroon violas at the base.

"Good morning, Special Agent Blackwell," she said as he strode forward to take her proffered hand.

"Mrs. Krowne." He accepted her hand. The CFO's firm grip didn't surprise him, but the bony ridges beneath his fingertips did. "Thank you for consenting to my visit. I know this is a difficult time."

This morning, he'd received permission from Lawson to join the multiagency task force Morgan was pulling together. Having federal, along with state and local, resources focused on finding the governor's killer gave them a fighting chance to succeed.

"Of course," Jillian said, looking lovely in a pale green blouse and beige pants. Red rimmed her eyes and sadness pulled at her pale features. "Anything to help y'all find the person who kill—" Her composure cracked at having to verbalize the word, possibly for the first time since the incident. She gathered herself. "Who killed Victoria."

"I won't take up too much of your time."

"All I have is time today." She waved him inside. "How is my daughter?"

"As well as can be expected. My brother Phin is watching over her today."

"I'm sure Phin's a very capable young man, but do you think we should contact a private security firm?" She led him through the lower part of the mansion.

He expected to see remnants of the previous evening's festivities, but the house was spotless. They must have had a cleaning crew on standby, waiting for the police to clear out.

"My brother is as capable as any private security firm, but the decision is ultimately up to Kayla." He thought he knew what the lobbyist would decide, but kept it to himself.

Jillian's features lightened for a moment. "I see you know my daughter well. She would not want her mother's interference."

He smiled. "Nor an FBI agent's."

"Please let me know if you need backup in the future." Their brief bout of camaraderie dissipated the moment Jillian's hands clasped the handles of the French doors that led to the veranda and the garden beyond.

"I can take it from here, Mrs. Krowne."

She gave him a grateful look before stepping away. "Jillian, please."

"Ash."

She frowned. "I thought your name was Cameron?"

Why had he offered Ash? While wearing his badge, he was Cameron. Period.

He reflected back on his exchange with Kayla this morning, on her insistence of using his first name and his pleasure at hearing it cross her lips. With some shock, he realized he'd made the mental shift of thinking of himself as Ash again. And the change didn't bother him.

"Professionally, I go by Cameron. My family know me as Ash."

A genuine smile lifted the grief-stricken shadows from her face. "What an honor. Thank you, Ash." She waved toward the garden. "I will leave you to it."

"Thank you. I won't be long."

"Victoria was precious to me." The large round diamond decorating her left ring finger drooped to the side as she placed a hand on his arm. "Please let me know if there's anything you need. I want to see whoever did this pay for their crime."

"Would you mind answering a few questions?"

"Of course." Wariness trickled into her eyes.

"Are there any security cameras on the garden?" He hadn't noticed any, but the nighttime gloom made for good camouflage.

She shook her head. "Only on the house's entrances and exits. Something we'll have to rethink."

"Do you have any thoughts on who might have killed Governor Stokes?" She'd already gone through this with the detective, but sometimes memories could spark after having some time to think.

Jillian folded her hands in front of her, silent for several seconds, as she seemed to be engaged in a mental debate.

"Vicky was a much-loved public figure. Even so, there were those who didn't agree with her politics."

"Anyone or any group in particular come to mind?"

Another thoughtful pause. Finally, she shook her head. "I would be speculating at best. Something I don't do."

"Any leads, no matter how unlikely, would be appreciated."

"I will let you know if I come across anything substantive."

"Call or text me anytime." He handed her a business card, even though his number would be in her cell's Recents log. "Final question. Any idea why Governor Stokes requested a private meeting with your daughter?"

Her attention shifted to the French doors' multipaned windows, to the garden beyond. "No, I'm afraid not."

An untrained observer would have missed the slight stiffening of her posture and the suspension of her breathing, but Ash catalogued each of her anxiety-ridden tells.

"If something occurs to you, please let me know."

Dropping her gaze to his card, she brushed a red-painted thumbnail over his name. "Life is such a wonder, don't you think?"

"In what way?"

"The fundraiser I threw last night met its goal. We saved Gorekin Cove and, in the process, sacrificed one of my dearest friends."

He stilled. "Sacrificed?"

"If I had not invited her, she would still be alive." A pair of tortured eyes bore into his. "Do you think a thousand acres of woodland was worth a life?"

"The governor's death rests in the killer's hands, not yours."

"Ambition, influence, power—they are the great motivators in politics and business. An arena I know very well." She swallowed with a hard, audible click. "Invite a governor and they will come, with their virtual checkbooks."

Grief counseling was not his forte. He would hand over his entire savings if silver-tongued Phin walked through the door, *right now.*

He cleared his throat. "I didn't know Governor Stokes, but from what I've gathered, she seemed like someone who would have been honored that her last evening on earth saved a valuable natural area."

The CFO's features teetered on the edge of collapse. She fought through the deluge of emotion and gave him a grateful smile. "Yes. Yes, she would."

When she disappeared into the house, he stepped out onto the veranda. Despite the reason for his being here, the spring day promised to be a beautiful one. Tulips rose from their hibernation to jumpstart the season. The waning purple-pink blossoms of a redbud tree occupied the back corner near a gurgling waterfall.

But for the most part, the garden had a barren quality to it. Many of the trees and shrubs were only now starting to break free of their winter sleep. A fact that would've made the shooter's job a lot easier, but also left them vulnerable to exposure. He followed the circular path around, looking for anything out of the ordinary.

Forensics would've already done a thorough search. But even the most stalwart could miss things. When he got to the gazebo, he stepped inside, expecting to find evidence of the governor's violent death. But like the mansion, the interior was now spotless.

On one level, he couldn't help but be impressed with the Krownes' cleaning crew. The large rug, where the governor's body had fallen, had been replaced by a nearly identical one.

Not a speck of blood spatter could be found anywhere inside the structure. On another level, the ever-present red flag at the back of his mind was slowly unfurling.

He understood that the crime scene and the detritus from the party would be painful reminders of whom they had lost the previous evening. But this level of cleanliness reeked of something less emotional and more strategic.

After finishing his first circuit, he ditched the manicured path and wove his way through triangles of rosebushes, hillocks of grasses, and tangles of leafless vines.

His efforts produced no fruit, not that he had expected them to. But he never underestimated what a fresh set of eyes could accomplish. Returning to the gazebo, he stood in the approximate spot the governor had occupied.

A mixture of trees, shrubs, and spring perennials surrounded the structure. A firepit was visible off to the left and a pool/hot tub combo was off to the right of the veranda.

Each area was surrounded by vegetation, offering the users a modicum of privacy during the growing season, rather than an open backyard, spring-break vibe. The Krownes' property wasn't fenced in, nor were their neighbors'. Which meant the shooter could have come in from any direction and taken up a spot behind one of the many trees dotting the property.

He hoped forensics found something that would give them a clue about the killer's identity, but he wasn't holding his breath. A shooter who could put a bullet in their target's forehead would know how not to leave any evidence behind.

Still, he took another circuit around the property. Every

fifteen feet or so he would pause and glance back at the gazebo, judging distance and line of sight. When he reached the southeast side of the structure, between the fire pit and pool, he paused near a large dogwood.

The understory tree's low hanging branches, heavy with its distinctive white blooms, would have given the shooter ample cover, yet an unimpeded sight line to where Kayla had stood with the governor.

As it always did when he recognized a breakthrough, no matter how large or small, blood pumped hotly into his ears. Dropping his focus to the ground, he could see evidence of other footprints in the vegetation. Several, in fact.

The forensic team had also found the spot. He nodded to himself, expecting no less.

A sixth sense, one he never ignored, compelled him to give a slow surveillance around the dogwood. He wasn't looking for casings, cigarette butts, or the like. If they had been here, which he doubted, they'd already been bagged and hauled off to the lab.

He was looking for something else, though he didn't know what until he spotted a small round object protruding from a crevice in the bark of a dogwood tree, just above his head.

Stepping back, he took several pictures from different angles with his phone. Then he fished an evidence bag out of his blazer's pocket, along with a pocket knife. Using the sharp tip of the knife, he eased the object from its resting place and let it fall into the bag.

Lifting his find to eye level, he identified it immediately.

A pearl stud earring.

13

"ANYTHING ELSE," KAYLA ASKED, HER ATTENTION TOUCHING on each team member seated at the long conference room table.

Their seasoned intern Gemma Niles piped up. "Tommy O'Connor called right before our strategy meeting." The smooth dark skin on her nose crinkled at the memory.

"Let me guess," Phin said. "He wants another face-to-face status update."

Gemma nodded.

Some clients, like Tommy, had an almost obsessive need to know every minute step the firm took on their campaign. Which was their right, but Tommy's check-ins had morphed from weekly to every other day to every day.

"He's growing concerned that we're not going to secure the final three votes needed to pass SB623," Phin said. "I'll give him a call."

Tommy's nonprofit was supporting legislation that would loosen housing regulations across the state in order to combat the substantial rise in housing costs caused by inadequate inventory. A recent census indicated North

Carolina was the third fastest growing state. Many attributed the growth to domestic migration, people leaving their home states for Tar Heel's more temperate climes and what used to be affordable housing.

"He, uh," Gemma hedged, "wants to hear from Kayla."

Phin's eyes narrowed. "Does he?"

Sometimes clients needed the extra reassurance only the top decision-maker could give. It sucked, for everyone, but part of Kayla's job was acting as a buffer between her staff and their clients.

"I'd hoped to be in Raleigh today to add some pressure to the holdouts, but—" No sense stating the obvious. Everyone knew why Kayla was still in town. She'd given the team a brief summary of Vicky's murder, cautioning them to be alert for anyone suspicious hanging around the office building, while also assuring them that the extra measures were likely overkill.

Given that Krowne and Associates occupied the ninth floor of the Robinson building in downtown Asheville, it would be difficult to identify strangers. Most of the businesses who leased space here had done so for a number of years, so they knew, or at least recognized, most of the employees. However, visitors were coming and going all of the time.

"I'll make some calls later this week." Not ideal, but Kayla couldn't leave Asheville, right now.

"Last night, I came across some information that might help sway two of the votes," Ryan Sorrano said with enthusiasm. He was a recent graduate of UNC and eager to make his mark. "I could head down to the Capitol, present it to Cindy, and assist with rallying the votes."

Cindy Barry had been with the firm for seven years. The veteran lobbyist would much prefer assistance by way of face-to-face meetings than long-distance phone calls. And Kayla knew Phin wouldn't make the trip. Not until Ash released him from guard duty.

Even so, she turned to Phin. "Your call."

He appeared to go through a mental debate before agreeing. "Keep me updated, Ryan."

"Will do."

"Thank you, Ryan," Kayla said. "Let me know if you hear any scuttlebutt on HB821."

"The Women Entrepreneur Empowerment Act, right?" At her nod, he said, "You got it."

She looked from Phin to Gemma. "I'll update Tommy."

Phin nodded, though he didn't appear too pleased by her decision.

Kayla glanced down the long conference room table and checked the clock above her office manager, Luke Handler's, head.

It was 12:42.

She'd picked this vantage point specifically so Guard Dog Phin wouldn't get suspicious if he caught her time-checking once too often.

A kaleidoscope of butterflies took flight in her stomach. A phenomenon that didn't happen to her much anymore. She'd survived so many skirmishes during her stint as a lobbyist that she'd gained a hard-earned confidence that allowed her to tackle almost any problem head-on.

Her anxiety hadn't bloomed out of fear but guilt. Guilt for what she must do. And to whom.

As if waiting for this exact moment, a stomach growled.

Kayla smiled at the woman sitting to her right.

Natalie Bryant, the firm's attorney and Kayla's BFF since college, placed a hand over her middle. "Sorry, I didn't get a chance to eat breakfast."

Kayla fought to keep her polite smile from turning into a knowing grin. Natalie had a new man in her life. Her normally buttoned-up, never late for an appointment employee had been acting and looking a bit disheveled of late.

Not in an I'm-in-over-my-head-stressful way, but in an I-can't keep-my hands-off-you-let's-do-it-one-more-time-before-work way.

She noted one side of the attorney's shirt collar was outside of her navy suit jacket, while the other side was still tucked neatly inside, and her normally smooth updo had several half-escaped strands in the back. Yeah, she'd been thoroughly pleasured before starting time.

Kayla couldn't have been happier for her friend. Like Kayla's, Natalie's love life was nonexistent, save for the random bed partner she'd pick up at after-hours cocktail parties. Exciting for a time, but nowadays, Kayla longed for something more meaningful, something more intimate than a one-night stand. She knew Natalie felt the same.

"I'm sure your stomach isn't the only one feeding on itself right now." Kayla gathered her phone and laptop. "I think that does it for now." Her gaze touched on each of her team members for confirmation. One by one, they nodded their agreement.

"Is anyone going out for a bite to eat?" She made sure her attention didn't linger on her office manager.

"I am," Luke said on cue. "I have a taste for a Reuben from Bailey's deli." He stood. "Want me to grab you something?"

"I'd love their strawberry spinach salad. Easy on the feta."

"You got it."

"Thank you, Luke. I'm going to be tied up in video conferences for the rest of the afternoon."

"No problem. Any other takers?"

"Since I kept y'all so late," Kayla said, "lunch is on the firm."

As expected, everyone chimed in with their order, including Phin.

"I'll call it in." Luke turned to Phin. "Wanna get some fresh air? I could use some help carrying everything back." He gave the youngest Blackwell a smirk. "Or has Romeo gone to fat now that he's off the market?"

Maddy Carmichael had swept the handsome charmer off his proverbial feet. Something many a gorgeous lady had tried and failed to do.

From day one, Phin and Luke, who were barely a year apart in age, had hit it off. Every team meeting seemed to be a competition on whose verbal slam would elicit the biggest reaction.

Luke's comment dislodged a chorus of whistles and anticipatory wide-eyed stares.

Phin didn't disappoint. "Juliet keeps Romeo far too busy for him to go to fat."

Kayla laughed as she made her way to the door. "Got your company credit card?"

Grinning, Luke gave Phin a good-hearted shove to the back of his shoulder. "Yes, ma'am."

"Try to behave yourselves at the deli. I don't want to lose access to my favorite salad."

She was nearly out of the room when Phin called her name. A question in his tone.

"I'll be fine," she assured him.

Phin assessed her for a long, uncomfortable moment before he said, "I won't be long."

"Oh, by the way," she said as if the thought just occurred to her. "Could you let Cilla and Cruz know that I spoke to my contact at the EPA? The attorney general's office is about to file a suit against Randolph Industries." The news would no doubt be bittersweet for Cilla, since her father was the CEO.

"So, it's happening."

Kayla nodded. "My source indicated the AG has a stack of evidence against the company. They'll likely settle out of court."

"Timeline?"

"Probably by summer."

"I don't know whether to celebrate or give Cilla a hug."

"Both might be in order. The hug especially. They just got the news that Brittany Tate, the little girl living on the farm Randolph wanted to buy, is cancer free."

"Cilla will be so relieved." He tilted his head, considering her. "You don't want to deliver the good news yourself?"

She shook her head. "I'll leave that pleasure for you, if you don't mind."

"Not at all."

"Good." She waggled her fingers toward the door. "Vinaigrette dressing, please."

Phin turned away, already texting Cilla with the good news.

Diversion accomplished.

Leaving the conference room, she went back to her office and busied herself for five full minutes before swiveling toward the bank of windows behind her.

She peered down at the sidewalk. Waited for a sandy blond head and light brown head to appear. Ten seconds later, Luke and Phin emerged and their tall, lean forms turned toward Bailey's.

Kayla opened the desk drawer where she kept her purse. She speared her hand inside to retrieve two items, then as casually as she could manage, she closed her office door and strode through the firm's common area.

Thankfully, everyone had returned to their desks or were using the restrooms after the long meeting. She left the offices of Krowne and Associates and headed for the row of elevators. The ride down seemed to take an eternity. When the doors pinged open, she shot for the front entrance.

The moment she pushed through the glass door, a breathtakingly handsome man wearing a tailored coat over a white button-down and black slacks pushed away from the granite column where he'd been leaning. Waiting for her.

Mason Wade nodded, matching her quick stride.

"Which way?" she asked.

"Left."

They strode side by side until they reached a sleek black Mercedes Benz EQS 450+ sedan parked along the road. He broke off, increasing his speed in order to open the driver's side door.

A commotion across the street snagged their attention.

"No handouts, I said." The thick-chested man inside the food truck shooed a mother and two small children away, like they were dogs begging at the table.

All three wore heavy backpacks and their clothes appeared to carry months' worth of grime. Kayla's heart contracted at the sight.

Asheville was a beautiful, eclectic city, full of warm people and live music on every corner. Like any tourist destination though, the mountain town had a number of homeless people populating parks, empty storefronts, and busy intersections.

Kayla had done what she could in the way of supporting local shelters, food pantries, and backing elected officials determined to execute real solutions.

"Asshole," Mason muttered before turning back to her. "Got your key fob?"

She held it up for him to see. "I knew better than to ask for yours."

His smile was full of mischief and sexy as hell. "Finally got you trained, did I?"

"Behave, or I'll drive through a mud puddle."

"Good luck finding one. We haven't had any rain for three weeks."

She gave him a sidelong glance. "Which means I have my pick of dusty gravel roads."

He made a sound in the back of his throat.

Grinning, she said, "Enjoy your extra-long lunch."

"I don't like this situation at all."

"I know. But sometimes I have to play the boss card. Today's one of those days."

"Phin's going to be pissed."

"With any luck, I'll be back before he notices I'm gone."

Her driver, friend, and, when needed, bodyguard gave her the *you're dreaming* stare.

"I'll make it up to him—and you."

"Don't forget Luke."

"Especially Luke." She nodded for him to step back. "Now buzz off. I'm going to be late."

"All the more reason I should drive you. I could drop you off at the door."

"Some secrets a woman has to keep to herself. See you soon."

"Text me when you're leaving," he ordered as she shut the door.

Waving her agreement, she hit the Start button and pulled away. It didn't take long for Mason's large figure to appear in her rearview mirror as he stalked across the street to the food truck. He drew bills from his wallet, said a few harsh words to the vendor, and motioned the small family closer.

Kayla smiled. "That's my softie." She pushed the accelerator and put the sedan's 329 horsepower to work.

14

On her third pass down Battery Park Avenue, Kayla sent up a *Thank You, Jesus!* when she spotted a blue Subaru backing out of a prime parking spot outside Hemingway's Cuba restaurant.

She could have gone to the parking garage off Otis Street, but that would've tacked on another ten minutes. Plus, the garage was right across the street from the federal building, where the FBI's Resident Agency offices were located.

Who knew if Ash was inside, but the last thing she needed was for him to glance out a window and catch her walking across the street. Alone.

Another wave of guilt filled her chest at having to conceal her activities from her team, especially Natalie and Mason. Natalie, along with Liv, had been her confidante since college. Her friendship with Mason was more recent, but she trusted him with her life.

There's nothing she wouldn't do for them, and they for her. But she needed to get a handle on what was going on without worrying about her friends becoming collateral damage.

She entered the restaurant and made her way to Hemingway's popular rooftop patio. The hostess on duty smiled at Kayla as she approached.

"Good afternoon, Ms. Krowne. Enjoy your lunch."

"Thank you, Aleta."

The hostess didn't need to escort Kayla to her party. She knew the way well. Nearing the familiar table, she noticed she was the last one to arrive. Not a complete surprise, given the machinations it had taken to get here.

Kayla never understood people who ascribed to the fashionably late mindset. Somehow those people had convinced themselves that being the last to arrive gave them a boost of power over the lesser, on-time mortals present.

Their inflated egos blinded them to the fact that the real power resided in the quiet one-on-one conversations of the early arrivals. Many plans had been cemented and much awareness had been seeded before a dinner or party ever started.

Being heard, being understood—that was power.

Not being seen.

Jillian's gaze locked on hers, and the conversation at the table halted. Unease put a hitch in her purposeful stride, and her mother's spine slowly straightened, as did her aunties'.

No one smiled. No one stood for their normal requisite hug.

Tension crackled in the air, like a bolt of summer lightning.

A distant part of her mind noted they each wore black,

though Elsie, being Elsie, added a splash of color to her mourning outfit with a chunky, multicolored necklace.

Kayla slid into the open chair next to Jillian. "Apologies for my tardiness. I had to do a bit of a dance to elude my protectors."

Sybil waved off her excuse. "Never mind that." Her dark midnight eyes clasped Kayla's in an unbreakable hold. "We have a problem."

Kayla breathed in a steadying breath, while she smoothed a linen napkin over her lap. "I'm listening."

15

As soon as Phin picked up the phone, Ash asked, "How's shadow duty going?"

"Fine. She's locked in her office doing video conferences."

Ash slid his index finger over the condensation coating the lower half of his glass of ice water. "When did you last lay eyes on her?"

"Right before lunch."

"You haven't seen her since?"

"I haven't, but Luke, one of my coworkers, delivered a salad to her not long ago. I've got a direct line to her door."

"Luke saw her?"

"I assume so. He came out of her office laughing like they'd been joking around." Phin's voice hardened. "What's with all the questions, Ash? I said I'd protect her and I am."

"Bro, she gave you the slip."

A short silence, then, "Bullshit. Quit fucking around."

"Go check her office."

He heard the squeak of a chair, then a sharp knock,

then, *"Sonofabitch."* Hard footsteps, metal rolling against plastic. "What the hell?"

"Speak to me," he said.

"Her purse is still here."

"What about her billfold?"

"I don't know, and I'm not digging around to find out. Give me a minute. I'll track down her accomplice and figure out where she went."

"Leave him alone. He was only following orders."

"You're taking this well," Phin said with suspicion.

"That's because I've had my eyes on our little pigeon for the past fifteen minutes."

"Fuck."

"I want to see where she's going with this. Let them think their little ruse succeeded."

"It would have, if not for you. " A heartbeat. "Listen, Ash. I'm sorry."

"Kayla Krowne is a professional manipulator. Her job is to find her foe's weaknesses and use them to her advantage. You trusted her to be where she said she would be. She knew you wouldn't question it."

He didn't want Phin to beat himself up over being outmaneuvered by his boss. "This isn't your fault. I should have never put her safety on your shoulders."

"I'm going to slay Luke. He took his role in this thing to Oscar-winning levels."

"He can't know that you know."

"He won't. But I'm going to love fucking with him."

"Have fun." He disconnected and dropped his phone into the interior pocket of his jacket. Sitting at the inside bar of Hemingway's, he had the perfect view of Kayla's clandestine meeting.

On his way to Kayla's office to ask her about the pearl

earring, he'd observed her walking out of her building, not with Phin, but with a large guy who had either been in the military or law enforcement. The whole time he'd been speaking to Kayla, the man's head had been on a constant swivel, assessing potential threats.

Pulling into a vacant spot a few cars down, Ash had watched Kayla get into a black Mercedes. The two looked to be having a disagreement, until she'd finally driven off. He'd waited until the guy strode toward a food truck before racing off after the birdie who'd flown the coup.

Why had she gone to such lengths to secure a private meeting with these women? Phin wouldn't have thought twice about escorting her.

Unless she didn't want Phin knowing about the meeting —or telling Ash about it.

Which raised the million-dollar question. Why?

They had picked a table well away from the other diners. Enough distance to ensure no one could hear their conversation.

An unwelcome thought burrowed into his mind. Did these women have something to do with the governor's death? Had one of them stowed a weapon in the garden, then waited for the right moment?

He couldn't see it. Or maybe he didn't want to. No, the expression on Kayla's face when he'd found her crouched over the governor's body couldn't have been faked. Shock, fear, devastation—they had all been there.

But he couldn't ignore Kayla's insistence that he not go after the shooter. Had she been giving one of the aunts enough time to rejoin the party?

He stared hard at the quartet, then blew out a frustrated breath. More likely, they had gathered together to mourn their friend in private, or maybe do some amateur sleuthing. Discuss potential suspects, make a list of names.

Who the hell knew. But he was wasting his time trying to divine their motives forty feet away. As he reached for his wallet, the fine hairs on the back of his neck snapped to attention.

He made a casual glance around, not seeing anyone acting unusual or looking out of place, until his gaze landed on a man sitting three bar stools down, his broad shoulders propped against the wall behind him. His dark brown eyes focused on him.

It was the same guy he'd spotted with Kayla outside her building.

While he'd been surveilling the ladies, Kayla's friend had been watching Ash. Had he spotted him on the street, despite his caution?

"Interesting view," the stranger said in a manner that could have been interpreted as a question or a warning.

The man studied him with predatory interest. The kind that warned the recipient to not run or turn their back on him.

Military, definitely military. He'd put money on special forces.

"Undecided," Ash said.

"Local cop or fed?"

His pulse snapped off, but just for a heartbeat. If he'd detected Ash on the street, it wouldn't be a big leap for him to figure out he was law enforcement. He considered ignoring his question, forcing him to work at finding the answer. However, one brief description of her "stalker" was all it would take for Kayla to identify him.

"Bureau. Special agent." He considered the other man. "Ranger, SEAL, or Recon?"

"Ranger."

"Boyfriend or bodyguard?"

The sharp edges of the Ranger's features softened, tilted toward amusement. "Whatever she needs."

A feral desire to smash his fist into the other man's face stole over him. Something in his expression must have given him away, because the Ranger produced a big, knowing smile. "You must be Ash Blackwell."

"Cameron," he said automatically, then cursed himself for giving any points to this—well, he didn't know what the guy was just yet. Right now, he'd classify him as a great big pain in the ass, but that could be due to some unfamiliar emotions he wasn't prepared to dissect at this precise moment.

Though brutal energy still simmered around the Ranger, his shoulders seemed to melt against the wall at his back and he lifted his drink—ice water, Ash noted—to his lips.

"Kayla didn't have anything to do with the governor's assassination," the Ranger said.

Ash's scrutiny intensified on the guy. Then it hit him. The Ranger hadn't busted his surveillance. He'd been following Kayla and, when he got here, his predator's instincts had zeroed in on a potential threat—Ash. He wondered if Kayla knew the guy had a tracking device on her Mercedes.

"You know this one hundred percent?" Ash asked.

"I'd bet my life on it."

"Because you were hiding in the garden bushes?"

"Kayla Krowne is capable of many things, even ruthless things, but not murder."

"I'm sure many wives never thought their husbands were capable of murdering them. And yet, so many do."

"Why would Kayla kill the one person who had veto power in the North Carolina legislature?"

"Desperate people do desperate, illogical things."

"What is it that you think you know?"

"If I knew, I sure as hell wouldn't tell someone I'd just met. I don't even know your damn name."

Leaning forward, he stuck out an enormous paw. "Mason Wade."

Ash shook the proffered hand, stood, threw a bill on the bar, and said, "If you come across any information that might help with my investigation"—he tossed him a card—"give me a call."

"Does this invite include a two-way communication?"

"No."

"You're sniffing down the wrong trail, Feeb. Kayla isn't the killer."

He was ninety-eight percent sure the Ranger was correct, though Kayla's clandestine meeting didn't sit well with him.

Nodding toward the women, he said, "Something smells off about their meeting, and I plan to keep my nose to the ground until I figure out what it is."

As he walked away, he noted the Ranger hadn't argued against his intuition or tried to explain away Kayla's actions.

Because he, too, could smell the rot.

16

KAYLA STARED AT THE THREE WOMEN SURROUNDING HER. They were more dear to her than anything in this world. Which was why she couldn't believe they were asking her to prostitute herself.

Having no alcohol of her own, she snatched her mother's mojito and took a sizable gulp. Partly because she craved the resulting numbing sensation and partly to give herself time to process what was happening.

A long time ago, she'd made a promise to herself that she would push the proverbial envelope up to the line. One side, the side she operated on, allowed her to sleep at night with a clear conscience. The other side, the side that took a piece of one's soul each time one crossed over, promised sleepless nights, hours of self-recrimination, and the kind of guilt one carried to the grave.

Until recently, Kayla had kept her feet firmly on terra pleasant dreams. But thanks to an ill-thought-out decision, she was already wrestling with one demon. She would not add another.

In the end, she could only come up with one thing to say. "You can't be asking of me what I think you are."

Sybil and Elsie shared a glance. Jillian sat stone-faced, twirling the base of her now near-empty cocktail. Dark shadows still haunted her eyes and her skin seemed thinner, almost translucent, and she'd barely touched her lunch.

Elsie cleared her throat. "All we're asking is that you gather as much intelligence as you can."

"It's imperative that we stay abreast of his investigation," Sybil said. "If the authorities dig deep enough, there's an unacceptable risk of exposure."

The muscles in Kayla's chest constricted to the point she feared her blood would stop pumping. "Even if I were willing, which I'm *not,* the gentleman in question can barely tolerate my presence."

Sybil laughed. "You're out of practice, my dear. The sexual energy pulsing off that man when he looked at you last night was far from disinterest."

"And he's protective of you," Elsie added. "I thought he was going to tear into that detective a few times."

Kayla tried to read Ash's body language the same way they had, but all she could see was a man who wanted something from her. And it wasn't keep-you-up-all-night hot sex.

More's the pity.

"Mama?" Kayla prompted, not understanding her parent's unnatural silence.

"I think"—Jillian's eyes met Kayla's—"that we need timely information about the investigation."

"Are you kidding—?"

"But," Jillian interrupted, and she cast a hard lioness look at the other two women, "on your terms."

Sybil smoothed the napkin on her lap. "Naturally, that's the desirable course." She hooked her cobalt gaze on Kayla's. "However, we've all had to make sacrifices for our cause. Some far more devastating than sleeping with a handsome man."

Kayla had thought she'd known what betrayal felt like. She'd been struck by it from so many different directions. Legislators who told her one thing and did another. Lovers who left her for more attentive models. Friends who broke confidences.

Yet none of those former disappointments in humanity had shattered the hard, protective casing around her heart.

Until now.

Snapping on her lobbyist mask, the one that revealed nothing but conveyed everything, she said, "I wonder what Aunt Vicky would think about this assignment?"

"If Victoria were still h-here," Sybil said, her voice catching, "she would be the one broaching this awkward but necessary topic with you, instead of me."

Kayla stood. "I have given and will continue to give much for our cause, but I hold ownership over my body." She jammed a thumb into her chest. "Me." She looked each woman in the eye. "I will get the information we need. But not with this," she tapped a finger against her chest, "with this." She pointed to her temple.

Elsie's small hand encircled Kayla's wrist. "Please sit down. We have much more to discuss."

Kayla rotated her wrist to break the fashion designer's contact. "Another time."

It was all the response her emotion-thick throat could manage.

17

Ash spent the rest of the afternoon on the Internet, reading through articles about Victoria Stokes.

He had a peripheral understanding of the governor's politics and the direction in which she'd been leading the state for the past three years. But those were things that had already happened.

Right now, he was more interested in her current initiatives. What social issues was she tackling? What had she done to fire up the opposition recently? Was she on record to veto anything that would put her in someone's crosshairs?

Ash snorted. It seemed everything was crosshairs-worthy these days. But he would look to see if one target stood out among the others.

The governor had signed twenty-two executive orders last year, six so far this year, and countless bills. All pretty standard. Real estate, background checks, drug penalties, nature trails, Indigenous rights; the list went on.

It would take months to root through everything, which

is why he'd leave them for the State's investigators to evaluate.

When his search failed to produce anything heavy enough to trigger his red flag meter, he moved on to Kayla Krowne.

While he waited for the Secretary of State's website to load, Ash stared at the murder board he'd set up against the side wall of his cubicle.

In the center of the board, he'd affixed photos of both Victoria and Kayla. He couldn't shake the idea that Kayla had been the original target and Victoria an unintended casualty. Yet he knew better than to build a case toward a hypothesis.

He would follow the evidence. The "spokes" on his board.

Instead of one wheel, his board had two. He would see where each one led. Would they veer off in opposite directions? Follow the same path? Or intersect?

At the moment, pitiful few spokes jutted out from the center of either wheel. But one very important, very unusual clue—a picture of the pearl earring—hovered between the two.

What did it mean, if anything? Had the killer placed it in the tree as a calling card? Or had it been there for months?

From his brief inspection, he ruled out the latter. The earring didn't appear to have been in the elements long. Maybe a drunken socialite had pinned it there the night of the benefit as a joke.

When rich people got bored, they did weird shit. Sometimes illegal shit. Sometimes dangerous shit.

Sometimes shit for shit's sake.

An hour later, and his mind once again wandered back

to his recent phone conversation with Detective Morgan. Not to the fact that forensics hadn't been able to lift any latent prints from the earring. No surprise there, though it had been impossible not to harbor a thimble of hope.

What he hadn't expected to learn about was the blood spatter discovered *outside* the gazebo. Forensics had located four fresh droplets streaked across the base of a tree, approximately eight feet from where Ash had found the pearl stud.

The finding made no sense to him. Did the shooter have a run-in with a rose bush? He couldn't imagine a professional killer, capable of a head shot, would be careless enough to leave DNA behind.

Morgan had also mentioned that forensics found evidence of a fight. Had there been more than one assassin in the gardens? Had someone gotten cold feet, and Plan B was initiated? Or had the disturbance been caused by wild animals or a secret tryst gone bad?

Ash reined in his vivid imagination. He'd learn more once the crime lab finished their analysis.

Redirecting his attention to the monitor, he pulled up the most recent Lobbyist Directory, which included a monthly catalog of lobbyists and their registered principals. He scrolled down the alphabetical list until he located *Krowne, Kayla* and read through the client names, not really knowing what he was looking for, but hoping he'd recognize it when he saw it.

All appeared to be organizations, rather than individuals. Avalon Addiction Recovery Care, AI for Tomorrow, Benoit Public Utility, Carolina Game Reserve, but not Engel County School Board or any other school board, for that matter.

He could guess what sort of lobbying she was doing for

each principal based on their company names. All except one.

HCVS.

No Inc., no action fund, no nothing tacked on the end. Just four letters.

Ash swam through his memories for any mention of HCVS. When he surfaced, he had nothing to show for it.

Had Kayla, or a member of her team, used the acronym as a shortcut? Or were the letters the company's actual name? He skimmed the full list of Krowne and Associates' sixteen principals. Some of the names were quite long, so shortening HCVS to an acronym wasn't consistent with how they'd registered other clients.

Unless the company had been registered by a new intern who didn't know any better and decided to speed up tedious paperwork.

Ash could sympathize.

He searched the Krowne and Associates' directories for the past twelve months, then expanded to two years, then three. HCVS appeared in every one, going back a decade.

Opening another browser tab, he typed in the four letters and hit enter. A melting pot of results popped up. Human Coronavirus Sensitivity, Hamilton Valley Community Services, High Conservation Values, Hickory County Virtual School, and High Clarity Vanilla Stable, which seemed to be a vegetable soap base.

He dug deeper into each hit. All were out-of-state. None of them seemed likely candidates for Kayla's clients.

But he couldn't be certain. He assumed she focused on issues affecting North Carolina, but that's all it was, an assumption.

Ash sat back and released a frustrated breath. A voice inside his head nagged him to stop wasting his time on the acronym company. Someone in Kayla's office had probably taken a shortcut while filling out the lobbying registration form. Simple as that.

Form.

Ash shot forward in his chair and clicked back over to the Secretary of State's website. He drilled down, link after link, until he came across their lobbying division database.

He selected the current year's term, searched for Kayla Krowne, then HCVS. A number of PDF icons appeared.

He double-clicked on the first one, and *voilà*!

In the second section of the Lobbyist Registration Statement, the first line requests the complete name of the principal.

HCVS.

Ash cursed, feeling as if he'd won the lottery, only to learn the jackpot was four bucks. He read further and smiled. The form listed an address and the contact details of the principal's representative, Larissa Maywood.

Finally, something he could work with.

He snapped a screenshot of her information before scrolling farther down. A grid of codes and subjects filled the page, requiring the lobbyist to select their lobbying areas.

Typed into the columned rows were codes ten through sixteen, which translated to elections, equal rights, government financing, and governments at all levels—county, federal, municipal, and state.

HCVS was starting to feel a lot like a political action committee, also known as a PAC. Organizations who shelled out big money to sway votes and legislators' minds.

Ash wondered how far back the Secretary of State kept lobbyist expense records. He backed out of the form and pulled up something called a compilation report. The spreadsheet had over four thousand rows of expenses, sorted by principals.

He located HCVS and frowned. Next to the principal's name was a column for the lobbyists each organization worked with. Many of the organizations listed five or six.

But not HCVS. All of their initiatives went to one lobbyist.

Kayla Krowne.

Ash followed the row totaling the expenses paid out for the previous year. His eyes widened. He scrolled up, then down several pages. None of the other organizations came close to the two million dollars HCVS had paid to Krowne and Associates.

"What the hell are you working on, Kayla," he whispered.

After several minutes of staring and coming up with no answers, he scrubbed a hand over his face.

"Sweet Jesus." In a matter of seventy-two hours, Kayla Krowne had become embroiled in two significant cases, both of which he was investigating.

He wished he could pawn both onto a colleague, but he knew if given the option, he'd keep them. Despite how he felt about Kayla, she was especially important to Liv and Phin.

Which meant she was important to him.

18

LIFTING THE STEAMING MUG TO HER NOSE, KAYLA INHALED the rich French Vanilla scent of her coffee as she shuffled across her kitchen, toward the double glass doors. This morning's mug had a cartoon Tasmanian Devil, with its massive teeth on full display, blood dripping from its canines.

SMILE
While you still have all your teeth.

Crispy the calico trotted at her heels. Her tail was in the air like a periscope, at the prospect of entering their favorite spot in the whole house—the screened-in porch.

She loved sitting out here. Loved listening to the absolute silence of predawn giving way to the first chirp of an eastern phoebe, Carolina wren, red-eyed vireo, or the ubiquitous American crow.

The avians' good morning chatter never failed to nudge out the groggy effects of a restless night. Their rhythmic staccato songs always gave her renewed hope. Encouraged her to forget about the travails of yesterday and tackle today with fresh vigor.

Until now.

Birdsong, no matter how beautiful and inspiring, could not erase the aftershock of yesterday's soul-crushing meeting at Hemingway's.

She propped fluffy-sock-covered feet on the metal coffee table and set her cushioned glider into motion. Even now, hours later, the thought of her conversation with Jillian and her aunties still made her stomach cramp and her heart constrict. The confusion and pain she'd felt yesterday remained sharp and steady.

As if sensing her mistress's inner turmoil, Crispy stood on her rear paws, bracing her front ones on Kayla's chest, and snuffled her cheek. The cat's long, white whiskers tickled her nose and lips.

Kayla set her coffee on a glass top table near the glider to avoid drinking cat hair before smoothing her hand down the feline's silky back. At her touch, Crispy's spine arched and her motor rumbled to life. She rubbed the side of her soft face against Kayla's.

"I'm okay," she whispered, trying to convince herself as well as her furry protector. "I'll get through this letdown the same way I have all the others."

Crispy's nose twitched against hers, as if she detected the fishy scent of deceit.

The doorbell rang, interrupting their feline therapy session. Crispy's head snapped in the direction of the front door, then to Kayla, as if asking, "Are you going to get that?"

"No, I'm not." She rubbed the cat's back again. This time, raking away a few white, black, and orange hairs. "I'm not in the mood to speak to anyone. This is the first Saturday I've taken off in two months, and I have no intention of interrupting my pity party."

Crispy whipped her tail back and forth like a kid stomping their feet when denied their favorite treat.

"You don't care who it is. You only want to amuse yourself against their leg."

The doorbell rang again.

Glowing yellow-green eyes stared at her.

Despite her determination to ignore the outside world today, Kayla's curiosity got the better of her.

"Fine." She dug her phone out of her robe's pocket and scrolled through several screens until she found her doorbell app. She tapped to open it and frowned.

No one was at her front door.

She searched the porch for packages, but found none.

Crispy jumped on her stomach, and Kayla let out an *"oomph"* at the unexpected move. The cat stood on her hind legs again. This time, facing away, her front paws steady on Kayla's upraised knees.

"Looking for me?" a familiar masculine voice said.

Kayla lowered her phone and looked right into Crispy's butthole. The calico's tail slashed left and right, as she assessed the potential threat. Unlike most cats who run and hide when faced with strangers, Crispy went on guard. As if she'd been a dog in another incarnation.

Stretching her neck to see past the feline bum, Kayla found the absolute last person she'd wanted to see today. Especially this morning.

Out of character, she'd gone to bed without taking off her makeup, not caring about clogged pores and morning raccoon eyes. She couldn't even recall if she'd brushed her teeth. Certainly hadn't yet this morning.

Freaking great.

"What do you want, Ash?"

"To come in. If your guard cat will let me."

"You realize it's barely seven on a Saturday morning, right?"

"What better time to have your undivided attention?"

If she wasn't so heart-weary this morning, she would find his determination to be in her company provocative and would have taken great pleasure in tweaking his fragile ego. However, at the moment, she simply wanted to be alone. "I'm not up for company right now."

"We need to talk."

Lowering her feet, she placed Crispy on the floor and stood. "No, we really don't." She met his gaze. "Unless you have new information on Victoria's murder?"

"I have something else I need to discuss with you."

She didn't miss his slight hesitation. Or the fact that he didn't confirm whether or not he had new information. What was he keeping from her?

This was where Sybil would want her to use her female wiles to tease it out of him. Kayla's stomach roiled at the thought.

Grabbing her mug, she turned to go into the house. "Stop by my office on Monday." She slid open the sliding screen door. "I'll try to squeeze you in."

"Kayla."

The low hammer-drop way in which he said her name made her pause and look back.

"The Bureau received a complaint. About you."

"Me?" Somehow she managed to inject the right amount of incredulity into her features and voice.

"I've been tasked with investigating the complaint. I'll hang here until you're"—he waved toward her robe—"decent."

She studied him for a moment. "Curious." Striding across the porch, she unlocked the door. "Have a seat. Crispy will keep you company."

19

DESPITE THE WISE VOICE IN HIS HEAD, WARNING HIM TO LOOK away, Ash couldn't do it. He couldn't tear his gaze from what he, in his professional career as a full-blooded male, considered a perfect ass.

The lightweight robe Kayla wore barely reached mid-thigh, exposing well-toned legs and incongruous blue, gray, and white striped crew socks. Her hair fell in sloppy waves around her face and over her shoulders, sealing her warm, fresh-out-of-bed look.

In the dark, primitive depths of his lizard brain, he knew it was a sight he would never get tired of seeing. Not in a day, a year, or by the next ice age.

He'd tried like hell to ignore his attraction to the lobby-ist. After all, she was the architect of his current misery.

For the most part, he'd been successful, until the incident with his brother Rohan and his girlfriend, Lena, when Kayla had helped them corner a killer and take down a vindictive hacker. And the time she'd used her connections to assist Liv in shutting down a high-profile drug scheme, which had the added benefit of helping Zeke track down a priceless family heirloom.

She'd put her life and reputation on the line for his family, making it impossible for him to dislike her.

He muttered a curse and scrubbed a hand over his face. He'd hardly slept last night, worried about how he would balance the demands of his job with the duty he owed his family. A position he'd prayed he would never be faced with, but seemed to fall into every time he turned around these days.

Whether either of them liked it or not, Kayla was an honorary Blackwell now, deserving of his protection, no matter the cost.

Family first.

Through blood.

Through hate.

Through fear.

Through joy.

No exceptions.

Zeke and his brothers had come up with the mantra, not long after Ash had left for the FBI. At a time they'd needed it most, the mantra had bonded the brothers together. Gave them the reassurance they needed to run the family business without Ash.

He'd been both proud and envious.

He'd tacked on the *Through joy* after overhearing them chant the mantra one day. Zeke had nodded his acceptance at the time, but Ash was under no illusions that his contribution had survived longer than that moment.

Although he would never regret his decision to leave, he was keenly aware of the many degrees of separation between him and his family now. That mound of uncertainty, awkwardness, and distance he experienced every time he went home made him want to return to the city, to his job. To safety and familiarity.

He wished he could find the balance between being a Blackwell and being a special agent. But Ash knew that day would never come until he and Zeke had a long, hard talk.

He'd hurt his brother—his best friend—when he'd left. The *way* he'd left. They both had things for which to apologize, things to get off their chests. Things to forgive.

Yet the timing never seemed right. Maybe the way things were now were how they'd always be, and he just needed to accept the new norm and move on.

Family first . . . no exceptions.

He clasped his hands behind his neck, wishing he had the strength of Thor to rip off his head and the regenerating ability of Beetlejuice to grow a new one. A better, undamaged-by-life's-poor-choices model.

When his head remained firmly attached to his neck, he blew out a harsh sigh and tilted his head back to stare at the painted timbers above.

As soon as he finished with this case, he would set up a time to meet with Zeke. Maybe he'd talk to Reid Steele or Gage Barber about renting a block of time in the boxing ring at their Law Enforcement Training Center.

Might be best to blow off some steam before their conversation. Controlled violence was preferable to out-of-control, hotheaded violence.

Ash became aware of eyes on him. Malevolent eyes.

Slowly, he lowered his hands and began a three-sixty until he spotted the source of his unease.

Sitting on the center cushion of the glider Kayla had vacated was a laser-focused, unblinking cat.

The feline who had thrown a literal hissy, scratching fit

every time he tried to check on Kayla's injury, the night he bashed her on the head.

The cat stood, arched its back, then prowled toward him. Close enough for him to notice the scar tissue running over its hip and down its leg.

The pain must have been excruciating. Had a fire consumed one of Kayla's properties? Or was this cat another one of her charity cases?

A memory of the first time he'd met Kayla slipped into his mind. It had been a Saturday. Phin had crashed at his place the night before, and the two brothers had stayed up late, reminiscing, drinking, and staring at the night sky.

The next morning, foggy-brained and bloodshot-eyed, they had dragged themselves out of bed for a late-morning run. As they made a circuit through Pack Square Park, Ash had spotted Liv sitting with a friend at a picnic table and had signaled for his brother to follow.

As they jogged closer, it hadn't been his red-headed colleague who'd held his attention, but the stunning blonde at her side. With her focus on stuffing items into what he would later learn were care packages for residents of a local nursing home, he'd been able to catalog her exquisite features—high cheekbones, dimpled left cheek, delicate jawline, slender neck, and a long, curvy-in-all-the-right-places body. Though he wouldn't have the pleasure of seeing anything below her neck until sometime later, because of the damned basket sitting in front of her, he knew with absolute certainty that he wouldn't be disappointed.

Then her green eyes had lifted, met his for a gut-clenching moment, before they made a quick, yet thorough sweep of his bare torso, glistening with sweat. He'd seen appreciation and interest in those beautiful, bold orbs.

After he'd confirmed her ring finger was bare, he'd determined to do everything in his power to leave the park with her phone number.

Until Phin had called out to her, followed by Liv's introduction. Every hormone vibrating with glee in his body had turned to stone as if they'd looked upon a molecular version of Medusa.

Kayla-fucking-Krowne. The lobbyist who had helped mobilize enough North Carolinians eight years ago to elect Eileen Tao as Attorney General, then lobbied for Tao's appointment as the FBI Director.

Tao the harbinger of new forms, procedures, policies, anything to make her mark on the department.

"Is this decent enough for you?"

Kayla's voice pulled him back before his thoughts spiraled down the death and dismemberment lane.

She stood in the doorway, with her long, blond hair pulled back in a simple ponytail, minimal makeup, and sporting a long-sleeved peach and white tee over a pair of white calf-length yoga pants. Different fluffy crew socks. This pair had swirls of pink, yellow, and white.

No one should look that good in such casual clothing. But Ash had a suspicion she'd make any outfit look amazing. And hot.

"Do you want to talk out here?" he asked. "Or somewhere else?"

"Since you're here in an official capacity, how about we move to my office."

He gave her a quick nod. "Lead the way."

Crispy jumped off the glider and trotted after her mistress, her regal back straight, and left Ash to follow in their collective wake.

20

RATHER THAN SIT BEHIND HER MASSIVE GLASS DESK, KAYLA led Ash to a plump sofa and matching chair near a white marble-framed fireplace.

"Make yourself comfortable," she said, indicating the chair. "I hope you don't mind such informality. I don't normally entertain business associates in here."

"Hence your lack of guest chairs around your desk," Ash said, running his fingers over the soft beige fabric before sitting down. "I would've thought you were one of those twenty-four-seven corporate types."

"I suspect there's much about me that you have wrong, Special Agent Blackwell."

He ignored her obvious taunt. "It's good to know you're at least part human."

"Only twenty-five percent, I assure you." She made her way to a well-stocked sideboard. "Can I interest you in coffee or tea?

"Coffee would be appreciated. Black, please."

"Of course."

He didn't miss the smile that shimmered across her

face. His gaze lingered on her full bottom lip and noted a light gloss across the surface. Lip balm? Or had her tongue moistened—

Ash ripped his attention away, as desire flamed through his veins. He forced himself to study her personal workspace, to take in every detail until his blood cooled.

A mix of business books weighed down the shelves behind her desk. A clock with a black stone base sat on the mantel with an engraving of a large X and some lettering he couldn't quite make out. Enough windows lined one wall to provide hours of procrastination. An escape door led to a backyard patio, complete with a pool, Jacuzzi, and colorful lounge chairs. Giant boulders rose up from one end of the pool to create a two-story waterfall.

It looked like something you'd stumble across in a tropical rainforest. A hidden grotto with a natural spring pool. Ash had the sudden urge to shed his clothes and dive in to see if it felt as warm and inviting as it looked.

Continuing his visual sweep of her office, he noted the predominant color was more of an off-white than beige, highlighted by mauve, olive, and hints of a light blue.

Soft, feminine, timeless.

Comfortable.

"One black coffee." She handed him a large mug, handle side toward him.

Was she being polite? Or avoiding potential contact with their fingers?

Ash gave himself a hard shake, irritated by his questioning of her style of mug handoff. This woman, this master manipulator, was going to drive him to the brink of insanity and kick him over the edge.

Unable to help himself, he checked the illustration on the ceramic mug. A kangaroo peered over its shoulder at the viewer, while shoving jewels from a safe into its bulging pouch.

Nothing to see here.

He raised a brow.

She grinned. "Appropriate, don't you think?"

Bold, irrepressible, hot-as-hell woman.

"Not even a little."

Curling up on one end of the sofa, she tucked her stockinged toes in between the two seat cushions. "Now, Special Agent Blackwell, tell me what transgression of mine has brought you to my back door."

"Why are you doing that?"

"What?"

"Using my title."

"You're here on official FBI business."

"Stop, okay? Just . . . I'm Ash. Just Ash." A wave of self-consciousness barreled through him. "Or Cameron. Anything but the title."

She regarded him for a moment, then one of her freaking smiles appeared.

He frowned. This one seemed different. On anyone else, he would've labeled her fleeting emotion as gratitude. With Kayla though, he suspected she'd already catalogued how to use this moment against him.

After taking a sip of the strong brew, he set the cup down on the oval coffee table and settled his forearms on his knees. All of a sudden, he found the casual atmosphere disarming. She acted as though she was having a cuppa with a dear friend and they were embarking on a bout of scandalous gossip.

Rather than stir up family drama, he'd decided to leave Zeke and Aunt Joan out of their conversation. He hoped keeping this Bureau-driven would resolve it faster, satisfy his supervisor, and preserve—or at least not worsen—his familial relationships.

But Kayla always had a way of pissing on his best-laid plans.

Until this moment, he'd known exactly how he would begin questioning her. Knew the tone and timbre he would use to tease out the truth. All of his planning seemed wrong now, though his inner monologue berated him, told him to stick to the script.

"Ash?"

Staring at her, he battled with an intense urge to cuddle up with her on the sofa. To take her fuzzy feet into his hands and massage them. To lay his head in her lap just so he could feel her long fingers trail through his hair.

Suddenly, he understood why she was so successful at persuading those in power to support her clients' initiatives. Find their weaknesses, their passions. Tempt them beyond reason.

A soft, pliable, fuzzy-socked Kayla Krowne was his weakness, his secret passion. His undeniable temptation.

And they were alone.

She's off-limits, Blackwell.

Would her hair be as soft and silky as it looked? Would her breasts be heavy in his hands? Would her aureole be petunia pink, dusky rose, or some other mouth-watering hue?

He shot out of his seat. Distance. He needed distance. A helluva lot of it.

"Ash?" A note of concern entered her voice.

The sound of his given name from her lips sent a bolt of heat straight down his spine. He prowled the room until he could no longer smell the scent of the soap she'd used during her quick shower. Could no longer calculate the width of her sofa to determine if it would accommodate six-plus feet of aroused male.

Pausing before her floor-to-ceiling bookshelf, he skimmed the titles, while he gathered the melting parts of his brain and molded them into a semblance of an intelligent, fact-finding, objective mind.

"Your silence is starting to unnerve me," Kayla said. "Not at all like you."

The volatile emotion constricting his throat eased. He turned away from what appeared to be a very rare book collection and gave her a pained smile.

"I find myself in a unique situation, where two sides of my nature are at war with how to proceed."

"Based on your reason for being here, I can guess the one side."

"My role as a federal agent, yes."

"And the other?"

A volcanic mix of desperate words and long-suppressed actions battered at him from the inside, demanding release. Pressure pulsed in his temple, his chest, his damn eyelids.

He turned toward the rare books again, squeezed his eyes shut. Gathered himself. Once his control was mostly restored, he leveled her with a steady, no-nonsense stare.

"Look, I'm not going to beat around the bush about this. It's come to my attention that you might have a personal interest in an agenda item going before the Engel County School Board next week."

She returned his stare with a speculative one of her own. "I have a personal interest in every initiative Krowne and Associates takes on."

"But Engel County School Board isn't one of your principals. I checked."

Surprise skittered across her features, and she tried to cover it by taking a sip of tea.

"You have no children in the school district. Why the personal interest in passing a Parents' Bill of Rights, in compliance with state law?"

"Children must be allowed to explore new worlds, to express themselves without the banner of danger hovering over them."

"Whose liberty are you protecting?"

"Every child's."

"Who specifically?" he pressed, though the answer came to him a split second before she answered.

"I'm godmother to Liv's son, Brodie."

"You're afraid of the domino effect. Whatever decision they make in Engel County might also be adopted in Haywood County."

"It's happening all over the country."

"Does your protection extend to loaning a twenty-five-hundred-year-old Celtic artifact to a board member's son?"

A beat of silence. "You have yet to tell me of what I'm being accused."

"I believe I just did."

"Where did you come by your information?"

Ash ground his teeth together. "Are you really going to play it this way?"

"I'm not playing it any way. I've learned it's best to make sure we're on the same page, is all."

"Let's start at Chapter One, then," he said, allowing his irritation to shine through. "An Engel County School Board member overheard another board member bragging about how a wealthy benefactor had loaned her son a priceless artifact for display at the grand opening of his natural history museum. Based on the proud mama's description, the other board member believed it's the one from your private collection." He tilted his head. "Ring a bell?"

"I'm not sure you could've been any more vague if you'd tried."

"Chapter Two," he ground out. "The complainant has suggested the artifact is payment for an upcoming vote addressing book bans and parental rights, and she conveyed this concern to others until the information reached my desk."

"Sounds like a great deal of speculation." Her head tilted to the side. "Let me guess—Joyce Ann Carlson, the so-called complainant, gave Joan Steele an earful about this *conspiracy*."

So much for keeping his family out of this. Kayla-fucking-Krowne was already several steps ahead of him. Did she know Lawson would send him?

It shouldn't have surprised him that she would have thoroughly researched each member of the school board, to determine the yeas and nays. But how had she made the link to his Aunt Joan?

"You've done your homework," he said at last, knowing it would be fruitless to probe at her methods.

"Always."

"Chapter Three—"

"The personal chapter," she interrupted. "I'm aware that Joyce Ann has already informed her *cousin*, Resident Special Agent Mitch Lawson, about her *concern*. Who did your Aunt Joan discuss it with?"

"Her sister-in-law." He raised a brow.

She sent him a don't-waste-my-time look. "Lynette Blackwell, your mother."

"Just checking."

"It's amazing, I know, but I'm still following this endless, epic tale."

"She thought Liv could talk to you and find out if the accusation was true."

"At least she gave me the benefit of the doubt." She eyed him as if to say, *Unlike her nephew.* "Liv never spoke to me."

"Zeke intercepted Mom before she could fill her in."

"How did Zeke know?"

"The size of Zeke's ears could rival yours." His brother's office was beside Lynette's, so he probably overheard enough of her conversation with Aunt Joan to trigger his protective instincts for his fiancée. "How did you know Joyce Ann talked to Lawson?"

A short visual battle ensued before her expression turned knowing. "Zeke decided to take matters into his own hands and sent his FBI brother to what, intimidate me?"

"If you knew anything about my recent history with my brother, you'd understand that he came to me for assistance as a last, desperate option." He hardened his tone. "Zeke doesn't want his fiancée worrying about her *alleged* idiot best friend, right now."

The perpetual humor that curled at the corner of her eyes fell away. "That's what friends do. Worry about each other, whether for valid reasons or not." Her gaze sharpened. A hyperalertness that wasn't there seconds ago. "Why right now?"

"Pardon?"

"You said Zeke doesn't want Liv worrying about me 'right now.' Is something going on with her?"

Who's the idiot now, Blackwell?

"If something was, I'm the last person my brother would confide in."

Something like empathy softened her expression. But

only for a second. She was a dog, at the moment. He, a bone. "You suspect something." When he didn't respond quickly enough, she demanded, "Tell me."

"And have you running to Steele Ridge? No thanks. I have enough disappointment"—*betrayal*—"piled at my brother's feet."

Her cup clattered against the end table when she set it down. The lobbyist unfolded her long legs from beneath her and set her feet firmly on the floor. She leaned toward him. "Liv's my best friend. If something is wrong, I have a right to know."

His gaze clashed with hers. "Like she has a right to know if her friend is about to throw away her career, maybe even her freedom?"

She didn't flinch, didn't avert her eyes. Didn't even hitch a breath. "Tell me, Ash."

She wasn't going to let it go. The last thing he needed was for her to blast Liv with a bunch of questions she wasn't ready to answer, because of something he let slip.

"You're a damn annoying woman."

"And you're a self-righteous stick-in-the-mud."

"I don't need you causing me more trouble with Zeke. If you run out there, telling them I told you—"

"I won't," she cut him off. The hand resting against the sofa's arm rolled into a tight fist, but not before Ash noticed her trembling fingers.

"You have my word. Tell me, please."

He drew in a deep breath, hoping he wasn't digging a deeper hole for himself with Zeke. The realization that he'd gladly pay the price if it meant allaying her fears made his voice rough and angry.

"I think my brother is protecting the mother of his soon-to-be-child."

21

Kayla burst from the sofa, her hands making the WTF gesture in the air. "For shit's sake, Ash. You had me thinking my best friend was dying."

"Don't get fired up at me. I didn't say a single word that would indicate Liv was at death's door." He frowned at her. "You've got one wild imagination."

Kayla plopped back down on the sofa. Face in her hands. She worked to control her wildly beating heart, while envisioning herself putting Ash Blackwell in a head-lock and giving him the noogie of a lifetime.

Five, four, three, two, one.

Once again, the silent chant helped calm her.

Straightening, she eyed her guest. "What makes you think Liv is pregnant?"

He shrugged. "Small things."

"Such as?"

"Zeke's steady. The most solid man I know. Nothing rattles him." Except leading the family business. But according to Rohan, Zeke had conquered his earlier fears of failure. "But when we spoke, his knee bounced like a jackhammer the entire time and he kept checking the time, as if he were anxious to get back home."

"Maybe he had another appointment. Or his nerves at having to ask you for a favor were getting the better of him."

"When it comes to me, the only visible emotions Zeke reveals are anger, disappointment, and, on really good days, irritation."

"What happened between the two of you?" She could recall being in the same room with the two brothers at the Blackwell estate, also known as the Friary. It was last year, when they were all searching for Lena Kamber's family while devising a plan to extract a confession from a killer, and the two had swapped dagger stares during the entire meeting.

Lena's situation hadn't been the first time Kayla and her connections had helped the Blackwells, and she hoped it wouldn't be the last. She enjoyed removing bad politicians from office through political activism, but there was something especially exhilarating about assisting the Blackwells take down dangerous criminals.

Her thoughts traced back to that day. There had been tension between Ash and Zeke, but nothing combustive. Nothing overtly hostile. Just a crackle of discontent in the air.

But everyone had been charged. Ash had just delivered some life-altering news to Lena, and Sheriff Kingston, Lena, and Kayla had gone rogue on the guys, and they hadn't liked it much. Especially Rohan. She imagined Lena had sent Rohan's heart into hyperdrive more than once since that excitingly terrifying day.

"Don't try to distract me from the reason I'm here," Ash said.

Back in familiar territory, Kayla resumed her former

relaxed position and took a drink of her chamomile and honey tea. "I'm curious if Joyce Ann mentioned to your aunt that she's been trying to discredit Dee Rhodes ever since she caught Dee and the superintendent *in flagrante delicto*?"

A muscle twitched in his cheek. "Are you suggesting Ms. Carlson fabricated the entire story about the artifact?"

"Joyce Ann isn't sharp enough to craft something so delicious."

The muscles on his face solidified before her eyes. "I'm not one of your politicians who gets off on your mind-fucks," he said in a savage voice. "Stop wasting my time. Did you, or did you not, loan a Celtic artifact to Lyle Rhodes?"

She could've given him an answer in a few short words. Had made up her mind to do so while upstairs, getting "decent."

But all of her life she'd had to put up with men trying to control her actions, her thoughts, her freedoms. Do women need advice, from time to time? Absolutely. But so does a brother, a nephew, or a husband.

What they don't need are orders, overprotection, and mansplaining.

Kayla rose and strode to the patio door, opened it, and settled an uncompromising look on her guest. "You can inform Zeke that you have fulfilled your familial obligation." She opened the door wider. "As for the rest of it, I never give petty gossips a stage on which to perform. I suggest you do the same."

He rose with chilling slowness and stalked toward her, pausing near enough that she could feel the wisps of his angry breaths against her cheek.

"Speaking of performance," he said in a low, thoughtful voice. His gaze dipped down to her mouth, lingered there long enough to hike up her heart rate by a hundred BPM. "Your Houdini act yesterday was just short of magnificent. I wonder what was so important, *so secretive* that you felt the need to lie to your employees." His eyes met hers for a breath-stealing moment.

How had he found out? Phin hadn't let on that he'd been aware of her vanishing act. Had Mason said something? She dismissed the idea. He might not have liked her scheme, but he never would have betrayed her trust.

He straightened and walked away, but not before tossing a veiled threat over his shoulder. "Something worth investigating."

Kayla's hand trembled as she shut the door.

22

ASH SAT ON A HARD-CUSHIONED CHAIR THAT LOOKED LIKE IT had been plucked out of a Jane Austen novel.

Every time he moved, the wooden frame squawked beneath his weight. He wondered if his hostess positioned him here, knowing he wouldn't be able to snoop around without alerting her.

The chair wasn't the only piece of ancient furniture. The room had an Old World feel. Hunt scene paintings lined the walls, a chaise longue, similar to the Krownes', but gold and gaudy, rested inside the bay window. Striped wallpaper surrounded him on all four sides, and when Joyce Ann Carlson entered a few seconds later, she carried a tea service, silver tray and all.

The metal clattered against the low coffee table when she set it down. Tiny, hand-painted pink roses covered the teapot and dainty porcelain cups and saucers resting beside it.

Ash flexed his hands, imagined himself snapping the handle off as he tried to maneuver the puny drinkware to his lips. He now regretted his "Whatever's easiest" response to her earlier inquiry of "Coffee or tea?" and gained a new appreciation for Kayla's quirky mugs.

Ms. Carlson asked, "Sugar or cream?"

Cream? He wouldn't be surprised if she started speaking in the King's English next.

"No, thank you," he said.

She added a generous splash of cream to her cup, then used a set of tiny silver tongs to extract two cubes of sugar from a matching floral bowl and dropped them into her cream.

Hot tea flowed from the teapot into an empty cup that she placed in front of him, complete with a matching paper-thin saucer, before pouring the liquid into her doctored cup. Using a dainty spoon, she swirled the concoction together.

Ash picked up his drink by the rim and took a sip. More out of politeness than any need to quench his thirst. He ignored his hostess's look of horror over his lack of pinky-up etiquette.

Social niceties done, he got started. "I understand you overheard a disturbing conversation between the lobbyist Kayla Krowne and fellow board member Dee Rhodes."

Ms. Carlson folded her hands in her lap. "That's correct."

He drew a small notebook and pen from an inner pocket of the jacket he kept in his vehicle for unexpected meetings such as this.

After leaving Kayla's house, he'd called Detective Morgan to get an update on the forensics for the earring he found at the scene, but his call had gone to voicemail. Still wound up from his confrontation with Kayla, he found himself driving west, toward Maggie Valley.

The compulsion to get to the bottom of this Celtic gift issue was strong. As was his regret.

He shouldn't have raised his voice and accused Kayla of mindfucking him. But something about her attitude, the way she seemed to be amused by the entire situation, amused by *him,* had burrowed beneath his skin like a tainted sliver that refused to be tweezed out. Which pissed him off.

He was a seasoned special agent with the FBI, trained in the art of interview tactics. And he'd allowed the lobbyist to manipulate his feelings.

With a damned smile.

"Walk me through what you heard, Ms. Carlson."

"Well now, this goes back a few days. The county held an arts and crafts competition last weekend at the fairgrounds. There were ten categories—mixed media, ceramics, jewelry—"

"I'll take your word for it, Ms. Carlson." He sat forward, arms resting on his knees, pen and paper at the ready. "Where does Ms. Krowne come in?"

She frowned. "I was about to get to that before you interrupted me."

"My apologies." He forced the words between his teeth. "Please go on."

"As I was saying." She lifted her teacup to her lips, her pinky extended, sipped, and returned the brew to its saucer. She squared her bony shoulders. "Ms. Krowne is a great patron to the school library. Has been for years, so the events committee chair asked her to be one of the competition judges." She paused, assessing his reaction.

"Very generous of her."

The board member sniffed. "Dee decided Miss Krowne needed an escort while she went from booth to booth. Like the woman couldn't walk down the street by herself." She seemed to shake herself. "Anyways, it was at this time, I heard the two conspiring."

Finally, they got to the meat of the issue. "Tell me what you can recall of their conversation."

"My memory is excellent, Agent Blackwell. I remember every word."

He gave her an encouraging smile—he hoped. "Proceed when you're ready."

"I heard Dee mention the grand opening of her son, Lyle's, natural history museum." The corners of her mouth turned down. "I'm sure you've heard of it. The billboards on I-40, between here and Asheville, are littered with advertisements about the new museum."

Ash recalled seeing one tasteful advertisement on the drive here. But maybe the "litter" was on the eastbound side.

When he didn't respond, the board member's pinched expression deepened. "Dee complained about the fact that one of the museum's donors had pulled their Celtic piece and her son was scrambling to find a replacement." She leaned forward, her eyes narrowing to angry slits. "That's when Kayla told Dee she might be able to help her son out of his predicament."

A cold blast of foreboding blew across the back of Ash's neck. "Did the conversation end there?"

"Of course not." She looked at him as if half his brain was oozing out of his ear.

Maybe it was.

"Dee said she would be *indebted* to Kayla if she could get her son a new showcase piece."

"Did you hear Miss Krowne say she would loan her artifact to the museum in exchange for her vote?"

"No, but they were whispering amongst themselves at one point."

"Whispering? Or were you too far away to hear everything? Or maybe fair-goers crowded in between you and the two women?"

The board member grew silent as if sifting through her memories. Then her vertebrae snapped into the upright position. "What does it matter? They were obviously speaking at a confidential level."

Ash let her absurd statement hang in the air for three heartbeats. "Why do you suspect the artifact for the grand opening belongs to Miss Krowne?"

"Because she had a Celtic piece displayed in her home last spring, when she hosted a St. Patrick's Day fundraiser for the county library."

"Have either of the women confirmed the artifact loaned to the museum belonged to Ms. Krowne?"

"Nooo." She drew out the word while she considered her answer. "Not specifically."

Ash stared at the board member and wondered how the good citizens of Engel County could have voted to put such a petty, vindictive, wildly unqualified person into office.

For the school board, no less.

Under his unwavering gaze, she fidgeted and searched the air for a particle of logic she could latch on to. "Who else could it be? Few could afford such a priceless piece. Maybe you should search Kayla's home. If the artifact is missing, then we'll know she loaned it to the museum." When he continued giving her the silent treatment, her tone turned hostile. "Kayla's wealthy, but not wealthy enough to possess more than one twenty-five-hundred-year-old treasure."

Kayla Krowne could own a hundred Celtic artifacts and it would barely put a dent into her fortune.

Enough was enough. Kayla had been right about Ms. Carlson wanting to discredit her fellow board member. He returned his notepad and pen to his pocket. "Anything else, Ms. Carlson?"

Recognizing a dismissal when she heard one, her eyes flared and her lips compressed. "Are you going to speak to Dee about this? Or her son?"

"More than likely."

"Good, she needs to be reminded of her sacred duty. Could you imagine the damage to our institution if it became known our votes could be bought for a bauble?"

Ash rose to leave. "Thank you for your time, Ms. Carlson." A thought struck him. "You believe Kayla Krowne is using the artifact to sway Dee Rhodes's vote on the Board's response to the state's new law on book banning and the parents' bill of rights?"

"Yes."

"Do you know how Ms. Rhodes was going to vote prior to her conversation with Miss Krowne?"

Silence stretched between them.

She took a drink. "Not specifically, but rumor indicated she would vote yes."

"Rumor." Ash bit the inside of his cheek to keep the explosion of words from escaping. "So it's possible the artifact might not have had an impact on Ms. Rhodes's vote, one way or the other."

"Dee said she'd be *indebted* to Kayla. Says it all, does it not?"

"Not by a long shot, Ms. Carlson."

He left her sputtering in her tepid tea.

23

KAYLA PUSHED THROUGH THE GLASS DOOR OF KROWNE AND Associates with less enthusiasm than normal.

Ten years of running her own lobbying firm hadn't dampened her daily excitement. She loved the many challenges and enjoyed pitting her intelligence against some of the most brilliant and cunning minds in the world.

Contrary to what Ash said, she didn't play psychological games with people. But she did find amusement in watching folks chase their own tails. The door closed behind her and the automatic lock snicked into place. She wove her way through the office, lit only by a few twenty-four-seven safety lights in the ceiling.

After Ash's abrupt exit, she'd gone to her in-home gym and tried to work off the nervous energy his visit had pumped into her body. But the free weights, 5k run, and yoga did nothing to diminish her feelings of restlessness.

Nor had strolling through the collections in her museum. Which was a first.

She'd considered texting her mom to see if she wanted to power walk a portion of the mountain-to-sea trail near the Folk Art Center, but couldn't bring herself to send the message.

After the disastrous meeting at Hemingway's, she had avoided any contact with her and the aunties. The memory of her aunties' edict, and Jillian's near silence, made bile rise into her throat.

Needing to fully engage her mind, Kayla abandoned her day off and went to the office. The scent of paper and progress flushed out the negative energy she'd been carrying and replaced it with purpose. Her sluggish footsteps found new life, and she was fairly flying to her desk when her intern's placating voice stopped her in her tracks.

"I'm sorry you feel that way, Mr. O'Conn—"

"I can assure you, sir—" Anger edged Gemma's next words. "If you continue with the name-calling, I'll be forced to hang up."

Kayla course-corrected and made her way to the Pit, where the intern desks were stationed. The low-walled cubicles, four in the center of the office, allowed for a constant flow of communication and team engagement.

"I'm hanging up now. Call back when you're more rational." Gemma Niles clicked her computer's touchpad to disconnect the angry caller and tore out her wireless earbuds. "Jerk."

"Are you okay?" Kayla asked.

Startled, Gemma jumped up from her chair, sending her gorgeous black curls bouncing. "Kayla! I thought you were taking the day off."

"So did I." She waved a hand at the computer. "What was that all about?"

Gemma sighed. "Tommy O'Connor. He's upset about our"—she made air quotes with her fingers—"lack of progress on his campaign."

Kayla closed her eyes a moment and swore. "I'm sorry, Gemma. Calling him back fell off my radar."

O'Connor was understandably invested in the firm's success in ushering SB623 through the complicated process of the North Carolina General Assembly. Relaxing tight housing regulations could help local communities construct more housing, which would bring costs down across the board. Locals would stop losing their homes because they could no longer afford the taxes on a home they'd lived in for decades.

She understood Tommy's passion. Until recently, all of the activist's encounters with her staff had been cordial and collaborative. But he was starting to unravel.

The intern shrugged. "It's not as though you don't have a ton going on." She hesitated a moment. "He's getting more insistent and loud each time we speak."

"I'm sorry he upset you."

"No worries."

"I'll take care of Tommy. When he calls in the future, forward him to me, even if you have to pull me out of a meeting."

"Thanks, Kayla. But if I'm going to have a career in political activism, I'll encounter a lot more Tommys and need to develop ways of dealing with angry clients or the other strange birds who like to orbit the firm."

Kayla smiled for the first time in hours. "True, but hold the line like you did with Tommy. Don't let anyone speak to you in a way they wouldn't to their grandmother."

Gemma's expression lightened. "Okay."

"Now," Kayla said, tapping into her boss voice. "May I ask what *you're* doing here on a Saturday?"

Gemma held seniority over the other three interns employed by Krowne and Associates. Two nurtured relationships on the liberal side of the aisle and two on the conservative side. If the interns came back the next year, they would work the opposite aisle.

Kayla believed the only way the firm could support their clients' many initiatives was to understand both perspectives. Both factions had their challenges, but one thing they shared were citizens passionate about their causes. Some to the point where a switch flipped in their head and they would say and do things they never would have in their right minds. Like Tommy's behavior today.

It was no less tricky to placate the activists than it was the policymakers.

"I—um. Sorry, I—" Gemma's expression turned sheepish as her attention dropped to the stacks of paperwork on her desk. "I didn't get everything done that I'd hoped to, yesterday." Her eyes slashed to Kayla's. "Don't worry, I won't log today on my time card."

Kayla stepped closer to the wall separating them and held her hand out to the young, promising woman. She didn't blink an eye at Kayla's unusual action. She simply stood and grasped her boss's hand.

Modulating her voice to that of a mentor, Kayla said, "Never apologize for ambition. The desire to get ahead, whether for one day's work or for a new position, isn't the sole right of men. And your time has value, even if it wasn't sanctioned in advance." She gave the intern's hand a squeeze before letting go.

Straightening, she switched to her no-nonsense voice. "How much time do you have before your friends cart you off for a bit of Saturday fun?"

"All afternoon."

"Beautiful. Bring everything we have on SB623 to my

office. Let's see if there's something more we could, or should, be doing."

Excitement infused Gemma's response. "I'll be there in a sec."

Kayla's lips twitched. She'd been an intern once and knew the prospect of working one-on-one with the boss would send a rush of adrenaline through the young woman's body.

Equilibrium restored, she marched into her office and didn't think about the FBI agent once over the course of the next few hours. Not until she found a spine-tingling message etched into the paint of her beautiful Mercedes.

24

THE SCENT OF ROASTED COFFEE AND BUTTERY PASTRIES tripped Ash's olfactory senses the moment he stepped into Blues, Brews, and Books, better known by the locals as Triple B.

One side of a soundproof wall housed a restaurant and bar, the other a coffee shop and oversized Little Free Library. Steele Ridge patrons had their pick of atmosphere and locally-sourced vittles.

When Randi Shepherd opened the doors beneath the iconic blue awnings, the coffee shop had operated only in the mornings. But in the era of *How do you want your coffee —hot or cold?,* she now kept the shop door open until 8:00 p.m., requiring Randi to double her staff.

Another win-win for Steele Ridge.

After placing his order, Ash skimmed the wall of library books for something to read while he waited for Liv to arrive.

Since he was in the area, he couldn't pass up a chance to check in on his former colleague. He'd thought of her often after his meeting with Zeke, and wondered how the possible mother-to-be was doing.

The barista called out his name. He grabbed a hardback by T. J. Newman, picked up his black coffee, settled into one of two seats at a postage-stamp-sized table near the window, and flipped to page one.

"Must be a good book," a familiar female voice said.

Ash blinked away visions of passenger planes sinking to the bottom of the ocean and glanced up to find Liv Westcott.

She raised an eyebrow, a smirk playing on her lips.

He used the dust jacket to mark his place, stunned to find that he'd already ripped through the first five chapters. With surprising reluctance, he set the book aside and rose to greet his brother's fiancée.

It took every molecule of control in his body not to glance down at Liv's stomach to see if he could detect the beginning of a baby bump. Instead, he gave her a swift hug before resuming his seat. "Thanks for seeing me on such short notice."

She set her to-go cup on the table, a testament to how engrossed he'd been in Newman's singular thriller that he hadn't noticed Liv come in, let alone place an order.

Sliding into the chair opposite him, she said, "Of course."

She displayed an unfettered smile and looked strangely radiant in her leggings and sports tank top beneath a sleeveless T-shirt.

"Did I interrupt your workout?"

She shook her head. "Brodie has a baseball game today and the weather gods believe we'll hit mid-eighties. So I dressed for sweat."

"I'm keeping you from your family." He pushed his

chair back from the table, the metal legs screeched in protest. "We can do this another time."

She waved off his concern. "Don't get me wrong, I love watching my son play, especially after he'd forsaken the game for so long. But he's in travel baseball, and it can be . . . a bit much."

"But—"

She shook her head and gave him a reassuring smile. "I'll be back in time to see the last few innings. No worries."

"If you're sure."

"One hundred percent." Her smile faded. "What's on your mind?"

"I see the private sector hasn't vaporized your powers of observation."

"I don't need FBI training to notice something is weighing hard on my friend's mind."

"I'm here to see how civilian life is treating you."

"Bullshit," she said in a low voice, so as not to disturb the other patrons.

He placed his right hand over his heart, as if she'd shoved a knife into the organ. "Ow."

"If you were checking in on me, you would've simply stopped by the Friary." She sipped her drink. "Which, by the way, you haven't done for several weeks. Stop by the Friary *and see your mother*."

"I'll pay a social visit soon."

"You'd better. Grams and Lynette are on the verge of storming your bachelor pad."

A smile pulled at the corner of his mouth. "Thanks for the warning."

"Welcome. In keeping with your charade, I'm doing fine. Best decision of my life. Now, what do you want to ask me?"

He could see she wasn't going to say any more. In one sense, he was relieved. They were friends, but they had never mucked around into each other's personal lives. Hell, he hadn't even known she and Zeke were a thing until she'd resigned from the Bureau.

On the other hand, she was a friend, and he needed to know she was okay. He'd figure out how to circle back around to the baby topic later.

For now, Ash slid into agent mode. "You've obviously heard about the incident with the governor."

"A bullet to the brain is more than an incident."

He wished she was still with the Bureau so he didn't have to guard every word. Although he trusted her implicitly, he was still a special agent investigating an active case and she was a civilian.

"Look," she said, keying in on his dilemma. "I know how this works. Why don't you just ask me what you want to know, and I'll do my best to answer."

He studied her for any obvious signs of stress or debilitating morning sickness, but he found none. In fact, she looked healthier and happier than he'd ever seen her.

"Why are you staring at me like that?"

He blinked. "Like what?"

A ridge formed between her eyebrows, and her gaze lasered into his. "Zeke told you, didn't he?"

Shit.

"No." He lifted his hands in the air, shaking his head. "No, he didn't tell me anything." His phone pinged with a text message. Even though he itched to high-tail it out of this conversation, he didn't dare look at the screen. Not with Liv's gaze slicing him in half.

"If he didn't," she said, "how do you know what I'm talking about?"

"Dammit, Liv. He didn't tell me. You know we don't have that kind of relationship." *Anymore.*

As if she'd heard his silent qualifier, empathy softened the suspicion in her eyes. A little. "Then how did you know?"

The jig's up.

"I guessed."

Her hand smoothed down her T-shirt, as if to test the size of her bump.

"Not visually. When I saw Zeke a few days ago, he was hyper-protective of you."

"He's always protective of me."

"Hence the added 'hyper.'"

"Please don't say anything about my pregnancy," she said in a low voice. "We're waiting until the end of the first trimester to make an announcement."

"Understood. Can I offer congratulations?"

"Are you kidding?" Her face brightened as if spotlighted by ten thousand lumens. "The delay is just a precaution. In case, you know, anything goes wrong. But I've been dying to let folks know."

He rotated his paper coffee cup clockwise several times. "Is Zeke . . . happy?"

"Amidst the worry, yes. Every evening, he kisses my stomach and says, 'Good night, little agent.'" Pink flushed her cheeks, nearly matching the red in her hair.

The endearment surprised Ash, given how much Zeke hated the Bureau.

But he still fell in love with Liv, despite her being a special agent, at the time.

A petal of hope unfurled.

Until he realized Zeke could have been referring to asset recovery agent.

The petal wilted.

"I'm glad," he said, shoving back his inner turmoil. "Zeke, both of you, deserve all the happiness in the world."

Her hand closed over his and squeezed, and Ash felt the prick of tears. He swallowed hard, and slid his hand away.

A heavy silence fell between them, then she asked, "Was your meeting by chance?"

He had to shut down this line of questioning. Zeke would never forgive him if she found out the reason why his brother swallowed his pride and came to him. "No."

"Did you talk out whatever's still going on between the two of you?"

"No, but soon, I think."

"What made Zeke turn into a cave man?"

When he didn't elaborate, she said, "You're not going to tell me, are you?"

"There's nothing to tell." He took a drink of his coffee. "He asked me for a favor. I accepted. End of story."

She didn't look happy, and he couldn't blame her. But he'd promised Zeke not to get Liv involved in the school board issue and he would stick to it. That didn't mean he couldn't use this opportunity to find out more about Kayla.

"Talk to me about the relationship dynamic between the Krownes and Governor Stokes."

She spoke in a rush, as if she'd been waiting for him to broach the topic. "The governor and Jillian Krowne were tight, along with two of their classmates, Sybil Barclay and Elsie Henshaw. I believe they all went to the same boarding school or university."

Sybil's last name sparked a memory. "I met them the night of the murder," he said. "Does Sybil have a son?"

Liv made a face, nodding. "Evan."

He'd been too pre-occupied with figuring out how to get

Kayla alone to make the connection at the benefit. "Don't care for him?"

"I crossed paths with him once. That was enough."

He wondered if Kayla was equally put off by Mr. No-Neck. Shaking off the twinge of jealousy, he prompted her to continue. "Didn't mean to sidetrack our conversation. You were saying?"

"Kayla's close with all of her mother's friends. Even refers to them as the 'aunties.' However, I always sensed she had a closer bond with the governor. Maybe because Victoria was her godmother and took her role seriously."

Godmother? Interesting.

"A seriousness she passed down to Kayla, who is Brodie's godmother."

"So I recently heard."

"Don't sound so skeptical. I don't think there's anything she wouldn't do to protect my son."

"Even breaking the law?"

"That, and more, if she had to. Kayla's fiercely protective of those she loves."

"Besides her political rivals, can you think of anyone who would want to kill Governor Stokes?"

She shook her head. "I've been thinking about it a lot since hearing the news. Believe it or not, Victoria was well liked by both political parties. She didn't make empty promises. Knew the art of compromise. Kept a cool head. She cared about North Carolinians and wanted to enrich everyone's lives, not just the wealthy. Pretty incredible, considering she came from old—very old—money."

"What do you mean?"

"She was good. Selfless. Didn't have any of that entitlement crap most of the wealthy have stamped on their foreheads. She spent a lot of time traveling the backroads of this state. Getting to know the challenges and concerns of all her constituents, not just the ones who helped fund her campaign."

"Sounds almost too good to be true."

"She does. But she was the real deal, and North Carolinians had Kayla to thank for such an amazing governor."

"How so?"

"Kayla's lobbying firm focused almost exclusively on Victoria's election for two years. If not for her team's relentless efforts, Daniel Puge might have been our current governor."

Hollywood handsome, charismatic, and missing his right eye, Danny Puge had won the hearts of many voters by his gut-punch tale of fighting off a trio of gangbangers before they could rape a fifteen-year-old girl.

A smug look crossed Liv's face as she continued, "Not long after Puge announced his candidacy for the gubernatorial race, Kayla's team tracked down the real story behind his horrific accident."

Ash knew about the video that had brought Puge's campaign to an epic halt. But he hadn't realized Kayla was responsible for making it public. "You've got my attention."

"I don't know the fine details, but someone tipped her off about the video that refuted Puge's heroic claim. It took her months to locate Luis Flores, the videographer."

The infamous video revealed Puge hadn't lost his eye in a heroic street fight, but in a collision with a busted bicycle spoke hidden beneath the murky waters of a local swimming hole. An intoxicated Puge, and his two buddies, had decided that jumping from a rope swing at midnight into dark, impenetrable water would be a blast.

Once the video surfaced, Puge had found himself

treading water and no one had been willing to throw him a life preserver.

"Sounds like Kayla approaches lobbying with the same passion as she does art collection."

"Has she given you the tour?"

He'd noticed numerous artworks before a black-clad Kayla interrupted his sweep of her home.

"Quite a collection."

"What's in her house isn't the half of it. If she pulled all of her paintings and artifacts from the various museums where she has them on loan, she could probably fill a floor at the Met."

Ash's grip on his coffee cup tightened, denting the sides. "I thought she had an in-home museum where she kept her collection."

"Not so much a museum. More of a gallery where she displays her, and some of her mother's, favorites. The rest are loaned out to museums across the country." Liv smiled. "Kayla believes art appreciation shouldn't be reserved for the wealthy alone. She likes the idea that one of her pieces might inspire generations to come."

Something untwisted in Ash's chest. He'd always avoided talking about Kayla with Liv, because of her close friendship with the lobbyist. Now he wondered if that might not have been a mistake.

Then he recalled the stack of paperwork on his desk and the upcoming changes Director Tao had announced last week, all thanks to Kayla Krowne's meddling, and decided donating a few art pieces didn't qualify her for sainthood. Especially if she'd participated in dozens—maybe even hundreds—of pay-to-play political schemes.

"I heard a rumor that she has a piece that dates back twenty-five hundred-years." His phone vibrated in his pocket. An incoming call. He ignored it. He ignored every-thing, including breathing, except for Liv's next words.

"A partial truth," she said.

"Partial?"

"She does have an ancient Celtic statue, but it belongs to her mom, Jillian."

25

AFTER CONTACTING HER INSURANCE COMPANY AND FILING A police report on the damage done to her Mercedes, Kayla made the humiliating drive home.

She'd put in a call to five different body shops, but all of them were closed up tight for the weekend. Moving to Plan B, she transferred her older model Audi from the third garage stall to the first, then backed her Merc into the farthest stall.

She stared at the ragged letters carved into the driver's and passenger's side doors.

TRAITOROUS BITCH

The sight drove her back fourteen years, to her undergraduate days as a poli-sci major, to the time she'd raised more funds for a charity drive than her fellow students. One of her classmates, who didn't like the number two spot, decided to take his frustration out on her vehicle.

In red paint, he'd written *BITCH* on the hood. A parking lot camera had captured the incident, but one call from his senator father to the school's leadership had squashed any possibility of discipline.

An act that had sparked Kayla's political activism. Anyone who could pick up a phone and cancel repercussions for someone's criminal act had been in office too long.

She flashed back to the moment she found the vandalism to her Mercedes, to the terror, to her knee-jerk reaction. A panicked text to Ash.

Someone vandalized my car while I was at the office.

Now, she'd give anything to pull back the message.

Another moment of indecision had passed before she dialed APD's number. After the police had come and gone, she'd called Ash on her way home to tell him to disregard her earlier text.

He hadn't answered, nor had he responded to her message, so she'd left him a voicemail, repeating the same. Even now, an hour later, finishing up a batch of stir fry, she still felt ridiculous for her automatic reaction.

If she hadn't witnessed a murder, she would have reacted to the vandalism the same way she had all those years ago. Search and destroy. Not fear and uncertainty.

When Alexander Brighton had desecrated her car, he couldn't have known the shitstorm his petty jealousy would unleash. But he found out when his father entered the Senate race for another term.

Prior to the incident, Students for a Better Tomorrow had been courting Kayla to join. She'd resisted the group's recruitment efforts because they acted like a bunch of puppies searching for their mama's teats. After Senator Brighton worked his phone magic and had the parking lot's video feed deemed too grainy to identify the perpetrator, Kayla joined SBT, not as a member, but as their president.

In a few short months, she'd rallied thousands of passionate college students all over North Carolina to register, then vote for Brighton's opponent. Stephanie Foxwood won the Senate seat by 20,933 votes.

A lobbyist was born.

Kayla removed the colander from the sink and prepared to dump the peppered shrimp in with the veggies, when her door bell chimed. Grabbing her phone from the island counter, she checked the video feed.

Ash.

She turned off the burner and engaged the intercom. "What do you want, Agent?"

"I got your text." He stared straight into the camera's lens, and Kayla's heart skittered around in her chest.

"Then you also got my voicemail, telling you to disregard."

"I came by to make sure you're okay."

"As you can hear, I'm alive and kicking."

"Show me the damage."

"Not necessary. The incident has been reported to the police."

He moved in close to the camera. Determination bracketed his eyes. "Stop being a brat and show me your damn car."

She thought about ignoring his command, but the reality was she'd been jumpy ever since she'd parted ways with the police. A part of her wanted Ash Blackwell close. Needed his strength to reenergize her natural confidence. Which aggravated her to no end.

"To your left," she grumbled. "I'll meet you at the third garage door."

Thrusting her phone into the pocket of her gray lounge pants, she turned toward the half bath to check her appearance, then stopped and reversed course. He'd already seen her at her worst, with bed head and scaly teeth.

A cami with an overshirt and cotton pants wouldn't blow his mind. She opened the door leading to the garage and hit the button for the far stall.

Cranks and pulleys slowly lifted the door, revealing a pair of brown shoes, widespread, then a set of thick quads in casual pants. Lean hips. Strong hands anchored on each side of his waist. Broad chest. Squared, tense shoulders. Stubbled jawline. Piercing blue eyes.

At some point, Kayla's brain had instructed her slippered feet to halt their march to her fouled vehicle and take in the wonder being unveiled for her, inch by tantalizing inch.

Her breath had stopped, too. The only part of her body working, including her mind, was the organ thrashing against her rib cage like a wild animal desperate for a midnight snack.

The clatter of mechanisms stopped and the cool night air swept in, sending goosebumps up her legs and arms. Neither of them said anything for a potent second, then the hesitant trill of a bluebird penetrated the silence, breaking their visual connection.

Ash dropped his hands from his hips and strode to the passenger side of the Mercedes. Kayla followed like a magnet attracted to steel.

26

Ash did his damn best to block out the image of Kayla's ruched nipples pushing against the thin fabric of her camisole.

He was here to inspect the damage to her vehicle and to make sure she was all right. Not ogle her invade-his-dreams body. His stomach still hadn't fully reseated itself after the free fall it had taken while reading her text.

Using a key or some other metal instrument, the perp had carved *TRAITOROUS* on the upper panel of the passenger side door. He angled around the sleek black Merc and found *BITCH* scrawled on the driver's door.

Ash clenched his teeth, furious with the weak-minded asshole who got their jollies off terrifying women. "Where was your car parked when this happened?"

"In the parking garage near my office building."

He wanted to ask where the hell Mason was, then recalled she only used his services during the week. Something he'd have to persuade her to change or hire a security firm to fill in the gap.

"Are there cameras in the garage?"

She nodded. "The police are working on getting a copy of the video."

"I'll check in with them tomorrow and see what I can find out."

"Don't trouble yourself. I'm sure they'll let me know if they get a clear picture of the vandal."

"Whether they do or don't, I'd like to see the footage."

"Why?"

"Because a person can give away their identity in more ways than facial recognition."

She stood only a couple of feet away, close enough for him to reach out, pull her to him, and claim those tempting lips that were even now pursing to make some inane argument. You would think a lobbyist, especially one running such a successful firm, would know how to accept help.

A thought struck him. One that made his already tortured stomach clench tight. Maybe it was *his* help she didn't want. The realization bothered him, more than it should.

What did he expect? Her undying gratitude? When he'd pushed, no—shoved—her away at every opportunity.

Disgusted by his conflicting feelings, he made a mental note to ask Detective Morgan to review the surveillance video to see if there might be a connection, no matter how slim, to the governor's assassination.

"Do you have any thoughts on who did this?" he asked, finally turning to her, keeping his attention on her face.

Which was damn hard.

She stepped closer, and Ash's pulse shot to one-fifty in a single bound. Her hand reached out, and she smoothed her fingertips over the crudely etched letters on the door.

Ash had never been so envious of a hunk of metal before.

"I've been called bitch a few times in my life. Once, in almost the exact same way." She produced a smile, but there was no humor in it. "A hazard of the job. At least, for female lobbyists." Her expression turned serious. "But I can't think of any reason why someone would fling *traitorous bitch* at me."

"Rewind a sec. Someone has written trash on your car before?"

She nodded and lowered her hand. "At university."

"Give me the details."

"The one has nothing to do with the other."

"You're a detective now, are you?"

Her brows bunched together. "You can't really believe a hotheaded young man from my past had anything to do with this." She pointed at the etching.

"I've learned to rule out nothing. Some criminals have exceptionally long memories, especially if they believe they've been wronged." A hard lesson Zeke had learned not long ago.

A hint of vulnerability penetrated her features, but she seemed to thrust the emotion away to make room for the ever-present, mocking curl at the corner of her mouth.

"This must be one happy week for you," she said.

"I'm not sure what you mean."

Her eyes lifted to his. "Someone hates me more than you."

The slap of her words had the same stinging effect as one of his grandmother's pointed looks. "I don't hate you."

"You don't like me, either."

His attention shifted to her mouth, to the infuriating curl at the corner. If he pressed his lips there, would it disappear or deepen? Welcome or repel? "You're wrong."

"Sometimes, but not in this."

After his meeting with Liv, he'd shucked his jacket and tie, rolled up the sleeves of his white shirt, and unfastened the top two buttons. Now, he cursed his decision to expose the flesh at the base of his neck. If he'd left his armor on, he wouldn't now be tortured by the whisper of Kayla's warm breaths against his skin.

Had he stepped closer? Or had she?

"I've got a problem with your profession. Not you."

"I am my profession, Ash," she whispered. "You cannot carve it out of me and expect me to survive."

Hadn't he said something similar to Zeke a few days ago?

Unable to stop himself, he brushed the backs of his fingers over her cheek, startling her, and continued the caress across her jawline to her chin. The tip of his thumb skimmed upward to her lower lip. He skirted the edge until he reached the curl.

He smoothed the mock away. Did the same to the other side. "I don't know. I'm pretty good with a fillet knife."

Then he did the last thing he should, and kissed her.

KAYLA FROZE AT THE FIRST PRESS OF ASH'S LIPS AGAINST hers.

His touch was tentative, as if seeking permission—or waiting for the violent rejection of her palm across his face, a kick to the shin, or a shove against his chest.

She sensed all of this, even as shock speared through her bloodstream, making her limbs heavy, her thoughts nonexistent, and her organs unsteady. The only part of her body that seemed to be functioning as intended was her mouth.

Instinct controlled her. Months of anticipation, of wanting, of imagining, guided her through one of the most erotic moments of her life.

When his tongue slid inside her mouth, she could no longer passively participate. Her body broke free of its strange paralysis. She moved in closer, snaking her arms around his middle, sliding her hands upward until she felt the ripple of muscle across his back.

Her G-man worked out. A lot.

The embrace brought her body flush against his. He

moaned in response, cradled her face in his hands, and deepened the kiss.

When she realized his hunger matched her own, her pulse stuttered and her breathing put on the skids. From the first moment she saw him, she'd wanted him.

His continual hostility toward her had only heightened her attraction, especially once she'd detected interest beneath all his male posturing. But something had changed in the last few days.

Beneath the hostility, beneath the interest, thundered a heart that cared for her. Truly cared. Cared enough to drive her home and check for intruders, cared enough to show up on a weekend to ensure she was safe.

Could she make love to Ash Blackwell and walk away, unscathed?

No. Absolutely not.

The answer squeezed out what little juice she had left in her heart, and she became lightheaded with fear. She didn't want to let him go, but she also understood the inevitable suffering she would endure if she allowed herself to indulge in one night with him.

Slowly, gently, reluctantly she brought their kiss to an end.

As soon as she stepped back, her stomach knotted with regret and longing.

Would his caress have led to the most amazing love-making of her life? Or would he have been one more romantic disappointment in a long line of disap-pointments?

Of its own volition, her gaze tracked over his body. Somehow, she didn't think anything about Asher Cameron Blackwell would disappoint.

Except for his annoying tendency to judge her.

He cleared his throat. "Forgive me. I don't know, what—"

She held up a hand. "It was a moment. No need for excuses."

He scowled. "I wasn't going to offer any."

"You don't know what came over you? You don't know what you were thinking?" She raised an eyebrow. "Those non-excuses?"

"You have a knack for pissing me off, you know that?"

"We all have our talents."

"You're right," he all but growled. "I shouldn't have come here." He stormed away, then paused at the garage door opening to look back at her. "Did any of your mother's guests report losing a pearl stud earring the night of the murder?"

The change of topic jolted her. "Pardon?" His words clicked into place. "No, not that I've heard."

"How about you?"

"What about me?"

"Have you misplaced a pearl earring?"

"Not that I'm aware, but I haven't worn my studs in weeks." She set her jaw. "Why do you ask?"

"An earring was discovered in the garden."

"You believe it's connected to Vicky's murder?"

"It's probably nothing, but we have to follow up on it. Let me know if you find an earring missing. And text me the name of your university vandal." He gave her a hard nod. "Good night."

"Do you have a picture of the earring? If it's not mine, I can ask around."

"No." Another command. "You sleuthing around is the last thing I need."

"But wouldn't it be better—"

"Stick to fucking up people's lives with your lobbying. Leave the investigation to the professionals."

Once the door closed behind him, Kayla backed up until her vehicle absorbed her weight. A mix of emotions pounded through her, making her unsteady on her feet. Fury and shame battled for the top position.

He had no idea what she'd sacrificed for the citizens of this state, *this country*. Every molecule in her body has been focused on fixing what was broken with the political system. Why did he hate her profession so much?

Stick to fucking up people's lives.

She flashed back to Alexander Brighton and his notable absence senior year.

28

LEAVING THE RESIDENT AGENCY'S BREAK ROOM, ASH CROSSED paths with Peppy Patsy and saluted her with his brimming cup. "Thanks for putting on another pot."

"My pleasure, hon. Now that we have a fancy coffee maker, it's as easy as buttering biscuits." She stopped a few feet away. "Need help with anything?"

He gripped the mug a little tighter as he prepared to take a drink. Unlike most communal coffee, the brew here was good. Didn't matter who made it, all they had to do was follow the detailed instructions Patsy had taped to the new coffee maker.

"I'm good." Ash blew into his cup before taking a tentative sip. The hot liquid was a few degrees shy of scalding as it slid over his tongue and down the back of his throat. Perfect.

He continued toward his office.

"If anything comes up, just give me a holler," Patsy said. "Now that I have a part-time assistant, I can take more off all y'all's plate. I can't imagine the number of balls you have in the air with the Stokes case."

"Thank you, Patsy. I—" He paused and turned back to the office assistant—manager. "Actually, there is something you could help me out with, if you're game."

Her smile grew wider. "I was born ready to play. You can ask my poor aggrieved mother. She could tell you story after story about my rollicking teenage years."

Ash couldn't help but grin. "I'll keep that in mind when I need blackmail material on you."

"Oh, I've gone and done a number on myself now." Laughing, she nodded toward her desk a few feet away. "Let me grab something to write on."

Ash followed and waited for her to get settled in at her desk.

"What's on your mind, hon?"

"At the governor's crime scene, I found a pearl stud earring pinned to a tree branch."

"Sounds like someone took Pin the Tail on the Donkey to a whole new level."

Ash suppressed a smile. He'd learned not to acknowledge Patsy's sometimes inappropriate, always amusing, one-liners. She could shoot off one right after the other like clay pigeons.

"Based on the line of sight, I believe it's where the shooter set up to make the kill shot, though forensics has yet to confirm my suspicions."

"A calling card?"

"Signature," he corrected. "Either that or a drunken socialite got stuck in a tree."

Patsy chortled. "Want me to check to see if a pearl earring pops up in any other cases?"

He nodded. "Widen the net. Search for any jewelry, not just pearl studs. It's a long shot, but worth looking."

"Got it. Anything else?"

"Not at the moment. If you get a hit, let me know immediately. I don't care if the director herself is in my office."

"I need to finish something for Mitch, then I'll jump on this."

He recalled the research he'd done yesterday on the Secretary of State's website. The organization who'd paid millions of dollars to Krowne and Associates, over a number of years. "One more thing?" he asked.

"Name it."

"See what you can find out about a company named HCVS and the company's rep, Larissa Maywood."

She scribbled the information on her pad of paper. "Is HCVS an acronym for something?"

"Maybe."

"How deep do you want me to go?"

"To the ninth circle of Hell, if necessary."

"I love it when you talk Dante."

Ash strode back to his desk, risking another sip while in motion.

He'd barely managed two hours of sleep last night. After his mind-scrambling kiss with Kayla, his body had remained strung taut for hours, until he'd finally taken himself in hand.

Regardless of what Kayla thought, he didn't regret the kiss. The revelation surprised him as much as it would her. What he did regret were his parting words.

Stick to fucking up people's lives.

For nearly two years, he'd done his best to stay out of her orbit. Primarily, because of Phin's and Liv's close relationship with the lobbyist. But he'd also been unable to suppress his irritation over how her lobbying efforts had impacted his day-to-day life and was concerned that his lack of control would cause a deeper rift in the family.

Something he did not need. Or want.

But something elemental had changed.

He wasn't sure when or how she'd managed it, but the woman inside the lobbyist attracted him like a bee to pollen. Maybe it was her selfless efforts helping his brothers or the stories of her generous philanthropy. Maybe it was her sharp, amused intelligence that seemed to always be directed at him or the grief in her eyes after witnessing her godmother's murder.

Or maybe, just maybe, it had been the way she looked yesterday morning. Casual, slightly disheveled. Sexy as hell.

Several times today, he found his thoughts trailing off. Moving from the important work in front of him to reliving the feel of Kayla's lips against his. Their softness, their warmth, their need.

A need that matched his own.

Ash threw on the mental emergency brake and sagged into his chair. She kept him on an emotional roller coaster. It was damn exhausting, which was why he'd made a third trip to the break room for caffeine.

Fishing his phone out of his pocket, he scrolled through his favorites until he found Rohan's name. While the line connected, he anchored a white Airpod into his right ear, pushed out of his chair, and strode to the far window, away from curious ears.

From this vantage point, he could see Otis Street, the public parking garage, and a sliver of the Battery Park area. Vendors occupied the permanent outdoor stalls, hawking their handmade crafts or popular tourist bric-a-brac. Tourists inched by them, deciding whether or not to part ways with their hard-earned money.

After three rings, his brother picked up. "Hey, Ash."

"How's it going?"

"Quiet for a change."

"Got the office to yourself?"

"In part. Phin and some of the ladies are busy planning a surprise birthday party for Grams and the rest of us are hunkered down, trying to stay out of their honey-do sight."

Ash's chest constricted. "Party?"

"They're brainstorming dates, but it'll probably be on the Saturday before her actual birthday." His brother paused as if realizing something. "It's all preliminary right now, Ash. Mom threw out the idea to Liv, Maddy, and Lena yesterday. The guys and I learned about it last night." Another brief pause. "I'm sure Mom was going to text you today."

Ash swallowed to ease the tightness in his throat. "Yeah."

"Don't worry, bro." A lighter, teasing note entered Rohan's voice. "Distance won't exempt you from Mom's to-do list."

"Whatever she needs." Ash brushed a hand over his face. "Mind if I ask a favor?"

"Name it. I still owe you one for helping us find Lena's family."

He wanted to ask how the reunion was going, but didn't feel this was the right time. "Before you commit, you need to be aware that this request requires a high degree of sensitivity, confidentiality, and the dark web."

"Noted."

The tension pulsing through his body dissipated. "I'm part of a multiagency task force working the Stokes case."

"Any leads on who killed the governor yet?"

"Not yet. That's the reason for my call. Can you scrape the dark web and see if there's any chatter about the hit?"

"Why not use the FBI's team of intelligence analysts? Surely, the governor's assassination takes priority."

"They're working on it, but . . ." Ash struggled to say the words he never imagined saying after leaving the family business.

"Your colleagues have to color between the lines?" Rohan offered, taking pity on him.

"Exactly." Ash expelled a breath. "I know you have lines you won't cross, too, but yours are more flexible."

"You're talking a lot of scraping, Ash."

"I know it's a long shot, but I have reason to believe—" He stopped himself before revealing details of the case. Outside of a few favors recently, it'd been years since he'd worked with his brothers. Yet he'd almost shared sensitive information with Rohan without a second's thought.

"I'll need to understand what I'm searching for, or this won't work," Rohan said after the silence stretched between them. "Whatever you share stays between you and me. I've never betrayed your confidence, as evidenced by my two decades of silence about who was responsible for the discarded condom in the back of Mom's vehicle."

Ash smiled at the ancient memory. He turned away from the window and headed back to his desk, pulling out the Stokes case file. "I believe Kayla Krowne might have been the intended target."

"Kayla?" his brother echoed, incredulous. "I didn't hear anything about her being present."

"So far, we've managed to keep her name out of the news. If she hadn't tripped over a rug, she would have taken a bullet from behind."

"That close?"

"She was damn lucky."

"How's she doing?"

"Hurting. The governor was a close family friend. I don't think she took the threat to herself seriously until her vehicle was vandalized yesterday."

"What about protection?"

"Her driver is a former Ranger, so she's covered during weekdays. I touched base with APD this morning and they agreed to schedule a regular patrol of her street in the evenings. Her mother is going to speak to her about hiring a private security firm to cover the weekends."

"What else can you tell me about the shooter?"

"He left what appears to be a signature embedded in a tree."

"What kind?"

"A pearl earring."

"Unique. Anything else?"

"There might have been another intruder. Forensics discovered fresh blood not far from where I found the earring."

"You think the two did some hand-to-hand?"

"It's the only scenario that makes sense. Plus, there were other signs of a fight. Why there were two intruders and why they went at each other is the bigger question."

"Hopefully forensics will get a hit on the DNA and that will answer your why."

"I have a feeling whatever the lab finds is going to create more questions than it answers."

"You want me to search the web for any mention of assassination plots on the governor or Kayla and jewelry left at the crime scene signature? Is that all?"

"See what you can find out about a company called HCVS. They've been pouring millions into Krowne and Associates for years. The only details I could find on them was the information Krowne listed on the lobbying statement form they're required to submit to the Secretary of State." With the task force and Rohan searching for clues, something had to pop. He hoped.

"Do you have that information handy?"

Ash rattled off the address and Maywood's contact info.

"Give me a couple of days, and I'll see what I can find."

"Thanks, bro."

"Family first."

Emotion pressed against the backs of his eyes, and he snapped his lids closed. Only once before had he been included in his brothers' mantra and that was only because he'd inserted himself into the mix.

Rohan had just invited him in. Without hesitation or prejudice.

"Ash?"

"Yeah," he swallowed hard. "I'm here." He released a breath through his aching throat, lifted his head as if he could see into his brother's eyes. "Go slow and easy on this one. Don't leave a single crumb for anyone to pick up. I don't know how deep and dark this goes."

"The last thing you need to worry about right now is my level of caution. This is my schtick. I know how to cover my tracks. Kayla is the one who needs your attention and energy."

"I hear what you're saying, and agree, but that won't stop me from worrying about my little brother."

Another silence fell between them. This one didn't contain the awkwardness of before. This one nodded toward fellowship. Brotherhood.

"Talk in a few days," Rohan said, and the line went dead.

Ash pulled the Airpod from his ear before opening the

bottom right drawer of his desk. Inside was a five-by-seven, black-framed picture, lying face down.

He lifted the photo from where he'd dropped it unceremoniously five years ago after finding it stashed in his moving box the day he'd left the family business behind.

No note. No explanation. But Ash recognized Grams's trademark *everything will work out* symbolism, all the same.

Turning the frame over, he stared into the smiling faces of him and his four brothers.

He couldn't even recall the occasion or what the hell they were so happy about. But he was certain of one thing. It was their last happy moment captured on camera before he'd ripped the family apart.

Bending back the frame's easel, he set the photo on the left corner of his desk. New beginnings had to start somewhere.

He just hoped it wasn't too late for this one.

29

Kayla scrambled to find her ringing phone as she exited the elevator and stepped into the marble-tiled foyer of her building.

In a hurry, she'd dumped the device into her handbag, along with a few file folders, rather than slipping it into its normal side pocket. Bad decision.

Frustration tunneled her vision into the black abyss of her purse, while she fast-walked to the doors leading outside. A sixth sense of an impending danger saved her from plowing into a man going the opposite direction.

She screeched to a halt mere inches from Tommy O'Connor. The same client her intern had to hang up on two days ago because of his belligerence. She'd called him back minutes later with an update and an admonishment about his treatment of her staff.

Now he was here, at her office, looking as though he wanted to do some serious verbal damage. Or worse.

A string of silent curses trailed through her mind as her fingers finally closed over her phone. With as much nonchalance as she could manage, she put an arm's length of distance between them.

"Just the person I was coming to see," he said. Irritation hardened his tone.

"Excuse me, Tommy." She lifted her phone. "Let me just acknowledge the caller." Hitting the green button, she said, "Hi, Jillian. I'm on my way."

"Jillian?" her mom echoed, aghast.

"Can you hold a moment? I'm with a client." Kayla didn't bother waiting for her mother's consent before hitting the mute button. A savvy businesswoman, Jillian understood there were times when clients must be prioritized over family.

"At least I'm not the only one you're keeping waiting," Tommy said.

Dressed in black slacks and a tan polo, with his group's logo embroidered on the left side of his chest, he stood at eye level with Kayla. Crimson flushed the top of his ears and his normally smooth forehead was scrunched into forbidding folds.

Where once she had admired the leanness of his square jaw and the flicker of his bulging biceps, she now found herself wary of the sight. The young man behind the building's reception counter offered Kayla a modicum of comfort. But she was all too aware of how much damage a fit man like Tommy could do before the police arrived.

Tapping into a decade of experience, she plastered on her de-escalation smile. "Campaigns such as yours take time. There's a legislative process—"

"It's been nearly a year, Kayla, and your team still hasn't secured the votes necessary to get our bill passed. If it doesn't pass this session, we'll be forced to start from scratch, because we'll be dealing with a number of newly elected legislators."

She almost shot back that she knew how the process worked. Instead of inflaming the situation, she said, "As I mentioned on the phone, there's still plenty of time to get the support we need."

"One month doesn't sound like 'plenty of time' to me."

"Tommy." She kept her voice low, modulated, confident. "You hired Krowne and Associates to shepherd your cause through the political process, because of our incredible success rate." She deepened her hold on his gaze. "Trust me."

"A lot of people are going to lose their homes if you fail." His eyes stretched into predatory slits. "And we know what a small community North Carolina politics is. A fail of this magnitude would be a big blow to your credibility."

As veiled threats went, it wasn't bad, but it had little effect on her. Over the years, she'd encountered this same scenario hundreds of times. Her client's feelings of impotence.

With every project Krowne and Associates took on, there came a time when the client had to put all their trust and faith into her firm's hands. Some campaigns flew through the process with little pushback. And some, like Tommy's, could take months or even a couple of legislative cycles to get the requisite votes.

Whatever a bill's journey, she always prevailed.

"I'm aware of the stakes, Tommy."

"Is your team?"

"Absolutely."

"What about this new governor? Do you have the same relationship with her as you did Stokes?"

She didn't know Gayle Cabrera as intimately as Vicky,

but the former lieutenant governor's ideology was similar to her godmother's. It was why Vicky, and other powerful individuals, had backed her for the number two spot.

"Governor Cabrera will support SB623."

"How do you know? Have you spoken to her about it?"

"Not yet. She's been a little busy settling into her new role."

"Sounds like the perfect time to approach her. Before the other vultures surround her."

"Vultures?" she echoed in a quiet voice.

Tommy's stormy gaze arrested, shifted from hers. "I'm sorry. I shouldn't have said that."

"No, you shouldn't have. My staff are working their asses off for you, Tommy. For your cause. They don't deserve your verbal abuse."

"I know. I know." He raked a hand through his hair. "It's —there's a lot of pressure right now."

Although she wanted to tie a bowling ball to his damn tongue, she understood more than anyone how it felt to have other peoples' lives, livelihoods, happiness, all of it, hanging on a yea or a nay.

Kayla drew in a breath, then checked her smart watch. "Look, I'm running behind for an appointment." She forced a conciliatory note into her voice. "I'll check in with my team in Raleigh and get back to you."

The tension radiating through Tommy's shoulders eased just as a large figure approached him from behind.

"Is everything okay, Ms. Krowne?" Mason asked, smoothly putting himself between her and Tommy.

Mason had at least six inches on her client and probably thirty pounds of muscle.

"Everything is fine, thank you." She leveled a look at the other man. "Mr. O'Connor and I were just wrapping up."

Tommy gave her a curt nod and strode away.

"What was all that about?" Mason asked.

Kayla waved for him to follow and headed for the door. "A stressed-out client. Nothing to worry about."

"Nothing to worry about?" Jillian Krowne exclaimed through her phone's speaker. *"Who does this Tommy think he is, threatening my daughter?"*

She'd forgotten all about putting her mother on hold. In her flustered state, she had evidently hit the Speaker button rather than Mute.

Kayla mentally reviewed her exchange with Tommy for any worrisome comments Jillian would call her out on later, once she got past this protective mama bear stage. When she recalled none, she said, "He's just worried, Mom. It happens."

"Kayla Cornelia Krowne, you and I know that if you'd been a man, he would have been more circumspect with his language."

She tilted an apologetic look toward Mason, who merely grinned, then increased his pace to open the back passenger side door for her. Today, he was driving the Audi, since her Merc was at the auto body shop.

"Mom, we can discuss this more when I get to the restaurant."

"Which will be when, exactly?"

Kayla glanced at Mason as she slid into the backseat. He flashed ten fingers, twice. "Twenty minutes."

"I'll be the woman seething in the back corner."

"A glass of champagne will help cool your ire. Later, Mama."

She clicked off and leaned against the headrest.

"You're going to pay for that last comment," Mason said, unable to suppress the humor in his voice. "Cornelia."

Jillian Krowne's fascination with Cornelia Stuyvesant Vanderbilt was legend. Heiress to the largest private home in the United States, Cornelia used her immense influence to raise much-needed funds for the community and was instrumental in opening portions of Biltmore House to the public.

"If you ever repeat that name again, I'll buy a twenty-year-old, rusted-out station wagon in lime green for you to drive."

"Roger that."

Kayla changed the subject. "How's college scouting going?"

"Slow and painful."

"Is your daughter leaning toward one in particular? Maybe one where all of her friends are going?"

"Jozi isn't one to follow the pack."

"A lone wolf like her dad?"

"It's not the worst of my attributes that could've rubbed off on her." His tone turned serious. "Do I need to alert APD or Agent Blackwell about O'Connor's visit?"

"No, he just needed to blow off some steam. Listening is part of my other duties as assigned.'"

"You're a better person than me. It's my opinion that rational discussion produces far better results than an excess of steam."

"Wise, as always, my friend. Unfortunately, social media has all but obliterated 'rational' from our vocabulary."

30

THE MOMENT KAYLA STEPPED INSIDE THE LOBBY OF THE Hilton at Biltmore Park Town Square on the south side of Asheville, her phone chimed with a text.

To the right of the bar.

Nodding to the ponytailed host, she entered Fork Lore, an upscale restaurant that specialized in Southern fare and locally-sourced food. According to their website. Kayla knew nothing of the place and wondered why her mother had selected an eatery so far from their offices.

The CFO of Krowne Hotels and Resorts sat at a small table, nestled between two giant planters with towering tropical plants. After the obligatory cheek peck, Kayla took the seat across from Jillian, then bypassed the glass of red wine to reach for the ice water, already sitting in a pool of condensation.

"Sorry I'm late." Kayla took a drink. "As you heard, the delay was unavoidable."

"I certainly did. We'll get to that later." She placed her hand over Kayla's. "Thank you for meeting with me at the last minute."

She frowned at her mother's bare finger. "Where's your wedding ring?"

Jillian removed her hand. "I took it to the jeweler to have the setting checked and cleaned."

"Didn't you do that just a few months ago?"

"It's been longer than a few months, darling."

Kayla didn't think so, but she would concede the point.

"Now, knowing your time constraints," Jillian said, "I took the liberty of ordering you a wedge salad."

Although she appreciated her mother's thoughtfulness, Kayla hated the bleu cheese dressing that normally flowed over the lettuce like white, clumpy lava. Hopefully, she had instructed them to put it on the side or had chosen a substitute.

"Thank you, Mama." She rested her forearms on the table and leaned in. "Now tell me why the clandestine location."

"I don't know what you mean. I thought you'd be delighted to get away from downtown."

"Maybe for dinner, but this is the middle of a very busy workday. All of which you know and would point out if our roles were reversed."

Jillian re-draped the linen napkin over her lap. A delaying tactic, while she no doubt grappled with how to respond.

The food arrived, buying her more time.

"Here we go, ladies." The server set a plate down in front of Jillian. "Smoked salmon for you and," he placed a rimmed plate before Kayla, "a wedge for you."

Thick white dressing dripped over the sides of the quarter cut chunk of iceberg lettuce.

Great.

She imagined herself scraping off the disgusting dressing, but it had soaked into the nooks and crannies of the cut sides.

"With a ranch substitute," he continued.

Relieved, Kayla picked up her fork and knife, suddenly starving.

"Thank you, Mark," Jillian said. "We're all set."

Once the server departed, Kayla said, "You remembered."

"Of course, you are my daughter. I remember every-thing about the past thirty-five years."

Kayla lifted an eyebrow. "Everything?"

Jillian's eyes narrowed. "All of the important bits."

Kayla shook her head, smiling. "Can we get back to why you're acting like Evelyn Salt? I know it's not so you can ask me about the investigation. We could have done that downtown."

Jillian finished chewing a bite of salmon. "Your father and I would like to engage a private security firm on your behalf."

Had they somehow found out about the vandalism to her car? Kayla shoved the question away. Only three people knew about the etchings. And none of them would have informed Jillian or Gordon Krowne.

She finished stabbing lettuce, tomato, and bacon onto her fork. "Why would you want to hire bodyguards for me?"

"To protect you, of course. I—we take threats against our family seriously." She toyed with the stem of her wine-glass. "I'm even more keen on the idea after overhearing your conversation with Mr. O'Connor."

"Tommy is scared, not violent." She hoped. "I will deal with my client." She gave her overprotective mother a pointed look. "Understood?"

Jillian cut her broccoli into perfect bite-sized pieces. "Very well."

Kayla evaluated her parent's body language for a good five seconds before letting the subject go. "As for the other, the police have yet to confirm that I was the intended target."

"While they're confirming, a murderer is running around Asheville, who may or may not want you dead."

Kayla could see it then. A mother's terror.

Over the years, there had been instances of overzealous activists, disappointed clients, ego-bruised politicians, or lobbyist haters who crossed the line.

For each incident, Jillian had gone through a battery of emotions, but never fear. Simmering anger fed her actions, which always boiled into satisfying retribution.

One time, her mother made a mouthy politician pay for his sin by holding her annual masquerade gala on the same night as the councilman's biggest campaign fundraiser of the year. He barely took in enough money to pay the electric bill.

When a trio of extreme activists hacked into and plastered gruesome pictures on Kayla's business website, Jillian had notified their employers. All three hactivists lost their jobs.

Jillian's extreme actions had forced Kayla to stop telling her overprotective mother about the darker side of lobbying in order to protect her attackers from their moments of poor judgment. But an unknown shooter at large was a scenario Jillian Krowne didn't have a retributive response for.

Setting down her knife, Kayla reached across the table and took hold of the older woman's hand. "Mama, you don't need to worry about me." She nodded toward the hotel's reception area, at the large man standing erect near one of the enormous columns. "I have Mason."

To her surprise, tears crowded in the corner of Jillian's eyes. She could count on one hand the number of times she'd seen her mother's iron grip slip.

"Mason can't be with you twenty-four-seven." A note of pleading took hold of her voice. "Please let me do this for you. For us. I can't lose you."

Kayla's heart twisted in a tight rope as she watched her freedom disappear. "All right, Mama. But I can take care of it myself." She would talk to Mason, or maybe Ash, about a reputable company.

Ash.

As annoyed as she was with him the previous evening, she found it impossible to remain so today. All she could think about was how every part of her yearned to mold itself around him. Absorb his warmth, his strength, his everything.

"Where'd you go, Kayla?"

She blinked.

"I asked if you're sure? I have time to do this for you."

Kayla straightened and resumed her methodical shaving off bites of salad. "Positive."

"You'll take care of it today."

"Yes, ma'am."

Jillian smiled. "Thank you, sweetheart. I'm sure it will only be for a little while."

With Ash on the case, Kayla tended to agree.

She glanced at her mother's barely touched plate. "Aren't you going to eat your salmon?"

"I'll take it home and eat it tonight. Seems I've ruined my appetite by making a mid-morning stop at Percolator."

"Currant scone?"

"Guilty."

They shared a smile.

"Do you have pearl studs?" Kayla blurted out.

"Of course." Jillian frowned. "Why do you ask?"

"Have you seen them lately?"

"What a bizarre question. Do you need to borrow them?"

"Please answer the question, Mama. It's important."

"I wore them two nights ago." She tilted her head to the side, assessing. "Why? Does this have anything to do with the murder investigation?"

A large hand constricted around her chest. "Why would you think that?"

"I know you, daughter. The location of my jewelry would be the furthest thing from your mind, under normal circumstances."

"Forget I asked. Ash wouldn't be happy if he learned I'd been sleuthing."

Amusement fluttered across Jillian's features. "It's not like you to customize your actions to please a man."

"I'm not being careful for *him*. It's the case I'm worried about. I don't want to screw up anything."

"It's best that you not form too deep an attachment to the agent."

"Not that I am, but why the warning?"

She waited for her mother to explain, but the board-room-savvy woman merely stared back with calm authority.

"Speaking of the agent," Kayla said, suppressing the automatic, teenage-style revolt bubbling in her stomach, "are you in agreement with Sybil and Elsie? About the method with which I should keep tabs on the FBI's investigation?"

Jillian folded her linen napkin and placed it on the table. "No, I'm not."

"You were unusually quiet at lunch the other day."

"As I said, I know my daughter."

"What does that mean?"

"It means," she said with quiet emphasis, "I raised you to use your mind to develop solutions to a problem. Not boudoir tricks."

Kayla's heart hammered in her chest. "But?"

"To my regret, I failed to teach you one important lesson." Jillian reached across the table to cup her cheek. "How to protect your heart."

31

Asн paced inside the circle of the veteran's memorial near Pack Square Park. Not far from where he'd first spotted Kayla at a picnic table, packing baskets for a generation often forgotten or who found themselves alone in a sea of unfamiliar faces.

He thought of Grams, of how long it had been since his last visit, and vowed to see her on his next day off.

Checking the clock on his phone, he groaned. Minutes ticked by with all the speed of a slug race.

An inner monologue revved up until it became a hammer inside his head. *This was a mistake. This was a mistake. This was a mistake.*

Two women watching over a clutch of barefooted children romping through a geiser-like splash fountain eyed him with more and more wariness. He knew he should sit down, be calm, and stop frightening the park users, but a nervous energy had taken over his movements and he couldn't seem to regain control.

He'd had more finesse in middle school, asking Mindy Wyatt to the school dance, than he had smoothing things over with the lobbyist after their explosive kiss and his cutting words.

What had gotten into him? Special agents don't get involved with witnesses. Yet he'd crossed the line. Hell, he'd leaped over it headfirst.

Eighteen hours later, and he still couldn't muster a proper apology or an appropriate amount of regret for the kiss. His shitty comment was another story.

The best outcome he could hope for was Kayla agreeing to forming a platonic, noncombative working relationship, until he—or one of his colleagues—tracked down the killer.

"I didn't realize they allowed tigers in the park," a flat female voice said from behind him.

Ash stopped his prowling and turned to face Kayla. Even dressed in a no-nonsense business pantsuit, she looked amazing.

Kissable.

Beddable.

He blinked the get-your-ass-in-trouble thoughts away and nodded at Wade, who stood sentinel several yards away, before addressing the lobbyist. "Thank you for agreeing to a last-minute meeting."

"It's a last-minute kind of day." She sat on a granite bench and clasped her hands loosely in her lap. "Do you have news to share? Or are you about to attempt another non-excuse for kissing me?" Her eyes dug into his. "Or an apology?"

He grasped the base of his skull as if he could squeeze out the right words. "All three, I guess."

A blond eyebrow rose. "You guess?"

His hand dropped back to his side. "All, dammit."

"How about I knock the list down for you."

"By all means."

"As with last night, I have no interest in hearing your apologies or assurances that you won't kiss me again." Her mouth curved into a secretive smile. "You know as well as I do that we've been circling each other since we first met and, if an opportunity presents itself, we'll be naked and consumed."

Ash went hard and aching, in an instant. If they'd been alone, he would have ensured her prediction came true. He buttoned his suit jacket, despite the warm March day. "You cannot say shit like that with little kids around."

Her gaze flicked down to watch his movements and her smile widened. "I noticed you didn't disagree with my assessment."

"You know how much I enjoyed our kiss?" He moved closer. Lowered his voice. "How badly I want it to happen again?" Her amusement dimmed, and he took unbelievable pleasure in the effect his words had on her. "What it did to me last night as I lay in bed with nothing but the memory to keep me company?"

She swallowed and sat straighter.

"For now, I'll keep it professional," he continued, having no intention of doing so. She'd opened Pandora's box, and he was keen to see what was inside. To hell with the Bureau's code of conduct. "But I do want to apologize for lashing out at you last night. No excuses. I lost my head for a second."

"Apology accepted."

He raised a brow. "That's it?"

"What did you expect? That I would hurt you in kind? Make you grovel to win my forgiveness?"

"I'm sorry, Kayla. I didn't mean to hurt you."

She nodded, then glanced down at her clasped hands before meeting his eyes again.

He tilted his head, allowed a teasing note to enter his voice. "I thought I'd have to work a little harder."

Her features softened, a little. "We're both adults, Ash. Neither of us have time for teenage games."

Leaning down, he kissed her forehead, lingered there long enough to pull her honey-vanilla scent into his chest. "Thank you," he whispered.

He brushed a finger over the spot where his sidearm injured her. "Still painful?"

"A bit tender."

Guilt stabbed through him as he straightened and shoved his hands into his pockets.

She cleared her throat. "Since we're clearing the air, I should tell you that I asked my mother if she was missing a pearl stud earring."

Ash gritted his teeth. "We haven't released that information to—"

She raised a hand. "My mother would never jeopardize your case by discussing it with anyone. She understands the value of some secrets."

"All it takes is one misplaced word to the wrong person."

"She wore her studs two days ago, after Vicky's murder."

"What about yours?"

"I don't own studs, exactly, but the pearls I have are still in my jewelry case."

He lifted his chin, stretching the tension from his neck, as he stared at the sky. "We got a hit on the earring."

"What exactly do you mean by 'hit'?"

Lowering his gaze, he said, "Patsy located a record for an

ex-con who liked to break into his target's home, steal a piece of jewelry, and place it at the hit site a day or two before he killed his target. If anyone found the jewelry before the hit, he took it as a sign from God to abort the mission."

"It's plausible he could have stolen the pearl earring from Vicky and planted it before the benefit."

"The task force hasn't been able to verify if the governor was missing an earring."

"What's the ex-con's name?"

Ash hesitated a moment, then recalled the scanned newspaper articles Patsy had shown him. Knowing the lobbyist, she'd just google the details he'd already shared with her and come up with a name. "Seb Grimball. Familiar?"

She shook her head. "How many missions did he abort?"

"Zero."

"You think this man is Vicky's' shooter?"

"Anything is possible. According to Patsy, he was released from prison a year ago after spending the last three decades behind bars. Maybe something triggered him and he went back to killing."

"Thirty years? How old is he?"

"Sixty-one."

"Wouldn't he have lost his . . . skillset after being dormant for so long?"

"He's had a year to hone it back into shape."

She didn't look convinced. and, frankly, neither was he, but it was the only lead they had at the moment.

"Why Vicky?"

"That's what I need to find out."

"You?"

"Tracking down bad guys is what I do."

"Who's your backup?"

"I'm going to feel out Grimball first, before I get the task force involved."

"No, sir, you're not. That's why there's a task force. Safety in numbers. Many minds avert disaster, and all that."

He fished his phone out of his pocket to check the time. "I have to go."

"To talk to the ex-con?"

"Come on. I'll walk with you to Wade."

She stood. A resolute expression on her beautiful face. "I'm going with you."

"The hell you are."

"I'm not letting you go alone." She started toward Wade. "And besides, I want to hear what this guy has to say."

He set his jaw and followed, regretting the bone he'd thrown her after his harsh treatment. "And I'm not allowing you to accompany me while I talk to Seb Grimball."

"I'll have Mason follow you."

The bodyguard glanced between them, tension radiating through the veteran. "Need me to grab the car, Ms. Krowne?"

Kayla looked up at Ash, raised a brow. His gaze flicked between her and Wade. The last thing he needed was an emotionally-compromised civilian sitting in on his interview with Grimball.

But he had no doubt that she'd follow up on her threat to have Wade track his vehicle. Then he'd have an Army Ranger of unknown background and temperament in the mix.

"Fine," Ash growled. "But the bodyguard stays."

Wade shifted closer to Kayla. She put a hand on his bicep as if to forestall violence. "Agreed."

The Ranger's hard gaze swiveled toward his employer. "I go where you go."

"Not this time." She nodded toward Ash. "I'll be perfectly safe."

A muscle worked in the Ranger's jaw before he stepped back. He locked eyes with Ash. "If anything happens to her, I'm coming for you, Feeb."

32

After passing a fourth barely standing matchbox-sized house on the narrow gravel mountain road, Kayla started reassessing her decision to join Ash while he interviewed the ex-con.

The vehicle's GPS announced, "In one thousand feet, your destination will be on the left."

Relief that they'd finally made it without any no-trespassing bullets zinging their way dissipated the moment she saw the large black and red BEWARE DOG sign at the foot of Grimball's driveway.

Before parting ways with Mason, she'd grabbed her workout bag from the trunk of her vehicle. Even though she had an in-house gym, she kept a membership at her local YMCA. They had a larger variety of equipment and an enormous swimming pool. The Y was also a great meeting place for the community and a practical, yet strategic, way of monitoring the needs of everyone, not just her wealthy peers.

Now she wore running shoes, though she preferred not to have to test them against an angry dog.

Ash was constantly scanning the area, which only heightened her growing anxiety. "Do you have to do this often?" she asked in a near whisper.

"Only a couple times a day."

"Not funny."

"It's not too late. I can drop you off at that antique mall you gushed over a few miles back, while I speak to Grimball."

"I don't gush, and no thank you."

"At least stay in the car."

"And become dog bait?"

"It would increase my chances of getting to the front door with all my flesh attached."

She backhanded his hard bicep, eliciting a full grin. After years of seeing nothing but scowls on his handsome face, it was disarming when snatches of humor appeared.

"What are the rules?" he asked, switching back to cop mode.

"We've been over them twice, already."

"Third time's a charm, right?"

"No talking, no emotion, no interruptions, no nothing."

"Except?"

The words clutched at the back of her throat. "Do as you say, when you say it. No arguments, no negotiations."

He nodded. The vehicle rolled to a stop, and Ash killed the engine. He didn't say anything for several long seconds, while checking his rear- and sideview mirrors.

She realized he was waiting for the guard dog to appear. "Clear?" she asked.

Another nod. "The sign must be an empty deterrent."

"Probably effective for sane people."

He sent her a sideways glance. "Last chance."

Pushing open her door, she said, "Let's go, Special Agent."

As they approached the sagging wooden porch, Kayla took in the graveyard of rusted-out vehicles, plastic jugs, crumpled beer cans, mangled kiddy pool, windowless camper with an oak tree growing out of one end, and two stocky painted horses eating the patches of grass growing around all the abandoned detritus.

Poverty was a disease in the United States. An epidemic. Thirty-eight million affected, according to the U.S. Census.

In her work as a lobbyist, Kayla had helped put forth several important bills that would raise the tide for all Americans. Not just those born into privilege, as she had been, or those with white skin or perfect vocabulary. But everyone who wanted to live their best life, however that looked.

Ash pointed for her to take up a position on the hinge side of the front door, while he stood on the opposite side, near the door handle. He rapped his knuckles hard on the door, whose white paint had aged into a moldy gray.

The sound seemed to thunder through the air. Kayla rotated her upper body, expecting the guard dog to shoot out of his resting place at hearing evidence of intruders. She caught a glimpse of something dark arrowing across the driveway, about three quarters of the way down.

Staring at the spot for several seconds, she tensed, waiting for more movement. When none materialized, she decided it must have been a wild animal. A black bear or maybe a fawn scampering after its mama. For some reason, the idea of a wild animal concerned her far less than a domestic guard dog.

Footsteps pounded through the interior of the house

and a second later she heard the snick of a dead bolt retracting into its cave. Then another, and another.

The door cracked open, inch by slow inch, until an older man filled the space. He wore his iron-gray hair short, military-style. His bare, corded forearms sported tattoos that had dulled with time. His fit body filled up all the space in his green polo and cargo pants. She now knew how he'd spent his days in lockup.

In short, if this was Seb Grimball, he met none of her expectations as she'd approached the ramshackle house. He wore sixty-one well, even with the swollen nose and blackened eyes.

"Sebastian Grimball?" Ash asked.

"That's right. Who's calling?" He kept his right hand tucked behind his thigh.

"I'm going to reach into my jacket for my credentials."

The grooves at the corners of the ex-con's eyes deepened before he gave a sharp nod.

Ash fingered out a square-ish bifold wallet, opened it, and said, "I'm Special Agent Cameron Blackwell and this is my associate Kayla. We would like to ask you a few questions about the night of March twenty-first."

Had Seb's eyes flickered in recognition at the mention of her name?

"What about it?" Seb asked.

"May we come in? We won't take up much of your time."

The ex-con seemed to be mentally weighing his options. After a long, pregnant silence, he opened the door and stepped back.

Grimball warned, "I have a gun in my right hand—"

The ex-con's words cut off as the top of his head disappeared.

33

Ash's body burst into action before his mind fully assimilated the facts.

He grasped Kayla's arm and thrust her inside the house. "Get down on the floor and stay there."

To his surprise, she didn't hesitate. She dropped to the hardwood floor, her face inches from blood spatter and brain matter.

A quick scan revealed they'd spilled into the front room. Unlike the outside, the inside of the small house was tidy and modern. A leather couch and matching recliner faced a seventy-inch TV and a white marble fireplace nestled into one corner of the room.

He kicked Grimball's feet out of the way and slammed the door shut. Crouching low against the wall between the door and large bay window, he drew his service weapon and checked the chamber.

"Stay there," he said.

"Where are you going?"

"To clear the rest of the house."

Her terrified, yet controlled, gaze slashed from the dead body to the front door. "I'm coming with you."

"I'll be able to clear the place faster if you stay put." He hardened his voice. "No going rogue like last time."

Embarrassed, she glanced away.

"I'll be back in under two minutes."

Her gaze snapped to his, their eyes locked for a long moment, then she jerked her head once. The amount of trust and bravery it took for her to let him go wasn't lost on him.

Using the toe of his shoe, he slid Grimball's gun over to her from where it had fallen at the ex-con's side. "Shoot anyone who comes through this door." He didn't question her ability with the Glock, recalling the way she'd handled her own.

She nodded, grasping the weapon with confidence and checking its load.

"Keep your head down," he said.

"You, too."

Pushing away from the wall, he kept to a low crouch as he dashed toward what appeared to be the kitchen.

He flinched as a bullet blasted through the front window and embedded into the wall separating the front room from the kitchen. Two more holes appeared, each one getting inches closer to his position.

Ash ducked into the hallway, listening for movement in the kitchen. Hearing none, he made quick work of the two small bedrooms and shared bathroom before returning.

He took a knee near what were probably once lemon-colored cabinets, but had now taken on the hue of yellow squash left on the counter a week too long. The new wood flooring in the front room extended down the hall as well as the kitchen. Grimball appeared to be putting his murder money to good use.

When no bullets *thunked* near his head, he moved to clear the kitchen. A single glance confirmed the room was empty. But a familiar scent caught inside Ash's nose. He inhaled again, to be certain.

Gas.

"Kayla," he whispered.

She lifted her head. Glass shards from the shattered window tinkled from her hair to join the other thousand on the floor around her.

"Crawl to me, quickly. Now."

She snaked her way toward him. Thankfully, she'd kept her suit coat on or her forearms would've been shredded. "What's wrong?"

"One of the bullets hit the gas line." He motioned for her to hurry. "We need to get out of here. His next shot could spark an explosion."

"You want us to go through the kitchen?" she asked, guessing his intent.

"It's the only other exit. Unless you'd prefer to take your chances through the front door."

Taking one last lungful of clean air, he crouch-ran through the breakfast area, bypassing the small dining table and two chairs, his senses split between the path ahead of him and Kayla's rapid steps behind him.

He flicked the lock on the slider, pushed it open wide, and waited for another barrage of gunfire. When none came, he turned back to Kayla, who squatted at his six.

"There's a pile of old tires fifty feet out. I'm headed there to draw their fire. If all stays quiet, run like hell to my location. I'll cover you."

"You think there's more than one shooter?"

"I always expect the worst."

"I don't like this plan."

"It's the only one we've got." He kissed her swiftly. "Ready?"

"Do I get one of those at the other end?"

He liked that she used humor to defray the tension. The woman was solid. Fearless.

Despite the pressure of the clock ticking in his head, he threw her his cockiest grin. "As many as you can handle."

She coughed, the gas choking the air. "Don't die, G-man. I have plans for you."

Ash surged forward.

34

KAYLA'S CHEST CRATERED AS SHE WATCHED ASH DASH toward the pile of tires. Arms extended, his pistol followed his upper body as it rotated side to side, searching for threats.

The gas swelled in the room behind her. She coughed again, even though she had her face pressed close to the slider's opening. Every second that slogged by, she prayed it wouldn't be her last.

The moment Ash reached his destination, he motioned for her to join him. Gathering the frayed ends of her courage together, she shot out of the house.

She hated running. Hated every bone-jarring, brain-bruising, sweat-inducing slap of the feet. It made her wonder what mind-altering drug runners took in order to put their bodies through such torture, every day.

Today's torment took less than five seconds, but her breaths heaved and her muscles quivered as if she'd run a marathon. Once she reached Ash's side, he cupped the back of her neck as if he could stop the rush of adrenaline sweeping through her body.

She hadn't heard any gunfire, but her blood was like a thunderclap in her ears. "Anything?"

Ash shook his head, though he continued to surveil the surrounding tree line. She knew with absolute certainty that if she hadn't been present, he would have gone after the shooter.

The realization made her equal parts thankful she'd insisted on coming and regretful. Just thinking about him hunting a predator capable of blowing off a man's head made her stomach revolt. On the other hand, allowing a murderer to escape set her brain on fire.

Kayla's muscles became heavy with her relief. She leaned back against the nearest tire, closed her eyes, and exhaled a long breath. Seconds ticked by, and her mind switched off, like a tunnel of lights blacking out, section by section.

Until a low vicious growl snapped her back to consciousness. She stared into the brown eyes of a large dog of indeterminate breed. Long nose, narrow face, wiry black and white hair, stocky build, matted tail.

The BEWARE DOG sign wasn't an empty threat to keep strangers away. It had been there to protect idiots like her from dismemberment. Beside her, still facing toward the opposite direction, Ash tensed, then slowly turned his head. His gun syncing with his movements.

Despite everything she'd witnessed since arriving, she couldn't watch Ash shoot down a dog who'd been trained to protect the property and its occupants. It was a brutal image she didn't want joined with the others she had accumulated.

The dog's growls deepened at Ash's movement. The canine's gaze banked to the right, then back to their position, as it prowled toward them at an unrelenting pace.

Power bunched in the dog's massive muscles, and Kayla knew it was seconds away from lunging.

Before Ash could twist around to take down the mutt.

So she did the only thing she could. Kayla lifted her gun and let bullets fly.

35

Ash kept an eye on his guest while he waited for the kettle to boil.

After they'd given their statements to Detective Morgan, he and Kayla had watched animal control wrangle the dog into the back of their van. Along with a box full of the pups they'd found denning inside the stack of tires.

The dog hadn't been protecting Grimball, but her litter. And Ash had almost taken her down.

If Kayla hadn't rapid-fired those shots into the air, he'd be mangled, the canine mother would likely be dead, and the pups orphaned.

They'd driven most of the way to her house in silence, until Wade had called. She briefed him on what had transpired at Grimball's.

Although Ash could only hear one side of the conversation, Kayla's responses made it clear that Wade had wanted to come to her. Ash had taken more pleasure than he should when she'd declined the driver's offer and told him she would be staying at Ash's place.

While Kayla had gathered items for an overnight bag,

Ash took the opportunity to call Phin to let him know Kayla wouldn't be returning to the office.

The conversation hadn't gone well.

"What the fuck was she doing with you?" Phin had asked.

"Do you even know your boss?"

"You should have ditched her and paid the piper later. That's what I'd do and I'm still standing."

"Ditched her how, exactly? Kicked her out of my car? Tied her up? Knocked out her driver?"

"Uh, *yeah*."

Gritting his teeth, Ash said, "This is a courtesy call, bro. Not an invitation for you to read me the riot act. Something I already know by heart."

Phin's tone changed. Softened, as understanding overtook his worry. "What can I do?"

"Keep things running at the firm for a few days."

"No problem. I have a go-bag in my car for times when I work late and don't want to trek home. Give me thirty minutes to finish up a few things here, and I'll relieve you of duty."

"Don't worry about it. We're at her place now, gathering some personal items, then we're headed back to my apartment."

"She's staying with you?"

"For tonight, at least."

A charged silence. "Don't hurt her."

His brother's words dropped into his stomach like rotten fruit. "Why do you think I would?"

"I don't—It's just—You've never been a fan—" Phin blew out a series of curses. "Listen, I know how you feel about her, but she's important to me—and many others."

"I'm not a damn barbarian. I'm surrounded by people

on a daily basis whose politics or opinions are not my own. Besides, she's been through hell. I know how to keep a civil tongue, when necessary."

"You're right. I know that. Sorry for being an ass. Your call . . . I-I guess it caught me off guard." He seemed to be struggling for words, which was very un-Phin-like. "Just keep her safe tonight, and let me know what else I can do to help."

Even hours later, the memory of his conversation with Phin burned. The thought that Phin, even for a second, believed Ash could harm Kayla—anyone—under his protection hurt like hell. Had the distance between Ash and his family grown so much that they believed him capable of such a thing?

The water in the kettle roiled. He swallowed back a lump of emotion, shifting his complicated relationship with his family aside.

He poured hot water over the tea bag, while snatching a glimpse of Kayla. Snuggled beneath a light throw, she lounged on the couch, with her stockinged feet propped on the coffee table and her head turned to the side, away from him, staring at nothing.

At least not anything of this physical world. He had no doubt Grimball's horrific death mask was replaying in her mind, over and over.

"Here." He held the mug out to her. "It's herbal and might feel good on your stomach." He stopped short of saying "settle your stomach," not wanting to draw more attention to what she'd survived.

She pushed up into a sitting position and tucked her feet beneath her before accepting the hot, medicinal drink. "Thank you."

"Can I get you anything else? Something to eat, maybe?"

She shook her head. "I'm not up for food yet, thanks." Patting the seat next to her, she said, "Stop hovering, Agent."

Lowering himself, a full cushion away, he asked, "Do you want to talk about it?"

"Yes," she said, without hesitation, "but not about what I saw or how I feel. I'll make an appointment with my therapist to discuss those things. I'm due for a check-in, anyway."

The matter-of-fact way in which she approached her exposure to trauma surprised him. He didn't know if he should be concerned that managing extreme self-care was old hat for her or thankful that she wouldn't break apart in front of him.

"What would you like to discuss?" he asked, though he thought he already knew what she'd say.

"I need to walk through all that's happened since my godmother's murder."

Her confirmation of what he'd expected sent a series of his own questions blazing through his mind.

36

"Okay," Ash said, "let's go through what we know."

The tension quivering through Kayla's body like a low-grade earthquake eased a little at his acquiescence.

Facts, brainstorming, and action plans, she could handle. They were the foundation on which her business thrived. Familiar, comfortable, solid. But delving into what she'd witnessed at Seb Grimball's place could open up a sea of emotions that might drown her.

"We're searching for one, maybe two, assailants," Ash continued.

"Two?"

"Forensics discovered droplets of blood where we believe the shooter set up, waiting for Governor Stokes to appear."

"Why does the presence of blood suggest a second person?"

"They also found signs of an altercation at the site. It's possible the shooter had a disagreement with his partner."

"Or a guest caught the shooter and tried to stop them." Kayla immediately shook her head, dismissing the idea.

"No one from the party came forward and no one is missing."

"Correct."

Kayla recalled Seb Grimball's battered face before someone blew off the top of his head. Swallowing, she twisted around to face Ash, propping her feet on the cushion between them. "Seb looked as though he'd been in a recent fight."

Ash closed a hand over her right ankle, as if sensing her distress. "Further confirming our hypothesis of a second assailant."

"I could understand having a backup assassin, but why would they have fought?"

"Good question." He anchored his forearms on his knees and clasped his hands together. "Now that you've had time to consider it, can you think of anyone who would want the governor dead?"

"A lot of people are settling differences of opinion with extreme violence, these days. Her killer could be anyone who didn't agree with a bill she signed into law or didn't share her ideology or—"

"Yes," he interrupted her, "but who could've guessed she'd visit the gazebo?"

"Maybe they got lucky—" Kayla's heart dumped into her stomach. "That came out wrong. I d-didn't mean—"

"Easy." He brushed a thumb over the top of her foot. "I got your meaning."

Kayla drew in a breath and released it slowly. "You visited the spot where the shooter set up?"

He nodded.

"Could you see the veranda?"

His eyes unfocused for a moment. "Yes."

"No matter what time of the year, guests always step

outside to escape the noise from the masses. I'm sure it's the same for any large gathering." She stared into her tea. "The shooter simply waited for her to appear. Vicky's visit to the gazebo was like hitting the lottery, I'm sure."

Releasing her ankle, Ash scrubbed a hand over his face and settled his back into the V of the sofa. "What can you tell me about her security detail that night?"

"I don't know what else I can tell you."

"Why'd they leave the garden?"

"I'm sure they were following orders. If she said scoot, they scooted."

"They could've given her some privacy and still kept her in sight."

" I can't see Glenn and Ford being a party to her murder. They were devoted to her. "

"You know better than anyone that money and power are the Great Motivators. All someone had to do was find a weak link in the governor's circle. A guard with a gambling problem or drug habit. Or maybe an assistant with medical bills stacking up, a chief of staff with an eye on a federal appointment, a lieutenant governor with more ambition than patience—"

Kayla held up her hand. "I see your point." Every sinew in her chest tightened as another possibility rose in her mind.

Eerily attuned to the slightest shift in her mood, Ash asked, "You've thought of someone else?"

"Maybe," she hedged.

"Someone you care about?"

She nodded. "Though I doubt she could kill a spider."

"But could she get someone else to step on it?"

"What are you going to do if I give you a name?"

"Have a chat."

"A civil chat? Or a bad cop interrogation?"

"Bad cop is always the most fun."

"A-ash."

"I'll ask some questions."

"I want to be there when you do."

"Or?"

Kayla folded her arms. "I'll have to do some sleuthing without you."

"Don't you have a job of your own to do?"

"I have an amazing team who can pick up any slack I might leave behind. Thanks for your concern."

On a long, aggrieved sigh, he draped an elbow over the sofa's arm and snaked a hand across the low back. The relaxed position stretched his white dress shirt taut over his broad chest and flat stomach. His right foot rested on the floor, while his left leg lay at an angle on the cushion separating them. Dark stubble covered the lower part of his face and finger tunnels rumpled his thick, black hair.

She'd never seen him look so at ease, so comfortable, so delicious. A tingling sensation stirred between her legs, and she squeezed her knees together to keep her arousal at a low simmer. But she could do nothing about her thundering heart.

As if sensing her biological shift, his eyes hyperfocused, and she got the distinct impression he was trying to visually drill into her brain and pick out her erotic thoughts.

The one moment she needed it most, her lobbyist mask failed her, disintegrating beneath his intense scrutiny, exposing the rawness of her need.

"It occurs to me," he said as his gaze lowered to her mouth, "that I owe you a kiss."

Kayla pressed her knees together so hard her bones stabbed each other. "Oh?"

She recalled his quick kiss of reassurance before they'd been forced to sprint across an open area, exposing them to the shooter's sights and her ridiculous comeback of getting another kiss if they survived. Even though he'd displayed confidence and an odd combination of calm urgency, she'd sensed the terror lurking beneath. Terror for her.

The realization had made her want to soothe his fear, let him know she trusted him with her life. She'd spoken spontaneously, honestly, and received the smile she'd been hoping for.

It was then her attraction to him shifted, deepened, transformed into something her heart recognized but her stubborn mind refused to acknowledge.

Until now.

She'd fallen for a man who reviled her profession, a calling that had fed her soul for most of her adult life. An insurmountable obstacle for any relationship.

Like a tiger rising from an afternoon nap, Ash pushed away from his den and leaned toward her, his eyes never leaving hers. The tip of his index finger traced an invisible line down the center of the cushion separating them.

"Meet me, Kayla."

Halfway.

The unspoken word tugged at her, as if he'd attached a string to her chest and pulled it taut.

Before she knew it, they were nose to nose, forehead to forehead. She drew strength from his warmth, the hard breaths he tried to control.

"I won't give up lobbying," she warned.

"I won't ask you to."

His promise whispered against her lips a moment before he fulfilled his promise.

37

ASH WAS IN BIG, FUCKING TROUBLE.

This revelation came to him a nanosecond too late. But a battalion of semiautomatics pointed at his head couldn't force him to reverse course.

Only one person had that power, and Ash prayed to every version of the Almighty that Kayla wouldn't deny him, deny *them* this moment.

The kiss started slow, tentative, then exploring, consuming. He gripped the sides of the sofa's cushion with both hands, letting her set the pace. Though he applied the slightest pressure against her lips, her tongue, letting her know he was all-in, ready to hit the accelerator.

Much to his amazement, so was she.

With pressure of her own, she urged him back into the crook of the sofa, prowling on all fours, until she hovered over him. She braced her right hand on the sofa, near his head, while her left methodically unbuttoned his dress shirt.

Being the helpful lover he was, he dragged the tails of

his shirt from his dress pants. He hissed out a curse and nearly jacked her over the side of their makeshift bed when the backs of her fingers brushed against his hardness.

"Problem?" she teased, between one sultry kiss and another.

"Yeah," he growled, "we're not naked."

"I'm working on it."

"Work *faster*."

She moved from his lips to the sensitive hollow of his throat. Her tongue and mouth took turns, exploring the expanse of his chest. She laved his right nipple, then rolled it beneath her thumb until it was hard and aching. Sitting back on her heels, she scraped her nails down the center of his torso.

His toes curled, and his hips lifted, seeking her warmth, needing the connection.

Ash's control was slipping.

A mantra started up in his lizard brain, and he didn't know how much longer he could remain in this passive state.

Enter her. Enter her. Enter her.

More than anything in this world, more than his next promotion, more than finding the governor's killer, more than making amends with Zeke, he wanted to be balls-deep in Kayla-fucking-Krowne.

"Are we doing this, beautiful?"

Surprise flared in her eyes. "Isn't it obvious?"

"Just checking." He surged forward, kissed her hard, and in an impressive feat of strength, he lifted her into his arms and stormed toward his bedroom.

"Impatient, are we?" she laughed, circling her arms around his neck.

Impatient didn't come close. The level of urgency firing his muscles was unprecedented. He wanted her naked and screaming his name before logic prevailed over lust.

Once they reached his bed, he lowered her feet to the floor. She gave his bedroom a quick scan, taking in the starkness of it.

Outside of the furniture and a single memento from home, the room was unadorned. The outer rooms weren't much better. The only difference was a couple green plants he'd somehow managed to keep alive.

They toed off their shoes and alternately unbuckled, unbuttoned, unzipped each other's and their own clothes until there were no more physical barriers between them.

Ash slowed his raging heart long enough to take in the woman who'd haunted his dreams for months. His imagination had not done her justice.

When he reached out, he realized his hand was shaking. He curled it into a fist, then unfurled his index and middle fingers enough to slide the backs against the base of her throat, down her chest, between breasts that would fill his hands, along her smooth stomach to the light brown patch at the apex of her legs.

Her breath caught, and she grasped the back of his neck, bringing him down for a mind-melting kiss. A millennium might have passed before she pulled back, he didn't know. All he recalled of that moment was hearing the three most beautiful words in the human language.

"Enough foreplay, G-man."

ASH'S ANSWERING GRIN MADE KAYLA'S HEART LIGHT UP IN A way she'd never thought possible. Her body's reaction was fleeting, for her special agent hooked his big, capable hands beneath her arms, lifted her until she wrapped her legs around his lean waist.

She pressed her heated, wet center against his scalding length. The fiery touch untethered his invisible restraints.

Mouths fused, their tongues tangled and writhed together, searching, priming.

In two erotic steps, he was at the side of the bed, bending forward until her back rested against the soft, cool duvet. Then he lifted his head, his eyes clashed with hers, burning with need.

"Last chance," he whispered.

She reached between them, guided his smooth, blunt tip to her entrance. "No regrets."

"Never."

Then he was inside her, over her, *with her*.

She cradled his massive body in her arms. Her hands smoothing, gripping, clawing to the pinnacle. She shattered into a mosaic of a thousand stunning pieces.

Tightening her inner muscles, she kissed-licked her way from the hollow of his neck to the indent beneath his chin. Her name ripped from his throat on a final thrust before he jerked free.

They lay clasped together for a long minute, then he shifted onto his elbows, easing some of his weight. A knuckle traced the line of her jaw, the edge of her lower lip. A smile played at the corners of his mouth before he bent to kiss her forehead, her nose, her left eyelid, and finally her mouth.

"Do. Not. Move," he ordered in a soft, sexy tone, before rolling away and striding into the bathroom.

She turned her head and watched the play of muscles moving beneath all that gorgeous flesh. The moment seemed almost ethereal. Real, but not. Imagined, but solid.

The sound of running water reached her, and she allowed her attention to wander around his bedroom. It was as austere as her quick glance upon entering had suggested.

Except for the wooden walking stick propped in one corner. The knotty, somewhat misshapen hiking tool appeared to be DIY. A young tree he'd cut down or a small branch from a large tree. The bark removed and the wood sanded down to prevent splinters.

For some reason, she hadn't pegged Ash as one of the many weekend trailblazers. Locals, as well as folks from across the nation—the world—enjoyed the region's vast trail systems, breathtaking waterfalls, and long-range, blue-hazed mountain views.

She'd traversed many of them herself, but none so rugged as to need an assistive stick.

Ash interrupted her musings, carrying a warmed wash-cloth he used to wipe her clean. It occurred to her then that neither one of them had considered protection.

Something that had never happened to her before. Not even during her fast and furious introduction to sex.

A bolt of fear speared through her as the multitude of consequences flooded her brain. Pregnancy wasn't among them. She'd been on the pill since her teens.

But STIs?

Her lover kissed her mouth softly before dropping the wet cloth on the floor beside the bed. "Everything all right?"

Plumping the pillows behind her, she sat up, pulling the sheet over her damp, chilled torso. "We were careless."

He motioned for her to scoot over, then climbed in beside her, drawing her into the center of his corded embrace. Resting a cheek against his chest, she closed her eyes briefly at the press of his lips against the crown of her head.

"I'm sorry, Kayla." He kissed her hair again. "Logic has never been my friend, where you're concerned."

"Finally, something we share." The tips of her fingers brushed over his chest. "I'm on the pill."

"Then you have nothing else to fear from me."

"Same."

"Do you want children?"

She stilled. Did he just ask—

"Not with me," he rushed to clarify. "In general. Are kids part of the Krowne master plan?"

"You think I have one?"

Humor rimmed his voice. "I know you do."

She kissed his chest. "Children aren't part of it, but they're not not part of it, if that makes sense."

"Weirdly, yes." His embrace tightened and his fingers made lazy circles on her bare hip. "A busy life and no Mr. Soulmate. Yet."

"Exactly." Would Ash be a good father? Husband? She forced her thoughts to safer territory. "I noticed your walking stick. Do you do a lot of hiking?"

The muscles beneath her hand tensed and an uncomfortable silence blanketed them. When he finally spoke, regret edged his words. "Not in a long while."

"Too busy?" she ventured, knowing instinctively that wasn't the reason.

"On the fourth Sunday of every month, without fail, my dad would take me and my brothers to a new hiking spot. Sometimes we finished the trail in thirty minutes, sometimes it took us hours."

"What a great bonding experience. I'm sure you cherish those moments more now than you ever did at the time."

He rested his cheek against the spot where his lips had been only moments before. "In ways I can't even articulate."

"Did your dad make the stick for you?"

He lifted his head. "On our first hike, Dad ordered us to go into the woods and find a five-foot long by one-and-a-half-inch branch."

Glancing up, she caught his smile. "Boys will be idiot boys?"

"Bigger is always better, right?"

She straightened into a sitting position, brushing her hand over the growing bulge beneath the sheet.

A hiss escaped his lips, and Kayla took pleasure in the effect she had on him. "How old were you?"

"Ten, I think. Phin was a little guy, riding on Dad's back for the first year or two. But he still had his own wand-sized stick."

From her conversations with Liv, she knew pancreatic cancer had taken Duke Blackwell's life thirteen years ago. Ash took over the family towing/repo business and kept it running for eight years until he decided to follow his dream to work for the FBI.

His departure hadn't set well with Zeke, which seemed to be a sore spot between the two brothers, to this day. It was plain to see why he'd held on to the length of wood all these years. A symbol of family, of unity.

Squeezing her hip, he changed the subject. "Now, about that name . . ."

His meaning didn't immediately sink in, then she recalled their conversation before their hormones had taken over. Her heart tripped and stumbled before it settled into a steady gallop.

"I want to repeat that I don't think this person was

capable of killing Vicky, yet I don't want my bias to leave a stone unturned."

"Noted."

Kayla took a breath and forced the name out. "Linda Collier." The walking stick drew her attention. A symbol of a family's better times. "Vicky's daughter."

38

ASH CHECKED HIS SURPRISE.

He'd anticipated a political rival or a disgruntled aide or even a sexual relationship gone bad. But he'd never considered that the governor's only child could be responsible.

"Why Linda?" he asked.

He watched in amazement as she gathered herself, setting aside whatever personal feelings she had for the woman in order to answer his question.

"She had such hate in her heart for her mother."

Ash turned her limp hand over and wove his fingers between hers. His pulse quickened when she clutched tightly to the comfort he offered.

"Do you know why?" he asked.

She molded her free hand over the top of his. "Things between them started falling apart not long after Linda's father died." Emotion thickened her voice. "At the time when they needed each other the most."

"What happened to Mr. Stokes?"

"Carbon monoxide poisoning, of all things."

"Vehicle or home?"

"A faulty fireplace in their home on Lake James. He'd gone out there to spend the weekend. When he didn't return Sunday evening, as planned, and Vicky couldn't get a hold of him, she asked the local PD to do a wellness check."

"How long had he been dead?"

"The coroner believed he'd succumbed Friday night, so two-plus days."

"Didn't the carbon monoxide detector go off?"

"Near the master suite, the investigators found the detector disassembled on the hallway table along with a package of new batteries."

"Let me guess," he said, seeing the scenario play out in his head.

"The alarm was going off, and Mr. Stokes assumed the device needed new batteries. When that didn't shut it up, he thought the detector was faulty and ripped it from the ceiling."

"That's what the investigators pieced together."

"Why in the hell wouldn't he have concluded the alarm was real?"

"About a month before, he'd had the HVAC system serviced." She shook her head. "I guess the fireplace in their bedroom never crossed his mind."

Ash raised both brows, wondering how someone could have missed such an obvious connection.

She gave him a pained smile. "Jonathan wasn't what you'd call handy around the house. And . . . "

When she didn't continue, he coaxed, "And what?"

"Jonathan's blood alcohol content was three times the legal limit."

Ash bit back a groan. "Might he have confused the carbon monoxide alarm for a smoke detector?"

"The investigators suggested as much."

"Linda took the news of her father's death especially hard, I imagine."

"At first, she acted as any daughter faced with such devastating news. She helped her mom with the arrangements, put together a slide show, and gave a heart-wrenching eulogy. But a few weeks after his death, Linda came to me in tears. She'd found out that her dad had been diagnosed with Parkinson's a month earlier, but her parents had decided to delay telling her. She'd just started her dream job, and they wanted her to enjoy the moment and be able to focus on learning her new responsibilities."

"Linda didn't agree with their decision?"

She shook her head. "Linda thought they robbed her of time with her dad."

"But his death and the disease had nothing to do with each other."

"Which Linda eventually came to realize once the raw edge of her grief dulled."

Ash frowned. "Then why was she so angry with the governor?"

"A few months later, she learned Vicky and Jonathan had been arguing before he left to go to the lake house. She reasoned he wouldn't have been there at all if it weren't for their fight."

"One strike too many?"

"I suppose. The Stokes were a tight-knit family. Losing her dad would have been devastating, then to learn that her parents had been quarreling might have flipped a nuclear switch in her head." She drew in a resigned breath. "I don't know. I find it hard to believe those two events led her to contracting a killer. But there's no denying the depth of her anger toward her mother."

"Who told Linda about her father's illness and her parents' fight?"

An unsettled stillness gripped her as she plowed through her memory. When she surfaced, she looked at him with a mixture of surprise and self-recrimination. "I don't know. I always assumed Vicky told her, but I don't recall Linda saying so."

"Sounds like we have even more to discuss with her."

"We?"

"Go get dressed before I change my mind."

She kissed him hard, then catapulted her lush body off the bed, shooting into the outer room to grab her overnight bag before darting into the bathroom.

Ash threw off the sheet, checked the level of wrinkle on his discarded clothes and decided he could live with them. As he finished pulling on his pants and shirt, a sharp knock echoed through the condo.

Collecting his handgun and holster, he padded to the front door barefoot and checked the peephole. Before he could bring his visitor into focus, a fist slammed against the door again. He lurched back and ripped his gun from the holster.

"Open the fucking door, Ash."

Zeke.

Ash reholstered his weapon and set it on a nearby table. His brother either wanted an update on the situation with Kayla or he'd found out about Ash's meeting with Liv. Small towns loved their gossip.

Either option wasn't ideal for him with Kayla in the next room.

Considering the amount of violence pulsing against his door, Ash put his money on the latter. Which meant he was about to get his ass kicked.

39

THE MOMENT HE DISENGAGED THE DEADBOLT, ZEKE PUSHED it open.

Although they were the same height, his brother had a good twenty pounds of solid muscle on him. Where Ash leaned toward Captain America, Zeke bulged like Thor.

His dark brown eyes looked almost black in the fading light and his thumb beat against his thigh like a bat's wing, a sure sign of his agitation.

"You've got some explaining to do, brother." His hand still rested on the door as if he didn't trust his welcome.

"Now's not a good time."

Zeke scanned the room, stopping on Kayla's sneakers by the sofa and her handbag hooked around the back of a dining room chair, then noting Ash's bare feet and rumpled clothes.

"I'll make this quick." Zeke shouldered his way past Ash, then stood in the center of the living room, arms crossed.

Ash blew out a frustrated breath. Of all the times his brother could have picked to visit for the first time in five years, he'd chosen the day Ash had crossed a professional ethical line. "Zeke—"

"What the hell were you meeting with Liv about?" The fury in his voice might have shaken the heavens.

Closing the door, Ash stepped into Zeke's personal space. "Keep your voice down."

Zeke bent close enough that Ash could've head-butted him into next Tuesday. "Answer the question."

Ash hoped Kayla was making use of his shower. "I had finished an interview in Maggie Valley and took the opportunity to stop in Steele Ridge to see how my former coworker was doing."

His brother's nostrils flared, sensing deception. "Why now? She left the FBI months ago."

"Which confirms my reason for stopping. My visit was long overdue. Who told you we met? Liv?"

"That answers my next question. You met at Randi's place to avoid the Friary. Why?"

Old grievances clawed up the back of his throat. He squeezed muscles and swallowed until they returned to the pit of his stomach. "You know why."

"Avoiding me?"

"In part."

"Why else?"

"None of your damn business." No way was he sharing how he felt like a stranger any time he walked into the Friary or Annex.

"My source said your convo with Liv looked serious. Did you talk to her about the issue I brought up about Kayla? The one I *specifically* told you to keep her out of?"

Ash slanted a look at the bedroom door he'd pulled closed, but not completely shut. He envisioned Kayla standing on the other side, listening. But he prayed she was oblivious to the volatile conversation a room away.

"We were talking about something more personal."

That cranked his brother's back into the upright position. "Personal to whom?"

Ash hesitated. Before Zeke's arrival, he assumed Liv would have given her fiancé an earful about how his overprotectiveness had let their secret out of the bag. Unless she was Zeke's source, which he doubted, Liv had kept their discussion to herself. He almost wished she hadn't. Maybe this entire uncomfortable conversation could have been avoided.

"Ash, personal to you or Liv?"

"To you and Liv."

Zeke stared at him for what felt like a full rotation of the sun. "Liv told you?" His voice held notes of confusion and jealousy.

"No."

"How'd you figure it out?"

"You."

"I didn't fucking tell you."

"No, you wouldn't, would you?"

"Can you blame me—?"

Ash held up a hand, cutting off his tirade. "I used my investigative skills. Why else would you have been acting so squirrelly and way overprotective at lunch the other day."

"Bullshit."

"Believe me or don't. Doesn't change the fact."

Zeke scraped thick fingers through his dark brown hair. "Was she pissed at me?"

"No, bro," Ash said. "She seemed relieved to be able to talk to someone about the baby." He forced a smile. Not because he wasn't happy for him, but he doubted the gesture would be welcomed or returned. "Congratulations."

A grin split across his brother's face, surprising Ash and revealing a set of white teeth that he hadn't seen for way too long.

"I still can't believe it. We've been dying to notify everyone. I'm sure Liv mentioned we're waiting until the end of the first trimester, which is just a few weeks away."

"Understandable. It'll be great having a little Blackwell running around. With any luck, Phin, Rohan, or Cruz will produce a cousin or two pretty soon."

Zeke's attention strayed to the women's sneakers next to the sofa. "What about you?" The question seemed reflexive. A ghost of the past, when banter between them was as common as breathing. As if realizing the same thing, Zeke winced. "Never mind. None of my business."

"Well," Ash said, "if that's all, I need to get back to my guest—"

The bedroom door swung open and out walked Kayla, wearing a lightweight cream sweater, skinny jeans, and brown booties.

She snagged her handbag from the chair and stopped by Ash to kiss him square on the lips. "I'll meet you downstairs." She eyed Zeke, a slight curve to her mouth. "Congratulations. I expect to be invited to the baby shower."

Zeke's gaze sliced to Ash. "You told her?"

Once again, his Bureau training kicked in, and he slammed the gate down on the flood of words bursting to be heard. But further inflaming an inferno would only lead to one thing.

Total destruction.

Unfortunately, Kayla wasn't on the same de-escalation page.

"Pillow talk, the vessel for so many wondrous secrets."

Fucking hell.

To his regret, the lobbyist wasn't done. She paused at the door and aimed one more salvo at Zeke, though the hit was really meant for Ash.

"You should trust your fiancée more. Women aren't as breakable as you seem to believe. Especially not Liv."

Revenge delivered, she looked at Ash and the contents of his stomach curdled. The lively brown eyes he had a love-hate relationship with were blank and her breezy facade transformed into a dead calm.

"Don't be long." Then she was gone.

"Kayla—"

When the door clicked shut behind her, Ash braced himself for Zeke's right hook. But the blow never came. He chanced a glance at his brother, who stared at him as if he were an ugly-ass extraterrestrial life force.

"What the actual fuck, Ash?"

ASH CLOSED HIS EYES.

Kayla had been listening at the door and she'd just delivered the payback of all paybacks.

He couldn't even blame her. The evidence of his betrayal was damning. She'd already figured out that Zeke had come to him about her alleged pay-to-play, but somehow hearing Zeke talk about it had made the whole thing feel sordid and underhanded. She didn't know the Blackwells had asked him to intervene because of their love and concern for her.

He stared hard at the door. Why the hell did he have to complicate things by sleeping with her? Why was he vibrating with the need to go to her, to apologize, to explain his part until she forgave him?

"I asked you to talk to her, not fuck her."

Ash surged forward, his face in Zeke's. "Watch your damn mouth."

Some of the flame left his brother's eyes, and he nodded. Ash stepped back.

"What's going on, Ash?"

"I've asked myself the same question a million times."

"Well, what's the answer?"

He turned toward the bedroom. "Don't have one."

"Is this thing between you two serious?"

He retrieved his socks and shoes, then sat down on a living room chair to put them on. "Whatever it was, it's no more, thanks to your stubborn ass."

"Why didn't you tell me she was in the other room?"

Ash tipped his head up just enough to shoot laser beams from his eyes straight into his brother's thick skull.

Zeke exhaled. "Liv's going to rip my balls off for this."

"A little less testosterone wouldn't be a bad thing."

"This isn't funny, asshat."

"Do you see me laughing?"

Standing, he threaded his arms through his shoulder holster, tossed on his jacket, and grabbed his keys and credentials from a handwoven bowl on a table by the door.

Twisting the door handle, he motioned for his brother to precede him. "To be continued—in another five years."

Zeke didn't budge. "Why'd you tell Kayla"—he waved his hand in the air as if he could conjure the right words—"about all of it?"

"You're not going to believe anything I say, so why waste energy on this?"

"Be square with me, no matter how damning, and I'll take you at your word."

Ash didn't bother pointing out that he would have no way of knowing if he was being square or otherwise. "I didn't betray your confidence, but Kayla and Liv are . . . " Now he was the one searching for an appropriate word.

Zeke lifted a brow, waiting.

"Perceptive. They key in on the slightest anomaly, then go in for the kill and don't stop shredding you apart until they get to the juicy marrow."

"You caved. They put the pins to you and you sang like a soprano."

Ash gritted his teeth, unwilling to go into the complexity of his verbal boxing sessions with Kayla and Liv. He bolted through the door. "Lock up when you're no longer drowning in your disappointment."

He strode away, figuring it would be the last time his brother graced his doorstep and envisioned the small foothold he had in Zeke's life inching back and the door closing with a solid thud.

40

———

BY THE TIME ASH EMERGED FROM HIS BUILDING, MASON HAD arrived with the Audi and Kayla was ensconced in the back seat. Although she was still keen on participating in Linda's interview, she had no intention of driving the thirty minutes to and from the woman's home with the agent.

As soon as Ash cleared the building's steel door, he keyed in on her transportation change and didn't look happy about it. Too bad.

The small part of her that didn't want to strangle him was pleased to see his encounter with his brother hadn't left him bruised or bleeding. Maybe the same couldn't be said for the absent Zeke.

When he reached her car, one of his big hands gripped the open window frame. No split or bruised knuckles. Another good sign.

"We need to talk," he said, bending at the waist to look her in the eye.

"Not today." She nodded toward his vehicle parked along the curb ahead of them. "Mason will follow you to Linda's. You have her address?"

"Come with me. We'll talk on the way."

A sensation of pain made her glance down, take note of her white-knuckled clasped hands. She spread her fingers wide and placed her palms on her thighs before meeting his gaze again.

"If we talk now, you won't like what I have to say."

"That may be, but—"

"And neither will I." She nodded toward his vehicle again. "We'll follow."

He wanted to argue. She could see it in the clenching and unclenching of his jaw. Instead, he pushed away and marched to his SUV.

Kayla rolled up her window, released an unsteady breath, and waited for the avalanche of questions from her driver.

They never came.

Relief compressed all the oxygen from her lungs. As Mason pulled away, she saw Zeke standing outside the building's entrance, arms crossed and a pensive expression on his handsome face. How long it would take for Liv to text, demanding details?

Despite everything, Kayla couldn't muster a proper rage. She'd understood Ash's objective from the start. Had expected Joyce Ann Carlson would run to her cousin. Knew by-the-book Mitch Lawson would forward the complaint to the Bureau's local art crime team.

Had anticipated Ash's knock on her door. Dreamed of it. Planned it?

No, not that far. But she'd certainly seized the opportunity to bring Ash into her orbit. Her mother's invitations had fallen into a black hole. But she knew he couldn't ignore a twenty-five-hundred-year-old Celtic artifact.

Then someone had murdered her godmother, and all of her maneuverings seemed trite, self-serving. Desperate.

What she hadn't expected was the Blackwells' lack of faith. The notion pierced a part of her heart she'd hidden away long ago. Ash's family—the same people she'd gladly helped over and over, the ones who'd become a second family to her—had sent their duly sworn son to find out if she was buying votes.

What did they expect him to do? Give her a stern lecture? The man sworn to uphold the law. The man who had avoided her like a cloud of mosquitoes.

A broken laugh escaped her throat.

"Are you okay?" Mason asked.

"Not really."

"Anything I can do?"

"Got a time machine?"

"If I had one, I'd get first dibs."

Mason always had a knack for calming her. Despite the hollow space expanding in her heart, her eyes crinkled at the corners when she met his gaze in the rearview mirror. "What's the matter? Did a bird poop on the Audi?"

He gave her an answering crinkle. "Worse, I got dirt on the floorboard."

A thought struck her, and just like that, her humor faded. "Tell me, Mason. Would you sleep with a woman knowing it would jeopardize your career?"

"Since I don't have a career, absolutely."

Though he worked for her during the week, he sometimes did contract jobs on the weekends or participated in war games or training or whatever they called it. He had the kind of professional freedom many would envy.

"You have a career. Just not the nine-to-five variety. Would you jeopardize that for a woman?"

The car slowed to a stop, and he glanced in the mirror again, no doubt weighing the seriousness of her question. "Depends on the woman. There aren't many men who wouldn't give up everything for you, Kayla. Cameron Blackwell included."

"Why do you say that?"

The stoplight turned green, and Mason's attention switched to the road. "I've seen the way he is with you. The way he looks at you and the way he gets when other guys show you attention."

Kayla's pulse quickened, recalling an exchange she'd had with Rohan and Phin when the former had been a bit short with her after she'd comped a thousand-dollar, last-minute ticket for him to attend a political benefit so he could ensure Lena Kamber was safe.

"I recognize the Lost Blackwell look by now," she'd told Phin, who'd apologized for Rohan's bad manners. "Once a Blackwell man loses his heart to a woman, he wraps his entire, protective universe around her."

Mason continued, "So I asked around. My sources say he lives and breathes for the Bureau. Even gave up the family business for it."

From what Kayla had observed, he'd lost more than the business. There was a deep fissure between Ash and his family, or more specifically, between him and Zeke.

If being a special agent was important enough for him to lose so much, why would he sleep with a woman he'd openly disdained and was currently investigating?

Only one reason came to mind and it both elated her and froze her pulse.

The Lost Blackwell.

"I'LL DO THE TALKING," ASH SAID AS HE AND KAYLA approached Linda Collier's front door.

"Okay."

He looked at her for what seemed like the hundredth time since she'd stepped out of her car. On the drive here, he'd gone through a battery of emotions, not the least of which were frustration, fear, shame, and jealousy.

His nerves felt like a too-tight bowstring, ready to snap if handled without care. He'd expected Kayla to be walking the edge, too. Filled with righteous anger and eager to deliver more verbal lashes. Instead, she seemed hesitant, unable to look him in the eye. Beta to his alpha.

It was unnerving.

He took another shot at reviving the lobbyist. "You're here to reassure Ms. Collier."

She nodded.

"Not to play investigator."

A muscle in her jaw twitched, restoring some of his equilibrium.

"Got it."

He bounded up the two steps leading to Collier's front porch and depressed the doorbell. Linda and her husband Gene lived in the quaint town of Black Mountain, situated due east of Asheville. Her two-story white wood-framed house sat in the midst of an eclectic mix of homes. Not a cookie cutter in sight. The neighborhood was within walking distance of a bustling tourist mecca as well as the town's popular Tailgate Market, where local artisans and farmers hawked their wares.

A pretty brown-haired woman, heavy with child, opened the door. She wore a long-sleeved floral maxi dress, revealing bare feet and slightly swollen ankles. Her wary gaze snapped from him to Kayla, who stood to his right.

The woman's eyes were red-rimmed and bloodshot. Either she had bad allergies—a good possibility in a region with millions of pine trees blooming at once—or she'd been crying. Also a distinct possibility, given she'd lost her mom.

"Kayla?"

"Hi, Linda," she said, "Sorry to show up unannounced." Kayla stepped forward and gave her friend a hug. "This is Special Agent Cameron Blackwell, with the FBI. He'd like to ask you some questions about Aunt Vicky."

He held up his creds before shaking her hand. "Pleased to meet you, ma'am."

"I already spoke to APD and State, when they notified me about M-mom." Her voice broke on the last word.

Kayla wrapped a comforting arm around the woman's shoulders and guided her inside. "Come on. Let's have a seat."

The Colliers' living area had an upscale farmhouse motif like something Joanna Gaines would design. Neutral tones with a pop of yellow here and there. A natural stone fireplace propped up a corner of the living room and one of the Colliers had a definite green thumb. A variety of plants, some he recognized, some new and bizarre, were stationed around the room, adding another level of warmth.

"Can I make you a cup of herbal tea?" Kayla asked the woman as she helped her get settled on a plush ivory sofa.

"No, thank you, but please make one for yourself and Mr. Blackwell."

Kayla glanced at him, and Ash shook his head. She took up a spot on the sofa, and he sat on an adjacent chair.

"First," Ash said, "allow me to extend my condolences on your loss. I'm aware of how difficult it is to lose a parent."

"Thank you." Linda looked at Kayla. "I'm sorry I haven't returned your calls. I just needed some time to process things."

"No worries. Do you need help making any of the arrangements?"

Linda's features turned stony. "The State is taking care of everything. Even down to the flowers draping Mama's coffin." Her eyes welled. "Shouldn't a daughter be able to do at least that much to honor her mother?"

Kayla shot him a confused look while she rubbed circles on the other woman's back.

Based on what little he knew about Linda Collier, most of it from Kayla, he hadn't expected the governor's estranged daughter to be quite so grief-stricken. Evidently, Kayla hadn't either.

Hate didn't always negate love.

"Seems like a reasonable expectation," Kayla said.

"Don't handle me, Kayla. You know as well as I do that ever since Mama became governor the State has owned her. I can't even get a clear answer as to what happened the night she was murdered." She turned pleading eyes on her friend. "I want to know, yet I'm so afraid. I can't count the number of times I've picked up the phone to reach out to you, only to set it back down."

Kayla folded a hand over her friend's. Her chest rose on what could have only been a fortifying breath. "I'll tell you as much as you feel comfortable hearing."

Ash's pulse snapped to attention and he fought the urge to remind her of their agreement that he'd do the talking. But he sensed both women needed this moment. He would trust Kayla to know what she should and shouldn't share and pray his faith wasn't misplaced.

"Did she suffer?"

"No, it was over quickly." Although her tone was empathetic, Kayla had tapped into her lobbyist persona for the strength to deliver the words.

Tears tumbled onto Linda's cheeks. "What was she doing in the gazebo by herself? Where was her security detail?"

"She wanted to speak with me privately, so she sent her guards away."

"What did she need to talk to you about?"

"I don't know."

"How can you not know?"

"She sent me a text, requesting to meet. I showed up, and—" Kayla struggled to finish or find the gentlest words; either way, Ash couldn't stand watching her suffer.

"And that's when the assassin shot your mother." Ash's contribution didn't appear to have any impact on the woman.

She kept her focus on Kayla. "You have to have some idea."

"We were working on several projects together,

including her reelection. There's no way to pinpoint which one she wanted to discuss."

"Why don't you *pinpoint* it down to the one where she was willing to put her life at risk."

Kayla grew still, as if Linda's words had cut through her, clear to her backbone and hovered there, ready to make the final slice.

When the lobbyist spoke again, her voice was low, raw. "I've tried. Believe me, I've tried. But I can't even be sure Vicky wanted to discuss one of our ongoing campaigns. It could have been something completely unrelated to our working relationship."

"Like what?"

A brief hesitation. "You."

Linda pressed deeper into the sofa's cushions. "Me?"

"I understand the two of you had a falling-out," Ash said, reinserting himself into the conversation.

"Falling out? Who told you we'd had a falling-out?"

Her head swiveled *Exorcist*-style toward Kayla. "You?"

When Kayla said nothing, the pregnant woman shot up from the sofa. Well, more like hoisted herself to a standing position.

Ash kept his attention square on Linda. He couldn't think of any reason why Kayla would lie to him about the governor's relationship with her daughter.

Unless it was to cover for someone else.

"Ms. Krowne is here to offer you support, while I spoke to you, knowing your husband would likely be at work."

He hoped his comment would direct her attention away from Kayla. When the woman continued to stare down her childhood friend, Ash decided to try a different tactic. But first, he needed to get the mother-to-be to sit or they'd all be standing in an awkward circle. Lynette Blackwell would've rapped the back of his head if she found him sitting in the presence of a pregnant woman.

He gestured to her spot on the sofa. "Please sit down, Ms. Collier."

She placed a hand over her baby boulder before reluctantly doing as he requested.

"Are you disputing an estrangement with Governor Stokes prior to her death?"

"You mean murder, don't you, Agent Blackwell?"

He said nothing. Simply stared at her. Most people were uncomfortable with silence. Conversation voids tended to be an investigator's promised land. Interviewees attempted to fill them with chatter, which often turned up the best morsels of information.

"Look," Linda said a few seconds later, proving him right. "I might not have agreed with all of my mother's policies, especially her more recent ones, but I loved her and she loved me."

"No one's questioning your affection for your mother," Ash said. "But your relationship with Governor Stokes changed after your father's untimely death, correct?"

Her pale blue eyes narrowed on him. "Why exactly did you come here today?"

"My job is to help the police track down the governor's murderer. We have to search beneath every stone, no matter how unlikely."

Her wariness turned to shock. "You think I had something to do with her murder?" She turned on Kayla again. "Is this what you told him? That I hated my mother enough to kill her?"

"No!" Kayla reached for her friend's hands. "It's just . . . you've been so angry of late."

She batted Kayla's hands away and lurched to her feet again. "Leave now."

"We're only trying to get answers," Kayla said, rising.

Ash followed suit. "Who told you about your parents' argument?"

"What argument?"

"The one that sent your father to their home on Lake James."

Linda closed her eyes. "Get out."

"I'm sorry to upset you, Ms. Collier, but the more I know, the better able I am to do my job."

"Someone who cared enough to tell me the truth." She turned on Kayla. "I suppose Mom told *you* about Daddy's diagnosis."

Kayla swallowed. "It was necessary in order for me to form a strategy around—"

"I don't want to hear about her damn political maneuverings." Linda swiped away a stray tear. "He was my father!" She slapped a hand over her chest as if stopping her heart from exploding out of her ribcage. *"Go."*

He placed a business card on the coffee table. "Thank you for your time, Ms. Collier. If you think of anything that could help with our investigation, please give me a call."

"Yeah, I'll be sure and do that. Now, get out of my house."

"Linda, please understand—" Kayla began, but Ash cut her off, motioning her toward the door.

They'd just reached the sidewalk leading to their vehicles when Linda wrenched open the front door.

Kayla turned back to her friend, hope in her eyes.

"Don't ever, *ever* come back here, Kayla. We're done."

The door slammed shut, and Kayla closed her eyes for a

moment. When they reopened, moisture glistened at the edges, but no tears fell.

Ash followed in the lobbyist's wake, placing himself between her and the anger pulsing from within the house. Regret clamped around his chest.

He should never have brought her here. Kayla was strong, but the human body could only take so much trauma before it either broke apart or shut down.

In the span of five days, Kayla had experienced a lifetime of shock and heartbreak. Much of it because of him and his need to keep her close—and his evident inability to say no to the woman.

Both of which, he must change.

42

"I thought I'd find you here."

Kayla glanced over her shoulder to find her longtime friend and her firm's attorney Natalie Bryant.

"How?" Kayla said, sipping her wine.

"It's rare for you to leave work early, so I figured recent events were weighing on your mind. You've said more than once that Blue Cellar's relaxed vibe helped you think."

Natalie didn't know the half of what was replaying in her mind like a stream of bad horror movies. Kayla hadn't come here to think. She was here to forget. Forget about Linda's parting words, forget about Ash's hungry lips, and forget about Vicky's vacant eyes.

"I didn't realize I'd become so predictable."

"Only to me, my friend." Natalie slid onto the stool next to her and ordered a beer.

"It's been a rough few days." Her index finger made swirls in an overlooked water ring left on the bar's wooden surface.

Natalie grasped Kayla's hand, halting her repetitive motion. "I'm sorry, Kay. Sometimes I forget you're as destructible as the rest of us. I should have checked in more often to see how you were doing."

Kayla squeezed her friend's hand, taking comfort from the gesture before releasing her and continuing the swirls. Any more than that, and she wouldn't be able to hold back the tears.

"You've done more than enough. Between you and the rest of the team, I have a refrigerator full of food and enough hearts and hugs emojis to carry me through each day."

Rather than be reassured, Natalie's expression became even more concerned. "Let me see your left hand."

Shit.

"Come on. Palm up."

When Kayla remained frozen, Natalie reached across her lap and gently unrolled her fingers from their tight ball to reveal four deep crescent marks in her palm.

Kayla's lie detector.

"Oh, Kay." Natalie smoothed a finger over the pain points. "You know you don't have to be the *strong one* around me. Talk, please."

Her confrontation with Linda had been the proverbial straw that broke the camel's back. Mason had taken her to the office, but she'd managed little more than staring out her window, torturing her brain. She relived every detail of her encounter with Vicky, her devastating discussion with Jillian and the aunties, her confrontation with Tommy, her shoot-out with Seb's killer, her night with Ash, and her guilt over misunderstanding Linda's feelings toward her mother.

Could Linda's anger have been nothing more than the jealousy of an only child losing her mother's attention?

The vehemence in Linda's voice when she'd spoken

about the State owning Vicky had rattled loose another conversation she'd had with the expectant mother.

Seven months ago, when Linda shared her baby news with Kayla, Jillian, and the aunties, Vicky had been thrilled. Through glistening eyes she'd talked about all the ways she was going to spoil the babe. The Linda before things went wonky would have sent her mother an indulgent smile and an admonishment about spoiling her child. The new, but not improved, Linda had snorted.

Prompting Sybil and Elsie to trade glances before Elsie deftly changed the topic. When Kayla had asked Linda about her reaction later, she'd confided, "The State won't retract its claws long enough for Mom to see her grand-child, let alone spoil it. She's going to miss all my baby's firsts."

Now, a ripple of awareness tracked down Kayla's spine. She'd felt it before. Most women had. That moment when you realized you were being watched.

Picking up her wineglass, she casually scanned the room while she took a drink. Her perusal came to a halt on a man sitting kitty-corner from her at the bar. He lifted his chin in that way men do to acknowledge someone in greet-ing. Only the black-haired Adonis accompanied his with a sexy-as-hell smile.

Kayla returned it. What red-blooded woman wouldn't? But she immediately experienced an odd sense of guilt. She didn't understand her reaction until she recalled her night with Ash and her astonishing self-revelation that she was falling for a man who would never be able to accept all of her.

One more heartache to add to the pile.

"Take my mind off the shitstorm that's my life," Kayla

said. "Tell me about this new guy who likes to muss your hair before work."

Heat crept into her friend's cheeks. A biological reaction Kayla hadn't witnessed since Natalie's first brush with sex their freshman year of college.

The rim of Natalie's longneck hovered near her red-painted lips. "We can find something more titillating to talk about than my love life."

"Nothing comes to mind." Kayla angled her body toward her friend. "Name?"

"Alexander."

The name conjured a bone-deep revulsion that Kayla had never been able to overcome. Ever since her run-in with Alexander Brighton her junior year at university, she'd hated the name.

"Good Lord, Natalie. Out of the four billion men in the world you had to shake the sheets with one named Alexander?"

"I knew this would be your reaction, which is why I've kept the relationship to myself."

"Aren't you reminded of what that asshole did to us every time you moan his name?"

"Did to *you*," Natalie corrected. "It was your car."

"You were as outraged as I was at the time."

"What he did was shitty, and he eventually paid the price."

When Senator Brighton had lost the election, the family's financial resources slowly dried up and Alexander dropped out of college. She knew she should feel some guilt about his interrupted education, but she couldn't muster the emotion.

"He wasn't the only student," Natalie said, "who'd lost their mind after that competition."

"Are you condoning what he did to my car?"

"I already said what he did wasn't cool. But the professors in our poli-sci program seemed to take an inordinate amount of glee in pitting student against student during the fundraising project."

Kayla frowned, then swiveled on her stool until she faced Natalie. "Your Romeo. What's his last name?"

The attorney froze like a rabbit hoping the eagle wouldn't spot her munching away in the center of the field. "Why do you want to know?"

"Why wouldn't I? You've been seeing this guy nonstop for the past month. It's time I met my friend's new beau."

"And have you react the way you did just now when I introduce him? I don't think so."

"I'm a professional at controlling my emotions. I won't dry heave at the mere mention of the name Alex—." The name stuck in her throat.

Natalie lifted a brow.

"Okay, maybe you could just mumble his name or sneeze at the opportune time."

"It won't matter." Natalie closed out her tab.

"Wait. You're leaving?" Her friend stood. "Come on, Nat. Stay for another drink. I'll behave."

"It won't matter because this is who you'll meet." She held her phone in front of Kayla's face.

Staring back at her was an older version of the shithead who'd painted *BITCH* on her car fourteen years ago. Alexander Brighton.

43

Ash stared at his murder board with a growing sense of helplessness. Instead of eliminating suspects, he'd added two more—Linda Collier and an activist named Tommy O'Connor.

While speaking to Phin earlier, his brother had let it slip that O'Connor had taken his need for updates to a harassing level, and Kayla was taking on the brunt of his displeasure. Phin had also denied knowing anything about HCVS, the company pouring millions of dollars into Krowne and Associates.

No matter how much he wanted it otherwise, the evidence kept dragging Kayla's name back to the board. The State Police still hadn't reported back yet on whether the governor had been working on anything that could have led to her murder.

His phone rested on his desk, silent. He willed it to ring. Didn't even care who as long as they gave him a new lead to follow.

Another person he'd like to hear from ghosted through his mind, but he shut down the longing before it could take root and make him do something stupid, like call her. After their disastrous interview with Linda Collier, he'd made a promise to himself to keep it professional with Kayla. Talk to her only if the case warranted the exchange.

He could already feel the ache of withdrawal.

A knuckle tapped against his cubicle, and he turned to find SRA Lawson.

"When I advocated against regular updates, I didn't expect a complete blackout."

"I'm not tracking, sir."

"The alleged pay-to-play situation with Kayla Krowne. What can you tell me about it?"

He'd become so wrapped up in the governor's case that he'd failed to send his report to his supervisor. "Apologies, sir." Keeping in mind that Joyce Ann Carlson was Lawson's cousin, he chose his words carefully as he laid out his findings.

He walked Lawson through his investigation, including the interviews and the revelation that the artifact belonged to Jillian Krowne, not Kayla.

"It's a degree of separation," Lawson said, "but maybe Mama Krowne wanted to help her daughter secure a vote."

"Possible, but Ms. Krowne is known for loaning pieces of her collection to museums and a curator in need would've been like catnip to her. Plus, there's nothing to indicate that the loan changed Mrs. Rhodes's mind. Even Ms. Carlson admits to this."

"What else?"

"Mrs. Rhodes confirmed her affair with the superintendent."

Lawson eyed him. "And?"

Ash cleared his throat. "She believes Ms. Carlson has a crush—her word, not mine—on the super."

"Good God, what a soap opera."

"Generally is."

"Send me your report." Lawson scrubbed his face. "Anything new on the governor's case?"

"I have a couple irons heating up, just waiting for some callbacks."

Thirty minutes later, Ash's cell phone rang. "You got something for me, Detective?"

"Grimball and DNA," Morgan said. "Which one do you want first?"

Slumped in his chair, Ash sat forward. "Grimball."

"The only living kin he has is an older brother in Winston-Salem. Three weeks ago, the brother supposedly opened a new savings account in Marion with a hundred-thousand-dollar deposit."

"You're assuming Grimball opened the account to stash his hit money."

"Bull's eye. The brothers have an uncanny resemblance. It would be little effort to snatch his brother's ID for a day and copy his signature."

"Or the brother was in on it. You going to Winston-Salem to have a chat?"

"Can't. I need to follow up on another lead. Two of my colleagues are headed there now."

Ash wondered if the lead was for this case or another. Before he had time to ask, Morgan said, "The State's crime lab got a hit on the DNA forensics found at the scene."

"Got a name?"

"Mason Wade."

44

"Alexander Brighton?" Kayla said, her voice thick. "Why?"

"I don't know," Natalie said. "It just happened."

She pushed her friend's phone away, unable to look at her nemesis's face, no matter how handsome. "He's living in Asheville?"

Natalie nodded. "For about six months now."

Betrayal burned in her chest. She took a large swallow of wine in an attempt to diffuse the pain. It didn't help. "How did you meet?"

"By accident." She downed the last of her own fortification. "My niece and I made our monthly trip to the bookstore. Alex and I were both in the thriller/mystery section, and he recognized me."

What a cliché.

"He moved here to be an aide to Senator Maria Alvarez."

After the arrest of the previous senator who'd held Alvarez's seat, Vicky had consulted with Kayla on who to appoint in his stead. Like Vicky, Alvarez was well-liked and she did what was best for the community, even if it meant crossing party lines.

Which meant Kayla could only blame herself for inviting the viper into her home.

"Is Mason waiting for you outside?"

Kayla shook her head. "I didn't know how long I'd be, so I sent him home. I'll ride share when I'm ready."

Silence fell between them.

"Someone wrote *TRAITOROUS BITCH* on my vehicle Saturday night."

"So I heard. *From Gemma.*"

She ignored her friend's accusatory tone. "You don't find the circumstances of that odd?"

"I would if I couldn't account for Alex's whereabouts Saturday. But I can." Still standing, Natalie sighed. "I'm sorry my relationship with Alex is hurting you. We can talk about it more when it's not so raw."

"That would be never."

"People change, you know."

Kayla swiveled on her stool. Betrayal turning to anger. "Do they? Maybe they grow wiser. Maybe they become more understanding or empathetic. But could a man who's a dickwad to his core ever stop being a dick?"

"I'm leaving before we say something we'll truly regret."

Natalie made it two steps before Kayla did just that.

"Nat, did it never occur to you that Brighton bumping into you at the bookstore was strategic? That he knew getting into your pants would be the perfect revenge on me?"

Anyone else would've taken attorney Natalie Bryant's stillness as shock, maybe even a slow, seething rage. But Kayla recognized the devastation, the kind of hurt that only a close friend could inflict.

"Nat, I'm—"

"Maybe the vandals got it right, after all."

Kayla followed Natalie's stiff back until she disappeared from sight. The heart thundering in her chest urged her to chase after her friend, explain what she was feeling, apologize for being so cruel. But all those same feelings kept her seated and mute.

Unbidden, her hand reached for her phone to call Ash. She froze. What would she say?

I just destroyed one of my most valued relationships?

He already thought she was ruthless. This incident would only serve to prove him right.

Maybe he was.

Something inside her broke.

"Mind if I sit?" a deep cognac-smooth voice asked.

She turned to find the black-haired Adonis standing next to the stool Natalie had vacated, with a whisky in hand and a killer smile.

"I wouldn't be great company," she said.

"In these situations, alcohol and conversation with a stranger you'll likely never see again is the best balm."

"'These situations'?"

"Pissing off your best friend."

"Been there?"

"More than once."

Kayla released a long breath before swiveling back to the bar. She opened her mouth to refuse, but was caught by his brown, knowing eyes. A twinkle at the edge vaporized the words and she found a smile twitching at the corner of her mouth.

"Have a seat."

45

Ash stormed into Blue Cellar in search of Kayla.

After he'd hung up with the detective, all he could think about was how upsetting this new development with Mason Wade would be for Kayla. She enjoyed a close friendship with the Ranger. To learn he'd been a party to her godmother's murder would be total heartbreak.

Before he knew what he was doing, he'd gone to Kayla's house. She hadn't answered the doorbell, nor was she ignoring him on the screened-in porch. Fear crawled into his throat and wouldn't back down. It didn't matter that she'd been driving around with Wade for months, unharmed. He needed to put eyes on her. Make sure she was okay.

He'd called his little brother, and Phin helped him locate Kayla through a series of texts with a colleague named Natalie. The attorney revealed Kayla was at the bar and being a real shit. Whatever that meant.

He paused inside the door to scan the room for Kayla's blond head. A sixth sense zeroed in on her immediately.

Ash's stomach dropped ninety stories at the sight of a

dark-haired man leaning forward and kissing Kayla. She smiled, then slid off her stool. After a quick exchange of words, she collected her purse and made her way toward the exit.

Toward where he stood frozen, except for his thundering heart. Their eyes locked, and her smile faded. Not trusting his words, he nodded for her to follow him outside. He stopped at the curb, drawing in deep, painful breaths. The kiss replaying in his mind like an apocalyptic mushroom cloud.

"Ash, what are you doing here?"

"Good question." Heat thrust from his chest, up his throat and into his ears. His hands rolled into steel hammers, ready to smash everything in sight. "Dammit, Kayla. I thought we had something going."

He ignored the mocking voice in his head, reminding him of his vow to keep her at a professional distance.

"Honestly, Ash. I don't know what we have. One minute you hate me, the next we're making love, and now—"

Whipping around, he fired back. "I don't hate you. Never have. Sometimes, I wish to God I did."

She crossed her arms, ignoring the gawking tourists and the rapt panhandlers as she joined him at the curb. "Oh, that's right, you dislike my job, not me."

"Exactly."

"Why?"

"You used your lobbying influence to get Director Eileen Tao appointed, and she's made my life and every other special agent's miserable."

"How?"

"I'm doing so much damn paperwork now that I'm spending more time on reports than investigating cases."

"Did Eileen explain why she's requiring so much documentation?"

Ash crossed his arms, mirroring her stance. Her calm insertions were slowly pinching out his lit fuse.

He thought back to the field visit Director Tao made to the Charlotte office not long after her appointment. She'd laid out her plan for the next five years, but most of what she'd said was a gummy mess in his head. Like everyone else in the room, he'd turned off his hearing and stayed focused on her last words.

We'll be collecting more data on what you're doing via required forms...

"Data," he said with less heat.

"What reason did she give for needing the information?"

He clamped his teeth together with such force a sharp pain arrowed straight into his temple. "I don't know." Possibly the three hardest words he'd ever uttered.

The look she sent him made the fire return to his ears, but for a completely different reason.

"How do you not know?" she asked a moment later. "Eileen showed me the talking points she intended to deliver to y'all. Her reasons for the extra work were clear."

"Why don't we get back to the reason I broke up your love fest."

"Love fest?" Confusion raked over her beautiful features, then she half-looked back at the bar and her expression turned incredulous. "Nick?"

"If that's the guy you were kissing, yes."

She shook her head, as if he were a boy pissing against a tree at a family reunion. "I understand now why you missed the important part of Eileen's five-year strategic plan. The vital part where she explained that good data leads to increased resources. Your damn brain shuts down when you hear—or think you see—something you don't like."

Increased resources? Ash recalled Patsy's promotion and her new assistant, the establishment of an art crime squad, the fancy coffeemaker, his new computer with its duo monitors. Shame gripped his heart, but it was nothing compared to the jealousy already consuming his chest.

"I saw the kiss as plainly as I see you now."

"Did you?"

The confidence in her challenging words made him review the painful memory again. The guy—Nick—had been sitting on her right, then he leaned in to kiss her. Had she kissed him back? Or had Nick's head blocked his view?

Much to his shame, he couldn't recall. The second their positions became *intimate,* a red haze of territorial fury had blinded him until Kayla stood before him, staring at him in surprise.

"I'll answer the question for you. No, you didn't see a passionate kiss. You observed a friendly peck on the cheek as a thank-you for a mutually beneficial conversation."

"Mutually beneficial how?"

"We're both having relationship issues." Her gaze roamed over his face. "Sometimes an unbiased stranger can help you see things those close to you can't."

Ash blinked twice in quick succession. "You didn't kiss him?"

"No," she said in a suddenly harsh voice. "It seems all my passion is tied up in a frustratingly hardheaded special agent."

The jealousy trembling through his body stilled and, despite feeling like a teenage fool, his cheeks widened into a grin. "A frustratingly *handsome* special agent with a hard head?"

"I will not be cajoled by an ass who doesn't trust me."

His grin fell away, and he took a step toward her, brushing his knuckles against a flush of red on her slender neck. "I'm sorry."

At his admission, her eyes widened, then narrowed. "What strategy are you playing, Blackwell?"

"No strategy. Just a man flooded with feelings for a woman and no idea what to do with them."

"Why?" she whispered.

Another step closer. "Because he's uncertain where he stands with her."

She closed her eyes and leaned into his touch before looking up again. "He stands beside her, if that's what he wants."

"He does—"

She placed a finger against his lips. "Don't say it, unless you mean it. Unless you can accept all of me. Even the so-called despicable parts."

"I'm beginning to see there's more to your *parts* than I realized."

Her lips twitched. "About damn time." She shuffled closer until their bodies touched. "I think your investigative skills need honing, Agent."

"Are you offering your assistance?"

She nuzzled her nose against his. "I think I could show you a thing or two."

Unable to deny himself any longer, he hooked one hand around her waist and drew her in until their breaths were one.

46

KAYLA STRETCHED UP ON HER TOES AND PUT EVERY LONGING, every lonely night, every lingering glance she'd had for this man into the kiss.

She didn't know how long they stood there wrapped in the moment of hope and happiness, but she eventually became aware of male whistles and giggling teens.

With reluctance, she pulled away and was gratified to see he wasn't keen on the separation either. He threaded his fingers through hers.

"May I ask you something?" She had difficulty getting the words around her thickening throat.

"Of course."

"Your family. They sent you to investigate me—"

"No, sweetheart," he interrupted. "Not investigate. No one really knew what to do with the information from Aunt Joan."

"Liv would've known."

He nodded. "They love you, Kayla. Their intentions, no matter how misguided, were pure."

"And yours?"

"Probably less so . . . in the beginning. But I always knew you were too smart to sink your career on a single vote."

Kayla closed her eyes, and felt shame singe her ears. "Maybe I'm not as smart as you think."

He studied her for a long moment. "Maybe," he kissed her forehead, "you protect your family as passionately as Zeke protects his."

He knew she was Brodie's godmother. Her G-man didn't need any assistance honing his investigative skills.

"Maybe." She rose on her toes again and kissed him. "What did you need to speak with me about?"

A shadow darkened his features, and he glanced up and down the street. "Is Wade with you?"

"No, he dropped me off."

"Is he coming back for you?"

She shook her head. "My ride share should be here any second."

"Cancel it. I'll drive you home."

A thrill of anticipation set her heart racing as she retrieved her phone and called up her app. She would happily pay the cancellation fee for a night of makeup sex.

"Done. Where'd you park?"

He raised their clasped hands and kissed her knuckles, then he folded his other hand over the area as if to seal it in place.

Kayla's conflict meter triggered. "What's wrong?"

"There's something I need to tell you. Something upsetting."

She threw up her mental shields and locked in each vertebra. "I'm ready."

"The police got a match to the blood spatter left at the scene."

"Someone I know?"

"Mason Wade."

"Mason?" She could see no deception, no trickery, no personal agenda. Just a messenger with bad news.

Wrong news.

She slid her hand from between his, needing distance to think, to analyze. "There must be some mistake."

"I'm afraid not. The DNA lab ran the sample twice."

Kayla's mind swirled with images of Mason. His laugh, his bad jokes, his fierce protection.

"You think he—" She couldn't form the words.

He set a palm on her shoulder. Evidently needing to provide comfort as much as she needed the space in order to process such devastating news.

"Let's take this one step at a time. See where the evidence leads."

Strategize.

Plan.

Results.

This she could follow, absorb, act upon.

"Have the police taken Mason into custody?"

"Not yet. He wasn't at his residence. Can you think of where he might be?"

Kayla worked through what she knew about Mason. He had a teenage daughter named Jozi and—. Stunned, she couldn't recall another family member's name, nor a friend's. She couldn't with any measure of confidence recount what he did for fun or what he liked for dinner.

"I have no idea," she admitted.

"None?"

"I'm only just realizing how little I know about him."

"You told me once that he wasn't available on the weekends. Do you know why?"

"He does personal security contract work a few week-ends per month, and one weekend he goes to some camp in the Piedmont."

"Camp?"

"A place where he gets range time and can keep his tactical skillset up-to-date."

"War games?"

She shrugged a shoulder. "They act out different scenarios, like SWAT teams."

The moment the words were out of her mouth, she grasped their implication. Shocked, she stared at Ash, feeling a volatile mix of disbelief and betrayal. "He couldn't have, Ash. I can't believe he would do something so cold-blooded to someone I loved."

"There could be a reasonable explanation for why his blood was on the tree trunk." He hooked a knuckle beneath her chin and lifted until her unfocused gaze met his. "How did you come to know Wade?"

"My previous driver moved to Charleston when his wife's company transferred her."

"Did you go through an agency or was he a referral?"

"Referral."

"From your previous driver?"

She shook her head. "Aunt Sybil. Her son served with Mason."

"I need you to do me a favor."

"Anything."

"Call Wade and have him pick you up."

47

KAYLA LOOKED AT HIM IN HORROR, AND ASH'S HEART constricted as if he'd delivered the shitty news about Wade all over again.

"We need to bring him in for questioning, but the task force hasn't been able to locate him. If we can get him to come to us, it'll be easier for everyone, including Wade."

"But he'll know I betrayed him."

"He's a potential killer. I don't think betrayed is the right word."

"Either way, our relationship ends."

"I can't say that chokes me up."

"What if you're wrong? What if he's not the killer?"

Two women exited the bar, releasing the erratic thump of nineties music.

"Wade's a big boy. He'll understand the situation. If anything, he'll blame me for pressuring you into doing it."

She squeezed her eyes closed and drew in several deep breaths. "There has to be a better way."

"There are other options."

Her eyes hooked into his. "Which are?"

"A team could hit his place tonight, while he's asleep. Or they could snag him tomorrow morning, during breakfast with his daughter. Or they could—"

She held up a hand. "I get it. I don't need any more visual images of him being treated like a criminal."

Guilt arced through his body. He hated playing off her loyalties toward her employees, but Ash couldn't stomach the thought of Kayla being alone with the Ranger again.

Wade probably had his place drowning in security and had a failsafe escape plan. But Kayla calling him for a pickup? As common as grass growing.

"Make the call, and I'll take care of the rest."

"You're not going to take him in yourself, are you?"

"I've dealt with a fair number of bad guys. No need to worry."

"I'm not calling him unless you get Morgan, Lawson, or another cop here to assist. If he killed the governor in cold blood, he'll have no problem taking you out."

"You don't appear to have a lot of faith in my abilities."

"I work in the realm of odds and I don't like yours going up against a combat veteran who's a suspected murderer." She covered his heart with her palm. "If Mason is who you believe him to be, he lacks an essential part of his humanity. You do not."

"I want it noted for the record," he trapped her hand against his chest, "that I could kick Wade's ass twice on Tuesday. By myself."

"Duly noted." She smiled. "Now call for backup."

"After you ring Wade."

"Ash—"

"Let's make sure you can get him here first."

She stared at him for a long, contemplative moment. "I confirm, you call?"

"Promise."

"I absolutely hate this plan." She lifted her phone and tapped Wade's name.

"Speaker."

She hit another button and the ring tone seemed to rattle the air around them. It rang several times, and Ash feared his imperfect plan was DOA.

Then . . . "Hello, Kayla."

"I'm sorry to bother you, Mason, but I'm going to need a ride home after all."

"Is everything all right?"

"Yes and no." The tips of her fingers holding the phone turned white. "I feel really ridiculous, but there's a guy who's creeping out on me and I'm afraid he's going to follow me out of the bar. I'd rather have you waiting for me at the curb rather than some unknown, muscle-challenged driver."

When Wade didn't immediately reply, they glanced down at the screen to make sure the call clock was still ticking. It was.

"Mason, did I lose you?" Kayla asked.

"I'm here."

"Did I come through okay?"

"Loud and clear."

Pinpricks of unease skittered down Ash's spine. Something about the Ranger's voice was off. He didn't display the normal emotion of being called back to work. No irritation, exasperation, or joking comment about what would she do without him.

He was calm. Too calm. Focused. His words penetrating.

"Are you able to pick me up?"

"You and Special Agent Blackwell?"

Shit. Ash scanned the road both ways, across the street, the buildings above. Nothing.

"I didn't kill Governor Stokes."

"I believe you."

"If you didn't kill her," Ash said, "why was your blood found at the crime scene?"

"I didn't say I wasn't in the Krowne's garden."

"Mason, what's going on?" Kayla asked. "Why were you there?"

"To fulfill a contract."

"Someone hired you to kill Vicky?"

Silence.

"Me?" she whispered.

"No, Kayla," he said in a rough voice. His first sign of emotion. "I would never hurt you. Not for any amount of money."

"Why Victoria?"

"I can't answer why."

"If you didn't shoot the governor," Ash said, still searching for the Ranger, "who did?"

"Seb Grimball."

The ex-con with a compulsive need to announce his intentions with carefully placed jewelry stolen from his victims.

"Did you murder him?" Kayla asked.

More silence.

"My God, Mason. You nearly killed us."

"If I'd wanted you dead, you'd be cold and rotting now."

"You hit the gas line!"

"Regrettable, but as good a distraction as any to keep your agent from following me."

"Who ordered the hit on Governor Stokes?" Ash asked.

Preparing for the evening crowd, the decibel level of the

music inside the bar seemed to have ramped up a good 10dbh.

"Have you told Blackwell about Service yet?"

What little color was left in Kayla's face drained away. "How do you know about Service?"

"Drivers are like domestic servants." Wade's voice rose as he fought to outloud the background noise swelling around him. "After a while, they disappear from their employer's landscape. Become air. Necessary, but unseen."

Unease forced Ash's attention toward the bar. He peered into the large window and scanned the clutch of tourists, locals, and bleary-eyed suits. "Who ordered the hit, Wade?"

"Someone very close to Kayla. Watch her back."

"Already done. Give me a name."

A shadowed figure inside the bar moved closer to the window. Tall, broad-shouldered, predatory stride. His left hand held a phone up to his ear.

Ash's feet carried him closer to the window until he was staring into Mason Wade's hard eyes.

The bodyguard dropped his phone, mouthed a name, and disappeared into the crowded bar.

"Stay here." Ash threw the sharp command at Kayla before ripping open the Cellar's door and giving chase.

He recalled another time, at Hemingway's, when the Ranger had sat inside the establishment to ensure his employer's safety. Why hadn't he considered the possibility the second his unease surfaced?

Sprinting through the bar, he ignored the bartender's shouts and crashed through the rear entrance that led to a back alley. A jean and black T-shirt clad figure caught his attention.

"Wade, stop! We can work something out."

The Ranger didn't acknowledge his command. In fact, he seemed to turn on the damn turbos. For such a big, muscle-bound guy, the Ranger could book.

Ash pursued, wishing he had worn his HOKA running shoes rather than his thin-soled Oxfords.

The Ranger burned around the corner and descended a set of stairs that led to a public parking lot.

Ash pumped everything he had into his legs. If Wade made it to his vehicle, he would go so far off the grid they'd never track him down.

He screeched to a halt as soon as he hit the lot and searched for the Ranger's dark head. Nothing.

Dammit.

"Ash!" Barreling around the corner, Kayla ran down the sidewalk, parallel to the parking lot, pushing her way through pedestrians. She pointed at a gunmetal Ram truck roaring up the hill toward Haywood Street.

He bit out a string of curses before hustling to Kayla's side.

Breathing hard, the lobbyist balanced on one foot while she locked a four-inch heel onto her other. She'd taken her damned shoes off in order to chase after him and Wade.

"Didn't I say to stay put?" he bit out.

"Do I look like someone who takes orders from a man?"

"I'm not just any man." He jammed his fingers through his hair. "I'm a law enforcement officer in pursuit of a suspected murderer. I cannot focus on my job if I'm worried about you getting hurt."

Her defensive stance eased, and she threw her arms around his neck. "You scared me when you took off."

Wrapping his arms around her waist, he pulled her in

close. Kissed her neck. "I can handle myself, but only if I know you're safe."

She nodded. "Where's your car? We should go after him."

"Wade's in the wind. The only way we'll find him is if he wants us to."

"What about his daughter?"

"As soon as we tracked down Grimball, Wade knew his days were numbered. Jozi's no doubt tucked away with someone he trusts."

"What do you suggest we do, then?"

He brushed a stray lock away from her cheek, then curled his hand around hers. "Come on, we need to talk."

48

——————

AFTER COLLECTING CRISPY AND A HASTILY PACKED OVERNIGHT bag, Ash found himself rocketing down I-40 west toward the one place where Kayla would be safe.

Steele Ridge.

The closer he got to his family's compound, the more knotted his stomach became. He was about to ask his brother Zeke for a favor and he had no idea of his reception after their falling-out yesterday.

Getting Kayla away from the city and all of her responsibilities would also give them an opportunity to have a long, uninterrupted chat. His pulse kicked up a notch when his mind flashed back to Wade mouthing the name of who put a hit on the governor.

HCVS.

The company that had been pouring buckets of money into Krowne and Associates.

Ash rolled up to the Friary's security panel, entered his code, and waited for the large gate to crank open. When nothing happened, he glanced at the panel and noticed an error message.

Invalid code.

He reentered his number.

Same result. A growl erupted from his throat.

"What's the matter?" Kayla asked.

"Dear brother deactivated my code."

"Because of your argument?"

"Because of a hundred thousand different reasons." Ash hooked his wrist over the top of the steering wheel and thrummed his fingers against the dash.

He could either sit out here like an idiot all night, call Zeke and grovel until he opened the gate, go around the asshole and narc on him to their mother, text one of his brothers and put them in the middle—again, or turn around and deal with Wade and Co. by himself, placing Kayla in greater danger.

"What are you doing?" Kayla asked into the silence.

"Thinking."

"About?"

"The most painful way to end my brother."

"Want me to call Liv and have her buzz us in?"

"No, that would put her in an awkward position."

"We could stay in a hotel tonight and deal with this in the morning."

He shook his head. "I want you on the other side of that gate. It's the only way I know you'll be safe until we figure out who's behind all this."

"What did Mason say to you, right before he took off?"

He'd avoided talking about this on the ride here, not wanting his attention divided by driving, watching for tails, and concentrating on not only what she told him but what she would no doubt leave unsaid.

Now, his only distraction was his near overwhelming need to pull her into his arms and cover her mouth with his. For months, she'd been traveling around in a vehicle with a contract killer. One moral code away from death.

He didn't know where the hell they were going from here, but a niggling fear told him he was about to lose her.

"Ash?" she prompted into the silence.

Angling his head toward her, he drew in a breath to share Wade's confession, only to be interrupted by a gruff voice. "You gonna sit out there all night?"

Ash closed his eyes for a fortifying second before he stuck his head out the window and spoke into the panel's intercom. "I'd be at the house already if someone hadn't deactivated my code."

"No one canceled your code," Zeke said. "You're family. A pain in the ass, but family."

"Explain why my number isn't working, then."

"Rohan sent out new ones last month. Did you update your records?"

Heat laughed its way up his neck and revved around his ears. He sagged back in his seat and knocked his skull against the headrest.

A soft, feminine chuckle broke out beside him.

"It's not funny," he growled, pulling up Rohan's text.

"Watching the two of you is the best show on earth."

Ash clamped his teeth together, entered the new code, and eyed the gate's opening with intense annoyance.

As he pulled away, Zeke's amused voice reached through the window and flicked his ear. "We're all in the Great Hall."

Wonderful. Group humiliation. His favorite.

49

Leaving Crispy in her carrier and the windows cracked, Kayla led the way from the parking lot to the large residence the family called the Friary in honor of its original Franciscan monk residents.

Soon after purchasing the behemoth, the Blackwells sank a significant amount of money into its renovation, creating large suites for each family member as well as guest rooms. The property also included a gorgeous chapel, an office building called the Annex, several renovated cabins that were erected when the property was owned by a church camp, and a number of outbuildings. Surrounding the living space was nearly a thousand acres of forested land, also under restoration, and a state-of-the-art security system.

Kayla stepped onto the expansive front stoop at the same time one of the ten-foot-tall front doors opened, revealing Zeke. His eyes shifted from Ash to her before he wrapped her in a warm hug.

"Hello, Trouble."

No questions, no raised eyebrows about her presence,

not even an annoyed tone, considering their accidental meeting yesterday.

"Sorry to barge in on y'all," she said, stepping away.

"You're welcome anytime." He nodded toward the interior where a bevy of excited voices could be heard. "Liv and the other ladies will be happy to see you." Niceties done, he focused his considerable attention on his brother, who'd remained below on the pathway. "Ash."

"Zeke."

She wondered how long they would've stayed that way if Zeke hadn't realized she'd failed to take his hint.

He tried again. "We won't be long."

"If you think I'm going to leave the two of you alone, you've learned absolutely nothing about me in the past two years."

"Your balls still intact?" Ash asked from the sidewalk.

"Yeah, no thanks to you."

Ash directed his next words to Kayla. "Last time we spoke, he was certain Liv would make him a eunuch for spilling the baby beans."

"We agreed not to share the news until the end of her first trimester."

"Smart, but hard," Kayla said, "especially for first-timers."

"Did you announce it to everyone yet?" Ash asked.

"Just tonight." The hard edge around Zeke's jaw softened. "Can't you tell?"

Another wave of excited chatter rushed through the open door.

When the two men fell into another staring contest, Kayla sighed and waved Ash forward.

He hesitated a moment, then joined them on the stoop.

"Zeke," she said, "Ash is sorry he figured out your secret and against his will told me what was up with my BFF."

Both men opened their mouths to protest. She held up a hand. "I'm sorry I pushed him into telling me, but his hedging made my mind go to the worst possible scenarios." She lasered in on the soon-to-be-father. "Your brother did me a kindness. Now accept his apology."

A muscle in Zeke's jaw flexed. "I understand your dilemma now, bro."

"Ash," she turned to the equally headstrong man to her right, "Zeke is sorry he didn't trust his wife to be strong enough to hear distressing news about her best friend and sent you on a fool's errand."

Zeke fired up like an over-pressurized boiler. "Mom and Aunt Joan were worried about you, and I rightfully kept my pregnant wife out of the mess."

"Rightfully?" Kayla said in her best musing voice. "Did it not occur to you that if Liv had approached me she would have known straightaway the truth of the situation? Instead, you sent someone who knew me only as a so-called blood-sucking lobbyist."

Zeke glanced at Ash as if searching for support, only to find his brother smiling. Ash stuffed his hands into his front pockets and rocked back on his heels, enjoying the show.

"If Liv had come to me, you would never have given away your secret and Ash wouldn't have had to tell me, and your balls would never have been in jeopardy."

Rather than pop a cork, Zeke blinked twice, slowly, as if he were trying to identify an alien species. "Does this mean you didn't pay-to-play?"

A gurgle started low in her stomach. One look at Ash,

and the laughter erupted into her throat and burst passed her lips.

Ash joined in until they both had tears in their eyes. Zeke glared at them, but even tightening his lips into a thin line couldn't halt his amusement.

"If you're not a felonious lobbyist," Zeke said, "what the hell *is* going on with the Irish artifact?"

"She connected a board member, Dee Rhodes, with her mother, Jillian Krowne, who's the actual owner of the artifact," Ash interjected, surprising her.

"You knew?"

He winked. "I'm a trained investigator, remember?"

"Why the hell didn't you tell me this yesterday?" Zeke asked.

"Did you give me a chance, brother?"

Zeke's thumb tapped against his thigh several times before he lifted a brow and trained dark eyes on her. "Your mother's artifact? Not sure a prosecutor would buy into that bit of hairsplitting."

Kayla shrugged. "The day of the craft fair, I'd intended to ask Dee for her support, but she offered it before I could even open my mouth to present my pitch. There was no reason for me to dangle the artifact in front of her."

Kayla left out the fact that she was prepared to do whatever it took, even put her career in jeopardy, to prevent Engel County's ill-thought-out policies from spilling over the county line and affecting her godson.

"If anything," Ash said, "the board member took the opportunity to volunteer her support in the hope Kayla would offer a solution to her son's grand opening dilemma."

"She knew about your collection?" Zeke asked.

"Of course. I host many parties at my Asheville residence, where I display samples of my, and some of my mother's, collection. Dee—the entire board—has attended at one time or another."

She glanced between the brothers. "It's common knowledge that I have a soft spot for museums. Asheville has the makings of being a cultural mecca. Having a natural history museum would be a wonderful boon for the city." She crossed her arms. "I would've put her into contact with my mother, regardless of upcoming agenda items, but I had no way of knowing if Mom would part with it."

"Your mom doesn't have the same patron of the arts mentality?" Ash asked.

"As generous as she is, she's notoriously hesitant to loan out her pieces to museums."

"Why?" Ash asked.

"I don't know. But for reasons I'm not sure even she understands, she prefers to keep her collectibles in the family's possession."

Zeke blew out a breath, then placed his hand on her shoulder. "My apologies."

"For not believing Liv was strong enough?"

He shook his head. "I am who I am. I can't—I won't apologize for protecting those I love. Though I will give your perspective more thought." His big hand squeezed, and she might have heard a bone snap. "I'm sorry for not having more faith in you. You've been a good friend to this family—and me. You've been there for us without hesitation and with a shocking amount of enthusiasm." He flicked a glance at Ash before returning his gaze to her. "I should have spoken to you myself."

Her throat tried to close on her. She had to swallow several times in order to eke out a single word. She clasped a hand over Zeke's extended arm and twined her fingers with Ash's. "Are we good?"

Ash and Zeke looked at each other. Neither said a word.

"For now?" she amended, knowing their injuries ran much deeper than this one issue.

"For now," Ash agreed, clamping a hand on his brother's shoulder.

Zeke nodded, then mimicked his brother's action.

Kayla smiled. It was a start.

50

Ash followed Kayla into the Friary, a slight smile on his face. The knots that had been twisting ever tighter in his gut eased their torture, strand by strand.

For the first time in years, he entered a family gathering without feeling like an *other*. A member by blood but not of mind and body.

He had Kayla to thank for this miraculous transformation. With stunning efficiency, she'd showed his black-and-white brother the world of messy gray. And opened the door enough for Ash to slide his foot inside again.

Kayla made a beeline for the group of ladies sitting before one of two giant fireplaces bookending the Great Hall. His attention rose to the gleaming sixteenth-century longsword suspended above the mantel on ornate iron hooks.

Lupos.

So called for the four-headed wolf decorating the pommel. Lost to the family for close to a century, Lupos became a symbol of strength and resilience to Zeke, which led him to conduct a yearlong search for the heirloom, unbeknownst to the rest of the family.

If not for Kayla's contacts and her active participation in the artifact's retrieval, his brother might still be searching for the hunk of steel.

Lynette and Grams appeared at the opposite end of the Great Hall. His heart clenched at the sight of his grandmother using a walking stick, a slight bow to her spine. Despite the stark reminder of her mortality, the soon-to-be-ninety-two-year-old moved toward him with purpose.

"It's good to see you, she'ashkii yázhi." *My little boy.*

He bent several inches to kiss her cheek. "And you, Grams." He straightened to buss Lynette's cheek as well. "Mom, how are you?"

"Growing old, boy. What brings you this far west?"

"She does," Grams inserted, nodding toward Kayla, who was currently enveloped in feminine hugs, as she moved to sit in her favorite chair near the fireplace.

Lynette craned her neck around him until she spotted the lobbyist. "Trouble?"

Because why else would Ash bring Kayla to his family's home?

Unlike Zeke, he wouldn't make the mistake of underestimating a woman's strength and intuition, especially not these two former war dogs.

"Governor Stokes might not have been the only target."

"Why?" Lynette asked.

"Unknown. We found out today that Kayla's driver, Mason Wade, was tangled up in it. Before he bolted, he revealed that a company named HCVS ordered the governor's hit. Before you ask, I have no idea if it's an acronym. But there were two shooters. Two targets? Or insurance for one?"

"Did you speak to Rohan?" Lynette asked.

"He's on it."

Peering over his shoulder, he watched Kayla place her palm over Liv's barely-there baby bump. Her beautiful face lit up, and he experienced an answering warmth inside his chest. When he turned back to the matriarch and super-matriarch of the family, he caught them sharing knowing glances with each other.

He pretended not to notice. The last thing he needed right now was to get into a conversation with these two strong-minded women about his love life.

"I have a favor to ask," he said.

"Of course, she can stay," Grams said in her usual eerie, read-your-mind way. "Kayla is family now. You do not need to ask. "

"It might be for a while. She has a cat."

"She and Crispy may sleep here as long as necessary."

Of course Grams would know about Crispy. Unlike him, she'd spent the past two years getting to know Kayla, rather than avoiding her.

"Or as long as she likes," Lynette added.

"As may you," Grams said.

"And face Zeke's disappointment every day? No thanks."

"Perhaps it is time for you to tell him the reason you changed your name when you left," Grams said.

"And all but disappeared when he needed you most," Lynette said.

Both precision knife cuts were delivered without inflection, without judgment. He didn't bother asking them how they knew. They would no doubt give him the *look,* making him feel like an even bigger ass.

"I will, but it's not going to change anything. The hurt is too deep."

A large, vertical plaque hanging above the mantle of the second enormous fireplace caught his eye. A combination of sans serif lettering and cursive words layered on top of each other covered the white-washed wooden panels.

Noting the direction of his gaze, Lynette said, "Beautiful, isn't it?"

"Our Lena made it," Grams added, "at Zeke's request."

Family first...
Through blood
Through hate
Through fear
Through joy
No exceptions.

It was the "Through joy" that produced the drop of moisture that bubbled at the edge of his lower eyelid. They'd kept his unsolicited contribution, after all. Zeke had added the line even though Ash had nothing to do with BARS, not to mention how raw his brother's feelings had been at the time.

"Still think a conversation won't change anything?" Lynette asked.

The too-heavy tear fell over the rim and tracked down his whiskered cheek.

51

"SORRY TO INTERRUPT THIS HAPPY MOMENT," LYNETTE SAID, her gaze landed on Liv and Zeke, "but there's a situation we need to discuss as a family." She motioned for everyone to join her, Grams, and Ash near the fireplace. "Gather around. You too, Kayla."

Kayla's eyes caught Ash's, and he gave her a small nod.

Cruz and Phin finished refilling their glasses from the extensive selection of amber choices. Zeke pushed away from the mantel at the opposite end of the Hall. Kayla, Lena, Maddy, Cilla, and Liv popped up from the plush leather couches and took up identical positions on this side of the room. Everyone was present, except for Rohan.

Noticing her fourth son's absence, Lynette looked at Lena. "Would you mind texting—"

"Already done." Lena smiled and winked at the older woman, who gave her an appreciative smile in return.

The front door slammed, and Rohan appeared. The rumpled nature of his dark hair and the laptop hanging at his side were testaments to what activity he'd been engaged in.

Lynette waved him forward. "Come sit, m'boy. Better yet, grab a glass of something that will ease the strain around your eyes."

Rohan complied, because that's what they all did when their veteran mother doled out orders. Even as grown men, they still had a healthy respect for—and fear of—their mama.

Once everyone was settled, Grams edged off her favorite chair. A three-stranded red coral bead necklace swayed away from her chest as she did so, until she reached her full four-and-a-half-plus feet. She joined her daughter-in-law standing before the fireplace.

Ash stood on the opposite side of Lynette. His hands sweating as he stared into a sea of curious faces.

"Asher shared with us," Grams said in a somber tone, "there's evidence to suggest that Kayla might have also been in the crosshairs of the governor's assassin."

"What?" Liv's expression was half-shock, half-reproach when she stink-eyed Kayla, sitting kitty-corner to her on a matching sofa. "You let me go on and on about nursery colors while you have a target on your back?"

Kayla, in turn, glared at Ash.

Zeke moved to stand behind the couch, where Liv sat, and rested soothing hands on her shoulders, then he cast a "you're dead" look at Ash.

Before he went up in flames with all the heat directed at him, Ash said, "There's 'evidence to suggest,' not to confirm. Some," he nodded toward Kayla, "don't believe she was an intended target."

"But your experience tells you otherwise," Liv pressed. As a former special agent, she would understand that fool-proof evidence wasn't always available during the early stages of an investigation. Often, law enforcement had to lean into their instincts to solve cases.

"Yes."

"Who put the hit on the governor?" Phin asked, worry for his employer knitting his brow. Maddy inched closer to him on the loveseat and threaded her fingers through his.

Ash's attention landed on Kayla. "We have credible information that points to a company called HCVS."

Her eyes widened. "That's not possible."

"You know them?" Cruz asked from his position on the sofa next to Cilla.

"They're one of my clients."

"Why have I never heard of them?" Phin asked.

She angled her head around. "I work with them exclusively."

Phin frowned.

Kayla addressed Ash. "There's no malice in the organization. They would have no reason to kill me or the governor."

Rohan's fingers danced across his keyboard, while Lena peered over his shoulder. "I've been searching all day for any mention of HCVS. So far, the only thing that pops up is what's on the Secretary of State's website."

"You're searching for HCVS?" Kayla asked, her voice sharp.

Rohan didn't lift his head as he peered at Ash over the rim of his glasses.

"I asked him to."

"But Rohan said he'd been searching 'all day.' How is that possible?"

This wasn't at all how he saw this play out in his mind. He thought he'd update the family on the situation and request their assistance to watch over Kayla while he continued to search for the shooter.

The current downward spiral of their conversation shouldn't have surprised him. Predictable was not a term he'd use for this eclectic group.

"Maybe you and I should adjourn someplace more private." He had no wish to interrogate her in front of everyone.

"*Maybe* you should have thought of that before getting your family involved." In one swift motion, Kayla stood. "If you'll excuse me, I need a bit of fresh air." She didn't rush out of the room, but strode away in her normal confident, purposeful stride.

Liv made to follow her best friend, but Zeke exerted the lightest pressure against her shoulders to keep her in place. She scowled up at him.

When the front door closed, Cruz asked, "She going to run or call her attorney?"

Cilla elbowed him.

"What? It's a legitimate question."

One Ash couldn't answer.

52

PANIC ATTACKS WERE REAL.

Although Kayla had never experienced one herself, she had a sorority sister who'd been plagued by them, and Kayla had learned how to help her work through the debilitating sensation of breathlessness and mind-numbing terror.

But she'd never understood—not really—how a person could cede control of their reality to fearful thoughts.

Until now.

Kayla's mind rotated around her conversations with dizzying speed. Her heart punched her ribcage with the strength of a heavyweight boxer, sweat steamed at the roots of her hair, and her stomach flip-flopped like a prize fish fighting a pro's line.

Her breath stopped.

Her mind spun from conversations and implications to fear and survival. From the depths of her mind, she recalled the mantra she'd established with her sorority sister.

Breathe, one, two, three. Exhale. Breathe, one, two, three.

She continued repeating the words, forcing her nervous

system to cooperate, to believe she wasn't dying. Finally, her lungs expanded and deflated and her heart rate scaled down until her body no longer vibrated from the impact.

Once she felt she could speak with control again, she called her mother.

The call went to voicemail. She tried twice more, letting Jillian know by sheer volume to pick up her damn phone. This was important. Still, her calls remained unanswered.

The sun fell below the treetops, and Kayla wrapped an arm around her middle to ward off the dipping temperatures. She considered taking the path to her right to the family's chapel for warmth and privacy, but her feet remained rooted in place while she dialed Gordon Krowne.

"Daddy, I'm trying to get in touch with Mom, but she's not answering her phone. Can you put her on?"

"Sorry, Pepper. Your mother left for Chicago this morning."

"Chicago? You're sure?"

"That's what she said. Now that I think about it, she hasn't checked in with me as she normally does."

"Is there an issue at one of our hotels?"

"Not that I'm aware. She gave me the impression that she's doing one of her periodic check-ins."

"Did she take Susannah with her?"

"No, she stayed back to finish up some research."

She could think of only one reason why her mother would make an unscheduled visit to the Windy City without her assistant. What she didn't know was why Jillian would need to speak with Indira Umar. Did it have something to do with Vicky's murder? Had Sybil and Elsie gone with her?

"Is she staying at our downtown hotel?"

"It's her favorite. Is everything all right, sweetheart?"

"Everything is fine, Daddy. I'm sure she's just busy with meetings. When I reach her, I'll make sure she calls or texts you."

She hung up and immediately searched her contacts for the Krowne hotel in downtown Chicago. "Gavin, this is Kayla Krowne. Could you put me through to the family suite?"

"Of course, Miss Krowne." A slight hesitation. "To my knowledge, none of the family are in residence."

An electric jolt slammed into her heart. "Could you please verify? Jillian might have checked in earlier today."

Rapid clicking echoed through the receiver. "I'm sorry, Ms. Krowne, but I don't see that your mother is staying with us. Could she be at—"

"Thank you, Gavin." She disconnected.

Kayla racked her brain for another reasonable explanation for her mother's trip. Maybe she and Harper traveled there to shop the Magnificent Mile for Gordon's upcoming birthday. That would explain why she'd called it a business trip.

Wouldn't she still stay at their downtown hotel, though? It would be the most convenient.

She called her sister. "Harper, did you by chance fly to Chicago with Mama?"

"Mom's in Chicago? She didn't say anything about a trip when I spoke to her last night."

"If you hear from her, will you let me know?"

"Sure, but—"

"Can't chat now. Give Jimmy a kiss for me."

Fear crowded in her throat as her fingers tapped out a frantic group text to Sybil and Elsie.

Is Mom with you?

Ten seconds went by with no answer. Thirty seconds. A minute. Two minutes.

Like her, the aunties lived and died by their phones. They always, *always* answered within a minute, if only to send her a "stand by" until they could respond more fully later.

What the hell was going on?

Kayla held her phone against her chest as snatches of conversation from the past week whisked through her mind. The low hum of anxiety that had started building in her chest after her first phone call was now a nine on the Richter scale.

She gripped the phone tighter to stem the trembling in her hand. With bone-deep certainty, she knew something had happened to her mother. And now her aunties weren't answering.

Had they all been targeted?

If so, that meant someone had found out about Service and was actively trying to destroy it. Kayla could be next. Had Ash been right all along?

Panic gripped her chest as she put the phone to her ear for one final call.

A cultured voice answered on the second ring. "Kayla, this is a welcome surprise."

"My apologies for intruding on your personal time, Indira. I will keep this brief."

"You have perfect timing. My next appointment has not yet arrived. What can I do for you?"

"I'm trying to locate Mom. Dad said she flew to Chicago. I wondered if she might be with you."

A long nerve-snapping silence followed.

"Indira, she didn't take her assistant and hasn't checked in at the hotel yet." She hated showing weakness to this woman, but answers to her questions were more important than her pride. "I'm worried."

The older woman released a heavy breath, as if she'd made a decision she didn't like but could live with. "I can confirm that Jillian requested a personal conference with me. We were to have dinner together at Oriole's tonight."

"What time?"

"Thirteen minutes ago."

Kayla's own breath shuddered between her lips. "Mom's never late."

"No, she's not."

"Have you tried contacting her?"

"Several times."

"What did she want to talk with you about?"

"She only said it was important and that . . ."

"Yes?"

"She was worried about your safety."

"From whom?"

"She wanted to discuss it with me in person."

"Any guesses?"

"None I'd be willing to share over the phone."

"Something's happened, Indira. No one has seen her since this morning. Sybil and Elsie haven't answered my texts either." She took a steadying breath. "According to my driver, someone within HCVS hired him to kill Victoria. Mason couldn't go through with it, but they hired a second assassin who had no problem with follow-through."

"Your driver, what's his name?"

"Mason Wade."

"Who was the other shooter?"

"Seb Grimball, but he's dead."

"You believe this Mason?"

"Yes, I do. The optics aren't good."

Silence settled on the other side of the call for several long seconds. "Did Jillian fly commercial or private?"

"I don't know. I'll look into it."

"Kayla?"

"Yes?"

"Do not contact any other Service members until you hear from me. I'll see what I can find out from my end."

"Thank you—"

The line went dead. She stared down at her now silent phone, wishing she could get a hold of Mason. He knew more than what he'd told them. She was certain of it.

"I think it's time you leveled with me, don't you?"

Kayla closed her eyes briefly before pivoting to find Ash leaning against the open doorframe, arms crossed.

A large lump rose in the back of her throat, doing its damnedest to suffocate her. She swallowed hard and nodded.

"Yes, it's time."

53

Once Ash ushered her into the family chapel, Kayla paused to take in the long, open room, with its high ceiling and stained-glass windows.

At the far end, wooden steps led to a dais housing a beautiful altar and elevated pulpit. Large organ pipes climbed a side wall, completing the picture of piety.

This wasn't the first time Kayla had visited here. Liv had given her the grand tour on one of her first forays to the Blackwell compound.

Despite its pristine condition, the family didn't use the chapel for worship, but more as a place of quiet reflection. A place where they could leave their stressful jobs at the door and be alone with their own thoughts.

Ash indicated a front pew. "Have a seat. I'll be right back."

He disappeared behind one of two hidden doors at the back of the dais. One led to a kitchenette and restroom, the other to a secret bunker below ground level full of canned goods and survivalist supplies that had been placed there well before the Blackwells purchased the property.

Ash returned a few seconds later with two black tumblers full of water and handed her one. "Drink up."

She smoothed the pad of her thumb over the silver BARS logo before quenching the thirst she didn't know she had. "Thank you."

"Now that you're hydrated, maybe you could tell me what the hell is going on."

"I'm sorry for running out on y'all. I . . . I had to make a phone call."

"You got spooked when I mentioned HCVS."

"I take it you made the connection between my company and HCVS, while snooping around the Secretary of State site."

He raised a brow. "*Researching,* yes. They've paid a significant amount of money for your services in the past decade."

"All legitimate, I assure you."

"Why didn't Phin know anything about them?"

"As I said, I'm the only one who works with them."

"Who is them, exactly?"

Going any further would force her to break a sacred oath. One she'd made at the age of twenty-five when she was welcomed into Service. An oath she'd gladly honored every day for the past ten years.

But when she followed Ash to the chapel, she'd made the decision to tell him everything. Even if it meant expulsion from Service and revulsion from him.

"Twenty-five years ago, my mother and aunties, a few years into their corporate jobs, got fed up with getting paid seventy-four cents for every dollar their fellow, sometimes less competent, male coworkers made. Of even greater importance to them was the fact that men across the world were making a muck of things. Had been for centuries.

Creating policy, killing policy—all for their own self-interest. Not giving a damn about their constituents, especially not the women."

She took a drink. "Until election time. Then they loved us. The quartet spent the next several years climbing the ladder, making friends with other women across the world with the same sense of *enough*."

"What was their plan?"

"Through activism and monetary influence, they would place women with honor, compassion, valor, and strength into political, corporate, governmental, religious, and social positions around the world."

"Honor, compassion, valor, and strength. HCVS."

"Very good, Agent." Her pleasure faded as quickly as it surfaced. "HCVS or, as we refer to it, Service, couldn't have killed Vicky. She was in a position to take women's rights to the next level in North Carolina. Eliminating her would've gone against our guiding principles. Service doesn't kill, threaten, undermine, or bully to advance our ideology. We use logic, facts, and persuasion through activism."

"And money."

She shrugged. "Welcome to a capitalist democracy."

"You don't sound wholly convinced Service didn't kill the governor."

"How could I be, when Mason identified HCVS as his employer? The only way he could have known about us is if someone from our organization approached him."

"I'll ask Rohan to check the dark web and see if Wade put up a shingle. But I have to say, it seems a little shortsighted for Service to introduce themselves when hiring a contract killer."

"They wouldn't have. Service is a group of highly intelligent women." Kayla gave it some thought. "Mason is even more strategic than I am. Knowing him as I do, he would've found out everything he could about an organization wanting him to assassinate the governor."

She lasered in more. "We don't have a website or business cards or offices. Everything we do for Service is in addition to our other jobs and responsibilities. They wouldn't have identified themselves, but they would have set up a communication system." She stared up at the pulpit. "I know how this will sound, but . . . I still trust him."

"You've got to be kidding me."

She bolted to her feet and began pacing. "I believe him to be an honorable man. Something forced him to become a contract killer. I feel it in my bones." Pausing beneath a stained-glass window depicting one of the fourteen Stations of the Cross—number six, where Veronica wipes the sweat-covered face of Jesus—she waited for Ash to point out the contradiction to her statement.

Mason could have killed her and Vicky, but he chose to break his contract instead. Yet he terminated Seb Grimball with seemingly no remorse.

"Let's set aside Wade's motives for now. What if a faction of Service developed a new plan, and you and Governor Stokes didn't play into it—or something you were working on together put a crimp in their playbook?"

Kayla turned around slowly, her mind running a million miles an hour. "Maybe Vicky found out about a rogue faction and that's what she wanted to talk to me about."

Ash rose and edged toward her as if any sudden movements would snap the thread she was mentally pulling on. Her mind flashed back to Jillian wanting to hire additional security for Kayla. Sybil and Elsie insisting Kayla stay close to Ash in order to get the latest on the homicide case.

Jillian's secret meeting with Service's Eastern U.S. Coordinator. Indira cautioning her to not discuss Jillian's odd disappearance with other Service members.

"You thought of something?"

"No one has seen or heard from Mom since this morning. She set up a last-minute meeting with our regional coordinator, but didn't show."

"You think Jillian intended to share her suspicions with —what was her name? Indira?"

Kayla nodded. "It's the only thing that makes sense. Sybil and Elsie have gone dark, too." Her throat tightened. "What if Seb Grimball had a partner?"

"Someone besides Wade?"

"Although he didn't admit to killing Grimball, it was clear he had."

"Why, I wonder?"

"Maybe he feared Grimball would go after me again."

"Or Grimball got a good look at him in the garden."

"You're determined to paint him as a villain."

"It's a flaw I have when people accept money to kill others."

Her phone chimed. She put the caller on speaker. "What'd you find out, Susannah?"

"Mrs. Krowne booked a first-class flight from Asheville Regional Airport to O'Hare International," Jillian's assistant confirmed, "but the airline has no record of her boarding."

The phone slipped from Kayla's hand, shattering against the chapel's wooden floor.

54

"WHAT DO YOU NEED US TO DO?" CRUZ ASKED, AFTER ASH finished filling his brothers in on the governor's murder and Seb Grimball, the vandalism to Kayla's vehicle, the blood spatter matching Mason Wade's DNA and his link to Service, and Jillian Krowne's disappearance.

Ash lifted his head from his hands and took in the various expressions on their faces.

Phin paced in front of the Annex's kitchenette, a worried expression replacing the charismatic smile he normally wore. Rohan sat hunched over his laptop, working his hacker magic on the new information Ash just supplied. Cruz leaned back in his chair, hands locked behind his head and one booted foot anchored over a thick thigh. Zeke stood at the end of the table like a thunder-cloud hovering over a city, deciding which meteorological torture device it would unleash on the denizens below.

After Kayla's devastating phone call with her mom's assistant, she'd collapsed in his arms and nothing he said or did had soothed her anguish and fear. So, he proceeded

the only way he knew how. Called in feminine reinforcements.

Liv and the other ladies had swept into the chapel, gathered up an inconsolable Kayla, and marshaled her back to
the Friary. Ash, furious and feeling more helpless than he
ever had in his life, had punched a hole in the pulpit.

A dry voice behind him had said, "You're going to hell
now, brother." Zeke motioned for him to follow. "Come on.
Let's get you bandaged and put your mind to work, rather
than your fists."

That was thirty minutes and two fingers of Defiant ago,
and Ash's helpless rage still simmered in his gut like acid.
"Hell if I know," he said, flexing his bandaged hand. "Everything has hit a dead end, and I have zero leads."

"We have leads," Rohan corrected. "They're just frayed."
He sent Ash a cocky smile.

The sight jolted him. Of all his brothers, Rohan never
displayed what they all knew. He was a bits and bytes
genius. Maybe his recent skirmish with the Collective had
given him an extra boost of empowerment. Ash didn't
begrudge his brother a dash of arrogance. He'd earned it.

Rohan's next words confirmed his suspicions. "I like
frayed."

Hope speared through his chest for the first time since
he lost Wade to the wind. Yet he couldn't just sit here and
watch Rohan dig up something actionable.

Kayla's tear-streaked face rocketed through his mind,
and he surged to his feet. "I need to check on Kayla. She
won't be weak with grief for long."

"Kayla is in good hands," Zeke said, still thundering at
the end of the table. "Six women who love her are
pampering and listening and doing all the other things

men suck at in these circumstances. We need you here and focused."

"*I am fucking focused!*"

"Easy, buddy." Phin appeared before him and placed a hand on his shoulder. "In this, I have to agree with Mr. Sensitive. Your mind is stuck in a loop of how you could have done things differently, how you could've prevented Jillian's disappearance." He nodded to the room at large. "We've all been there in the past couple years." His voice lowered for Ash's ears only. "It's what happens when the woman you love is hurting."

Ash raised his burning eyes and met each man's gaze, ending with his youngest brother's. Love for these turds filled the aching hollowness he'd been living with since the moment he announced accepting a position with the FBI. Today, for the first time in years, he felt like a Blackwell again. "When did you grow up, you little shit?"

Phin laughed and rumpled his hair like Ash used to do to him two-and-half decades ago. "Time to get to work, loverboy."

Ash lifted a brow in Rohan's direction. "Got a connection yet to any of those frayed ends?"

Rohan's eyes gleamed their triumph. "Does Phin wear pressed T-shirts?"

55

"I'M GOING TO RIP THEIR BALLS OFF AND HANG THEM FROM MY bumper," Kayla threatened as she paced before the massive fireplace. If she could reach it, she'd draw Lupos from its iron perch and begin the maiming now. If only she had a specific target on which to direct her ire.

Then she remembered who was in the room. "Sorry, Grams."

"You are in a circle of trust." The Diné woman smiled. "I've wanted to snip a few achó bizis in my time."

Unaccountably, the backs of Kayla's eyes burned. All six women were positioned in a semicircle around her, with Lupos at her back.

Lupus. Wolf.

Weren't most wolf packs guarded, at least in part, by an Alpha or breeding female? Their show of sisterhood drained the fury from her heart. But not her determination.

After her warrior angels had marched her back to the Friary, they'd supplied her with tissues and plied her with wine until her tears had dried up.

No judgment. No false platitudes.

Only patience and understanding and strength. The realization that they would make amazing members of Service whispered through her mind.

"Tell us what you know, child," Grams said, as if sensing her mental shift.

Kayla laid out every detail to these women, even the smaller bits that she hadn't yet shared with Ash. She told them about Tommy the activist and her guilt for the way she'd treated Natalie after hearing about her relationship with Kayla's college nemesis.

"Alexander Brighton," Liv said. "There's a name I'd hoped to never hear again."

Thank heavens Liv was on the same page. She didn't know what she'd do if Liv started spouting off about how people could change. Kayla knew this. She'd evolved over the years.

But Alexander Brighton would always be a dick in her book.

"A coincidence is a term our emotional side uses to justify our lack of action," Cilla said, referring to the profane markings on Kayla's vehicles, both past and present. "Your initial gut reaction to this guy showing up in Natalie's life has merit."

"What happened to him after you reported the vandalism?" Maddy asked.

"Nothing. His father, a former senator, made the incident go away."

"Former?"

"Unfortunately for Mr. Brighton, his response to his son's juvenile stunt triggered my activism gene. He lost his reelection campaign."

"Damn, girl." Lena smiled. "Glad you're on our team."

"Everything has consequences. Even so-called righteous actions."

Noticing everyone's confused expressions, Liv jumped in. "The family's finances collapsed, and Alexander didn't return for his senior year."

"Alexander might feel he has a score to settle," Maddy said. "Natalie falls in love with him, putting your friendship and your firm at risk."

"And kidnapping your mother," Lena added.

"But why now? All that happened fourteen years ago. And how is this linked to Vicky's murder?"

"Maybe it's not," Cilla said. "They could be separate incidents."

"That's a lot of bad luck in such a short amount of time," Maddy said.

"Vicky was your godmother," Liv said. "Another person close to you and someone who advanced your political ideals."

"But Mason all but confirmed Seb Grimball killed Vicky."

"Can you one hundred percent trust what Mason Wade told you?" Lynette challenged. "Should you?"

Kayla crossed her right arm over her middle and planted her left elbow on top, allowing her to drive her fingertips into her forehead. In the political arena, she thrived on strategizing offensive maneuvers to their opponents' various points of attack. Loved anticipating their movements and delighted in their resulting failures.

But with this living nightmare, she couldn't identify the enemy with any certainty and therefore wasn't able to develop a counterattack plan.

Liv approached and placed a warm palm on her shoulder. "How about we take this one step at a time?"

"That's the thing," Kayla said, her voice raw. "I don't know which direction to go first. There seems to be an infinite number of options."

Lena appeared on her other side and snaked her arm in the crook of Kayla's. "It's good there are six fabulous brains here to help you figure this out."

She lifted her head, realizing these women weren't here to just help her through a difficult patch. They were here for the long haul.

Emotion garbled her words. "Any suggestions?"

Grams looked at her daughter-in-law. "Clay?"

Lynette clicked her phone to sleep. "Just sent him a text."

"Step taken," Grams said. "Clay will look into this Alexander Brighton's background and see what he says when he thinks no one is listening."

Part of the Rios family, who had kept the estate running well before any Blackwell stepped foot on the property, Clay Neuman had become an essential element of the BARS team by taking over Zeke's duties in the field, allowing the CEO to focus on the administrative side of the multimillion-dollar business.

But what made Neuman even more valuable was his ability to bounce around to different jobs, filling in for the guys at a moment's notice.

Kayla focused on Grams's words, on what she hadn't said, and her stomach twisted. "Does that mean Neuman's going to bug his place?"

"That would be illegal," Grams said.

Which was neither a yes or no.

"I don't want anyone getting in trouble or hurt on my account."

"Your problem is our problem, Kayla Krowne." Steady

brown eyes bored into hers, and Kayla could see the matri-arch's resolve.

"Thank you, Grams."

"Is there anything else we should know?" Lynette asked. "Any other people of interest we should look into?"

There was another name that hovered on the tip of her tongue, but Kayla couldn't bring herself to say it. Not even in this circle of trust.

56

"You want the tech version or the short version?" Rohan asked.

"Dazzle me with your brilliance later," Ash said. "Give it to me short."

"I followed the convoluted trail of hit money to Seb Grimball."

"How convoluted could it be, going to Marion, North Carolina?" Phin asked, referring to the bank account Grimball's so-called brother had opened.

"Marion was the final destination. Getting there was like taking a grand tour through the worldwide banking system."

Impatience pounded through Ash's blood. "Who hired Grimball?"

"A company called Gradient Enterprises."

Recognition flickered in the back of Ash's mind, but he couldn't make the connection.

"The security firm?" Phin asked.

"Among other things," Rohan said.

"Why would Gradient contract a killer with a signature?" Cruz asked. "That's the height of stupidity."

"They knew law enforcement would find the earring, attach it to a known serial killer, and case closed," Zeke said. "They'd say Grimball acted on compulsion. No reason to look any further or excavate his finances, like Rohan did."

Ash clenched his teeth. "We're not all a bunch of bungling idiots, grasping at the first bit of evidence we find."

"If you have such respect for those in your profession, why did you ask for Rohan's help? Why not involve your colleagues?"

"I did, dammit. But the Bureau only has so many analysts and I'm one request in a long queue." He refocused on Rohan. "Who owns Gradient?"

"Evan Barclay."

"Barclay?"

"You know him?" Zeke asked.

His mind whisked back to the night of the governor's murder.

Mr. No-Neck. A friend of the family.

Shit, shit, shit.

Ash closed his eyes and pictured Kayla's expression at the moment she learned one of her beloved aunties was linked to her godmother's murder.

Devastation.

Opening his eyes, he pinned Rohan in place. "You're absolutely certain?"

His brother nodded.

"Sybil Barclay's son. He tried to recruit me the night Stokes was assassinated."

"She's one of the four founders of Service," Zeke said.

"Sybil, Elsie, Jillian, and Victoria," Ash confirmed.

"What would make this Sybil turn against one of her partners?" Phin asked.

"Maybe two partners," Cruz said. "With Jillian missing."

"Kayla said their mission was to place honorable, compassionate, valorous, and strong women in positions of power." His gaze tapped on each of his brothers as possibilities whirled around his mind. "What would drive Sybil to torch such a longstanding association?"

No one had an answer, and the room went silent but for Chris Stapleton's "White Horse" in the background. "I can think of one person who might know," Rohan said, a brow arched in Ash's direction.

Kayla.

"She's already lost her godmother, her mother is missing, and her bodyguard betrayed her. How do I break the news to her about Sybil?"

Zeke slouched back in his chair. "Wasn't it Kayla who recently climbed up my ass about trusting Liv to be strong enough to deal with bad news about her friend?"

"You can hardly compare the two."

"Oh, I can, brother."

Phin chimed in. "Kayla's at her best when she's working a problem. She's probably pulling out her hair right now because she," gleaming teeth flashed at Rohan," has a lot of frayed ends and nothing to grab on to."

"She has the support she needs to survive this," Cruz thumped his index finger against the table, "in here and an even fiercer group inside the Friary."

"She's got eleven semi-intelligent minds focused on this case," Zeke said.

"Semi?" Rohan and Cruz said in unison.

"You can make this promise to her," Zeke continued. "We'll get the bastards behind this. Every single damn one."

"Twelve," Phin said. "Don't forget Neuman."

Ash stared at the grain in the wooden table, overcome by their support. A large hand grasped his right shoulder and another his left. Their strength poured into him, lifting his head, straightening his back.

"Do me a favor," he said to Zeke.

"Name it."

"Figure out how deep this rot goes into Service."

Zeke glanced at the others, who nodded unison. "Consider it done."

Ash stood. "Thank y'all." Then he took the first step on the longest walk of his life.

57

KAYLA BURROWED DEEPER INTO THE VERANDA'S LOUNGE chair and readjusted her cashmere sweater against the evening chill. She smoothed a hand over Crispy's soft back, igniting the feline's internal motor.

After her conversation with the ladies, Kayla was escorted to a beautifully appointed guest room on the first floor by Henri, the Amazon-like woman who took care of the house and gardens.

The calming scents of jasmine and vanilla from a trio of candles inside drifted through the screen door, but Kayla wasn't ready to give up the ghost yet.

Staring at the clear night sky, she noted the constellations Orion and Big Dipper. She couldn't identify any of the others, astronomy not being her strong suit, but she found a strange comfort in the stars. Their familiarity, their consistency, their brightness.

Movement to her left had her upright in a split second. She grasped the edge of the chair, her heart in her throat. An image of her Glock nestled in her handbag on the bed flashed through her mind.

Crispy jerked away, shot toward the narrow opening in the screen door, and disappeared. Evidently her guard cat's territorial instincts had yet to kick in.

"I didn't mean to startle you," Ash said, slowing his approach. "Would you rather be left alone?"

She settled back, unaccountably happy to see him. "No, please sit with me. I feel like I'm going to burst from my skin."

He eased his large frame onto the adjacent lounger. Rather than lie back, he sat facing her, a troubled expression on his handsome face.

"I understand the feeling." He reached for her hand, where it still gripped the lounger's frame. "The ladies took good care of you?"

She nodded. "They're a formidable bunch."

The deep lines in his forehead softened. "They are."

Several seconds passed, and she watched burrows return to his forehead.

"What's wrong?"

His free hand covered their clasped hands and his gaze fell to the mound of digits. A low, hard thud of anxiety reverberated in her chest, and she found herself sitting up again and turning to face him.

"What is it?"

The audible click of his swallow confirmed her fear. He had more unwelcome news and didn't want to or didn't know how to tell her.

"It's okay, Ash. You can tell me." This time she swallowed hard. "No matter how terrible the information."

Five, four, three, two—

"Rohan figured out who hired Seb Grimball to kill the governor."

"Who?" she whispered, hoping Mason's accusation about Service was wrong.

"A company called Gradient Enterprises."

Kayla released a pent-up breath and she nearly collapsed against the weight of her relief. But then a pinprick of memory caught her attention, blossomed into a fully-realized conversation.

With Sybil.

About her son.

58

ASH SAW THE MOMENT KAYLA CONNECTED SYBIL TO Gradient Enterprises and what that meant.

All the color leached from her face and her breathing became more labored. Then she did something surprising.

Rather than rail at the Almighty or break into tears or isolate herself, she lifted her chin and stared into the night sky. She said nothing for several long seconds and soon her breathing returned to its normal rhythm and color entered her cheeks.

"You're sure?" she asked into the silence.

"Positive." He tried to catch her eye, but her gaze remained heavenward. "Can you think of any reason why Sybil would want the governor dead?"

"Dead? No. Removed from office, maybe."

"Tell me."

"One of the reasons people loved Vicky and why she made such an effective governor was her ability to mediate difficult issues. She could find that happy medium where both sides of the aisle felt as though they not only won, but also stuck it to the other side."

"Sounds like an impossible feat."

"For many in the political arena, it was. But not Vicky." Her gaze slid from the diamonds sparkling above to focus on him. "It was a gift that oftentimes put her in conflict with Service's tenets."

"Which are?"

"Service sees itself as a warrior against corruption— and, historically, men have been the corruptors, the polluters of society."

"Let me guess. Victoria worked well with men as well as women to get the job done."

She nodded. "Sybil and Vicky had been butting heads more and more lately. Sybil became vocal about her opposition to Vicky negotiating deals with the Senate leader and Speaker of the House, both of whom are men."

"Every negotiation strengthened Victoria's position, but also the State's male leadership."

"Exactly. Service has been working behind the scenes to position two women who could assume those leadership roles."

"But they won't get the votes if their male colleagues are bringing in the wins and getting the job done."

"Why upset the apple cart if all the apples are unblemished?"

"HCVS wasn't willing to wait out the three years remaining on the governor's term."

"Not HCVS," she said with uncharacteristic roughness. "Despite appearances, Service is responsible for some amazing political, social, and moral transformations around the world." Grief filled her voice. "If Sybil is responsible for Vicky's murder and my mother's disappearance, she's gone rogue. I guarantee you that her actions have not been sanctioned by Service. We don't do violence, especially against our own, to accomplish our goals."

If Service was as big and wide-ranging as Kayla led him to believe, it wouldn't be unheard of for a small faction to lose faith in the organization's methods and strike out on their own. Was Sybil acting alone? Or were there others in this region who shared her desire for a more expedient resolution to the Vicky problem?

Could Jillian Krowne's disappearance be of her own doing?

Kayla shot off her lounge chair. "I can't sit here and do nothing." She stormed into her suite, and Ash followed.

"What does that mean?"

"I'm going to see Sybil. Confront her with our findings."

"If she confesses, then what?"

"I'll demand she turn herself in."

"You think she'll go along with your plan? This is the woman whose son can mobilize an army of trained killers."

"Sybil used to change my diapers. She's not going to hurt me."

"She may have ordered her best friend's death. If so, what do you think she'll do when she's desperate and backed into a corner?"

"I guess you'll have to come with me." She pulled a Glock from her handbag, checked the chamber and mag like a pro, and tried for a smile. "Two guns are better than one, I hear."

59

"Turn into the gravel lot." Kayla pointed to the right, toward the small three-car space not far from Sybil Barclay's home. It was one of four trailhead lots in the expansive mountainside subdivision, where residents and their guests could pick up the six-mile loop trail.

Ash killed the engine. "What are you plotting?"

"About three-quarters of a mile down the trail, a foot-path leads up the ridge to Sybil's backyard."

Many of the homeowners whose land backed up to the trail had created spurs for quick access. Some even went so far as to put signs with their family name inscribed on it at the intersection, demarcating the footpath as private.

"Want to tell me why we're visiting Sybil through the rear gate?" he asked as they exited the vehicle.

Stepping out of the quiet SUV and into the concert arena of a thousand screaming insects forced Kayla to adjust the volume of her voice. "She has a guesthouse on the property. It's secluded and easily protected."

"A place to hold your mom?"

"Maybe. I don't know. I'm still not convinced Sybil had

anything to do with all of this. But I'm pragmatic enough to realize that if she is guilty of murder and kidnapping, one of the most likely places she could stash Mom would be her guesthouse."

Kayla didn't allow herself to consider why Sybil would hide Jillian away rather than kill her, like Vicky.

"Let's take a look." Ash opened the liftgate of his SUV and handed her a Maglite after replacing the clear lens with a red one. "This reduces our chances of being detected and preserves our night vision." He lifted a tactical belt weighted down by extra magazines and a large knife from a bin and fastened it around his hips.

The sight made Kayla long for her armored vest, though she took comfort in the handgun cradled at the V of her lower back and the extra clip shoved in her back pocket.

"Don't forget to silence your phone," he said.

"Already done."

He closed the liftgate. "Ready?"

She nodded, and they set off down the trail.

The loud crunch of their shoes against the gravel did nothing to muffle the crickets who seemed to be following them. As it turned out, a half-moon lit up the forest, making their flashlights unnecessary.

Five minutes into their hike, Ash wove his fingers between hers. "We need to keep an eye out for black bears. This is about the time they emerge from their dens."

His warning conjured images of the many photos Sybil had taken of bears in her yard over the years. Although black bear attacks against humans were rare, they did occur, especially when mama bear felt her cubs were in danger. And this time of the year was prime baby season.

Rather than worrying about running into wildlife,

Kayla focused on the warmth of Ash's hand. She took comfort from his strength and solid presence at her side. Other than his verbal skirmishes with Zeke—and her—he was one of the most steady, unflappable people she knew.

Whatever awaited them at the top of the hill, they would get through it together.

From the base of the spur to where it terminated at the back of Sybil's lot, the elevation rose a hundred and fifty calf-burning feet. They crouched behind a set of landscape boulders to catch their breath and give Ash a chance to catalogue his surroundings. Kayla had been here so often she could practically sleepwalk her way around the property.

To their right, about twenty feet from the main house, sat Sybil's two-thousand-square-foot guesthouse and a much smaller toolshed.

The guesthouse's stone and lumber façade was a near replica of her aunt's home. None of the exterior lights were on, which was odd, and the interior was dark but for the upper story bedroom and bathroom combo. She watched the curtained window for a familiar feminine silhouette, but Jillian never appeared.

"There's a guard at the rear door," Ash whispered.

Kayla dropped her gaze. For a moment, she saw only a deep penetrating darkness. Nothing distinct. Until a slight movement separated one shadow from the rest.

The man was massive and he appeared to be kitted out as if he were in a war zone. Kayla's heart *thunked* in the well of her chest. He was guarding someone or something important inside that building.

"Stay here," Ash said.

"Where are you going?"

"To see how many guards are around front."

"What does it matter?" She pointed at the guard's long gun. "We won't get within ten feet of the building without being mowed down."

"I like to know what I'm up against." He gave her a side-long glance. "I don't suppose you'll hike back to the vehicle while I assess things here."

"Not a chance."

He clipped her chin between his thumb and forefinger. "Do not move from this space, no matter what you see or hear." He pressed his lips to hers. "Promise me."

"Too many variables, Agent." She plucked his fingers from her chin and kissed his knuckles. "Hurry back."

"A dozen hairs on my head just turned bone white." He squeezed her hand in reassurance. "Stay low."

She watched him melt into the forest before returning her attention to the guesthouse. The light remained on upstairs. Still no signs of life.

Her back pocket vibrated, and Kayla backed down the hill until she could no longer see the house. Only then did she pull out her phone, dim the display light, and check her text message.

Liv: where'd you go?

Her BFF must have visited her suite and found it empty.

Kayla: To confront Sybil about Rohan's findings.

Liv: ur joking

Kayla: Snuck in back way.

Liv: ash with u?

Kayla: Yes. Armed guard outside guesthouse.

Liv: wtf

Kayla: Protecting something? Or keeping someone inside. Mom?

Liv: where's ash?

Kayla: Doing recon.

Liv: zeke's going to blow a gasket.
Kayla: I had to come.
Liv: i know but still don't like. stay safe. keep me updated.
Kayla: Will do.

She slid the phone into her pocket and scrabbled back to her hiding spot to keep watch. What she saw stopped her heart mid-beat.

A light now illuminated much of the downstairs and a dark-haired woman dressed in red silk pajamas and matching robe opened the slider.

She knew that face. She knew those PJs.

"Mama."

Tears gathered in the corners of Kayla's eyes at the sight of her uninjured mother. The urge to call out to her vibrated through every sinew in her body, but she tamped down her heart's desire to give her brain the airspace to think.

She would shoot Ash a text, confirming her mother's presence. Together, they would develop a plan for freeing her. Once they secured Jillian, she would call her father and let him know they were bringing her home.

The process to create her mental to-do list took no more than three seconds. Long enough for the guard to leave his station and move to the open door where his prisoner stood.

He said something to Jillian, and she laughed.

Kayla's hand paused in the act of reaching for her phone.

Laughed?

Instead of keeping her prisoner, the guard was there for her protection. *Why?*

The sour taste of betrayal climbed up Kayla's throat.

"No, Mama," she whispered. "Not you, too."

60

ASH PICKED HIS WAY BETWEEN THICK, MATURE TREES AND thin, wispy saplings. As he drew parallel to the front of the guesthouse, he searched for a place to exit without having to lose a layer of skin to the jungle of raspberry bushes at the forest's edge.

His luck proved to be frog shit. A thick perimeter of briars stood between him and a clear view of the house.

"This is going to suck," he said beneath his breath. He'd be pulling thorn tips out of his thighs for the next two weeks.

Filling his lungs with air, he plowed through the spindly plants, stepping on the ones he could and enduring the stab-slice of the ones he couldn't. The sound of fabric ripping marked his progress. He held his breath as he pushed through the last of them and that's when a long, hooked barb caught the tender flesh of his inner thigh and clung *tight*.

He stopped, barely holding back the curse that erupted into his throat. Reaching down, he disengaged the thorn, leaving a stinging—no doubt bloody—wound behind.

Clear of nature's torture chamber, he took a knee behind an Adirondack chair, one of six encircling a stone firepit. From this vantage point, he could see both the mansion and guesthouse. An armed guard stood sentinel near the smaller building's front entrance, while another peeled away to walk a surveillance round.

Ash noted the time, then scanned the entire backside of the main house for more guards, but detected none. Interesting.

The security detail wasn't here to protect Sybil, but to secure whoever was inside the guesthouse. The ache deep in his bones told him all he needed to know. Kayla had hit the target.

Jillian Krowne was inside.

Now he had to figure out how to free the elder Krowne while ensuring the younger one didn't jump into the fray and get herself killed.

He wished Zeke was here. His brother would've figured out the best path forward in two blinks of an eye. No matter how well Ash had planned out their projects, some unforeseen variable on-site would always blast his plan to smithereens. Zeke's quick thinking and ability to pivot on a dime had saved their bacons more than once.

A keen sense of loss barreled through his chest. He absorbed the impact, took the punishment, then refocused on the problem at hand. Zeke wasn't here, so Ash would have to depend on his own instincts tonight.

The surveilling guard returned, and Ash clocked the time it had taken him to make the full circuit. Another timer ticked in his mind, letting him know he needed to get back to Kayla. He didn't trust the headstrong lobbyist to stay put for long.

Gritting his teeth, he backed toward the tree line and

steeled himself for the swath of pain. Before his boot could ease into the briars, something hard dug into the back of his head.

"Toss your weapon," a no-nonsense male voice said. "Nice and slow."

Sonofabitch.

Certain the dense, thorny perimeter would alert him to anyone sneaking up behind him, he'd kept his senses focused forward. There must have been an opening farther down, because there was no way anyone could have traversed those raspberry bushes without him hearing, no matter how preoccupied he'd been.

The gun barrel jabbed at his head. "Toss your weapon, down on your knees, hands over head."

Alerted to an intruder, one of the guesthouse guards stormed toward them.

Great. Double the fun.

In a lightning move, Ash dropped low and kicked out. The guard behind him stumbled against the impact and crashed into the brambles. Thorny claws sank into his clothes, into his flesh in a thousand different places, holding him immobile but for his hands. The ones holding his assault rifle.

Ash dove to the side as bullets sprayed in an arc toward him. He scrambled for cover behind a giant oak tree and raised his pistol to the second guard. Rather than aiming for center mass, he took his time and targeted a knee-cap. He pulled the trigger and the guard went down, screaming in pain.

The first guard tore his way out of the raspberry bushes and rolled behind the stone firepit. Chunks of wood splintered off Ash's oak tree. He paused, then slammed three bullets into the stacked stones near the shooter's head.

A muffled curse echoed across the lawn, indicating a shard of stone had hit its mark. The guard was injured but not down.

Ash shoved away from the tree, running as hard and zigzag as he could toward Kayla's location. As much as it burned his gut, he'd grab Kayla, retreat to safety, and come back with more guns and shields.

But when he arrived at the boulder where he'd left Kayla, she was gone.

61

Kayla's hold around the flashlight Ash had given her firmed as she inched closer to where the guard and her mother stood chatting like old pals.

Jillian leaned one shoulder against the slider's door frame, her hands shoved deep into her robe's pockets to presumably ward off the chill creeping steadily into the night.

When the first gunshots rippled through the air, two thoughts *whooshed* through her mind in quick succession. One—*dammit.* She'd been less than three feet from the guard's unprotected back. Two—*Ash.* The latter thought had paralyzed her long enough for the guard's sixth sense to kick in.

He whipped around, his eyes widening at her close proximity. Then he raised his rifle toward her chest. Kayla struck out, hitting the long barrel with the flashlight and knocking the business end away from her.

A dull thud registered, freezing her hand as she reached for her handgun. The guard's body convulsed. His eyes rolled back in his head and his knees buckled.

Above him, Jillian stood as regal as ever, brandishing a metal meat tenderizer. "They removed all the knives, but left this." She rocked the hammer-like kitchen utensil back and forth. "Sloppy."

The guard rallied, sliding a serrated knife from a sheath strapped around his leg. Before he could free it, Kayla put the flashlight to use again and finished the meat tenderizer's job.

When he lay prone and bleeding between them, Kayla shared a smile with her mother. Until she recalled how friendly Jillian had been with her so-called captor.

"What's going on here, Mom?"

"Helping you rescue me, of course."

"I don't mean this." She swept a hand over the unmoving guard. "Why are you hiding out in Aunt Sybil's guesthouse?"

Jillian frowned. "Hiding out?" Something caught her eye and she sucked in a sharp breath before ordering, "Get inside!"

Kayla detected rapid movement in her peripheral vision. She reached for the handgun stuffed in the back of her jeans at the same time she flicked on the flashlight.

Rather than the bright, blinding beam she'd anticipated, a red glow lit up the guard. Ash's night vision saver.

Even so, the guy ground to a halt, throwing an arm up to protect his eyes. "Kayla, it's me."

Ash.

She immediately lowered the gun and flashlight. A tremor took root in the center of her stomach and worked its way through her body, until it reached her hand. Slowly, carefully, she slid the pistol into the back of her pants before she lost all motor coordination.

She'd almost shot him. A half-second away from

squeezing the trigger and shattering a man's life. Not just any man.

Ash.

"You had a gun and you chose to attack my guard with a flashlight instead?" Jillian said, oblivious to or blatantly ignoring the near calamity right beneath her nose.

Kayla peeled her burning gaze from Ash to address her mother. "Do I look like a guns-blazing kind of gal?" The words shook from her mouth, echoing the tremors she couldn't get under control.

Jillian sent her a warm, reassuring smile. "No, sweetheart, you don't."

Realization of what her mother was trying to do came to her by slow degrees, as if each neuron had to slog through thick gel before making a synaptic connection. Once she understood, Kayla tried to send her an answering thank-you, but her chin wobbled instead.

"Come on," Ash said, holding his hand out to Kayla, "we need to get out of here. The guards won't stay incapacitated for long."

Kayla looked back at the beautiful woman still standing in the slider door frame. She didn't know what to make of her mother being here, but she knew she couldn't leave her behind.

Lifting an outstretched hand, she said, "Mama?"

Jillian hesitated the slightest bit before clasping tight to Kayla's hand.

She turned back to Ash and nodded, just as another guard rounded the corner of the house and fired off a shot.

Ash's body bucked, then he slipped from her fingers.

62

THE BULLET SLAMMED INTO ASH'S SHOULDER WITH THE force of Drago's knockout punch.

Using his temporary imbalance as leverage, a small hand shoved him down before he could gather himself enough to return fire.

"Get down," Kayla yelled, and Jillian Krowne dropped to the ground beside him.

Two succinct, controlled reports splintered the air, and Ash twisted around in time to see the guard who'd shot him fall. Kayla stood in front of him, arm extended, weapon pointing in the direction of the downed guard. A warrior protecting her teammate.

He pushed himself into a sitting position, transferring his pistol to his left hand. The weight didn't feel foreign in his nondominant hand. He always made a point of shooting with both at the range. His forethought would pay off tonight.

A quick inspection revealed that the bullet had entered and exited his shoulder. Rather than the intense, gut-clenching pain he expected, the gunshot wound burned, deep and radiant.

"How bad is the damage?" Kayla asked, her breathing rapid but steady. Her attention shifted from one corner of the house to the other, constantly scanning the area for more armed men.

He reached behind his shoulder, fingering the coin-sized hole. "It's a clean exit."

"Mom, grab a couple kitchen towels to staunch the bleeding."

Jillian didn't balk at receiving orders from her daughter. She simply jumped to her slippered feet and ran inside.

"Can you walk?" Kayla asked, glancing at him for the first time.

"We'll soon find out." Ash climbed to his knees, then his feet. A surge of lightheadedness hit him at the same time Jillian reemerged.

But she wasn't alone.

Ash and Kayla swung their weapons toward the new threat. Out from behind Jillian, rose another guard. The guy was massive. His shoulder width nearly twice that of his captive's. Even with the light behind him, Ash could feel the heat of the man's gaze.

An older woman shouldered past Jillian and her guard and glided across the stone patio toward Ash and Kayla's location.

"Stop," Ash commanded.

The woman took two more steps to establish dominance of the situation, then clasped her hands before her.

He forced himself to keep his eyes forward, to not check Kayla's reaction to this reality that would no doubt eclipse her worst fears.

"You too, Aunt Elsie?" Kayla asked, horror dripped from every word.

"Too?" Elsie produced a slow, satisfied smile. "Me, my dearest Kayla. *Me.*"

63

As if a celestial being reached out of the sky, cracked open Kayla's skull, and used their little pinky to whisk her brain, Kayla could only conjure one word. "You?"

Elsie Hinshaw tossed a disgusted look over her shoulder at Jillian. "Some people don't have the mettle to do what needs to be done."

"Murder is never the answer," Jillian said. "It's not the Service way."

"The Service way is like pitting a slingshot up against an armored tank." Elsie, sweet Elsie, the woman who'd taught Kayla how to play Zelda and intervened when a pair of older girls attempted to steal her new bracelet, curled her fingers into fists, and her features contorted into anger. "No more losing ground because our tactics weren't tough enough. We will become the tank that mows over the rock slinger."

"What happened to you?" Kayla asked, unable to keep the strain of shock out of her voice. "You've become the very thing we've been fighting to suppress."

"Diplomacy and fair play would take us another life-time to accomplish all we desire. We need results now." Elsie eyed Ash with hatred. "Or men like him will pull the world into another war and, before you know it, they'll chase women out of the boardrooms and back into the kitchens."

Kayla's arm trembled with the effort to hold up her gun. "You're wrong. Men like Asher Blackwell are honorable, compassionate, valorous, and strong. The exact type of man our leaders need at their sides."

"Why? So they can watch for our weaknesses, then use them against us? Or sabotage us in order to take over our positions?" Elsie shook her head as if disappointed. "What happened to the young initiate who wanted women to rule the world?"

Kayla recalled the bold statement she'd made to her mom and aunties over booze and cards not long after she'd taken her oath to uphold Service's tenets.

Watch out boys. It's our time.

"Not rule the world," an older, wiser Kayla clarified. "Guide it with people who'll do the right thing even if it's the harder option. Men just so happen to have been bloody awful at it for the past three millennia."

"Exactly why we need to take more drastic measures now. In case you hadn't heard, we have only a handful of years left to reverse a million greedy decisions before this world becomes uninhabitable. I'm not going to let a few doctrines that four idealistic twenty-somethings devised stop me from protecting my grandchildren's future."

"You killed your friend to avert the climate crisis?" Ash inserted, skepticism dripping from his words.

Kayla had never known Elsie to be a proponent for the

environment, so her explanation fell flat. From a big-picture view, though, Kayla could empathize with the woman's logic.

Over the years, she had come up against political resistance that had nothing to do with the issue and everything to do with the candidate's reelection. Watching an important issue become a sacrifice to a politician's campaign agenda had been disheartening and, oftentimes, infuriating.

More than once, the thought had crossed her mind to combat politicians' machinations with a more direct, heavy-handed approach in order to accomplish a Service goal. She'd certainly skirted the line of ethical and nonethical, as with the case of the Irish artifact. But at her core, she believed in doing things the right way, the honorable way. No matter how many future headaches it produced.

"The climate crisis is just one issue of many on the cusp of imploding." Elsie clicked them off on her fingers. "Immigration, inflation, gun violence, tribal rights, racism, partisan cooperation, veteran benefits and reacclimation, health care costs. The list is endless."

"Bulldozing your ideology will only add fuel to extremists' propaganda," Kayla said. "You might achieve short-term wins, but the big important battles will always be out of your reach."

"Enough talk." Elsie held up both hands, flicking her forefingers in a silent *come here* command.

Ash whipped around, but not in time. Two additional guards appeared out of the shadows. One kicked Ash's arm with such force that his pistol went flying. The bastard followed the explosive move with a hard barrel stab into Ash's wounded shoulder.

A pained grunt *whooshed* from his throat, and he crashed to the ground. "Not. Again," he wheezed.

The other guard stormed toward Kayla, his assault rifle anchored against his shoulder and a red dot sighted on her chest. "Drop your weapon," he ordered.

Kayla's heart shook inside her chest, but she refused to lower her Glock. The black-clad guard stood eight feet from her, terrifying in his size and ferocity.

"Do as you're told, Kayla," Elsie said in a calm voice. "Or I shall have to instruct Marco to break your mother's fingers, one by one."

"You wouldn't dare." Even as the words left her mouth, Kayla realized this new Elsie would not only do it, but might even relish making an example of Jillian.

She glanced at Ash, and he nodded, as he slowly climbed to his feet. After ejecting the round in the chamber and pulling the magazine, she tossed her weapon and experienced an overwhelming sense of vulnerability.

Elsie said, "Get them inside the guesthouse and prepare them."

"Prepare us for what?" Jillian asked.

"For the tragic fire that will consume your bodies."

Jillian lunged for her old friend, but the large guard near her grasped her upper arm and dragged her toward the house.

"Elsie, you're insane!" Jillian screamed. "Don't do this."

Ignoring her, Elsie assessed Ash. "Change of plan for this one. Forensics will flag the bullet wound." She motioned to the man flanking Ash. "Do you have a suppressor?"

"Yes, ma'am."

"Take him down the mountain and bury him in a back

lot of one of my neighbors. Most of them live here part-time, so they've probably gone home for the week. Stay clear of the trail. I don't want his grave discovered by a curious dog walker."

Ash took a swing at his guard, but the contract killer had anticipated his move. He ducked to the side, then trained his red dot on Ash's forehead.

"Stop!" Kayla yelled, throwing herself in front of Ash.

He bearhugged her and swung her around, putting himself between her and the bullet. She struggled against his hold, not realizing she was crying until his thumb brushed against her wet cheek.

"Do you trust me?" he whispered.

She continued to squirm, terror for his safety deafening her.

He cupped her cheek, stilling her. "Do you trust me?"

"Y-yes."

"Go inside. Watch over your mom. I'll be back. Promise."

The guards wrenched them apart and zip-tied Ash's hands behind his back. The awful reality of their situation sank deep into Kayla's bones and melted her marrow. This might be the last time she saw him.

"Aunt Elsie," she pleaded. "This isn't you. You're not a killer."

The older woman smiled, and Kayla's heart shrank to the size of a raisin.

"I am more me now than I've been in nearly three decades." A line of perfect white teeth appeared, and her head tilted like a female praying mantis seconds before she chomped into her lover's head. "Did you never wonder about Vin's sudden change of heart?"

Confused by the shift, Kayla responded like an automaton. "He wasn't ready for marriage yet." Vincent Bonetti had been her first love. The only man before Ash that she imagined a future with. But once they started looking at rings, he all but disappeared.

"If that were true, why didn't he stick around until he was ready to commit?"

Kayla stared at her aunt, prepared for another emotional apocalypse.

"You stupid, naive girl. Your precious Vin wanted the multi-six-figure CFO position. I"—her pink-painted forefinger tapped her chest—"offered him more than he wanted you." She jabbed the finger in Kayla's direction.

Sadness blurred her vision. Not for losing Vin. She'd washed him from her life years ago. But for losing the people she used to know, like her aunties and Mason. "Why would you interfere in my private life?"

"When you started talking about rings, I knew I had to do something. Husband, children, career—too many distractions. Service needed your lobbying firm. We didn't need the others, so I cut them out before they bloomed."

Kayla was going to be sick. How could she have not seen this *other* Elsie? Was this how wives of serial killers felt when their husbands were caught? Was Elsie a psychopath? Or was she like most people who get too much power and begin thinking they're gods? Above the law?

She'd figure out the psychology of it later. Right now, she had a burning question in need of extinguishing. "Vicky's husband. Was he a distraction, too?"

Elsie smiled.

Emotion roughened her voice. "And Linda. Were you the one feeding her vitriol about her mother?"

"Can't take credit for the daughter. Sybil had fun with that one."

"How else does Sybil play into all of this?"

"No 'auntie' for us anymore?"

Kayla said nothing. Simply stared at the creature who was ripping out her heart with every word she uttered.

Elsie sighed. "Sybil started out promising. On board with my plan until it became obvious that Jillian suspected us of killing Victoria." She glanced back at the building where Jillian was imprisoned. "Losing Jill was one too many friends, I guess."

"Why did you kill Vicky?"

"She'd lost her way."

"Because of her working relationship with the Assembly's male leadership?"

"Men should've lost their right to lead decades ago, but the majority of the voting public cannot reason for themselves."

"Aren't you the one who put Vin in a CFO position?"

"Temporary, my dear. I fired him a year later for embezzlement."

"Evidence, no doubt, fabricated by you."

"No doubt."

Disgust and anger overrode her sadness. "Where's Sybil?"

"Snoozing away in her mansion. She'll be quite shocked when the drug wears off and she finds first responders swarming her property to put out a flame she set."

Kayla took in the armed contractors. "Evan Barclay won't let his men help you frame his mother for murder."

Elsie laughed. "Do you think I'm stupid enough to use Evan's men for this project?" She shook her head. "Tell me, does knowing all of this bring you comfort?"

"The only thing that will bring me comfort is shredding your *plan* and watching your face as you're sentenced to a lifetime in prison."

All humor fled the older woman's face, and she stepped close enough for Kayla to feel the hot vapor of her breath. "I was going to be merciful to you and Jill. Now, you will feel the flames licking your skin while you roast."

64

Ash accompanied his would-be killers deep into the forest.

Every so often, he would spot a flickering light through the new spring leaves.

Sybil's neighbors.

Which lot would these former commandos choose for his gravesite? How the hell would he get out of this, unarmed?

They'd packed his wound with hemostatic gauze to staunch the blood loss. Not out of compassion, but to prevent a blood trail that the authorities could follow. But the damage was done. He'd already lost a couple pints before they'd performed first aid.

Sweat pebbled his brow and ran down the center of his back. Every other step was a lesson in maintaining his balance and not heaving up his guts. Before long, his blood pressure would drop low enough to force him into blackout mode.

The scene at the guesthouse swept through his thoughts. Kayla had been engaged before. Did she still love him—Vin? Instead of jealousy, he felt sick for her. So many betrayals, so much pain.

He vowed, then and there, to spend the rest of his life making her feel safe, loved.

For a time, they traveled down the same trail he and Kayla had used earlier before veering off. He had trouble keeping his eyes open and worried he wouldn't be able to find his way back to Sybil's once he shucked himself free of these assholes.

If he shucked them. His confidence was withering with each labored breath. Grams's words from years ago whispered in his ear.

Negative energy attracts negative outcomes.

He'd first heard her wise words his freshman year of high school, when she'd found him sitting atop a picnic bench in Barron's Park, red-faced and alone.

"What's wrong?" Grams had asked on that long-ago day.

"I'm too small for football."

"Where is this written?"

"Nowhere. You just have to look at the other guys in my class."

"Do those big boys have the legs of a mustang and the heart of a wolf?"

He shrugged.

"You do."

Ash lifted his head and stared into her fierce brown eyes. Warmth filled his narrow chest, until an image of Freddy Molenski's beefy arms slamming him to the ground and his three massive friends piling on top of him surfaced. "Doesn't matter. They'll turn me into a hamburger patty."

Grams placed a finger beneath his chin and lifted. "Not if you *fly,* she'ashkii yázhi."

He'd gone on to be the fastest, most capable cornerback on the team for four straight years.

Now, Ash's drooping shoulders eased into the upright position. He had a promise to keep. Return, and get Kayla and Jillian to safety. Then he would make Elsie pay for putting terror in his lover's eyes.

His thoughts shifted from cataloging his limitations to formulating an escape plan. He flipped through scenarios like an eager shopper scrolling through an online store for the right gym shorts.

He thought about what his brothers would do if they were trapped in this situation. Zeke and Cruz would rush in and flatten anyone in their path. Phin would charm his way out of it by connecting with them on a personal level. Rohan would use specially made glasses to guide an armed drone into their midst and blast them to smithereens.

Maybe Ash could—

"Hold up," one of his executioners ordered.

He complied, a heavy dread filling his chest. He glanced around for possible weapons, but they'd picked their kill spot well. Except for several inches of decaying leaves and mounded burrows, the forest floor was clear of potential weapons. No fallen branches, no random rocks. Not even a thorny raspberry bush.

Outside of a large tree that had uprooted decades ago, there was no available cover nearby. The trees were small and uniform in diameter, indicating the area had been logged, probably within the past twenty years.

Leaves crackled behind him a second before cold metal raked against his inner wrist. The zip tie fell away.

Surprised, he whirled around, then had to throw his arms out to counteract a wave of dizziness that nearly dropped him face-first. He blinked several times to bring the two black-clad figures into focus.

Something heavy thudded at his feet. He looked down.

A shovel.

"Get digging, dead man."

Digging a hole would sap the last of his strength, the last of his hope for escape. He channeled Phin. "I'm an FBI agent, trying to protect American citizens. Same as you, when you were in the military."

They lifted their rifles from the low ready position. Two red dots crawled up his body, then pulsed against his chest.

"Dig," the guard on the left repeated.

So much for establishing a personal connection.

Ash's hands curled into fists, as he stared down the two hired guns.

In unison, they moved into a shooting stance. One leg braced behind the other. Rifle buttstock to shoulder. Upper body slightly forward.

Drawing in a breath, he eased his right hand open, bent toward the shovel, and toppled to the ground.

65

"TAKE OFF YOUR CLOTHES."

Kayla stared at the largest of Elsie's henchmen. Fear fluttered at the edge of her consciousness.

Do you trust me?

Ash's words came back to her. He had a plan to get them out of this. She didn't know what it could be though. The odds against his success were astronomical.

But she trusted him to keep his word. Until then, it was her job to make sure Jillian stayed alive. Even if it cost her a piece of her soul.

"Clothes," the guard prompted.

The flutters didn't beat faster. They hardened. Turned poker hot.

Kayla shook her head. "I'm not about to make your job easy, Marco." She braced herself. Waited for him to storm over and strike her or rip away her clothing.

He didn't bother. Didn't need to. With all the exertion of a slug, he strode to where her mother sat on a large, square ottoman and pressed the barrel of his weapon to her temple.

No more commands. Just a hard stare.

Jillian's back was ramrod straight. She didn't flinch, nor did her gray eyes plead with Kayla to comply.

She knew why. Her mother didn't have the benefit of knowing Ash would return to save them. She assumed their fates were sealed and had decided not to let her enemy see the terror that no doubt rippled through her body in ever-increasing waves.

Kayla hated the fact that she couldn't soothe her mother's fears. All she needed was five seconds alone with her, but the chances of that happening were less than zero.

Recalling Elsie's reason for sending Ash into the woods, she said, "Forensics would have a field day with a bullet hole through Jillian Krowne's skull."

Marco's response was so fast, so astonishing, so violent that Kayla didn't realize what had happened until Jillian cried out and crumpled across the ottoman, the skin covering her cheekbone splayed open to the bone.

"You sonafabitch!" Kayla rushed across the room, looking for something to staunch the blood. When nothing appeared, she yanked her cotton top over her head and eased the skin back together before pressing her shirt against the wound. "I'm sorry, Mama. So sorry."

Jillian sat up, holding the blood-soaked shirt to her damaged face. "It's okay, sweetheart. Best do as he says, though."

"Remove your pants." He motioned to a set of royal blue pajamas lying across the back of the sofa. "Put those on."

Kayla locked her jaw before standing and yanking the PJs from their perch. She toed off her shoes, while she unbuttoned her tight-fitted jeans with blood-covered hands. She shimmied free of them, never taking her eyes off the guard.

To his credit, Marco kept his attention on her face. Not once did his gaze drop down to her near nakedness.

If he hadn't just brutalized her mother, she would've taken his consideration as an indicator he still had a smidgeon of honor left that she could appeal to.

"Whatever Elsie's paying you, I'll double it. All you have to do is walk away."

"It don't work like that, lady."

"What doesn't?" She stabbed her hands into the arm holes and dragged the top over her head, not even bothering to unbutton it.

"I have a contract with Ms. Hinshaw. When it's completed, I'll consider your proposal."

"Hard to do if I'm dead."

"Then I won't consider your proposal."

Kayla pulled on the silken bottoms and sat next to Jillian and grasped her hands.

"Now what?"

Elsie entered the guesthouse, carrying a bottle of red wine. "We wait."

"For what?"

The house's open concept allowed Kayla to follow the other woman's movements. She drew two wineglasses from a cabinet, placed them and the bottle onto a large wooden serving tray before taking a seat on the L-shaped sofa behind them.

She slid the tray onto the ottoman. "For word of your lover's death. He's digging his own grave now." She patted the sofa cushion beside her. "Come sit with me."

When Kayla and Jillian ignored her, the guard grasped Jillian's upper arm and hauled her to her feet.

"Don't touch her!" Kayla ordered, shooting to her feet.

She tried to pry his sausage-like fingers from her mother's arm, but they didn't budge. She dove for the wine bottle to use as a weapon. He wouldn't hurt Jillian again. She'd make sure of it.

But Elsie beat her to the bottle. "Not this, dear. It's a special blend."

The guard forced Jillian toward the sofa.

An animal instinct combined with fury combined with one of Liv's self-defense moves exploded from her brain, rushed down her arm, and powered her fist.

She elevated two of her knuckles and drove them into the soft fleshy part at the base of his throat. The gagging sound he emitted was immediate and more gratifying than she'd expected. She wasn't a person who enjoyed inflicting pain, physically or emotionally. But the asshole had laid open her mom's cheek.

Kayla drew Jillian to the side and wrapped her arms around the older woman. She hadn't hurt him enough for them to attempt an escape. He'd be on them before they cleared the door.

Her little rebellion might have accomplished her goal of freeing Jillian from his crushing hold, but she'd likely shifted his transactional mindset to something more personal, something involving pain. When his watery eyes lifted to meet hers, she saw a promise in their hate-filled depths.

A promise of retribution.

Of pleasure.

His.

66

"Get up!"

When the guard's boot connected with his ribs, Ash swung the shovel in a high arc, smashing the blade into the side of the man's head.

He rolled, not waiting for the body to crumble. Bullets sprayed the earth where he'd been seconds before. Rather than flee from the danger, he advanced toward it.

Any sort of cover was too far away. He had one opportunity to take out the second guard. He wouldn't waste this small element of surprise. He plowed into the guard's legs, hooking them with his good shoulder.

They went down, and Ash barely avoided braining himself on the descent. He grappled for the knife sheathed at the guard's thigh. He pulled it free, then something slammed into his wounded shoulder.

His left arm went numb and he dropped the weapon, but his right had tightened around its load. Rearing up, he threw a handful of red dirt from a mounded burrow into the guy's face, peppering his eyes and filling his snarling mouth.

Blinded, the guard knuckled his eyes.

Ash retrieved the knife from the ground and plunged it into his executioner's throat. He stayed suspended over the thrashing body, using his bodyweight to keep the knife in place until silence filled the night again.

Breaths coming hard, Ash collapsed on his back and blinked up at the stars. He soaked in the night sky for a full minute, amazed to still be alive.

His left hand started tingling, and he took that as a sign to get his ass moving again.

Reclaiming his phone, he cursed at the lack of reception. Pocketing his device, he divested the dead guard of his weapons and spare ammunition. Did the same for the unconscious guard, tossing anything he couldn't carry into the forest. Using zip ties he found in one of their pockets, he secured the guard's hands and feet. He'd send law enforcement to retrieve him and his partner's body later.

After getting his bearings, he started the long trek up the mountain. He hoped he could find his way back to Sybil's house.

His internal navigation was normally spot on, but he'd never tested it under the haze of pain and near-unconsciousness. Once he located the loop trail, he was confident he could find the spur leading to Sybil's house.

As long as he didn't black out first.

A SHADOW SHIFTED BEHIND A LARGE, SMOOTH-BARK TULIP tree as the fed trudged by.

The shadow waited to make sure the agent didn't return before pushing away from the protection of the tree. The shadow crept into the clearing and loomed over the two heavily armed idiots who'd managed to lose a bound and wounded man.

One dead.

One beginning to stir.

The shadow lifted the suppressed rifle from low ready position.

Pulled the trigger. Once. Twice.

The shadow turned and followed in the agent's wake.

67

THE LARGE GUARD GLANCED AT HIS WATCH, THEN ANGLED away from Kayla to speak with his men through his throat mic. When he shifted back, his features were so hard an Olympian could've ice-skated across them.

"Status?" Elsie asked, her voice as calm as ever, though she leaned forward in her seat.

"My men aren't answering."

"Could the mountains be interfering with radio transmission?"

"No. Not with our technology."

Joy surged through Kayla and she squeezed Jillian's hand, silently communicating all would be well. The injury to her mother's right cheek was causing her eye to balloon. However, looking at her profile from the opposite side, one would never know she'd been brutalized.

Jillian's back hadn't lost a centimeter of its rigidity. She scanned the room as if looking for vulnerabilities. Opportunities to get them out of there. Kayla had never been prouder to be the daughter of such a strong and resourceful woman.

"Send more men to check on things," Elsie said.

"I don't have any more available."

"How's that possible?"

"Because Ash took them all out," Kayla said, smiling.

Marco set his jaw.

"You stationed three at the main house," Elsie said.

"Who need to stay there," the guard said.

"To guard one sleeping woman?"

"You're assuming the agent's working alone."

The first fissure in Elsie's calm façade appeared. It took her two blinks of the eye to pull it back together. "Send two men."

"It would be best—"

"I'm not interested in your opinion, right now. Send them."

"You're jeopardizing the mission and the safety of my men."

"The only thing in jeopardy is your bonus. Send. Them."

Terror crawled up Kayla's throat. Ash might have managed to survive his two executioners, but who knew what kind of toll the encounter had taken on him.

He'd lost a lot of blood before they patched him up. Had he passed out after his skirmish? Or did he die along with the guards? Was there another reason for their radio silence?

Every neuron in Kayla's brain was urging her to act, to stop the team leader from sending his men. One look at Jillian put a halt to any rash action, though. Kayla couldn't chance it.

Marco leveled a defiant glare on Elsie. For a split second, Kayla thought he might put his men's lives ahead of his bank account. Then he lifted a hand to his throat and barked orders into his radio.

"Now that Mr. Blackwell will soon be dispensed with," Elsie set two half-filled wineglasses in front of Kayla and Jillian, "we can get down to the real business at hand. Drink up, ladies."

Kayla stared at what was no doubt tainted wine for several pounding heartbeats before wrapping her fingers around the glass stem.

"Don't, Kayla," Jillian warned.

"I must." She gave the red wine a twirl, inhaled the fruity aroma, and tossed the contents into Elsie's face.

The fashion designer screeched, bounded from the sofa, and ran to the sink.

"Don't lick your lips, auntie. Could be deadly."

Kayla braced herself for a retaliatory hit from Marco. None came. A muscle twitched in his jaw. His version of a smile?

"My offer still stands," Kayla said to him. In answer, he picked up the wine bottle and refilled her glass. "You're as psychotic as your employer if you think I'm going to willingly commit suicide."

"Do you want a repeat of what happened last time you defied me?" He looked pointedly at Jillian's damaged cheek.

"Torturing us won't go unnoticed by the ME."

He leaned forward until his square face was inches from hers. "Fire can mask a helluva lot."

Elsie came storming back. Strands of wet red hair clung to her face. Thick smudges of mascara beneath her eyes gave her a deranged Elvira appearance.

"You stupid, reckless child. No wonder Victoria gave you up the moment you washed from her womb."

68

———

ASH LEANED ON HIS MAKESHIFT WALKING STICK, A BRANCH he'd picked up near a narrow ribbon of creek twenty yards back. A creek he didn't recall seeing on his way to the kill site.

A heaviness had settled in his legs and his toes felt as though he'd climbed Mt. Everest barefoot. Even more concerning in his catalog of aches and pains was the clammy film of sweat coating his body and his inability to feel his shoulder.

The copious sweat indicated his body was going into shock. Not good. The numbness he didn't even want to think about.

Instead, he scanned the darkened woods for the hundredth time, looking for familiar landmarks or signs of civilization. But a light mist was rolling through the landscape, obscuring everything and plastering his clothes to his body.

He was one hundred percent lost.

Where had he gone wrong? Should he retrace his steps? Or forge ahead?

If he made the wrong decision, Kayla could pay for it with her life. An unfamiliar paralysis kept his barely functioning feet rooted in place. His heart clamored in his chest, and the earth shifted on its axis without warning.

He spread his feet and closed his eyes until the wave of dizziness passed.

A cool breeze whipped between the stark tree trunks, sending the nimble branches overhead dancing and hurrying along the foggy mist.

The impenetrable gray cleared for several heartbeats, long enough for him to spot a twinkle of light in the distance. He wiped the moisture from his face, squinted through the ever-shifting fog.

He wasn't seeing things. That was artificial light high on the ridge.

Adrenaline surged through his weakened body, and he scrambled up what had to be a forty percent gradient slope. He didn't think about it, didn't worry about how he looked as he clawed, hands and toes, his way toward the light.

The only thing that mattered was getting to a phone and stopping Elsie from murdering Kayla and her mother.

About halfway up, the terrain leveled out and the crunch beneath his boots no longer belonged to layers of leaf litter but to gravel.

Through heaving breaths, he glanced left, then right.

He'd found the trail.

Relief pulsed through him, then quickly stalled out.

Which way? The wrong choice would cost him precious time.

Before he could make a decision, two black-clad figures appeared above him on the trail. Assault rifles locked against their shoulders.

Elsie must have sent reinforcements when his executioners had failed to check in. Given their high alert stance, they'd heard him crawling up the embankment.

"Stay where you are," one of the men ordered.

Once again, he had no cover. The scattered trees along the trail were barely thick enough to hide a child let alone a grown man.

But this time, he was unbound and armed. All he needed to do was survive the next few seconds.

Twin red dots flickered on his chest.

Ash made the only decision he could.

He dove off the edge of the trail.

69

"Vicky gave me up?" Kayla repeated. The meaning of Elsie's words just out of her reach. "What are you talking about?"

Elsie's wide eyes shot to Jillian, whose pained expression made something crack deep inside Kayla's chest.

Her captor's momentary shock dissipated. Elsie shrugged, though the action held no arrogance, no triumph. "Seems I set your little secret free, Jill."

"Secret? What secret?" Her psychotic aunt's meaning finally penetrated her confusion, but she couldn't bring herself to believe that her entire life had been a lie. A lie told to her by two of the most important people in her life. "Mama?"

Jillian lifted her tear-drenched gaze to Kayla's. "I'm sorry, sweetheart."

A lump the size of a beach ball lodged in Kayla's throat. It took her several attempts to work around it, to get the words out. "Vicky's my mom?"

"Biological, yes."

"Why?"

Why didn't she want me? Why didn't you tell me? Why? Why? Why?

"It's complicated."

"Actually, it's pretty straightforward," Elsie countered. "Vic found out she was pregnant right after she'd decided to run for county commissioner." She looked at Jillian as if to hand her the it's-your-story baton, but the distraught woman could only stare at Kayla, as if she were afraid her daughter would disappear forever.

Exasperated, Elsie continued, "Jill talked Vic into letting her adopt you rather than . . ."

"Abort me?" Kayla finished, when the other woman's bravado wavered.

Another lift of the shoulder. "Vic wanted a career. Jill wanted you."

Kayla looked to Jillian for confirmation.

"I loved you from the moment I heard your tiny, galloping heartbeat on the ultrasound."

The muscles in Kayla's throat constricted to the point of pain.

"Even though Vic chose her career over motherhood," Elsie smirked, "she couldn't quite let you go."

There had always been something special about her and Vicky's relationship. She'd mistakenly thought it was the godmother connection.

Did Vicky ever regret her decision? Or had she been content to be in Kayla's life as a beloved auntie?

Kayla dropped her head into her hands. The events of the past week whipped through her head like scattershot. It was all too much.

A warm, trembling hand settled between her shoulders. Rather than provide comfort, Jillian's touch seared her flesh, burned her nerve endings, incinerated every happy family memory from birth to truth.

"Victoria and I talked about telling you," Jillian said, rubbing a circle on her back like she used to when Kayla was younger. "Planned to do it very soon."

Heat poured into her temples, pounding at the thin barrier for release. "Why now?"

Jillian's hand stilled.

"Why after thirty-five years of deception would you decide to tell me?"

Silence met her query, and Jillian slowly removed her hand.

Kayla erupted from the sofa, putting more distance between them. "Tell me, Mama!"

The guard's casual stance stiffened, but he didn't force her back down.

Like a lioness sensing wounded prey, Elsie turned bright eyes on the quiet woman beside her. "What have you been keeping from me, dear friend?"

Jillian ignored her. Lifted tear-soaked eyes to Kayla. "I have stage four colon cancer."

STAGE FOUR.

To her shame, Kayla realized that she didn't know much about colon cancer. But she knew stage four was bad. Really bad. Terminal bad.

"Mama, no."

"I'm sorry, sweetheart."

The tired eyes, the weight loss, the lack of appetite. Why hadn't she added it all up before now? The clues were there, and she'd dismissed them. Blamed them on fatigue and stress. If she'd been paying better attention, maybe they could have caught the cancer before it metastasized to other parts of her mother's body.

Kayla sat next to her mother, held her hands. "I'm the one who should apologize. I assumed your heavy schedule was the cause of your exhaustion and changes in physical appearance."

"I fed your assumptions. It's not your fault."

"Why?"

"I needed to get second and third opinions, needed to speak with your father. Needed to wrap my own head around the illness so I could be strong when the time came to prepare everyone around me."

Tears ran freely down Kayla's cheeks as she dropped to her knees and folded her arms around Jillian. She buried her face in her mother's hair, inhaled her familiar shampoo-y scent. "All you need to focus on is your health."

Elsie took the moment to poke and stab. "How relieved you must be, Jill, for this opportunity." She gestured to the tainted wine. "This act of kindness."

"Kindness," Kayla sputtered.

"Months of pain and suffering reduced to minutes, seconds, even."

When her mother said nothing, Kayla eased away and looked into her red-rimmed eyes. Eyes of acceptance.

"No, Mama. No, no, *no*. You will not give up. I won't let you."

"I won't be the only one suffering through months of treatments that will only forestall the inevitable. You, Gordon, Harper—you will all feel the pain right along with me."

"A small, very small price to pay to have more time with you."

"Even if the time is spent in hospitals and treatment

centers?" Jillian shook her head. "I don't want that for you. For us."

"Mama—"

"Take heart, Kayla," Elsie said, impatient. "You enjoyed two moms for the first third of your life. Many don't even get one."

The tension in Kayla's head ratcheted until she was certain her eyes would explode. She transferred her full attention to the monstrous stranger. "Until you killed Vicky."

"Technically, Sybil ordered the hit on Victoria—"

Kayla launched herself at Elsie. "You killed her! You killed my godmother. *Your friend!*"

She slammed the heel of her hand into the woman's forehead. "How does that feel? Hurt? It's nothing compared to being shot in the head."

She hit her again. And again.

Marco grabbed both of Kayla's upper arms and flung her to the side. She flew across the room and crashed into a four-foot-tall pedestal holding a large potted aloe.

The spiny plant teetered, and Kayla attempted to roll away. But the hard landing had stolen her breath, and all her energy was consumed with jumpstarting her breathing again.

When the plant lost its battle with gravity, she braced herself for impact, already anticipating the excruciating crunch as her ribs gave way to the heavy ceramic planter.

A flash of red silk and dark hair rushed forward.

Jillian dove for the container, shoving it in an attempt to change its trajectory. But she miscalculated the speed of the falling planter—and the location of Kayla's left foot. Those two elements combined sent Jillian plowing headfirst into the unforgiving ceramic.

Kayla heard a dull *thunk* seconds before Jillian crashed to the ground. One of her mother's knees jabbed into her stomach, sucking what little air she'd scrounged up right out of her lungs.

Jillian's eyelids fluttered once, twice, before unconsciousness claimed her.

The planter missed Kayla and crashed against the hardwood floor. The perlite infused potting soil spewed out of the container and the succulent's dense, aloe-filled leaves sagged to one side.

Kayla drew in a pocket of air. "Mama!" She brushed a lock of long hair from her mother's face and held the backs of her fingers beneath her nose, while she watched for the slow rise of her chest.

When she felt and saw both, the elbow holding her up gave way and she slumped to the floor.

"Well," Elsie drawled from the sofa, "I guess there's no need to ply her with wine now."

70

WHILE ASH ROLLED, SLID, AND BANGED HIS WAY DOWN THE steep ridge, he wondered if he should've taken his chances with the armed men on the trail.

His momentum came to a jarring halt when he landed with a splash in the rocky creek bed. Spring water flooded his clothes and swept over his face, giving him a jolt, the arctic equivalent of a defibrillator. He flailed to his knees, then his feet, sluicing water off his face in order to assess his situation.

The pain in his shoulder made him nauseous, but he ignored the sensation as he slogged his way out of the knee-deep water. Something *thrumped* near his left foot milliseconds before he heard the muffled echo of suppressed fire.

He zigzagged to a rock outcropping forty yards away, reaching for his sidearm, the only weapon that survived his tumble down the mountain.

After doing a quick equipment and ammo check, he braced a hand against the cold gray stone protecting him from becoming Swiss cheese. He leaned out to get a handle on his enemies' location and drew back immediately, when more bullets rained down on his location.

He waited for their heavy volley to stop, but they continued on and on. Then he realized something crucial —the bullets were no longer drilling into the earth around him.

Confused, he chanced another look. Four individuals in dark clothing were descending the ridge, like giant spiders emerging from the mist to secure a juicy morsel hung up in their web.

He aimed his Glock at the nearest mercenary. His eyesight kept blurring out, making it impossible to get a good bead on the dark figure against a gloomy background. Blinking rapidly, to help clear his vision, he pulled the trigger. The man went down and the other three raced for what little cover they could find.

"Hold your damn fire," a familiar voice yelled.

"Zeke?"

"Yeah, and the others."

"The two mercenaries?"

"Got away." He spit the words out like a mouthful of livermush.

A VW-sized boulder lifted off his chest. He might survive this night, after all. Using the outcropping to steady himself, Ash gained his feet and staggered toward his brothers.

Rohan knelt beside Zeke and looked to be assessing his left thigh. The boulder returned to crush his chest.

"Did I hit you?" It would be a marksman miracle if he had, considering he was even now having trouble keeping his brother in focus.

"Lucky for Zeke, you're a shitty shot in the dark," Rohan said, not lifting his head. "The bullet grazed his thigh."

Ash didn't bother explaining about his warped vision. " Do you have first aid supplies?"

"Of course."

Rohan started to bandage Zeke's leg, but his impatient brother grabbed the gauze out of his hands and wound the white material around the wound several times before tying it off.

"Not that I'm complaining," Ash said, "but how did y'all find me?"

"By accident," Cruz said, "we were coming up the trail at the same time you took a header over the side."

"Why were you on the trail?"

"Liv couldn't find Kayla," Zeke said. "She texted her, and Kayla explained what the two of you were up to. Liv got worried." He leveled a stare at Ash. "For good reason."

"All we intended to do was check out Sybil's guesthouse, then ask her a few questions."

"But all hell broke loose?" Phin supplied.

Ash nodded.

"What's wrong with your shoulder?" Zeke asked, eyeing his bloody sleeve.

"Flesh wound, same as you."

"You look like you've been on a bender for a week."

"And you look like Mt. Vesuvius on the verge of eruption."

"Boys, now isn't the time to get into a pissing match," Phin said. "What can you tell us?"

Ash summarized the events of the last two hours, starting with his and Kayla's decision to confront Sybil about Victoria's death, Elsie's shocking revelation about her part in the governor's assassination, his death walk, and Elsie's endgame.

"Elsie intends to kill Kayla and her mother, then frame

Sybil for everything." Ash used his sleeve to wipe sweat and grit from his eyes. "I have to get back to Sybil's before it's too late." He didn't voice the fear that Elsie had already put her plan in action. He couldn't face that possible truth.

Zeke grabbed something off the ground, then used Rohan's shoulder to leverage himself up. "You're not going anywhere alone." He tossed the object from the ground to him. "You dropped this."

With one hand, Ash caught the rifle he'd taken from the dead guard.

"Let Rohan take a look at your shoulder."

"No need. The bastards stuffed the wound with combat gauze to staunch the blood. Shot was through and through."

"It appears you lost a significant amount of blood before they plugged the holes," Cruz said, a warning in his voice. "And from the way you're squinting your eyes, I'm guessing you sustained a head injury, too."

"I'll be fine." He started up the ridge. The pressure in his head pulsed with each sluggish beat of his heart. "A little lost blood and a bump on the head are nothing compared to the fate awaiting Kayla and her mother."

He sniffed the air and caught the acrid scent of smoke.

71

KAYLA WAS BURNING.

Flames licked at her stockinged feet and seared her wet cheeks.

Wet cheeks?

Had she been crying?

She tried to lift her hand, but it wouldn't budge from her side.

She attempted to sit up, but a hippo sat on her chest.

She made to raise her knees, but they remained locked in place.

Her head wouldn't turn.

The only thing she could move were her eyes. And she didn't like the view.

She lay prone on the sofa in the guest house's great room, a blanket of sweat covering her body. Fire consumed the area by the back sliding doors. Flames crept up the walls and slithered across the ceiling. Soon the inferno would be overhead and burning detritus would rain down on her, setting her hair and clothes aflame.

With extreme effort, she lifted her head a few inches

and turned it just enough to spot Jillian, where she still lay sprawled on the floor by the broken planter.

The sight opened the gates to more memories. Marco holding her head immobile while Elsie poured tainted wine into Kayla's mouth. Some of the brew slipped down her throat before she delivered a vicious kick to Elsie's stomach, sending her aunt and wine flying.

Elsie's fury.

Marco's anvil-like fist slamming into the side of her head.

Lights out.

Now, smoke billowed through the room, causing her eyes to water and her lungs to rebel. She tried to cough, but whatever paralytic Elsie had given her suppressed her ability.

"Mama!" Her scream came out more as a croaked whisper.

The woman lying face down didn't stir.

Wind pushed at the fire from the outside, feeding the voracious flames. They rounded the wall and headed straight for her mother.

"Mama!"

Kayla fought against her paralysis. Strained to reassert control over her body. Her heart skipped a beat when her fingers flexed and her shoulders shifted.

Hope surged.

She worked her way down her body.

The rest of her mass remained still as granite, except for her feet.

Fear extinguished her small spark of hope.

"Jillian!"

Had her scream been a little stronger?

Her mother's body jerked, as if startled, then settled again.

Coughing, Kayla attempted to roll off the sofa, get to lower ground, where the smoke was less dense. But her body sat like a boulder at the bottom of a hill, heavy and immovable.

Tears streamed from her eyes—part from smoke, part from frustration and fear.

"Jillian Helene Krowne, get your ass up!"

This time, her mother lifted her head, coughed.

"Mama! Run!"

Jillian raised up on an elbow and turned toward the great room. Her expression was one of confusion until she saw her daughter lying helpless on the sofa. "Kayla?"

"Mama, get out of here, now!"

Jillian shook her head and her fingers touched her temple to ease what was no doubt a raging headache.

Kayla concentrated on her neck muscles. Slowly, she angled her head until her neck hooked over the side of the seat cushion. The fingers of her right hand grabbed the edge of the middle cushion. She forced her right leg to move a few inches until her toes anchored against the front of the armrest.

Through tearing eyes, Kayla watched Jillian crawl toward her on hands and knees, hacking against the poisonous air filling her lungs.

Three, two, one—

Kayla commanded every available ounce of strength into her neck, fingers, and toes. They pushed against the side of the sofa. With frustrating slowness, the leverage elevated her body up and onto its side, like a sail catching a stirring breeze.

She just needed a little . . . more . . . to tip . . . her over.

But gravity's talons held tight, and her body stopped its forward momentum.

"*Noooo.*" Blood rushed to Kayla's head as she strained to get to safety. Her body teetered for a breath-stealing second, then tilted in the right direction. Kayla's triumph was short-lived.

Unable to break her fall with her hands, she crashed to the floor. Pain shot through her nose and what little breath she had disappeared on impact.

"Ow." Her smooshed boobs would never be the same.

She lifted her head and felt warm blood trickle down her upper lip, then *plop* onto the rug below. The air was better at this level, but still laced with smoke. And the heat continued to intensify. She couldn't imagine what it would feel like if she stood up.

"Kayla," Jillian said, swiping hair out of her daughter's eyes, "what's wrong?"

"Paralytic in wine. Small dose. I can use my hands and feet. Some."

"Let's get you out of here." Jillian grasped her beneath her arms and attempted to drag her toward the front door. She barely managed three inches before she *huffed* to a stop and fell back on her butt.

"Leave," Kayla pleaded. "Before it's too late."

As if the fire wanted to put an exclamation mark at the end of her sentence, burning plaster dropped from above and landed on the sofa where she'd been thirty seconds ago.

Jillian surged into action. She gained her feet, though she stayed in a low crouch. She flipped the ottoman several times until it cleared the accent rug beneath its wooden feet. Then she stepped between Kayla and the burning sofa, heaving it backwards, once, twice, not stopping until it had cleared the rug, too.

The physical effort must have sapped a good deal of strength in her already exhausted body. Kayla knew her close proximity to the flames must be burning her exposed skin. But the stubborn woman wouldn't listen to her pleas to leave.

Turning back to Kayla, Jillian flopped her over onto her back.

"What are you doing?"

"Getting you out of here."

"There's no time!"

"Let's hope you're wrong."

The older woman knelt near Kayla's head and curled the edge of the rug for a stronger grip. "Stay still, Kayla."

"Mama—"

"Shut up and don't move."

Kayla did as instructed, while her middle-aged, cancer-riddled mother dragged her dead weight across the hard-wood floor, toward the front door that Elsie had left wide open. No doubt to feed the flame.

She continued to wrest control away from the drug in her body. Now, her legs and arms could move, though the movements were jerky.

As they inched closer to freedom, an overwhelming sense of dread sank into Kayla's bones. "Not the front door. Bedroom."

Jillian coughed. "Why?"

"Not sure. Safer, I think."

Her mother didn't question Kayla's instincts. She simply altered course and headed toward the master bedroom, not far from the kitchen.

As Kayla slid by the open door, she caught sight of the

back of Sybil's house. A light illuminated the patio, and sitting on a cushioned chair was Elsie, sipping from a champagne flute, watching them burn.

The betrayer's eyes widened, and Kayla did the only thing she could have in that moment.

She jerked her hand into the air and lifted her middle finger.

72

By the time Ash crawled his way up the last few feet of the ridge behind Sybil's property, flames had completely engulfed the smaller guesthouse.

His heart did a freefall, not stopping until it hit the earth's core.

"Kayla!" He scrambled to his feet, a wave of dizziness forcing him to reach for the nearest tree.

"You need to sit down," Rohan said, grabbing his elbow.

Ash wrenched away, stumbled forward until he crashed into the tree trunk. The heat from the inferno warmed the entire front side of his body. His gaze raked over the area around the house, searching for a familiar blond head.

"I have to find her," Ash said through labored breaths.

"Ash," Zeke said, flanking his other side, "no one could survive—"

"She's alive." He couldn't bear any other alternative. "Kayla's smart. She would've figured a way out."

When Zeke's jaw set in an uncompromising line, Ash mustered enough strength to push away from his resting post. Only to be met with a large paw, shoving him back.

"You're not going anywhere, you damn stubborn fool," Zeke growled. "Rohan and I will check out the house."

On the way here, they'd picked up the trail of the two fleeing guards. Zeke had sent Phin and Cruz to track them down. Now, Ash wished they'd all stayed together.

"I'm not staying behind while you guys head into danger."

"Sit. Down," Zeke said, as he limped toward the mansion in the distance. "You're a liability right now."

The pounding in Ash's head was so strong now that nausea had begun to churn in his stomach.

Rohan winced and squeezed his shoulder. "We'll find her." Then he was gone.

Ash's legs shook and sweat dripped into his eyes. He watched his brothers filter away. Shame, helplessness, and rage immobilized him.

Was Zeke right? Would he be a liability? Would he divert their attention away from saving Kayla and taking out that witch Elsie?

Probably. His body gave him every indication that it was done. That it had nothing more to give.

But he'd made Kayla a promise. Blackwells didn't renege, and they sure as hell didn't cower in the woods while their brothers went to war on their behalf.

Ash straightened and willed his legs into motion.

The soft crunch of leaves was his only warning before a large hand grasped his hair and yanked his head back, while the mercenary's other hand rocketed toward his throat.

A six-inch blade leading the charge.

73

KAYLA LEANED AGAINST HER MOTHER FOR SUPPORT WHILE HER wobbly legs remembered how to walk.

After escaping the burning house through the bedroom's French doors, Jillian half-dragged, half-carried Kayla into the woods, fleeing in nothing but their pajamas and, in Kayla's case, stockinged feet.

So far, her tender flesh had found every jutting thorn, sharp stone, and hidden stump.

When she went down for the dozenth time, she took Jillian with her. The older woman released a bone-rattling cough, then sprawled back on the forest floor, her stamina no doubt reaching its end.

Who could blame her? Kayla wasn't a small woman. For Jillian to have gotten them this far was a testament to her mother's single-minded determination to safeguard her daughter.

And Kayla was her daughter, in every sense that was important. Vicky might have given her birth, but she hadn't guided Kayla through all the tricky parts of life. Sure, she'd swooped in and offered Kayla much-needed advice or uplifted her spirits, from time to time.

But she hadn't made the million and one sacrifices mothers did for their children, as Jillian had.

It was time for Kayla to make a sacrifice. "Mama, you need to leave me."

"No!"

"With the terrain the way it is, there's no way I'm making it to the nearest neighbor. But you can."

Jillian shook her head. "I'm not leaving you." Purple shadows smudged the underside of her eyes and deep hollows pressed into her cheeks.

"It's the only way we'll both make it out of this alive. I know you've already gone through the various scenarios and have landed on the same conclusion." Kayla fumbled for her hand. "But your motherly instincts are clashing with your logic."

Jillian's breaths were hard and fast, but Kayla could tell she was listening.

"Don't let your fear win," she echoed her mother's sentiment from what seemed like a million years ago, when in fact it had only been days since the fundraiser. Kayla lifted up onto her elbows and looked around. "I can stay hidden until help arrives."

"I don't like it."

"Neither do I. But it's our best chance of surviving this."

An image surfaced, of Ash being led away, injured, and with a promise burning in his eyes.

Along with something more.

Outside the bar, he'd been a breath away from declaring his feelings for her—until she'd stopped him. What had possessed her to stop him from saying words she wanted to hear, *needed* to hear?

Kayla drew in a slow breath and rolled the tension from her shoulders.

Whatever it took.

She would do whatever it took to get through this nightmare, then she'd demand the words from Ash. No, she would gift him with the words first.

No more hiding her feelings, no more playing it cool.

I love you, Ash. Hold on.

A small, insidious voice whispered along the smoke-drenched breeze. *You're too late.*

74

ASH THREW UP HIS GOOD ARM TO BLOCK THE MERCENARY'S knife from giving him a tracheotomy. He halted the blade's descent, but the guy was strong.

Out of the corner of his eye, he could see the merc had at least three inches and fifty pounds on him. If Ash hadn't been injured and exhausted, he wouldn't have blinked twice at the guy's size. Somewhere in his mid-twenties, both Zeke and Cruz had out-muscled him, but that hadn't meant they could outmaneuver him. To their annoyance.

But Ash's defense was already weakening, and six inches of steel were closing in.

"You're a hard fucker to kill, I'll give you that." The fingers anchored in Ash's hair rolled tighter, forcing Ash's head back until his neck refused to bend any farther. "Are all my men dead?"

"Only the"— he edged past the pain in his neck, forcing his attention on his hand while it worked to unsheathe his own blade"—assholes."

Once he slid the knife free, Ash jammed it into the

merc's hip so hard the tip hit bone. The other man cursed, and his hold loosened.

Ash withdrew the weapon and slammed it into the man's thigh, then twisted.

An earth-shaking scream.

When Ash pulled the knife out this time, blood spurted, arcing in the air with each of the merc's rapid heartbeats.

He'd hit the femoral artery.

Good for him. Bad for the merc.

Jerking away, he kept a wary gaze on the giant, unsure if he would try a last desperate rush or simply empty his magazine into Ash's body. "Hope you have a tourniquet."

The merc glanced down at his hand covering the wound, blood seeping between his fingers and draining onto the forest floor. Ash watched as realization dawned on his enemy.

"Did the two women in the guesthouse make it out?" Ash asked, knowing the other man would take the answer to his grave.

The merc staggered back, caught himself against the nearest tree. Slid down, landing on his ass with a hard *thud*. His head wobbled on his spine, as if it were suddenly too heavy. He let it fall back against the rough bark, his eyes closing.

"Hellcat," the merc muttered. The bloody hand covering the wound lifted, and one thick finger pointed into the woods, in the opposite direction Ash had been heading.

He could think of only one person who could earn that moniker in such a short period of time.

Kayla.

The merc's eyes closed and his hand fell to his side.

Ash stared at the hired killer, suspecting him of sending

him into an ambush. But something in the man's tone when he'd said hellcat sounded almost respectful. Reluctant, but respectful.

"I feel your pain, man," Ash whispered, then went hunting for a hellcat.

75

JILLIAN HELPED CAMOUFLAGE KAYLA BENEATH BOUGHS OF PINE and oak they'd taken from dozens of young saplings vying for a foothold on the crowded ridge. She allowed her mother this futile action, knowing she wouldn't leave Kayla's side without some assurance of her safety.

The repetitive work had allowed Kayla time to digest her mother's earth-shattering revelation. If she'd had her phone, she would've researched survivability rates, effective treatments, patient testimonials, anything to better understand the disease. And why Jillian had been ready to let Elsie poison her.

A new thought whirled to the surface. Was this the reason why Vicky hadn't wanted her to say anything about their meeting to Jillian? Because she knew her friend had enough stress on her plate already?

Sounded like Vicky's M.O.

Jillian dropped to all fours, and her dirt-covered hand reached inside the small den for Kayla's. "It'll take me ten minutes to reach the Rickerts' residence, five minutes to explain the situation and make the call—"

"I understand, Mama." Through a small gap in the leaves, she peered at her mother's weary countenance and experienced a surge of raw guilt. "It could be awhile before help arrives."

To her surprise, there had been no sign of Marco's pursuit. He must have figured that two unconscious women had no chance of fleeing a burning building and took the opportunity to conduct a perimeter check.

That'll teach him to never underestimate a woman again. Especially a mother.

"I love you, Kayla," Jillian said. "Be still."

"Love you, too."

Seconds later, she was alone.

Please forgive me.

Kayla gave her body another ten minutes to fight the drug before slapping the leafy branches away. Using the large, downed tree she'd been snuggled against, she leveraged herself into a standing position, taking a few seconds to brush off and shake out her loose clothing to rid herself of any four-, six-, or eight-legged passengers, while testing her legs.

Choosing a different direction than her mother's, she took one shaky step after another, using branches, shrubs, and trunks to help maintain her balance, until she had full control over her muscles again.

I'm coming, Ash.

Kayla followed her mental map of the most likely path Ash's captors would've taken him. She'd zeroed in on the small mountain meadow at the back of the Poehler property. Secluded, and far enough away from Sybil's estate so as to not draw attention to her.

The big question was—did either of Ash's guards know about it? Pushing away her doubts, Kayla set off in the direction of the meadow, pausing every twenty feet or so to listen. During her second stop, she heard the distinctive sound of cautious feet making their way toward her position.

Had Marco circled around in the opposite direction to cut them off? Was that two sets of boots rustling the leaves?

Heart climbing the wall of her throat, she backtracked to her spot and repositioned the branches to make them as natural as possible, though she wished they were brown rather than green. An observant person would notice the ruse within seconds.

Hopefully, the darkness would mask the odd suppleness of the so-called fallen branches. It wasn't unheard of for gusts of wind to rip limbs off trees and scatter them across the forest floor.

The crackle of leaves grew closer, and Kayla worked to modulate her breathing. She pictured herself prepping for a meeting filled with powerful, dismissive men. Used her breathing technique to calm herself before settling into her "annihilate them" mindset.

Five, four, three, two, one.

Through a space in the leaves, she glimpsed a pair of legs pausing right outside of her location.

Something plopped down on her head and immediately began to burrow into her hair. Revulsion skittered down her spine. Her hand shook with the urge to remove the creature. Another part of her squirmed at the thought of touching the thing.

Would it be encased in a hard shell like a beetle? Squiggly like a grub? Or leggy like a spider? Would its little feet grasp her finger? Bite it? Or scurry away?

Every centimeter the insect moved felt like a thousand

black widow spiders crawling across her flesh. Her every nerve ending vibrated with the compulsion to *do something* as the creature approached the base of her skull.

She braced herself for the first feel of it slithering onto the back of her bare neck.

At some point, she'd squeezed her eyes shut. She opened them and peered through the leaves. The guard's legs were no longer in view.

Was he standing just out of view? Or had he moved on? She didn't know what was worse—seeing his legs or not seeing them.

The creature made its move and now used her neck like a bridge. Every muscle in her upper body turned rock hard, as if that would protect her from the sensation of tiny feet trotting along her exposed flesh.

One moment, she huddled in darkness, warring with every instinct she possessed. The next, a large boot kicked the branches sheltering her away. Moonlight spilled into her hiding space. A familiar face filled her vision.

"Hello, Hellcat," Ash said, his words warm and gentle.

The relief she heard in his voice pierced the dam holding back her emotions and tears pooled in her eyes. Then the writhing creature used her spine like a ski run.

She bolted from her hiding place, wriggling her shoulders and tenting her pajama top. "Get it off me! Get it off!" she exclaimed in a loud whisper.

When she noticed his bewildered stare, Kayla ripped the top over her head and turned her back toward him. "Get it off! Please." She shook the garment hard.

Ash lifted her soot-covered hair and peered beneath. When he found nothing, he searched through the mass of tangles.

"Whatever it was, it's gone," he said.

"You're sure?"

"Positive."

She checked the pajama top thoroughly before putting it back on, then searched the area near her ravaged feet.

Nothing.

Kayla suppressed a shiver, still able to feel the insect's phantom dance down her neck.

Her eyes locked on Ash. Took in his filthy clothes, blood-coated shirt, sweat-slicked skin. How he was still standing, she didn't know, but he was here. With her. Tears blurred his image. "You made it back."

"I had a promise to keep."

He tilted a little to the left, and she grasped his forearm to steady him. Kayla didn't bother asking him to sit, she knew the stubborn man would decline.

Cradling his whiskered cheek with her other hand, she said, "As do I."

Ash frowned, clearly trying to recall her promise.

Blinking away the moisture, she produced a wobbly smile. Ignored the ticking clock screaming in her mind. "I love you, Asher Cameron Blackwell." She stepped closer, needing the connection of his body against her. "I promised myself that if I got away from Elsie, I would tell you how I feel. No more games. No more waiting for you to love me back."

"You never had to wait for me to love you. I fell hard the moment I saw you assembling care packages for the seniors' home."

"But—"

His thumb brushed over her bottom lip. "What you were waiting for was for me to get out of my own head."

Kayla leaned back. "Have you?"

"Yes, God help me."

"About damn time, Blackwell."

His teeth flashed. "Agreed. Now come here."

She hugged him close, as he covered her mouth, sealing their promise to each other.

ASH IGNORED THE SEARING PAIN IN HIS SHOULDER, AS HE HELD Kayla close. He inhaled and found a hint of her honey-vanilla scent amidst the smoke.

Before he'd located her makeshift den, he'd begun to think the dying merc had duped him, until he noticed several small trees had branches ripped from their wispy trunks. He followed the trail of sapling destruction to the downed tree.

Branches were placed willy nilly over the enormous trunk and scattered across the ground to give the impression a wind storm had ripped the fragile limbs from the trees above. Many would've been fooled by their ruse.

But Ash had *felt* Kayla's presence. Knew down to the cellular level that she was close by.

Adrenaline from his fight with the merc began to ebb, a bone-deep weariness taking its place. He couldn't give in to it yet. They still had a puppet master to apprehend and family to protect. He kissed her temple. "Where's your mother?"

"She ran to a neighbor's house to call for help."

He grasped her shoulders and set her away from him. "Why didn't you go with her?"

"Elsie forced me to ingest some sort of paralytic. At first, my body wouldn't cooperate and it was clear Jillian would be more successful in going for help if I stayed behind."

"All your limbs working now?"

"For the most part." She averted her gaze. "But it still feels like I have an alien inside me, operating the controls."

Something about her expression alerted his instincts. "Why do I feel like there's more to this story?"

Her face cleared, and she cupped the side of his face. "I'm so damn glad to see you alive."

Covering her hand with his, he lifted her soot-covered fingers to his lips, kissed their tips. "Same. Now tell me what scheme you've hatched."

She sighed. "I wanted to search for you, but needed to ensure Jillian would be safe first."

"You didn't trust me to keep my promise?"

"I did. I swear." She squeezed his hand, then swallowed. "It's just that . . . "

"What?"

"When Elsie's head mercenary couldn't get a hold of the two men tasked with murdering you, she had him send two more. The odds that you'd survived seemed rather steep at that point."

"Elsie could've sent an army, and I still would've made it back to you."

She rose up on her toes and kissed him. "Now I know."

He gave her a wry grin. "I have to admit, keeping my word would've been a lot more difficult if Zeke and the guys hadn't shown up."

She glanced around. "Your brothers are here?"

"Thanks to Liv. Cruz and Phin are tracking down the

two mercs you mentioned. Zeke and Rohan are clearing the big house."

"We should update them."

"In a second." He wrapped an arm around her and poured every fear he'd been consumed with, since the moment he left her standing outside the guesthouse until he discovered her beneath a tree, into the kiss.

Ash leaned into it, wanting to bury this nightmare and sink into her light. But a wave a dizziness struck, and he pitched into her, all one hundred and ninety pounds of him.

Not expecting the weight shift, her body buckled under his. She held on tight though, somehow guiding them into a jarring knee crash, rather than a face plant.

"Sorry," he whispered, resting his forehead against hers.

She steadied him, then turned her head to cough up a smoke-filled lung. "What's wrong?"

"Lost my balance for a second. I'm fine. You, on the other hand, sound like shit."

"Don't lie to me, Asher." She reared back, her gaze zeroing in on his bloody shoulder. "Your gunshot wound."

He nodded.

"What else?" He opened his mouth, and she interrupted him. "Don't give me any of your macho BS. Where are you injured?"

"Probable concussion, maybe a broken rib or two."

"Let's get you into my hiding spot, and I'll—"

"Not happening."

"You're hardly in a position to fight."

"I can hold my own just fine, as evidenced by the guy I left back there." He hooked his thumb over his shoulder, then pushed to his feet. "How many mercenaries are left?"

"One is guarding Sybil in the big house and there was a

big one, their commander, I think, carrying out Elsie's bidding."

"The same one guarding Jillian earlier?"

"Yes."

"He's out of commission." Grasping her hand, he headed toward the house. She stumbled, and he noticed her stockinged feet for the first time.

He bent at the knees, careful to keep his blurry gaze straight ahead. "Jump on?"

"Pardon?"

"Get on my damn back."

"Are you out of your mind? You're in no condition to carry me."

"Your socks are bloody, which means your feet are torn up. I'll carry you as far as the forest edge, then you can be your badass self again." When she stayed fixed in place, he said, "I can do this. Trust me."

Ash thought she would refuse him, but after another short hesitation, she scurried up on the narrower end of the fallen tree, then eased onto his back, taking care not to touch his injured shoulder. He focused on putting one boot in front of the other until, finally, they arrived on the east side of Sybil's mansion.

Once Kayla slid down and moved to his side, he retrieved his phone to send Zeke a text, when a message from his brother popped up first.

We have a problem.

77

Ash stared at the clusterfuck in front of him. "What the hell happened?"

"Damned if I know," Zeke said.

"This isn't good," Rohan said.

Understatement of the year.

A gasp sounded beside him, and he swung around, putting his body between Kayla and the macabre scene splayed out in the middle of Sybil's great room.

"I'm sorry, sweetheart," he said, clutching her to him. "I didn't hear you approach."

Upon entering the house, Kayla had peeled away to grab them some water and tend to her feet, while Ash joined his brothers in the family room. Zeke and Rohan had already cleared the house so he hadn't worried about her running into a merc.

Her arm tightened around him for a long second, then she drew back, tears in her eyes, and offered him a glass of water. "I'm good."

"What about you?"

"I drank my fill in the kitchen."

"Why don't you go back there and wait for us to sort through this mess? You don't need this in your head."

"And you do?"

"I have several degrees of separation."

"I'm good," she repeated in a stronger voice, but twin tears crested her lower lids.

Ash hesitated, unable to leash his protective instincts.

As if she understood his inner turmoil, Kayla cupped his cheek in her palm. "Thank you, but I need to see this through."

Gritting his teeth, he lowered his hands. She swiped the tears away, then strode around him to stand before the two back-to-back chairs in the center of the room.

Sybil sat facing her, zip-tied to a wooden dining room chair. Behind her, Elsie sat in a posture mirroring her friend's. Their necks were linked by a white silken sash. Pink sticky notes stuck to their foreheads. Trailing from beneath the paper, rivulets of congealed blood bisected their faces.

"For the one I couldn't stop," Zeke read out the note affixed to Sybil.

Kayla frowned. "I don't understand."

Ash drew up alongside her and pointed to Sybil's lap. Her killer had freed her right hand and propped it palm up on her thigh. In the center stood a spent bullet and its casing.

"Governor Stokes," Ash said.

Eye for an eye.

Rohan read the note on Elsie's forehead. "Debt paid."

"Sounds like we have a vigilante," Zeke said. "Ideas?"

Ash nodded, but said nothing, letting Kayla work it out in her own time. It didn't take long.

She squeezed her eyes shut as if enduring a terrible pain. Then she whispered, "Mason."

78

THE ROILING IN KAYLA'S STOMACH HAD NOTHING TO DO WITH the volumes of smoke she'd inhaled, the lacerations on her feet, the worry she carried for her mother, or the gruesome scene before her.

This sickness went deeper. It tried to debilitate her, and had nearly succeeded.

Mason Wade had killed Sybil and Elsie. Executed them. For her.

She lifted a fist and pressed it against her mouth in a feeble attempt to hold back the bile. Her other hand reached for the square of pink paper.

"Don't," Ash warned in a low voice. "Evidence."

Zeke's attention snapped to his brother. "We're well beyond that. Right, bro?" His eyes shifted to Kayla and back. "Family first."

If she didn't already love Liv's fiancé, his inclusion of her into the Blackwell clan would have clinched the deal. Words of gratitude lodged in her suddenly thick throat. The Blackwells were known throughout Steele Ridge for eschewing society, preferring their own company, and for being slow to trust strangers.

It was partly because the nature of their business required them to tiptoe over the legal line. Sometimes they vaulted over it. The greater reason they kept things tight-knit was genetics. While still in the womb, they were taught to put family before all else, no matter the consequences.

Realizing how quiet Ash had become, Kayla joined her gaze with the brothers' as they waited for him to fight a silent war in his mind.

A selfish piece of her heart shriveled when he didn't immediately agree with Zeke. But she batted away the emotion. She knew what it meant when your career pulled you in an opposite direction from your heart. Both didn't always align, but both made her—them—whole.

For Ash, setting aside the lawful way to handle this situation to protect her—and as a result, Jillian and HCVS—must have felt like severing an appendage.

"It's all right, Ash." She wrapped a hand around his hard bicep, felt his thundering pulse beneath her fingertips. "I'll find a way to explain what happened to the authorities." She reached for a note of humor. "Digging clients out of disaster zones is kind of my lane. Today, I'm the client."

His face turned stormy. "You think I'm capable of walking away?"

"It would be hard, but I know how important justice is to you."

"You are the most frustrating, most dangerous"—he raked a hand through his hair—"most . . ."

"Selfless?" Rohan offered.

"Loyal?" Zeke added.

"Yes," he ground out. "Fuck y'all, yes." He turned to her, leveled on her an uncompromising look. "All I'm interested in is protecting you"—without looking, he pointed in his brothers' direction—"and those asshats."

Rohan lifted a brow.

Zeke grinned, then frowned, then wiped all emotion off his face.

"That's it," Ash continued. "Got it?"

Emotion squeezed her chest like an ever-tightening tourniquet. A smile wobbled. "Got it." She kissed him softly on the mouth, then glanced at the remnants of her once-beloved aunties.

"Just heard from Cruz and Phin," Zeke said. "They found the two mercs."

"Are they headed back this way?" Ash asked.

"Their throats were slit."

Ash and Zeke shared a weighty glance.

"Mason?" Kayla asked.

"He gets my vote," Rohan said.

"We need to make this look like a burglary gone bad," Ash said. "Clean up all evidence to the contrary. Including the dead bodies."

"Agreed," Zeke said.

Kayla realized that Ash's internal monologue hadn't been a war between his FBI duties and protecting her. He'd been plotting how to get them all out of this mess. She hugged his arm, then stepped toward Sybil.

"First, I need to . . . " She reached for the pink barrier.

"It won't be pretty," Ash said.

"I know."

"It could have a lasting, negative effect."

Nightmares, mental flashes, sweats, panic attacks.

She'd already considered the consequences. None of them could hold a candle to wiping away the haunting image of Vicky dying in front of her. Tonight, she would erase one terror and replace it with a lesser one. "I understand."

"Make it quick. We're running out of time."

She plucked the paper off Sybil's forehead. Her stomach clenched at the familiar round, dark hole. Swallowing, she turned away and took a step toward Elsie's side of the macabre scene.

"Kayla," Rohan cautioned, "please reconsider."

Sirens echoed in the distance. Jillian had either succeeded or someone on the opposite ridge had noticed the orange glow against the night sky. Kayla hoped it was the former.

She paused. "What's one more?"

"It won't be one more. It's a new horror all its own."

Kayla frowned, her gaze jumping from one brother to the next, trying to divine their thoughts.

Zeke sighed. "The two wounds you've seen were entry wounds." He pointed at Elsie. "That's an exit wound."

Shifting her stance, she forced herself to look at the back of Sybil's head and nearly lost what little food she had in her stomach. The wound was gaping, messy, nothing like the near perfect hole on her face.

"How did—?"

Mason had used one bullet to kill them both. Now she understood why he'd tied the sash around their necks. To ensure a clean shot, through one head and the next.

Kayla maneuvered around until she faced Elsie's body. Held in place more by blood than glue, the pink square barely did its job of covering the wound. Her determination wavered, then she thought about what Elsie had done to Jillian and her reason for killing Vicky.

She ripped off the sticky note.

THROUGH THE LENS OF HIS RIFLE'S SCOPE, MASON WADE watched Special Agent Blackwell's hands remain at his side while Kayla plucked the notes from the two bitches' heads.

Relief poured through him, and he released a heavy breath.

If Blackwell had intended to play it by the book, he would never have allowed Kayla to tamper with crime scene evidence.

Mason experienced a twinge of guilt at Kayla being exposed to the brutal deaths of two women who'd played an important role in her life, but elimination had been the only option. The actions of a couple of rogue actors shouldn't be allowed to take down an important organization like HCVS.

With Elsie and Sybil out of the picture, Kayla, Jillian, and other Service members could continue moving the world in a more positive direction. One where his daughter could be anyone she wanted, including the president of the United States.

Thankfully, stick-in-the-mud Blackwell hadn't screwed up his plan.

Thoughts of Jozi made his eyes burn. From the age of eleven years old, when she met her hero, Jane Goodall, she'd been working hard to prepare herself for entrance into Duke. And his little girl had done it. Last month, she'd received her admittance letter from the university. Now Mason had to figure out how to pay for it. Tuition was fucking expensive.

Which had aided in his decision to take on the contract to assassinate the governor. But mostly, he'd wanted to protect Kayla. Make sure she didn't get caught in the crosshairs of an unknown shooter who wasn't bothered by human collateral damage.

In the end, he hadn't been able to pull the trigger. Not because he had any moral issues with killing such a high-ranking public figure. Politicians were like cockroaches. Smash one and another would crawl over its carcass to feast on the available power, licking its feet on the other side.

No, the reason he hadn't been able to follow through was the joy he'd witnessed on Kayla's face when she strolled into the gazebo. He understood the pain of watching someone you cared about die before your eyes. Had witnessed it more than once on the battlefield. Had watched his wife, Naomi, struggle to survive for days in the hospital before she finally succumbed to her injuries. He'd refused to put Kayla through that kind of mental torture.

But Sybil had had a backup plan. A brilliant one, as it turned out. Who the hell took a serial killer with *a signature* to an assassination? Someone establishing a masterful decoy, that's who.

He hadn't known about Grimball's jewelry fetish the

night of the fundraiser. All he'd been focused on was preventing the assassin from taking the second shot, the one intended for Kayla. If Grimball's weapon hadn't jammed, giving Mason time to locate the convict and smash his face before the bastard slipped his grasp but not before his knife slashed across Mason's forearm, the night would've had an even deadlier ending.

There were other targets, other ways to get the money for his daughter's tuition.

From the moment Jozi bellowed her way into the world, he and Naomi had put every extra cent into a college fund for their daughter. But his wife's medical bills had ripped through their savings, and Mason had joined the millions of Americans mired in devastating medical debt.

Once he'd clawed his way out, he started building Jozi's college fund again. He'd done what he could on a single salary, and Jozi received a few grants from essays she'd written, but they had only managed to cover the first two years of her undergrad degree.

Now, he was without a steady job and had only a short time to come up with the money for her junior and senior years. Once he got her settled into her dorm, he'd have the freedom to take higher paying contract jobs overseas.

Mason pushed away from the boulder and retrieved the bag of bullet casings he'd picked up in the forest and around the burning guest house, dropping them into his rucksack.

Once the ruck was situated on his back, he shouldered his rifle, grabbed a shovel from the toolshed, and slipped back into the shadows.

EPILOGUE

Three weeks later

THE MOMENT KAYLA AND ASH ENTERED THE FRIARY'S FOYER, Liv greeted them with enthusiastic hugs.

"What did you think of the streamers and lighting along the path leading up to the Friary?" Liv asked.

"Absolutely gorgeous," Kayla said. "Great way to get everyone in a festive mood."

"I thought so, too. Alejandro and Neuman outdid themselves. Wait until you see how they decorated the back patio."

Alejandro Rios was Clay Neuman's stepdad and managed the maintenance on the estate's grounds and buildings.

Liv reached for the present Ash held in the crook of his arm. "I'll put this with the others. Gorgeous wrapping, by the way."

"Can't take the credit." Ash smiled at Kayla and lifted their entwined hands to his lips.

Kayla's heart warmed. That's all it took, these days. Just

one loving glance, and she turned into melted butter at this man's feet.

"Wait until you see the Great Hall." Liv guided them into the expansive room. "Zeke, Rohan, and Phin came up with the idea to honor Grams's Diné heritage." She glanced at Kayla.

"Also known as Navajo," she offered, having done a bit of research after first meeting the Blackwell matriarch.

Liv nodded. "Lynette, Henri, and Clara worked on the menu. Cilla, Lena, and I figured out the decorations. Maddy and Sadie supervised the guys while they hung them."

Clara was Alejandro's wife and Clay's mom. She home-schooled her daughter Sadie and set up scenario rooms in the shoot house the guys used when fine-tuning their recovery plans.

White, blue, yellow, and black balloons filled each corner of the Hall, representing the four sacred mountains surrounding Dinétah, homeland to the Navajo, also known as the Four Corners in the southwestern region of the United States.

A giant rainbow arced across the entire room, from one fireplace to the other, a symbol of Diné's sovereignty, the tribal nation's right to govern themselves. Incongruously, music from the fifties—Grams's favorite—played over hidden speakers.

"How beautiful," Kayla said. "Did you manage to surprise Grams?"

"Believe it or not, yes. But it took curtaining off the entire Great Hall and watching her every minute. Who knew Grams hated surprises?" Liv smiled at them, then raised a brow at Ash. "Girl time."

He groaned, eyeing Zeke across the room. "Don't leave me."

"Grams will protect you," Kayla said, grinning. "Go give her a kiss."

Without another word, Liv whisked her away, leaving Ash to fend for himself. She added their birthday present to the pile of others on the way to what Kayla had begun to think of as the Wolf's Den, the side of the Hall housing Lupos.

Maddy, Lena, and Cilla jumped up from the plush, leather couches to offer more hugs and kisses. Once they'd all refilled their beverages and resettled around the fireplace, Liv demanded, "Tell us everything."

Kayla frowned. "About what?"

"Mason, mercenaries, and murders. What else?"

"Zeke didn't fill you in?"

Liv shook her head. "He said it wasn't his story to tell."

Kayla glanced at the other ladies. "Your guys, too?"

"Yes," Lena said, "so freaking annoying."

Maddy added, "Phin's never been this tight-lipped."

"What the hell happened out there?" Cilla asked.

Before leaving Sybil's estate, they had all agreed to keep what really happened to themselves, but she never dreamed the guys wouldn't tell their partners. After all, if somehow the truth ever surfaced, the women in this room would all be affected, too. Maybe the guys were concerned.

"I'm sorry, it wasn't my intent to keep y'all in the dark."

Liv waved off her apology. "Family secrets are a prerequisite when involved with a Blackwell. We all knew that when we signed on."

"But you're all my friends. You've trusted me during pivotal moments of your lives. I should have returned the favor."

"Sometimes, more than one hand in the cookie jar can cause a bottleneck," Maddy said.

"It's all good." Lena smiled.

Cilla said, "Next time."

"I'm all out of murdering aunties, I'm afraid."

Liv leaned over and squeezed her hand. "Before you get into the three M's, how's Jillian doing?"

Kayla covered her BFF's hand with hers. It was good to be surrounded by lady friends again. Other than spending time with Jillian and Harper, she'd had a dearth of female companionship since The Night.

"Doing her stubborn best to ignore her diseased body's limitations." Kayla had finally accepted her mother's decision to forgo medical intervention. Acceptance didn't equate to agreement, but Kayla refused to spend whatever time she had left with Jillian badgering her about treatment. "Yet her mind," Kayla searched for the right words, "is at peace in a way I never thought possible. Not for my workaholic mother and certainly not for someone who lost her friend support system and feels death consuming her, every day."

"Most of our fear surrounding death," Lena said, "revolves around not knowing how it will happen or when it will come. Your mother has the answers to those questions."

Mischief twinkled in Liv's eyes. "Which frees her mentally to focus on ensuring her family's happiness."

Kayla groaned.

Maddy glanced between the two friends. "Spill."

"Last weekend, Mom took Harper and me wedding gown shopping. Said she wouldn't be deprived of the pleasure of seeing her girls in white."

An emotional chorus of shock and delight flared around her.

Feeling her own throat tighten, Kayla changed the topic and filled them in on all that had happened, from the time of Vicky's murder to the moment they set the scene to look like a sadistic burglary-homicide.

When she finished, the ladies sat in silence . . . for about one-point-seven seconds.

"The State Police bought your story, whole cloth?" Lena asked.

"Why wouldn't they?" Kayla said. "Ash has an unblemished reputation."

"But didn't they wonder about who had hired Seb Grimball?" Maddy asked.

"Rohan erased the trail leading to Sybil's son and created a new one. A more radicalized version."

"Three friends getting murdered within a week of each other didn't raise any brows?" Cilla asked.

"It's possible, but they'd have to find a hole in our story."

"Will they?" Liv asked.

Someone, maybe Mason, had done a remarkable job of cleaning up the physical evidence, including burying the bodies. Had he been the one who killed the guard Ash left behind and slit the throats of two others? A question that would go unanswered, with him in the wind again.

Rohan had worked his magic on the digital trail and Ash had assessed everything with a law enforcement eye. The holes had been plugged to the best of the team's ability. Now, all they could do was wait.

To the ladies, she said, "Our story is as fireproof as possible."

Almost as one, the women relaxed into their seats, having complete confidence in their men.

"Did you find out who vandalized your car?" Cilla asked.

Kayla inwardly winced, still recalling the murder of crows she'd had to swallow during her apology to Natalie. "Using the parking garage video, Neuman worked with my intern Gemma to identify the vandal. Turns out, one of Tommy O'Connor's teammates, Jennie McIntyre, thought the scare tactic would incentivize me."

"Unbelievable," Lena said. "Did you notify the police?"

Kayla shook her head. "A lot was riding on the bill's passage. She had a valid fear. Several families would have lost their homes if the bill failed." Her team had secured the votes to pass Tommy's bill. A win. But Krowne and Associates wouldn't be partnering with his group again. "I strongly recommended that she work with a professional to find more productive means of expression."

"You're a damn saint," Lena said.

Kayla grinned. "Not even close."

"Did you figure out Mason's motivations? " Maddy asked.

"Not yet."

"How was the governor's funeral?"

"Amazing, heartbreaking. The State honored Vicky's memory beyond my wildest dreams. I think even Linda was impressed, though she would never say."

Not being able to tell Linda about Sybil and Elsie's scheme had been one of the toughest pills for Kayla to swallow. But doing so would have put them all in danger. She hoped Vicky would forgive her.

"How did, um, Ash and Zeke get along?" Liv asked, her attention on something behind Kayla.

"Outside of a few verbal jabs, exceedingly well. Best I've seen yet. Why?"

Male voices rose above the Penguins singing *Earth Angel.*

Kayla peered over her shoulder, and all the blood cooled in her veins.

Ash and Zeke stood before the bank of windows that overlooked the backyard. They each held a crystal tumbler half full of amber liquid. Tension radiated out from them, like a slow-moving poisonous fog, bent on killing the festive mood.

Lynette and Grams's conversation suspended mid-sentence. Phin glanced up from the board game he was playing with Sadie and Brodie. Rohan and Cruz peeled away from the liquor sideboard and headed toward the oncoming disaster. Henri, Clara, Alejandro, and Neuman slipped from the room.

The moment had come, the one the family had been encouraging for years.

Ash and Zeke would finally hash out their shit.

Dread filled Kayla's chest.

"EVERYTHING IS ALWAYS ABOUT YOU," ASH SNARLED, ignoring the startled stares of the birthday party guests. "What about me?"

Zeke snorted. "You got exactly what you wanted. Your *dream* job."

"And lost everything else. My name, my family, my home."

"Using your middle name was your damn decision."

"Guys," Cruz interrupted, Rohan at his side. "Maybe this isn't the best time."

Ash made brief eye contact with Cruz and Rohan before waving them off. If he and Zeke needed to get psychologically bloody to bring an end to their feud, so be it. He would apologize to Grams later.

"You're right, it was," Ash said. "Because I realized distance would be the only way to force you to become the leader I knew you could be."

"What a crock. You couldn't wait to divest yourself of the family business. Not lofty enough. Or was it the blue-collar taint you despised?"

"I didn't love towing and repoing. A truth I made clear the day I took Dad's place at the helm. But you did. You were the one with the grand ideas to transform it into something bigger, something more meaningful."

"If you thought my ideas were so great, why didn't you stick around long enough to help me see them through?"

Moments like this, he wished he could time travel back to his conversation with their father, when Duke Blackwell made the narrow-minded comments about Zeke not having the right mindset or temperament to run the company, that he was a great number two guy, and kick the old man's ass. Or at the very least shut the office door.

Only later did he realize Zeke had overheard everything, doing permanent damage to the teenager's confidence. Then and now, Ash had understood Zeke's capabilities, his commitment to the family business. But a brother's opinion was worth pennies compared to a father's.

"Because you were ready," Ash said.

"You threw me into the fucking frying pan."

Ash's gaze snapped to where Sadie and Brodie had been sitting by the fireplace with Phin. Gone. He glanced around the Great Hall. Cleared out.

He experienced another pang of guilt, but shoved it into

the box with all of his other regrets, embarrassing moments, and painful memories. Neither of them were leaving this room until this cancerous thing between them was settled.

"And you survived." Ash took a large swallow of his drink. "Hell, you thrived, Zeke. BARS is a multimillion-dollar business due, in large part, to your leadership and vision. You didn't need me."

Zeke stalked off toward the fireplace, where the ladies had been engaged in "girl talk" before a pall had settled over the festive mood. In a low voice, he said, "I needed your counsel more than ever."

Ash ignored the kick to his gut. He moved to the liquor sideboard, made a selection, and joined his brother. Palming the bottle, he held it out between them.

"Your story is a lot like Defiant's."

"Are you really comparing me to whisky?"

He gave his brother a sideways you're-an-idiot glance. "Not the liquor itself. The company's journey to its unique-ness, its success." He replenished both of their tumblers before setting down the bottle. "The owners took the tradi-tion of making single-malt Scottish whisky, added their own ingenuity, and created something all their own. Some-thing special." He clinked his glass against his brother's. "Like you did with BARS."

Zeke stared into the amber liquid like all the answers of the world lived in its depths.

"Two years ago, you realized that you didn't need to possess Lupos"—his glaze flicked to the heirloom mounted above the mantel—"in order to be a respected leader. All you needed to do was trust your team." He shifted to give Zeke his full attention and laid a hand on his brother's shoulder. "Just like you didn't need my help to transition your vision of Dad's repo business into an asset recovery empire." His grip tightened. "You needed to believe in yourself."

"Maybe," Zeke said after a stunned silence. "But I would've liked my big brother's—my best friend's—ear, support, encouragement, I don't know what. I just needed *you*. Except you not only cut the umbilical cord, you burned the fucker to ash."

Ash set his tumbler down on the coffee table and faced his brother. Zeke wouldn't make eye contact with him, preferring to stare over his shoulder at the far wall.

"Zeke, I'm sorry."

Silence.

"I did what I thought would help you be successful, but I realize now I made a big mistake. On many levels."

His brother's Adam's apple moved up and down as if he were battling to keep an emotion from rising to the surface.

Ash clamped a hand around the back of Zeke's neck. "I'm sorry, brother. Sorry I hurt you. Sorry I abandoned you. Sorry I'm the worst fucking friend and brother to ever grace this earth—"

"Shut the hell up." Zeke clamped his hands around Ash and pulled him into a bear hug.

Ash embraced him hard, fighting the rise of tears. He brushed away two escapees, then smacked his palm against his brother's back once, twice, three times before pulling away. "Forgiven?"

Zeke swiped a wrist across his cheeks. "Forgiving."

"Fair enough."

Ash frowned, arching his lower back, then rotating his shoulders. Something felt . . . damp down his spine. He reached behind, rubbing a hand over his shirt. It came away wet.

"Why is my shirt—?" He broke off, peering down at his brother's hand.

Zeke held up his mostly-empty glass. "Oops."

"You couldn't have held it away from me?"

"Our man hug wouldn't have had the same impact."

"Clearly." Ash untucked his shirt, fanned the tail in an inane attempt to dry it.

An amiable silence fell between them, the first of its kind in years.

"You know," Ash said. "I never did get a chance to make use of the gift you got me last year."

"I could say something right now about your shitty inability to recognize a peace offering when it's presented to you."

"And I could counter by saying a meaningful conversation costs nothing."

A slow smile spread across Zeke's face. "Touché, brother."

Without another word, they turned as one and left all their bad blood burning in the fire.

KAYLA PACED THE NEW COVERED PATIO, WHICH WAS connected to the Annex by a thirty-foot-long meandering path made of gorgeous flagstone.

The enormous addition was a near replica of the indoor Theater, except the outdoor version had a pizza oven and a gas firepit. Construction would begin in another month on the east side of the Annex, which would include three additional offices for Liv, Maddy, and Neuman.

Not knowing how long the brothers' argument would rage, Lynette had moved the entire party here. But the '50s music was gone and the joyous conversation had trickled down to monosyllabic words. Liv stood at the edge of the patio, arms folded over her center, staring toward the Friary.

"Do you think they'll work it out this time?" Kayla asked, joining her friend in her vigil.

"I don't know," Liv whispered. "They're wading through years of hurt and harsh words."

"And male stubbornness."

"That too." Liv gifted her with an amused glance before returning her attention to the house. Her friend's expression transformed into a frown. "This can't be good."

Kayla followed her line of sight and her heart skittered like a pebble across a murky lake. Ash and Zeke strode with purpose down the drive. Neither of them speaking. She couldn't get a read on their mood from this distance.

"Where are they going?" Kayla asked as they disappeared from sight.

"Cruz's garage is over there."

"I heard my name."

Liv glanced at the self-proclaimed gearhead over her shoulder. "Why would your brothers be going to your garage?"

Confusion crowded between his dark brows, followed by fear. "The Stutz is in there. I had to change out a hose." He bolted from his chair. "I'll break their fingers if they even think about touching Cilla's car."

The beautiful vehicle he'd spent years renovating to honor his dad, then gave to Cilla.

Like an amoeba, the entire group followed Cruz as he cut across the lawn to reach the garage in record time. Grams and Lynette piled into what looked like a brand new UTV, after a short skirmish over who would drive. Lynette won.

Kayla peeled off her shiny neutral-colored high heels and released a deep sigh when her toes threaded into the grass.

"Good idea." As the only other stiletto-wearing woman, Cilla followed suit.

Brodie and Sadie ran ahead, grinning and whispering like they were about to see blood spilled.

Clara, Alejandro, and Henri shook their heads in unison and returned to the Friary. Neuman snored softly in one of the cozy lounges.

Phin rubbed his hands together. "The finale we've all been waiting for. Where's the popcorn?"

Maddy elbowed him.

Rohan shook his head. "How did you ever survive adolescence?"

Lena laughed, weaving her arm through Rohan's. "I love this family."

Minutes later, even Phin was speechless. The garage doors stood wide open. Cruz's Stutz took up one side and the other housed several man toys. Six four-wheelers with custom paint jobs and what looked like a two-seater dune buggy.

Ash and Zeke had already rolled out two of the ATVs. Four windblown gray wolf heads screamed across the front of Zeke's and a distorted FBI seal stretched over the same area on Ash's, with Fidelity on the left side, Bravery in the middle, and Integrity on the right.

Brodie sat on a smaller, camo-colored ATV still inside the garage, with Sadie standing next to him, arms crossed and mouth set in a firm line. Someone was feeling left out. Kayla couldn't blame her. The off-road vehicles looked like a lot of fun.

Zeke had given the ATVs to his brothers last year as a

thank-you for all their hard work and his big heart hadn't been able to exclude his soon-to-be stepson. Although she didn't doubt gratitude played a part in the gifts, Kayla suspected the big lug simply wanted a way to spend time with his brothers, to knit their bond back together again.

Unfortunately, Ash hadn't been ready to accept the gesture yet. He and Zeke had too much unresolved stuff between them, and a man toy—no matter how cool and thoughtful—couldn't fix it.

Fast-forward to today, Ash and Zeke looked happy, as if they'd siphoned out all the bad blood from their system and found a new way forward.

Emotion ballooned in the back of her throat. She forced it down and teased, "Going on a joyride?"

Ash grinned at Zeke. "We have some dirt in the exhaust that needs to be blown out."

"Speak for yourself. My exhaust got cleaned out last month at the doctor's office."

Everyone stared at the normally warring brothers in varying stages of shock. Some laughed, some produced hesitant smiles, and some looked at them as if they waited for an alien transport ship to arrive.

Then a shift occurred.

The pivotal moment spread through the gathering like the sensation of hot cocoa sliding into your stomach on a cool evening.

Zeke put voice to what everyone was feeling. "Family first."

"Through blood," Phin chimed in.

"Through hate," Rohan said.

"Through fear," Cruz said.

The brothers all turned to Ash. His eyes flared, then he dropped his chin down, blocking her view of his face. His chest rose high and hard, once, twice, before he lifted his head. Moisture rimmed his eyes.

Ash cleared his throat. "Through joy."

Everyone smiled and a chorus of voices intoned through tight throats, "No exceptions."

"Ready?" Zeke asked.

Grinning, Ash nodded. "Lead on."

They started their rides. Phin and Cruz stepped aside, creating an opening in the familial circle.

Ash glanced at Kayla, and she blew him a kiss. He mouthed, *I love you,* then tore off after his brother.

Lynette, in full-on military mode barked, "Boys, make sure your brothers don't have a relapse."

"Yes, Mama," Rohan, Phin, and Cruz affirmed at the same time. They kissed their favorite ladies, then ran to their four-wheelers.

Phin jumped on the flashy red one, Cruz hit the black with metal flecks that perfectly matched the Stutz's paint job, and Rohan slid onto the blue with computer code embedded. Brodie roared after the men.

A silence fell over their group, each woman smiling and shaking their heads at the same time.

Sadie propped a hand on her narrow waist. "Why couldn't we go with them?"

No one said anything. Everyone was probably experiencing the same feeling of being left behind, like Kayla. Her phone pinged with a text.

Natalie.

During her eating-crow session, she'd managed to patch things up with her friend. Even promised to give Alex an opportunity to prove he'd changed.

At least she no longer gagged when she heard the man's name. That had to mean something.

A loud motor from inside the garage had her head jerking up. A tricked-out dune buggy, with Grams in the driver seat, rolled to a stop beside Sadie. "We can't let the boys have all the fun, can we?"

The illumination of a million stars couldn't have competed with Sadie's joy as she jumped into the passenger side of the two-seater.

"Grams," Lynette warned.

The older woman waved off her daughter-in-law's concern. "I won't go over eighty, promise." She turned to Sadie and winked. "Buckle up."

Once the girl complied, Grams hit the accelerator and the electric vehicle shot off after the others.

Lynette muttered something about a heart attack and ran toward the more sedate UTV, a few feet away.

"Don't worry," Cilla said, nodding at the dust cloud in the distance. "Cruz picked that style specifically for its low center of gravity." At their blank looks, she explained. "It's harder to tip over a dune buggy."

Lynette raised a brow at the rest of the group. "Who's coming with me to pick up the body parts?"

Lena, Maddy, and Cilla piled inside the four-seater.

Soon, only Kayla and Liv were left. An ache settled in her throat.

Liv placed a hand over her small baby bump. "You didn't have to stay behind to keep me company. They could have made room for you."

"Don't be ridiculous. Do you know how long it took me to get this wave in my hair?" She slid her hand over a blond lock draped over her shoulder. "Windblown isn't my best look."

Liv made a you-don't-fool-me-for-a-second face.

"Besides, I need to make a phone call. Do you mind?"

"Not at all."

She wandered a few feet away. Natalie picked up on the second ring. "Sorry to bother you, but I thought you'd want to know."

"What's up?" Kayla braced herself for whatever bad news her friend was about to impart.

"The governor signed HB821."

Kayla blinked, not prepared for *this* news. "On Saturday? You're sure?"

"Just received word from our Raleigh office. The new governor is working her ass off to get everything back on schedule. Cabrera signed eleven bills today."

Emotion tingled against the backs of her eyes. The Women Entrepreneur Empowerment Act would help women across the state with startup costs and professional development.

We did it, Aunt Vicky.

Pride in her team swelled in her chest.

"Are you in the office?"

"Yes, do you need something?"

"Can you leave a note for Gemma, asking her to book a private room at Capella on Nine for a team celebratory dinner next week?"

"She's here. I'll pass your request on to her, though it might be a hard one to fulfill on such short notice."

"Have her talk to Stan. He'll make room for us."

"The usual bonus for everyone?"

Kayla responded with a higher amount. This had been a particularly hard win.

"Consider it done."

"Thanks for the call, Natalie. Now go enjoy the rest of the weekend with that loser you hooked up with."

"I love you, too."

Kayla laughed and rejoined Liv.

"Good news?"

"Governor Cabrera signed HB821."

"Congratulations!" Liv hugged her tight. "Vicky would be so proud of you."

"She did most of the political legwork. It's more her win than mine."

"It's a win for you both." Liv released her. "Let's head back to the Friary and celebrate."

Kayla opened her mouth to brag about her team's efforts, when she heard the rumble of a distant motor. She squinted into the distance. "Is that?"

Liv grinned. "Yep."

Ash and Zeke were headed straight for them, clumps of grass and dirt arcing behind the tires as they descended a hill. They let off the gas a few car lengths away and circled around behind them. Ash pulled up next to her and Zeke next to Liv.

Ash's enormous smile lit up all the chambers of her heart. "Need a ride?"

"Always."

She climbed on behind him and circled her arms around his waist. "I love you, G-man."

"Love you too, World Disrupter."

Leaning back, he turned his head until their lips connected. He was warmth and hope and love all wrapped in a perfect-for-her body. She couldn't imagine a happier moment than this.

He drew the kiss to an end and revved the engine. "Hold on."

"Wait!" She glanced back at her friend, who now sat straddled across Zeke's lap. The father-to-be's hand resting on her bump.

When she turned back around, she saw Ash watching the exchange too, a smile playing on his lips. Kayla kissed his shoulder and rested her cheek in the V of his neck, comforted by the fact there would be happier times ahead for them as well.

"Hit it," she whispered.

EXTENDED EPILOGUE

"Is your Mace where you can reach it?" Mason asked, his chest tightening.

Jozi patted the small handbag slung across her body. "Yes, sir."

He surveyed the chaotic, yet organized, mess that was Freshman Move-In Day at Duke. Vehicles rolled in at designated times, enthusiastic volunteers helped unload mountains of belongings that would later be stuffed into sardine-sized dorm rooms, wide-eyed freshmen took in everything with varying degrees of wonder, excitement, and terror, and conflicted parents waved off their kids with an odd sense of relief, hope, and anxiety.

"You'll take it with you wherever you go," Mason pressed.

"Even the bathroom," Jozi said, finishing his mantra. She grasped his forearm. "Don't worry, Dad. I got this."

He'd done his best to prepare her for the world, to give her the tools needed to fend off predators. He'd taught her every self-defense move he knew, even the dirty ones. Now, he had to set her free on a campus the size of a small town. A place where she would become a woman.

"If you need me, text, call, whatever." He noticed the ache in his teeth and worked to relax his jaw. "Day or night."

"I know." She smiled.

"Emergency phrase?"

"It's Grandpa's birthday." She stood on her tiptoes and kissed his cheek. "I got this."

He swallowed hard, then pulled her in for a hug. "Your mom would be so proud."

She tightened her arms around him. "I'll see you at Thanksgiving." She lowered her voice. "Stay alive."

He stilled, then set her at arm's length. In her eyes, he saw an understanding of him that he never wanted his daughter to have. Something cracked inside his chest.

She threw her arms around his neck and whispered, "I love you, Daddy. All of you."

Mason snapped his eyes shut before any passersby could see the gathering moisture. He knew in that moment she would be all right. His strong, intelligent, beautiful girl.

When he had control again, he sensed eyes on him. He scanned the crowd once more, and froze. Two familiar figures leaned against a low stone wall, watching them.

Detecting his mood shift, Jozi stepped back and searched his face. "What's wrong?"

He tore his gaze away and looked down at his too-smart daughter. "Stay here."

"Where are you going? The family farewell event starts in fifteen minutes."

"I'll be back in five. Don't move, Jozi."

His daughter, like the men and women he'd served with, recognized his we're-in-danger tone. After another visual recon, he strode toward the pair who had the power to destroy the one person in the world he cared about.

"HE LOOKS PISSED," ASH SAID, AS HE PUSHED OFF THE LOW stone wall and anchored himself in a defensive position.

"As far as he's concerned, we're the enemy—and far too close to his daughter." Kayla flicked a glance at Ash, standing between her and Mason. "Please sit. Your battle stance isn't helping to dispel the illusion."

"Not yet."

Stubborn men.

The tension in her shoulders eased though, when she noted Ash shifting his weight to one leg and uncurling his fingers from their fisted position.

Mason halted six feet away. His attention slashed between the two of them. "What are you doing here?"

"Checking in on an old friend." Kayla still didn't know what to do with her conflicting emotions about Mercenary Mason. But the man who'd always anticipated her needs, made her laugh, and never judged her, him, she missed.

"How did you know we'd be here?" When neither of them spoke, Mason's attention fixed on Ash. "Let me guess. Rohan."

"He's a marvel," Ash said without inflection.

"What are your intentions?"

"To meet the young woman you would kill for," Kayla said.

Mason flinched.

"An introduction is the least you could do."

"If you recall, I paid my debt. My daughter is off-limits."

"What I recall," Ash said in a low, intense voice, "is the mess you left for us to clean up."

Mason glared at Ash. "I did more than my share of the cleanup."

Kayla thought of the shallow graves scattered around Sybil's neighborhood and had to agree with her old friend.

"But if you're talking about the ladies," Mason said, "I did what you couldn't."

Ash's hands curled into hard knots at his side, and he took a step toward the mercenary. "You don't know what I'm capable of."

Kayla pushed off the wall and stepped between them. "None of that."

"It wasn't an insult, Feeb," Mason said in an even voice. "You're law enforcement. Your integrity wouldn't have allowed you to do what needed to be done to preserve HCVS."

"How long have you known?" She understood he'd identified his anonymous employer and linked Sybil to Service, but she never imagined he'd penetrated their mission.

His unflinching gaze met hers. "Day One."

ASH WAVERED BETWEEN RESPECT FOR THE MERCENARY AND flat-out hatred. He had yet to fully understand why they were crashing Jozi Wade's move-in day.

Part of it was probably to do with Kayla shutting the door on a painful time in her life—the moment she'd lost not only her beloved aunties but someone she called friend. Ash knew there was something more to this visit than hashing up months-old pain, yet all he could do was go along for the ride.

Not that he was complaining. He enjoyed watching Mason Wade squirm.

"One last time, Kayla," Mason said. "Why are you here?"

"Dad?"

Mason closed his eyes for the briefest of seconds before turning around to find his daughter at his shoulder.

The auburn hair, freckles, and average height must have come from her mother. But the suspicious hazel eyes were all Wade.

"I told you to stay put," Mason gritted out.

"You also told me five minutes. It's been ten."

Ash smiled. He liked this young woman. A lot.

Jozi's attention skidded to Ash, then Kayla. The latter held out her hand. "I'm Kayla Krowne."

The younger Wade looked to her father, who nodded, before accepting Kayla's hand. Somehow Ash didn't think Jozi asked permission for much, but Wade must have indicated in some way to his daughter that he and Kayla were potential threats.

"This is my partner, Ash Blackwell," Kayla said.

Ash kept his hands loose at his sides and nodded, choosing the de-escalation route rather than riling the mercenary further.

"Business or romantic?" Jozi asked.

Mason groaned.

Kayla smiled. "Very romantic."

Jozi grinned. "My dad used to work for you."

"That's right. He was an indispensable part of my team."

"If he was so indispensable, why is he no longer on your team?"

"Jozi, for chrissake—"

"It's a legitimate question, Dad."

"A rude one."

"No worries," Kayla said. "I like a young person who isn't afraid to ask the tough questions."

Jozi lifted a brow, and waited.

"Business relationships are like personal relationships," Kayla said. "Sometimes they have an expiration date."

"Which doesn't really answer my question."

"Enough, Jozi. Why I no longer work for Kayla is between her and me. Just like why you and hippie-boy no longer hang out is between you and him."

"For the hundredth time, his name is Bodhi."

Wade leveled a look her way, as if to say, *Your point?*

A note of frustration rumbled in Jozi's throat.

Ash couldn't remember the last time he'd been so entertained.

"I understand you're majoring in environmental science," Kayla said.

"That's right."

"Do you have an internship lined up?"

"Not yet."

"I'll be losing my longtime intern, who dealt with environmental issues, at the end of this school year. I'm looking for someone to replace her, someone who could shadow her over the next year and learn the ropes. Someone unafraid of big personalities."

"Are you offering me a job?"

"If your dad approves, of course."

Jozi turned excited eyes on her father.

"What's the pay? My daughter isn't working her ass off for free."

"Dad!"

"No," Kayla said, "it's okay. This is a business arrangement, and you should always hear what's on the table." Kayla fingered a card out of the front pocket of her purse and handed it to Jozi. "I pay ten dollars over minimum wage—"

"*Ten dollars?*" Jozi interrupted, her eyes wide with excitement.

"Plus expenses, including mileage. If you don't have a vehicle, you can use a company car. My employment package also covers full tuition, room, and board."

A stunned silence swept over their small group, and all the color leached from Wade's face.

Ash now understood the reason for Kayla's visit, and he fell in love with the daft, big-hearted woman all over again.

"Yes!" Jozi said.

"No," Wade said at the same time.

"Dad, why not? What she's offering is unbelievable. Much better than being a server at a restaurant."

"Exactly."

"But if I accept, you won't have to take that job in the Philippines."

"How do you know about—?" He clamped a lid on the rest of what he was going to say. Seemed to count to three. "Dammit, Jozi."

Jozi swallowed hard, but she didn't back down. Simply stared at her father and waited for his decision.

Kayla said, "The package is the same one I offer all my interns. I'll give you their contact information, if you'd like to verify. I ask a lot from my staff and can't afford to have their attention diverted because they're worried about finances. My motivation is purely selfish."

"Selfish, right." Wade studied Kayla a long while before turning to his daughter. Took in her hopeful face. Blew out a defeated sigh. "If you don't like the work, you quit. And the job can't interfere with your schoolwork. Deal?"

"Deal!" Jozi hugged Wade, then Kayla, before tugging

on her dad's arm. "I'm sorry, but we're late for the family farewell."

"I'll see you at holiday break," Kayla said.

"Thank you," Wade said in a tone that conveyed regret and gratitude at once.

"No need. I'm always on the lookout for tomorrow's leaders. Jozi's name popped up."

"Right." Wade appeared as though he wanted to say something more, but merely nodded at them and strode away.

"Mason," Kayla said, her voice soft.

He glanced back.

"Stay safe."

A hint of a smile. "Always." Then his hard gaze turned to Ash. "Feeb." His gaze shifted from him to Kayla and back.

Understanding his silent message, Ash said, "I will."

Once the Wades disappeared into the crowd, Ash turned to Kayla and pulled her into his arms. "You're amazing."

"Military kids sacrifice a lot of things for this country. Their education shouldn't be one of them."

"Yet you still wanted to make sure she was a good fit."

"Of course, I'm a businesswoman."

"Probably didn't have anything to do with honoring an old friendship or wanting to protect the Krowne team you've created, right?"

Ignoring the first part of his comment, she said, "Everyone deserves to enjoy going to work."

"Will you be this fiercely protective of our kids?"

She jerked in his arms. "Is that a marriage proposal?"

"You do have a wedding gown ready to go."

Kayla groaned. "Who told you?"

He kissed the sensitive area behind her earlobe. The place that melted her defenses, every time. "Would you like to hear what's on the table?"

"Oh." Her hand traced down his torso as she tilted her head, giving him more access. "I'm intimately aware of the full package."

"Hmm, is that a yes?" he whispered.

She straightened until her lips met his and sealed the deal.

Thank you for reading our Steele Ridge: The Blackwells series. If you missed The Steeles and The Kingstons series, please read on for more information, including excerpts.

STEELE RIDGE: THE STEELES
Book 1

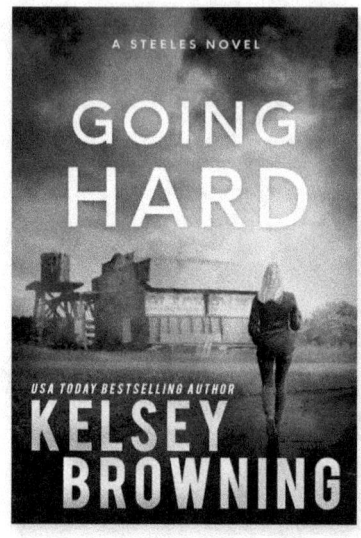

Will the fourteen-year-old secret she's been keeping from him kill their second chance at love?

When a scandal rocks professional football, a sports legend partners with a small-town sheriff to stop a ruthless killer.

GOING HARD EXCERPT
BY KELSEY BROWNING

Enjoy an excerpt from Kelsey Browning's *Going Hard*, Book One in Steele Ridge: The Steeles series:

A vee of sunlight splashed across the wood floor, signaling someone coming in the front door. Carlie Beth bolted behind the bar and crouched down. Maybe she could snag a drink and get out before whoever it was saw her. She grabbed a highball glass and quickly filled it from the soda gun. The sweet scent from the soft drink was too much of a temptation and she gulped down several swallows, making her head contract in a painful brain freeze. "Ugh," she moaned but went back for more, draining the glass.

"Dean," a male voice said from somewhere disturbingly close by, "I talked with the GM and straightened out the misunderstanding about your surgical consult. Believe me, he wants you back on the ice as much as you want to be out there."

At the man's rumble above her, every tiny hair on Carlie Beth's body did a Don King imitation. She hadn't heard that voice in years, not until his mom's sixtieth birthday party a few months back. He'd called out to her, his smile just as charming and sinful as she remembered. Panic had swamped her, and she'd hightailed it out of there, leaving her best Pyrex bowl in the middle of the food table.

But one night fifteen years ago that voice had whispered the smoothest dirty talk Carlie Beth had ever heard directly into her ear. While the man himself was sliding inside her.

"Yeah, this is exactly the reason you pay me the big bucks." His low laugh shimmied through Carlie Beth. "I'll check in with you when I get back to town."

His Carolina Boy drawl had matured into the intoxicating smoothness of expensive artisanal whisky. And she knew the risks of bingeing on it.

"Anyone here?" he called out. "Because I could sure as hell use a drink."

An arm came over the bar top to snag a glass and she squeezed closer to the shelves. The next time she had a craving for a Cheerwine, she would stop at the Sack & Snack before coming in here. But for now, she was trapped.

"Hope you don't mind, but I'm making my own." His words were accompanied by the sound of liquid being poured.

She could pretend she was in a bubble, unable to see or hear anything, and just waddle her butt back to the hallway. But she wasn't a timid little girl. She was a grown woman. A strong woman, who didn't hide from things. Okay, so maybe she'd *hidden* a thing or two, but she had to face the man she knew was on the other side of this bar.

Carlie Beth filled her lungs with air, then lifted her head.

He was leaning over the wood expanse, staring down at where she was crouched next to the extra shot glasses. Every molecule she'd just inhaled whooshed back out.

He shouldn't impact her this way. He couldn't impact her this way.

His eyebrows drew in over his nose. "Carlie Beth, what are you doing back there? And why do you look like you just lost a mud-wrestling match?"

Griffin Steele was one of those men born on a day when God was in an excellent mood. Artfully mussed golden-brown hair and eyes the blue of titanium welded too hot. A face that made angels break out into The Whip and a smile that made women like Carlie Beth lose their panties.

Fifteen years ago, those laugh lines around his eyes and mouth hadn't yet put in an appearance. Now, they hinted that he was a man who'd been around the block. Probably in a Mercedes Benz with a number of beautiful women riding shotgun. At that thought, something that felt oddly like jealousy sparked inside her midsection.

No, that was just her stomach growling from missing lunch. Because one look at Grif and she'd realized he was the masculine version of the Mad Batter Bakery's sinful hazelnut cream cheese puffs. Delicious, but so dangerous. Few women could resist that kind of temptation.

You can. You have. And you will.

With Grif staring, uneasiness swarmed over her. The sweat on her skin was cooling, making her shiver. Her hair was half stuck to her face, half a bedraggled tail hanging limp on her shoulder. No makeup. Not a speck. Seven-year-old jeans and a Canyon Ridge band booster T-shirt from Aubrey's drawer.

This was what happened when Carlie Beth put off doing laundry. Her face went hot because although she was a mere bra size bigger than Aubrey, that shiver had woken up her nipples, now clearly visible against her snug shirt.

"I...uh...wait tables here. I was just grabbing a soda before getting cleaned up."

She tried to get her legs to work, but the damn things were apparently just as affected as her lungs. *Get your shit together, you two.*

"Looks like yours is empty." Grif leaned farther over the bar top and held out the glass he'd already filled. "Here. Take mine."

She couldn't tear her attention away from his hands. Those long, talented fingers were able to finesse a curveball *and* a woman's curves. Tan and obviously strong, they did more for her than seeing another man's naked body. "No, I couldn't—"

"I insist."

So he was still a gentleman, something she'd found hard to resist years ago and couldn't seem to hold out against now, either. Her hand was shaking as she reached up and took the lowball glass. She tried not to touch him, but it was impossible. Her fingertips grazed his knuckles, shooting heat up her arms and into her torso.

Grif's gaze dropped to her chest, held there for long enough to make the soft fabric of her bra feel scratchy and binding, almost unbearable against her tight nipples. When he finally looked up, his eyes had darkened to navy.

She knew that color.

It was the color of sex.

**Find out what happens next and order
GOING HARD**

CRAVING HEAT EXCERPT

ADRIENNE GIORDANO

Enjoy an excerpt from Adrienne Giordano's *Craving Heat*,
Book One in Steele Ridge: The Kingstons series:

"Hey," he said, "can we talk?"

When she didn't respond, he took that as a green light.
Of course he did. One thing about Marlene Tucker, she'd
taught him how to capitalize on situations. Besides, by now
Maggie could have hopped into the cruiser and taken off.
Which she didn't.

"I'm sorry," he said. "My crazy life put you in danger.
You have no idea how much I hate that. And, let's be
honest, I like you. You're funny and smart and, well, you
carry a big gun. I'd rather you not be mad at me."

She shook her head, but the smile tugging at her lips
couldn't be denied. Score one for the jock. He pointed to
the corner of her mouth. "I think you're smiling."

Pushing his luck—what the hell?—he inched his hand
closer. Close enough that the tip of his finger brushed the
insanely soft skin at the corner of her mouth and he
wanted...Jesus, he wanted his lips there. Right at that spot.

She wrapped her hand around his finger and—wow—if she'd wanted to get his mind out of the gutter that wasn't the way to do it.

"That woman," she said, still holding his finger, "is stone-cold nuts. None of this is your fault."

"Then why are you mad at me?"

Finally, she let go of him. "I'm not."

"Yeah, you are."

"You don't even know me. How would you know if I'm mad or not?"

He'd spent half his life surrounded by amped-up football players. More than anything, he recognized when people were pissed. "I've spent a career working in a team environment. Learning people's signals and moods. You're right, I don't know you, but I know when someone is angry. At least talk to me. Not that you owe it to me after today, but —" Damn. He shook his head. How to say this without sounding like a douche?

"But what?"

"Nothing."

Which, of course, was total bullshit. It was definitely something. Something that began with him looking at Maggie and liking it more and more. He met her gaze and inched close enough to hook his finger into her belt loop, pull her forward and ...

He dipped his head, studied the slope of her top lip and the air stopped moving. Everything froze. Including his lungs.

"I..." She peered down at her feet, dug the toe of her boot into the ground, then rocked back.

He took a hard inhale, held it until his chest slammed, and blew it out. Lord, he felt like a middle-schooler trying to steal his first kiss. "You what?"

She lifted her chin and the street lamp shined in her lush brown eyes and he was gone. Totally smitten with this beautiful, strong woman so unlike the soft-spoken females he went for. The ones who let him call the shots.

Maggie, Maggie, Maggie, what are you doing to me?

"I got distracted," she said. "During the press conference."

"There was a lot going on."

"That doesn't matter. I had a job to do."

"Maggie—"

She squeezed her eyes closed, jabbed her open palms at him. "Shut up."

Whoa. Shut up? "I'm trying to—"

"My lack of attention could have gotten you hurt." She pressed the fingers of both hands into her forehead. "I've been shredding myself over this, thinking about all the things I did wrong, every second I could have done something differently and yet," she dropped her hands "I stand here, looking at you and thinking, 'Gee, I'd bet he looks mighty tasty fresh out of a shower.' How stupid can I be? That's what I'm pissed about. It has to stop."

Not one to let a grade A opportunity pass him by, Jay tipped his head closer. "If you're thinking those thoughts, I don't want it to stop. In fact, I'd throw myself off the top of this building to make it not stop."

She gawked at him. Literally stood there, mouth agape, and instinct kicked in. "Honey," he whispered, "if you want me, I'm all yours."

Find out what happens next and order
CRAVING HEAT

ACKNOWLEDGMENTS

Releasing *End Game* to the world has been a truly bittersweet moment for me. I'm excited to finally share with readers Ash and Kayla's story, but I'm sad that their HEA marks the conclusion of the series. Terrorizing Zeke, Rohan, and Ash Blackwell was a genuine delight, and I believe my amazing writing partner, Adrienne Giordano, feels the same about putting the screws to Phin and Cruz Blackwell. Our black sheep boys needed a good shake up, and we found the perfect ladies to upend each of their worlds. In the best possible way, of course!

Huge thanks to Adrienne for your enduring friendship, marketing genius, and villainous mind. I love ya, sister.

To copy editor Martha Trachtenberg and developmental editor Kristin Weber—thank you for digging deep and helping me make this story the absolute best it can be.

Enormous gratitude to beta readers Sandy Modesitt, Liz Semkiu, and Becky Burciaga. Your keen eyes have saved me much embarrassment, and I appreciate your thoughtful feedback.

As always, much love and appreciation to our powerhouse behind-the-scenes team—Maureen Downey, Donna Duffee, Heather Machel, and Sandy Modesitt. You're all freaking amazing!

Huge thanks to Elizabeth Mackey for designing such a stunning cover for *End Game*. You captured the heart of the story and chose the perfect color—purple!

Team Devlyn Review Crew members—thanks for taking the time to read Kayla and Ash's story, posting your reviews, and jumpstarting the algorithms.

My heartfelt thanks to every reader, reviewer, bookseller, librarian, influencer, and blogger for your enthusiastic support of my books. Y'all rock!

To Tim, my best friend and love of my life, thank you for sticking with me, despite all of my character flaws and tendency for plotting other people's deaths and spending pages in the sack with other men. You are the best.

ABOUT TRACEY DEVLYN

 Tracey Devlyn is a *USA Today* best-selling author of contemporary and historical suspense, often layered with mystery, romance, and environmental crime. Despite the thrilling, emotional journeys she creates for her readers, Tracey lives an annoyingly normal life in the mountains of North Carolina with her husband and rescue dog.

For access to exclusive content, new release notifications, special promotions, and behind-the-scenes peeks, join Tracey's VIP Reader List at https://TraceyDevlyn.com/Contact.

www.ingramcontent.com/pod-product-compliance
Lightning Source LLC
Chambersburg PA
CBHW070830260626
47170CB00007B/2329